MY MERRY MISTAKE

A HOLIDAYS WITH HART ROMANCE

COURTNEY WALSH

Swedhaven
Press

Also by Courtney Walsh

HOLIDAYS WITH HART
My Phony Valentine
My Lucky Charm

ROAD TRIP ROMANCE
A Cross-Country Christmas
A Cross-Country Wedding

NANTUCKET
If For Any Reason
Is it Any Wonder
A Match Made at Christmas
What Matters Most

HARBOR POINTE
Just Look Up
Just Let Go
Just One Kiss
Just Like Home

LOVES PARK, COLORADO
Paper Hearts
Change of Heart

SWEETHAVEN
A Sweethaven Summer
A Sweethaven Homecoming

A Sweethaven Christmas
A Sweethaven Romance (a novella)

STAND-ALONE NOVELS
Things Left Unsaid
Hometown Girl
Merry Ex-Mas
Can't Help Falling

For the eldest daughters.
You get it.

Chapter One

Raya

Halloween—two years ago

Morticia Addams is staring at me.

I'm standing in front of the full-length mirror in my bedroom, in my costume for a Halloween party.

Long, straight, dark hair. Dark, thick eyeliner. Black dress. Other than my less low-cut dress, I'm a dead ringer.

What this says about me, I'm not sure.

One thing I do know is that this whole get-up has me feeling like I'm about to make a huge, giant, colossal mistake.

And I don't make mistakes.

Why did I say I would go? A Halloween party? With a bunch of hockey players? Also, what brain injury did I sustain right before I picked this costume?

In my defense, it was Morticia or "Sexy Ninja."

I pick up my phone, ready to text Poppy and tell her I've changed my mind, but when I open our Hart sisters' group chat, I see her last text.

1

POPPY

> I'm SO GLAD you guys are coming with me tonight! We're going to have so much fun!!

Leave it to Poppy to turn an off-the-cuff white lie about dating a man she met in a coffee shop into a full-fledged relationship with a professional hockey player.

I can admit I'm a little jealous.

Poppy is known for believing the best about everyone, which means she gets her heart broken very easily. And *has* had her heart broken very easily. But Dallas Burke seems to be exactly who she needed in her life.

But he's the exception, not the rule. *Especially* when it comes to men. Double-especially with hockey players. When she started dating Dallas, I did my homework. Seventy percent of NHL marriages end in divorce.

Unlike my youngest sister, Eloise, I have no interest in opening my heart for a thirty percent success rate.

"You're doing this for Poppy," I say to my made-up reflection. "So suck it up, Raya."

I transfer a few key items—a credit card, my driver's license, and some cash—from my work bag to a small black purse, then glance down at my laptop as a work email comes in, when Poppy's *Be there in fifteen!* text pops up on my phone.

A candidate for a CFO position at a Fortune 500 company is *this close* to accepting a very good deal, and I need to stay in the know. I type out a quick reply to the email, then let my assistant know she needs to contact me immediately if she hears anything tonight. She instantly texts back:

SUZE — ASSISTANT

But it's Halloween . . .

RAYA

And? . . .

SUZE — ASSISTANT

. . .

I'll keep my phone on me

RAYA

Great!

I close my computer, pull out a bright red lipstick—which I had to dig out of the very back of my makeup drawer—and apply it to my lips.

Fifteen minutes later, as promised, Poppy and Eloise are knocking on my door.

I give myself a last once-over in the mirror, flip off the light, and walk downstairs. I open the front door to find Poppy dressed like a 1920s flapper girl and Eloise is Rainbow Brite, complete with colorful knee-high socks, her hair pulled up in a ponytail with a purple bow, and mid-forearm gloves that stretch over her middle fingers.

Poppy looks chic and timeless.

Eloise looks cute and bubbly.

I look like a vampire out for blood.

"Ray!" Poppy practically squeals. "You look amazing!"

"*Why* did I let you talk me into this costume?" I grab my purse and coat from the hooks by the door and step out onto the porch.

"Because you already sort of look like Morticia," Eloise quips.

I only stare.

"Seriously," she continues, blissfully oblivious. "I can't believe we haven't thought of it before."

"This is not a compliment." I walk past them and around to the driver's side of my Altima.

"I thought I was driving," Poppy says.

My car chirps as I click the button to unlock the doors. "I'll drive."

Eloise shakes her head. "Always have to be in control, don't you?"

I pause, pretending to think about it, then say, matter-of-factly, "Yes." I flash them both a quick smile, but they can't be surprised. I'm the responsible one. The practical one. The one who takes charge. Someone has to watch out for them—that's always been me.

That's not going to change just because I currently look like a person who breeds carnivorous plants.

We slide into the car, and I start the engine.

From behind me, Eloise says, "Catherine Zeta-Jones played Morticia in that TV show, and she's got to be one of the top five most beautiful people who's ever lived."

I scoff. "I don't look like Catherine Zeta-Jones." I pull away from the curb and out into the quiet Loveland street. Families are dotted up and down the sidewalks, walking behind groups of kids in costume, carrying bags and pails for their candy haul.

A wave of nostalgia washes over me—a flash of the three of us when we were kids—Eloise, dressed as a pirate, always running ahead, pulling Poppy by the hand to the next house, and me lagging behind, yelling at them to look both ways and make sure to say thank you.

Even then, I was taking care of them. Even then, I felt responsible.

4

"But it's not an insult, is what I'm saying," Eloise says. "You look hot. Who knew you had that hot body under those frumpy black blazers?" She shudders.

Catching her eye in the rearview mirror, she makes a face at me to let me know she's kidding.

I smile and shake my head slightly. She's maddening—the chaos to my order—but I couldn't love her more.

A half an hour and a *lot* of Eloise chatter later, I'm parking in a garage down the street from the location Poppy punched into my phone.

"Whose apartment is this again?" Eloise asks.

"One of the players—they call him Brookie—has a Halloween party every year," Poppy says.

"His name is Brookie?" Hockey players are ridiculous.

"It's a nickname," Poppy says. "He's super sweet. You guys will love him." She looks at me, then at Eloise. "Well, one of you will anyway."

I frown. "What's that supposed to mean?"

She shakes her head, an innocent look on her face. "Nothing, it's just—you know."

"No, I don't know," I say as we get out of the car, and I lock the doors.

"You don't really like people," Eloise says. Somehow, her bluntness manages to still come across as sweet. Like there's a hint of an apology, which is so Eloise.

"I like people," I object. "Some people, anyway."

We stop in front of the elevators and Poppy presses the button to go up. They look at each other, then Poppy says, "You're just sort of, you know . . ."

At the same time Eloise says, "Bossy," Poppy says, "Rude." Poppy winces.

I cross my arms over my chest and feel instantly self-conscious. My dress isn't staying where I put it, and it's way more low-cut than anything else I own.

I also very much regret the push-up bra.

"I'm not rude, I'm honest," I reason.

They look at each other, and then back at me.

"And quit ganging up on me, will you?" I don't *mean* to be rude. I'm focused. I have a million things on my mind and, more often than not, a million responsibilities. I can't help it —this is just how I am.

"Okay, rude is the wrong word," Poppy says. "Maybe . . . 'direct' is better? You just never turn your work personality off."

"Maybe just for tonight you could, I don't know—let your guard down a little?" Eloise reaches over and quietly unfolds my arms, pushing them down at my sides.

"Hubba, hubba," she says, raising her eyebrows up and down, looking at my chest.

I gasp and fold them back. "El! Seriously!"

The two of them giggle, and a part of me softens. I don't laugh, because for some reason I don't want them to know I thought it was funny too.

Even though it totally was.

Why do I do that?

As the numbers above the doors ascend, I can hear the elevator slowing. "You really want me to let my guard down at a party full of hockey players? No, thank you." We step into the elevator, and I blow out a breath.

I stand up a bit straighter and pull up the front of my costume, searching for an inch more of modesty. "Besides, one of us has to have common sense tonight."

"In case you missed it, Ray, we are actually full-grown adults," Poppy says.

I look at Eloise and raise my eyebrows.

"I am anyway." Poppy grins at me, and Eloise frowns.

"Hey! I'm an adult." She shifts her Rainbow Brite costume.

Poppy giggles, and this time, I do too.

After a pause, my middle sister looks at me. "Ray, all I'm saying is that maybe if you loosened up a bit, let your hair down, had a bit of fun, you might meet someone. You haven't dated anyone in months."

"I like being single," I say, but even I don't believe myself. Still, I double down on the lie. "I don't have to answer to anyone or be responsible for anyone else's feelings. I can do whatever I want—whenever I want. I can spend all night dancing around my house in my underwear, eating Chinese takeout, and leave the mess on the counter if I want to."

"Have you *ever* done any of those things?" Eloise asks, even though we all know the answer.

"The point is that I could."

"Just be nice, okay? These people are important to Dallas," Poppy says as the elevator doors open to the lobby of the parking garage.

"Poppy, I'm not *not* nice," I say.

Eloise barks out a laugh. I shoot her a look, and she snaps her jaw shut.

Poppy leads us out of the lobby and onto the street, but I'm still thinking through their assessment of me. Is it wrong that I like things a certain way? Neat. Ordered. Tidy. Everything in its place.

It's how I like my feelings too. I learned a long time ago that those need to stay tightly wrapped.

"Raya, what if you actually let yourself have fun tonight?" Eloise asks as we walk toward the skyrise apartment building. "What if you—" she gasps, for effect, per usual—Eloise is always dramatic— "flirt with a hot hockey player?"

I roll my eyes. "I don't flirt, Eloise."

"I know, Raya," she says, mimicking my tone. Then, she stops abruptly, takes me by the shoulders, and says, "But what if you did?" Her eyes are wild and wide.

"You look psychotic right now," I tell her.

She flares her nostrils and widens her eyes, then whispers, "*Hot. Hockey. Players.*"

"Not if my life depended on it," I whisper back.

Finally at the party, all cleavaged-up for my least favorite holiday, I'm struck with the horrible realization that I have to go inside.

Chapter Two

Raya

"Wow," Eloise says. "So, this guy is loaded."

We step into the darkened apartment, which, I now realize, is the entire top floor of the building. We're fourteen stories up, and there's a wall of windows with a stunning view of Lake Michigan on the opposite side of the room.

"They're professional athletes, Eloise," I say. "They're *all* loaded." *And that is another reason to steer clear.* The last thing I need is another man who's used to getting whatever he wants.

This makes me think of Rich, the corporate version of a professional athlete. Cocky. Full of himself. And used to getting whatever—and whoever—he wants.

I look around the room for a quiet corner where I can hide.

Eloise bumps my shoulder with hers. "I've already caught two guys checking you out."

It takes everything within me to not turn and walk back out the door.

Dallas emerges from the crowd and scoops Poppy into a hug. "Been waiting for you!" he says loudly, over the din.

She smiles at him like a lovesick teenager, and I look away—just in time to notice Eloise is no longer next to me.

If this were a cartoon, an Eloise-shaped cloud would be hovering where she stood two seconds ago. I look around and see she's already on the dance floor. She throws her head back in a laugh as she bounces around like she's having the time of her life.

She makes it look so easy.

I stiffen at the reminder that it's not so for me.

Some days I envy my youngest sister. Scratch that. *Most* days. She'd be lost in a boardroom, but she sure knows how to connect with people.

"Hey Raya," Dallas says.

I force a smile and nod. "Hello."

"Happy Halloween." He holds his hands out, as if taking in my costume. "Solid choice."

"According to my sisters I have Morticia vibes," I say without emotion, playing the part.

He laughs, and I see why Poppy is so enamored with him.

Despite my initial hesitation, Dallas Burke has proven himself over and over again. He's good to my sister—good *for* her too. They're not a power couple, they're a comfort couple. And somehow, I think that's even better.

For Poppy, I mean. Not for me.

Comfort has never been my goal.

"Can I steal her for a second?" Dallas looks at me. "A friend of mine was asking about caterers last week, and I wanted to introduce Poppy."

Poppy's eyes go wide, and I know her business needs this. Her restaurant is doing well, and Dallas's connections have taken it to a whole new level. But she's still trying to dig herself out of some unfortunate debt, so she needs to take advantage of every open door. Besides, she's an amazing chef. She deserves this.

She grabs my arm. "I'll be right back, okay? I promise." She looks at me earnestly, and I know if I don't convince her I'm okay, she won't leave my side.

I squeeze her arm and nod. "Go. I'm totally capable of handling myself."

She pulls me into a quick hug and whispers, "You sure?"

I pull back slightly and say, "If I get overwhelmed by the small talk, I'll go hide in the bathroom."

She laughs, but we both know I'm not kidding.

I might be strong and confident at work, but that's different. I know what I'm doing there. I'm prepared. If Poppy's a chef, I'm a baker. Give me the recipe, the plan, the order of operations, and I'm your girl.

If I have to wing it? Improvise a conversation that *isn't* about recruiting candidates for high-level executive positions? Bathroom time.

Poppy smiles at me, then I watch as Dallas leads her away in the direction of a small group of people near the kitchen. I fidget for a moment, tugging once again at the front of my costume, then take a few steps toward the windows. Maybe if I hug the perimeter, stay in the shadows, everyone will leave me alone. I can put in my time, then go home and work. I pull out my phone to make sure I don't have a new text from Suze, then quickly tuck it back in my tiny, black purse.

I slowly make my way around the room, doing my best to avoid the gyrating bodies, and walk over to the bar. At least if I'm holding a drink, I'll have something to do with my hands.

There are two Barbies and a "naughty" nurse (eye roll) in line, and a guy wearing a reddish leather jacket behind the counter, making drinks.

A firefighter gets in line behind me. I don't watch hockey, so he could be a star player, or a coach, or a guy who wandered in from the lobby, and I'd have no idea.

He leans in close. "You here alone?"

I straighten. "No." I search my mind for something—anything—else to say, but I come up empty.

I can practically hear Eloise begging me to *at least try* to have fun, but when I turn back to fumble through something else to say, he's gone.

I'm not disappointed.

Finally, it's my turn at the bar. Without looking, I lean toward the guy in the leather jacket and practically yell, "Can I just get a Coke?" without really looking at him.

"I thought your drink was a Long Island iced tea," he says.

Somewhere, in the recesses of my mind, I recognize that voice.

I look up.

I blink.

As the room shrinks and the background noises fade, my entire world collapses in on me. The bartender. From Christmas Eve.

Five years ago.

"Hey there, Hart." He pins me in place with a smile. "Remember me?"

Unfortunately, yes.

"What are you . . .?" But my voice trails off. Because it's Finn. Bartender Finn. The guy who witnessed my first—and only—full-fledged meltdown. The guy who knows things about me that nobody else knows.

He's filled out and bulked up. A man version of the boy I saw five years ago. If I walked into his bar today, I'm pretty sure I'd look twice.

"Love the costume" he nods at me. "Are you an undertaker?"

"Morticia Addams," I say, wishing I were *anyone* else. Someone with a mask, preferably.

"Morticia . . . right." He gives me a nod. "You wear it well." He opens a can of Coke and hands it to me.

"Thanks." I turn it around in my hands, then lean closer and hiss, "What are you doing here?" I'm not surprised he's still bartending, if I'm honest, but I am surprised he's doing it *here*. I mean—what are the odds?

He leans toward me and mimics my hiss. "What are *you* doing here?"

"My sisters dragged me," I say, inching back—our faces do not need to be that close. "One of them is dating a hockey player. Believe me, I'd rather be home with a giant stuffed-crust pizza and my pajama pants."

"Not into Halloween, then?"

I glare at him. "Do I seem like the Halloween type?"

"Not even a little bit."

I frown. "Who are you supposed to be?"

"Peter Quill," he says, arms wide, spinning around, pretending like he has a microphone. "*Come and get your love,*" he sings.

"Who?"

"Come on, man . . . Star-Lord? From *Guardians of the Galaxy*?"

"Never saw it."

"What?" He gasps, like this is the craziest thing he's ever heard. "That's a travesty. It's the best Marvel movie." He pauses. "Second best." Another pause. "Hmm. Top five, *definitely*." He watches me. "We should watch it sometime!"

"No thanks," I say absently. "I don't think it's my kind of movie."

He looks like he's fake pouting, and I catch a glimpse of Poppy and Dallas walking our way in the reflection of the mirror behind him.

I drop my gaze to him. "Listen, my sisters don't know about—"

"The night you tried to kiss me?" Finn cuts in, voice low.

My eyes go wide. "That is *not* what happened."

He pulls a face.

"Are you going to make this a thing?" I feel myself reeling.

"Probably." He grins. If I weren't so annoyed, I might find him attractive. Completely wrong for me, but the man is good-looking.

I look away, irritated.

"All right, I get it," he says. "You want me to keep your secret."

"That'd be great."

"Sorry about that, Ray," Poppy says when she reaches me. "Oh! I see you met Finn."

"I did," I say. "Just now, uh, right this second. He gave me this." I hold up the Coke.

"She's living on the edge tonight! Watch out!" Finn says.

"Brook-*ie*!" The firefighter emerges from the crowd and

14

claps Finn on the shoulder. "Don't you have people to do that?" He nods toward the bar.

Wait. Did he just call Finn "Brookie?"

My mind slides the pieces around, trying—failing—to slot them into place.

Finn laughs. "Yeah, she had to use the bathroom. I used to tend bar back in college, so you know—muscle memory." He looks at me when he says this.

I thought Finn was the bartender. But he's not the bartender.

He lives here.

This is his penthouse.

Because he's a *professional hockey player*.

The put-together pieces are unexpected.

A woman dressed in a white button-down and black pants walks up. "Thanks for the break, Finn, I thought I was going to wet my pants."

He nods, flashing her that cocky grin. "Glad to help. Only broke four glasses," he jokes, as he steps out from behind the bar. Poppy and Dallas move toward the counter to order, and he slides around the front of the bar next to me.

I feel my shoulders tense. Because Finn . . . is unfortunately very physically attractive.

"You look confused," he says.

"Brookie?"

"Oh, yeah. My last name's Holbrook," he says. "It's a nickname. I lobbied for 'Cowboy,' or 'Studcake,' but I was outvoted."

I frown, but assume that has something to do with the fact that he's from Montana. Are there cowboys in Montana? Also, why do I remember that little detail from five years ago? Hadn't I scrubbed that night from my memory?

Another guy appears out of nowhere and calls out, "Brookie!" and Finn high-fives him right over my head.

"So—you play hockey." The second the words leave my mouth, I realize how stupid they are. I'm probably the only person in this entire apartment who didn't know that.

"I do, as a matter of fact." He laughs. "Not a fan?"

I wince. "Sorry. I don't like sports."

He puts a hand on my shoulder, almost like he's talking to one of his friends, and the heat of it zips straight through me.

He shrinks to my eye level, and his expression turns serious. "What are you watching, Morticia, if you don't like Marvel and you don't like sports?"

"Literally anything but those two things."

"So, Amish romance, then?"

I make a face at him. He's easy on the eyes but wow, is he wrong for me. I'm wondering just how many other women he talks to exactly the same way.

He grins and stands back up, shaking his head. "You're still beautiful."

I tell myself this is just classic male ego, but the words still try to weasel their way in and soften my defenses.

"You can't say stuff like that." I look away.

"Why not?" He shrugs. "You are."

I look at Poppy, thankful she didn't hear him, then grab his arm and pull him through the bouncing crowd.

I hear someone say, "Yeah, buddy, get it!" as we make our way out of the crowd and into the kitchen. While it's still loud, it's considerably quieter than the living room. Muffled music and conversations still pulse through the walls. Once I'm sure we're safely out of my sister's earshot, I turn and face him.

He's still grinning. "Whoa, whoa, whoa, this is like déjà vu . . ."

I smack him across the arm. "Finn! You cannot tell anyone that we've met."

"I told you I won't," he says, matter of factly.

"Yeah, but I don't believe you." I go to push my hand through my hair, then remember there's about half a bottle of hairspray in it. I turn away and huff out a breath. "Is everything just a joke to you?"

"I mean, most things, yeah."

I stare daggers at him.

"Oh. Except this, of course."

I try to enhance my calm and talk slowly. "Look. Finn. My sisters don't know anything about that night."

"Why not?" The question is so earnest, it makes me laugh.

"Because I don't share my humiliations with people."

"They're not *people*." He frowns. "They're your family."

"Exactly."

"Are you afraid they won't love you anymore if they find out you're not perfect?" He leans toward me. "Because— newsflash—they probably already know."

I groan. "You don't get it."

"I have a pretty big family. I think I get it."

"You clearly don't."

"Then explain it to me."

I search my mind for a way to make this clear to him, but when I come up empty, I just let out a noise in frustration. "You are infuriating."

Because how do I get into it without *getting into it*? Someone like Finn will never understand someone like me. I'm driven by ambition and perfection.

I have a feeling he's driven by testosterone.

He reaches past me, opens a cupboard, and pulls out a canister of cashews. He pops the top, grabs one, and tosses it up in the air, catching it in his mouth.

"Have you grown up at all in five years?"

He shakes the can, dumps out a handful, then caps the canister and puts it back in the cupboard.

"I have, actually," he says. "But I'm still me, thank goodness. I'm not a college kid anymore but I still know how to have fun once in a while." He has an air of confidence that walks right up to the line of cockiness and dips a toe on the other side.

"Finn. I'm being serious."

"Oh, I know, Hart," he says. "I have a feeling you're always serious."

"And I have a feeling you never are."

"I wonder which one of us has better stories." He grins.

I roll my eyes.

And then we just look at each other. In those few seconds, my mind goes blank, and I wonder what it might be like if I were a completely different kind of person. A person who likes to have fun.

"You never texted me, by the way." He says, taking me out of my own head. He reaches over, takes the Coke out of my hand, and cracks it open. "After that night."

At that, I lift my chin and meet his eyes again, expecting to feel chastised, but instead, he looks amused. He hands me the can.

I'd done my best to forget that night—and everything that led up to it—over the years. And I'd mostly succeeded.

It's one of those things that pops back in late at night

18

when I'm trying to sleep, and my brain decides to take me on a tour of my most embarrassing moments.

The fact that Finn witnessed my first and only genuine meltdown is a very unfortunate reality.

"I was embarrassed," I say, honestly. "It was not my finest hour."

He opens the freezer and pulls out a frozen pizza. "It happens. No one's perfect, you know."

I watch as he moves around the kitchen, shocked at the way my past and present are colliding right here in this room.

I draw in a breath. "I . . . am . . . sorry I didn't text." A follow-up thank you would've been nice. Even I can't deny that he'd gone above and beyond for me that night.

"Are you, though?" He pulls a pizza pan from a skinny cupboard, and when he looks at me, I see the tease playing at the corner of his mouth.

"Yes," I say, honestly.

He smiles. I wish it weren't a nice smile. I get the feeling that Finn is used to being very well-liked. I've never had that knack with people, but I've convinced myself that being respected is more important.

"Apology accepted. Eat this pizza with me. You said you wanted pizza, so—" He walks over to the oven and sets it to preheat.

"Wait . . . what?"

"Eat. Pizza. With me." He acts out every word.

"You . . . just like that? Apology accepted?"

"Yep." He shrugs. "It's not deep dish, but it's pretty good."

I watch for a few seconds, then press my lips together, inhaling slowly. "And you won't tell anyone about before?"

He leans against the counter, on the opposite side of the

room. "I mean, forgiveness is free. *Keeping* a secret, though, might cost a bit more."

Great.

"Like what?"

"A real date."

I roll my eyes. "Please."

"I can do much better than frozen pizza in my kitchen," he says.

"Oh, I'm sure you think you can." I quirk a brow, feeling a little lighter.

He must see it as a crack in my armor because his smile brightens. "Oh, come on, Hart. Give me a chance to prove it."

"Be serious for once," I say.

"I am!" But everything about his tone says otherwise. The last thing I need is to fall for this act and end up as the butt of some locker room joke.

"I don't date hockey players, *Brookie*," I say.

"That's great, because I'm not a hockey player. I'm just a guy who happens to play hockey."

I steel my jaw, ignoring the wordplay. "Are you going to keep this secret or what?"

At that moment, the door to the kitchen opens and Poppy walks in, a curious expression on her face. "Keep what secret?"

My eyes dart from her to Finn and back again.

Her eyebrows are perked up, clearly expecting an explanation. My brain is completely blank. I'm not a great liar.

Finn picks up the pizza and shakes it. "We're ditching the party food and making frozen pizza. Don't tell anyone."

For a second, I don't think Poppy is buying it. But then the oven beeps, right on cue.

"It's your party," she says with a smile. "I don't think anyone cares." She looks at me. "You good?"

"I'm good," I say.

She glances at Finn, then back at me, then walks out of the room.

In the silence, I dare to meet his eyes, not at all surprised to find him smiling. "Oh, yeah. I think I'm going to like keeping your secret."

Chapter Three

Raya

Present day

Engaged.

I have a sister who is engaged.

I know that's supposed to make the parents feel old, but it sure does something to older sisters with no prospects too.

Today is Poppy and Dallas's engagement party, and while I'm ecstatic for my sister, I didn't realize until I was getting ready to leave my house that showing up here alone is a unique kind of awful.

I shift the rearview mirror so I can see more of my face and pull a lipstick from my bag. Before I apply it, I give myself a stern look and say, "This is not about you, Raya."

And it's not. I know it. I'm not selfish . . . just lonely.

I wish there weren't so many events where you're really supposed to have a plus-one. It's like finding a prom date once every few months, and that was stressful enough the first time.

I cap the lipstick, tuck it in my bag, and open the door of my Altima.

"Fancy meeting you here."

I glance up and see Finn standing beside my car, dressed in neatly tailored dress pants, a blue button-down, and matching tie. Even I can admit the man looks good. Since he grew up in Montana, I have a mental picture of him on horseback, lasso swinging, wrangling cattle.

And I wish I could say that made him less attractive.

I get out of the car, and Finn gives an overacted, presentational bow.

"You look stunning, as always."

I close the car door and straighten my shoulders, trying *not* to feel like a loser. Also trying *not* to let the compliment land. "Thanks."

"Okay! Sorry!" A voice calls out from behind us, and I turn to see a tiny woman wearing half a dress walking toward us. "That was my video editor. I forgot to send over the new workout,"—she winces dramatically as she walks up to Finn and grabs his arm, then flicks her free hand in the air—"it doesn't matter." She looks at me. "Hi! I'm Kaylee." She smiles with her full mouth, revealing teeth so perfect and so white I wonder if they're fake.

"Kaylee, this is Raya Hart," Finn says. "Poppy's sister."

She thrusts a hand in my direction. "Oh! I love Poppy! I sat with her at the game last night. She's *sooo* sweet!"

I shake her hand, but my face remains neutral. "Nice to meet you."

"Are you the one who works for the team?" she asks.

"That's me," I say, desperately wanting to get back in my car and drive straight home. "I should—" I make a move to go around them, but quickly realize there's really no easy way to get out of walking to the door with Finn and *Kaylee*. We're going to the same place.

"That must be so fun," Kaylee says as we start up the driveway. "Working for the team, I mean." She squeezes Finn's arm. "I don't think I'd get anything done though. Too much eye candy." She giggles.

Finn's gaze catches mine, and I quirk a brow. "What do you do, Kaylee?"

"I teach yoga," she says. "And I'm a fitness influencer?" She says this like it's a question. I try not to chalk it up to her age, which I'm assuming is younger than me.

"I'm really trying to grow my account and get a couple of brand deals." She looks up at Finn. "Hoping this one will make an appearance in a few of my videos."

He smiles uncomfortably, and I squint over at her. "He probably needs to check his contract and see what he's allowed to do publicly, and most likely without compensation."

Her eyes go wide. "Oh! I hadn't thought about that."

"With professional athletes, there's a lot to think about," I say, feeling the sarcasm brim over the words.

I have a bad habit of sizing people up in the first eight seconds, then believing that's who they are for the rest of the time I know them. I wish I were different.

Or wrong.

I nod as Finn pulls the door open and Kaylee walks in.

"Is this a networking event for her or . . . ?" I say under my breath as I walk past him.

"She's cool," he says, but he doesn't look sure.

In some ways, I feel sorry for the single guys on the team. It would be hard to find a real connection with anyone, considering how many women would love to say they're dating a pro athlete, regardless of who that athlete is.

In Finn's case, I have less sympathy. The man is a chronic flirt who doesn't seem to have any common sense when it comes to dating. In the short few months I've been working for the team, there's been a revolving door of women on his arm, most of them taking Kaylee and hitting Copy/Paste.

As soon as possible, I excuse myself and go find Poppy, who is in the kitchen hovering over the caterer, a woman Dallas hired so my sister could enjoy her party.

When she sees me, Poppy's eyes light up. "Ray! You're here!" She rushes toward me and pulls me into a tight hug. "Thanks for coming. I know social events aren't your favorite."

I pull back and look at her. "They aren't. But *you're* my favorite."

"I know." She smiles, with a twinkle in her eye. "I won't tell El."

I smile back, then the caterer shoots me a wide-eyed, silent plea, and I usher my sister out of the kitchen.

"Oh, I was going to help with the—"

"Nope," I say, moving her into the living room and out onto the back deck. "You're not working today, remember?"

Poppy nods. "Right. Not working."

"Everything is going to be perfect," I say.

When Dallas bought this house in Loveland, it was never supposed to be a long-term living situation. It was meant to be a place where his grandma could recover from surgery. But then my sister pretended they were dating, and that one interaction led to a fake relationship that turned real . . . and Poppy ended up with a guy who adores her.

Outside, there's a large deck that opens to a patio and a big yard. Quiet music drifts from a speaker, and further out in the grass, there's a long, rustic table decorated with the most stunning fall flowers I've ever seen.

Poppy and Dallas won't get married until next spring, but an early November engagement party, sandwiched between hockey games and restaurant events, is actually pretty perfect.

"Poppy, this is amazing." I take it all in. It's quiet and rustic and peaceful and so . . . Poppy.

"You like it?" she asks.

I turn to her. "I love it. It's all so beautiful. I'm just so happy for you."

Her face brightens. "We wanted it to feel like a big family dinner."

I spot Eloise with some of the hockey wives, and when she sees me, she lifts both her arms and waves with both hands. "Raya!" she calls out, and more than a few people look at me.

I smile and wave back, then look at Poppy. "Zero social graces."

Poppy laughs as Eloise rushes over. "Raya, you gorgeous queen, that dress is criminal."

I give myself a quick once-over. "Is it?" I frown, secretly thankful for the compliment. I don't need a lot of puffing up, but since I'm one of the only single people here, I did feel extra pressure to make myself look attractive.

That way maybe people think it was my choice coming alone, and not that no one wanted to come with me.

Which is ridiculous. I can't control what other people think, and I really don't care.

Except when I do.

People who know me would probably be shocked if they found out how much I actually want to fit in. Since I typically don't, I quit trying and convinced myself I was better off this way. And usually, I believe it. Lately, though, I've been more aware than ever of my aloneness.

I hate that stupid, superficial things like this still take up space in my brain.

"I saw Finn gawking at you," Eloise says.

I roll my eyes. "I guarantee that's not true. He's here with a yoga instructor." I glower at Poppy. "I think she's nineteen."

Poppy giggles. "She's twenty-five."

I quickly scan the group, and my eyes land on Finn.

Whose eyes are on me.

Instead of looking away, like a normal person caught staring, he lifts his drink in a "cheers," and gives me a wide smile.

And of course, my sisters see.

"He's so into you," Eloise says.

"Uh, look at who he's dating," I say. "The exact opposite of me. The literal photo negative. *That's* who he's into."

"I think you terrify him," Poppy says.

"I think you terrify everyone," Eloise chimes in, holding in a laugh.

"Good." I pump my eyebrows. "I like to be feared."

"He's a good guy," Poppy says. "I think you should give him a chance."

I look at her, incredulous. "A chance to do what?"

She stutters a bit. "I don't know, be your friend?"

"He's still looking over here," Eloise points out.

I peer over, meeting his eyes again, and this time, he quickly looks away.

Poppy puts a hand on my arm. "I want you to be with someone who makes you happy."

"Well, it's not Finn," I say, matter-of-factly. "He's too immature, and we're too different. Plus . . . *yoga instructor*."

The words have a little sting in them, but I don't know why. Maybe it's the reminder that men want women like the yoga instructor. Men do not want women like me.

I have receipts to prove it.

I grab Eloise's glass and take a sip, then quickly remember that I don't like champagne and hand it back to her—aware that my sisters are concerning themselves with something I don't want them to concern themselves with.

"I don't need a guy in my life, you guys. I'm really, really content with how things are right now. Plus, I don't have time. The transition to this new job is hard, and work needs all my attention."

"Oh, right, Dallas said you're in charge of the Denim and Diamonds fundraiser thing?" Poppy says.

I smile. "I am."

"Is that part of your job?" Eloise asks. "I thought you had a boring job, and that actually sounds fun."

"I asked to take it on," I say. "I like to plan events." *And I like to stay busy*. When I'm busy it's harder to examine what's missing in my life.

A few other people arrive, and Poppy squeezes my arm. "You good?"

"Yes, Poppy, this is your party—go mingle. Please don't worry about me."

She smiles, hugs me, then rushes off. I hate that she feels like she has to "make sure I'm okay" just because I showed up alone. They really should know I'm used to it by now.

If only it got easier.

28

"My boyfriend is so hot." I follow Eloise's gaze, firmly attached to Grayson Hawke, who's standing in a small circle of hockey players, looking—as expected—very serious.

But then he looks up at her, and the corner of his mouth tugs upward in a smile so subtle most people would miss it.

Another twinge of jealousy.

"I'm going to go see if he wants anything to drink." She looks at me, and I don't know what my face is doing, but she says, "You know you deserve to be with someone who adores you, but you'll never find him if you don't put yourself out there."

I frown. "I don't even know what that means, Eloise."

"Yeah, you do." She smiles, then walks off, leaving me standing there.

Alone.

Blech.

I try not to look the way I feel, which is awkward and a little out of place—reminding myself that this is my sister's engagement party, and I'm one of two maids of honor in her wedding. I *belong* here.

And yet, I feel like an outsider.

Like I don't belong.

"Thought you could use this."

I find Finn standing next to me, but not looking at me. He's holding out a brown bottle in my direction. I frown. "You know I don't drink."

He peers at me sideways, and my breath hitches in the back of my throat at a memory I've tried to bury—and the reminder that he knows something about me that no one else does.

"It's some fancy cream soda."

I take the bottle. "Thanks."

We stand there in silence for a few long seconds, close enough that I can feel the heat from his shoulder against my own. I take a drink, then look at the back of the bottle.

"It's basically a bottle of liquid sugar," he says, as if he knows what I'm looking at. "That's why it's so good."

After a beat, I ask, "Where's your yoga instructor?"

He chuckles. "She's talking to the wives. And she's not my anything." He nods toward a small group of women on the other side of the deck. It feels a little like high school all over again.

I always kept myself on the outskirts of popularity—too focused on where I was going after high school to trouble myself with what was happening while I was there. I never really fit in with girls my age.

As if on cue, Kaylee and a few of the wives burst into laughter.

A litany of criticisms rolls through my brain: *Too stand-offish. Frigid. Scary. Serious. No fun.* If you hear those things enough, you start to believe them.

More than that, I started to *own* them.

"She seems really nice," I say.

He laughs. "You're a terrible liar."

Ugh. I thought I hid it better than that.

"Just be careful, okay?" I look at him now.

He frowns. "Careful? Why?"

"Look, I know they probably don't have gold-digging content creators in Montana—"

"They absolutely do, they're just on horseback," he jokes.

I shoot him a look, and his face sobers. "She just seems like maybe she's looking at this as a networking opportunity, and not, you know, a celebration for her boyfriend's friend."

"I love how concerned you are about me, Hart." He takes

a drink from his own brown bottle—probably *not* cream soda. "People might start talking if you keep carrying on like that."

Flirty, as always. I brush it off, as always.

"I'm just thinking about the liability it could be for the team."

"Right. The *team*," he repeats.

"Yes, the *team*," I say right back. "If anyone's going to get swindled out of all of his money by trusting the wrong person—it's you." I steel my jaw. "And that would be a PR nightmare."

He frowns. "You really think I'm that stupid?"

"I mean . . ." I shrug a mock *if the boot fits.*

He lets out a laugh. "Huh. I didn't realize you had a sense of humor tucked in there."

I take another drink. "I'm full of surprises."

"No doubt."

There's a moment of silence, almost comfortable, and I default into telling-people-what-to-do mode.

"Look." I pat his arm, which is much firmer than I expected. "I think you're nice, and if I'm honest, a bit too trusting. You're nice. And that's one of your best qualities—but makes you an easy target."

His gaze drops to my hand, still on his arm.

I pull it away. "Just some friendly advice."

"All I'm hearing is that you have thoughts about my 'best qualities.'"

I roll my eyes. "Oh, for the love. Go back to your girlfriend."

He grins, leans closer, and looks so far into my eyes I can feel it in the back of my head.

"She's not my girlfriend."

My breath catches.

And then he walks away.

I stand there, on the perimeter, watching people move in and out of the space—laughing, smiling, having loud conversations. Telling jokes and making memories. And I'm on the fringes.

Just like always. And it's getting harder and harder to believe that it's my choice.

Maybe my sisters are right. Maybe it's time I actually put myself out there. To figure out what I want in a relationship —and what I don't—and then go for it. In a way that doesn't make me lose my head.

My phone buzzes in my bag, and I pull it out and look at it. It's a notification from an app that's a lot like Fiverr, but exclusively for young professionals, called Métier. Post what you're looking for, and you'll have twenty recommendations within ten minutes. Need signage for your next event? A caterer for a work luncheon? A new administrative assistant? It's a way to connect to people who have firsthand—and in-depth—knowledge for just about anything you need.

Anything I need.

I often need a date to these kinds of things.

And then an idea begins to form . . .

Métier isn't a dating app. It's more like job postings. But why can't it be both?

I'm not in this for romance. I'm not looking for a tradi-tional date—or even a traditional relationship. What I need is, well, someone like a business partner. A co-laborer. Someone who will agree to enter into a partnership with a clear understanding of the expectations.

It's just that partnership is dating.

I could make a post, take resumés, interview candidates, and potentially end up with someone to help take the pressure off events like this. If things go smoothly, there could be upward mobility—someone to eventually split the bills and the chores. After that, if they show promise, it could work itself into a marriage arrangement built on cordial feelings and mutual respect.

The more I think about it, the less romantic it sounds.

And I'm okay with that, honestly. After all, if I could bypass all the messy emotions, the over-the-top reactions, the blowups, the pining, the dramatic feelings, maybe I'd find stability, respect, and common goals.

Maybe I'd find someone perfect for me.

I like this. The possibilities excite me . . .

"Dinner is served!" Dallas calls out to the group. "Let's eat."

I tuck my phone away and catch Finn's eye as Kaylee grabs his hand on the way to the table.

My heart starts to buzz, and my brain says, *See? Exactly why this will work.*

No feelings. Just a simple, easy business transaction that will end in a solid partnership between two goal-oriented people.

It's perfect.

"Raya, you're sitting by me." Poppy motions for me to take the seat beside her. I glance down at the place card to my left and see Finn's name, written in perfect calligraphy.

I look up and find Eloise smugly watching me just as Finn finds his name. He picks up the card and looks at me. "Were you in charge of the seating arrangements?" He smirks.

I scoff. "In your dreams."

And, in a quick-witted callback, he says in the same tone

I used earlier, "*I mean . . .*" His shrug also seems to say "*if the boot fits.*"

I take a deep breath and let it out slowly.

He pulls out my seat, and I sit, side-eyeing Eloise, who looks like the cat who just swallowed the canary.

Yes, Finn is fun. He's good-looking and will probably make someone incredibly happy someday.

Just not me.

SOCIAL ENGAGEMENT TECHNICIAN

Early-thirties young professional woman with excellent 401K seeks professional man, preferably between the ages of 32–40, for plus-one events, social gatherings, and potential future personal partnerships.

Must be courteous, honest, and gainfully employed.

Duties include (but not limited to):
- Engaging in mutual accompaniment to work functions
- Attending all "plus-one" social events (i.e. work parties, weddings, and so on)
- Having a firm grasp of social interactions, sentence conjugation, and a wide variety of current events
- Maintaining excellent manners of decorum and hygiene, including but not limited to: person, vehicle, living space, and workspace

Candidates must also have no expectation of physical recompense for duties fulfilled.

Expenditures for all work functions, social events, parties, weddings, or any gatherings attended and fulfilled will be entirely covered.

Lastly, romantic gestures are not required or necessary.

If interested, please send your resumé and cover letter to: SocialEngagementTechnician@dropmail.cc.

Chapter Four

Finn

"All right, Brookie, level with me—what's going on with the yoga instructor?" It's after practice, a few days after Dallas's engagement party, and a perennially half-dressed Jericho Stephens is not going to let me go without a full interrogation.

It's like this guy never wears clothes.

We were on the road for two days, but now we're back, and for whatever reason—I'm in the hot seat.

I'm standing in front of my locker wrapped in a towel, hair still dripping from my shower. "Kaylee?" I grab a shirt out of my bag and tug it over my head. "We're just hanging out."

"But you've got a thing for Hottie Hart, right?"

Oh, *shoot*.

Dallas chucks his towel at Jericho, and it hits him in the face. Jericho stands. "What the—?"

"Watch it. That's my future sister-in-law you're talking about," Dallas says.

"It was a *compliment*." Jericho emphasizes the last word

36

to drive home his point. "Plus, my *wife* was the one who called her that."

"That woman is terrifying," Junior says. "I had to sign some papers for her last week, and my hand was shaking the whole time."

"Hot and terrifying—a lethal combination." Crosby shakes his head as he walks off toward the showers.

"So?" Jericho adjusts the towel around his waist, and I'm thankful he didn't drop it completely, per usual. "You gonna tell her?"

I frown. "Tell who what?"

"Tell the yoga instructor you're in love with Hottie Hart," Jericho says, then ducks as Dallas throws another towel at him. "Or—" he pops back, "Tell Hottie Hart you're in love with her!"

What? I think. *You mean tell her the truth?*

I pull my sweats on and lie. "Not in love with her."

"But it's something, right?" Kemp asks. "I mean, we were all at the party—"

"You stare at her, dude," Krush says.

"I don't stare—"

"You do," Gray says without turning around.

"I do?"

A collective laugh ripples through my teammates, each one mumbling something along the lines of "Seriously? You didn't know this?"

I turn toward my locker. I thought I'd gotten good at hiding my . . . infatuation, but I guess not.

I fell for Raya Hart the moment I slid her drink across the bar seven years ago.

No way I'm going to tell these guys that.

And no *way* I'm going to tell *her*. She's so far out of my league she may as well live on Saturn.

"Plus, her sisters are hooked up with two other guys on the team," Jericho quips. "Gotta go for the trifecta."

"Come on, guys." I toss the towel into a nearby bin. "She wouldn't give me the time of day."

"That's not a no," Kemp points out.

I muster my most convincing look. "It's a no."

"Well, maybe don't show up to her sister's engagement party with TikTok girl," Jericho says. "No way she's going to take you seriously."

"Good! I don't want her to take me seriously," I say. "I'm not a serious guy!"

"You're fooling yourself, man." Jericho shakes his head, and thankfully, reaches for his undershirt and starts to pull it on.

He and Monica got married when they were practically kids, and it's no secret how he feels about her. They're kind of gross—PDA wherever and whenever—but the truth is, someday, I'd like to be in a relationship like theirs. Like my parents'.

That would be the dream—a real partner. A best friend.

"We all know you're fooling yourself," Jericho says. "The only one who doesn't know it is you."

"I'm not—" and I stop. I realize they're all looking at me. And they've all read me like a book.

And nothing I say is going to convince them otherwise.

Because yeah. "Fine. Yeah. I like her."

Cue the chorus of "*Ohhhhhh!!*" accompanied by clapping and whistling.

I sigh. Because I know nothing will ever come of it.

The day after we met seven years ago, I went back to

her apartment, thinking maybe I had a shot. Sure, she was a couple of years older than me, but I swear we had a connection. She'd sat down at the bar, and the second our eyes met, I felt the spark. And yeah, I go on a lot of dates, but I'd never felt that spark before—and I haven't felt it since.

If those two drinks hadn't immediately gone to her head, maybe the night would've gone differently.

But in the light of day, all I got was rejection and closed doors. And you'd think that would be enough for me to get the hint, but every time I'm in the room with her, I'm drawn to her like a magnet. I stare because I can't *not* stare.

I want to watch out for her. To protect her. To make sure she's okay, because even though on the outside Raya Hart is one of the fiercest, strongest, most independent women I know, I also know there's a lot more to her than what she shows people.

But it doesn't matter. She doesn't see me as anything other than a joke—and that's not going to change.

"All right!" Jericho claps his hands together and shouts above the hooting and hollering. "Now we're getting somewhere! What are you gonna do about it?"

"Nothing?" I say, because really—what else can I do?

"Nothing?" Jericho's brows lift in surprise. "For real?"

"Do you know how many times I've asked her out?" I ask. "Probably a hundred."

"I don't think she knows you're being serious." Dallas pulls a hoodie on and tousles his damp hair.

I drop onto the bench in front of the locker. "Okay, so what else can I do to show her I'm serious?"

"Start by being straight with the yoga chick," Jericho says, "and stop bringing women like that to every party

Raya's at." He shakes his head like this is obvious because, well, it's obvious.

I look around the room. "Guys. Come *on*. I have exactly two chances with her. Slim, and *none*." I pause. "And Slim just left town!"

"Look." Gray, who's been completely silent in the back of the locker room, turns around. "You need to be honest with yourself about what you want. That's step one." He looks at me. Gray doesn't talk a lot, but when he does, everyone pays attention.

"What's step two?" I ask, pulling my hoodie from the hook in my locker, and tugging it over my head.

"Make sure you're good enough for her," he says.

"Dude, he's already scared of this woman," Jericho says. "You want him to be terrified of you too?"

"I just want to make sure he understands," Gray says to him, then turns back to me, eyes piercing. "She's not some fitness influencer looking for a little extra publicity, right? She's one of the good ones. From a good family. If you can't be the guy who's good enough for her, then don't even try."

There's more than just my ego or my feelings on the line here. If I screw this up—it could mess up the dynamics on our team. Maybe that's too big of a risk.

"I got it." I grab my duffel and sling it over my shoulder.

As I walk out of the locker room, I hear Jericho say, "Why'd you have to go and do that? You know he's never going to go for her now."

I'm through the door before I can hear Gray's response, but the whole conversation has me conflicted. Because yes, I have big feelings for Raya, but does that make me the right guy for her?

Nope.

As I walk down the hall, I catch my reflection in the glass of a display case.

I stop.

I try to stand a bit taller and suck in my stomach.

Man, I'm not her type.

I don't wear a suit. I don't have Dallas's face or Gray's abs. Heck, I don't even speak right half the time.

In all my twenty-nine years, I've never had a relationship that felt serious enough to think about engagement or marriage, but I do want those things. And I want them with the right person.

How do I know whether or not that's her?

I walk out to the parking lot just as Raya's Altima pulls in. I slow my pace because, even though three minutes ago I was sure the best thing for me to do was nothing—the prospect of seeing her is too tempting to ignore.

I walk over to her car and wait as she parks and turns the engine off.

I catch her eye in the rearview mirror and flash her a smile.

Her brow lifts, and she gets out and looks at me. "You know, Finn, sometimes I think you're stalking me."

I love it when she says my name.

"Stalking is such a harsh word," I say, grinning. "Are you just getting here?"

"Uh, no." She closes the car door and walks toward me. She's wearing a long khaki-colored coat and a deep green top, and I wonder if she has any idea how beautiful she is. "I just left for coffee."

She holds up a to-go cup from a little café I know down the street.

"You look pretty today." I test the waters.

Her mouth flattens into a straight line. "I bet your *girl-friend* also looks pretty today."

The guys were right. She's never going to take me seriously. My "harmless distractions" definitely need to go.

"She's not my girlfriend," I say.

"Does she know that?" She shifts her bag to her other arm.

"She does." I look away. "We've only been out a couple times anyway. It was never really . . ." My voice trails off.

"Never really . . . ?"

"Never really serious."

She gives me a quick, stern nod. "I'm guessing with you, most things aren't." She starts to walk around me, and I feel an impulse to stop her walk from leaving.

"Hey—" I say, sharply, reaching out and touching her arm.

She turns, looking at me expectantly.

I have no idea what to say. I didn't mean to stop her—I just don't want her to leave yet.

"You're wrong," I say, pulling my hand back. "About me."

"Am I?" She folds her arms. "How so?"

I take a breath, and it feels like a week before I manage, "I am serious. Sometimes."

Her shoulders soften and relax slightly, but she doesn't move.

I don't move.

But my eyes dip to her lips, and I swear I hear a hitch in her breathing.

I want her to say something. I want *me* to say something.

Words aren't working right now.

42

Raya's expression turns to disbelief. She smiles. It almost knocks me out.

"Keep telling yourself that, *Brookie*." She pats me on the shoulder, like I'm her kid brother, and walks away.

I stand there, caught—feeling vulnerable and stupid and staggered and swept up.

The smart thing to do would be to get over her and move on.

There's just one problem—I don't think I can.

Chapter Five

Raya

It worked.

I'm not sure what I was expecting from my post, but twenty-two resumés in six days wasn't it.

Eight of them were an instant NO, with the NO capitalized for effect.

Another seven went into a *Not Likely* pile, five went to the *Maybe* category, and two were very promising. And while I'll leave the post active a little longer, I'm not wasting any time getting on with the interviews—the holidays are right around the corner.

It would be really great not to shoulder those alone.

Judging by the keepers in the stack, it's refreshing to know I'm not the only professional, goal-oriented person who doesn't have time for niceties. I'm not looking to be swept off my feet here. I just need someone to be a plus-one for the events I have to attend, whether social or professional.

And later down the line, someone who pays enough attention to change the oil in my car when it needs it.

I think our ancestors were onto something with arranged marriages.

Got some cows? I've got a daughter! Boom. Done.

The only unfortunate thing here is the timing—because I'm absolutely slammed at work. The Denim and Diamonds fundraiser is set for the week between Christmas and New Year's, and since I volunteered to take it on, I'm handling all those details on top of my normal day-to-day.

Essentially, I asked them to hand me another full-time job for a few months because I love to stay busy. I also love that feeling when something I've planned goes off without a hitch.

Never mind that I'm only sleeping about four hours a night.

It's worth it. Once the fundraiser is over, I'll get back on schedule.

I walk into Meg's, my favorite little café and coffee shop, order a latte, and find a table in the back corner. I'm early, which is good, because I'm unexpectedly nervous to meet the two most promising candidates who replied to my ad.

I shift things around on the table to make room for Candidate One. Eric. I created a filing system on my iPad to keep track of resumés and responses, giving promising candidates their own folders. I pull up my settings and navigate over to Eric's folder. I click it open, thankful I gave myself a little extra time to review his details before our meeting starts.

The barista calls my name, and I stand to pick up my drink, returning to my seat just as the door swings open and a man I recognize from his photo walks in. Our eyes meet, and he lifts a hand in a polite wave. I watch as he makes his way back to the table.

Eric is tall and lean, with sandy-blond hair and glasses. He's three years older than me, graduated from the University of Illinois, and now works as a financial planner at a firm in the city. He's not handsome or unattractive, and judging by his reply to my ad, he has a limited sense of humor.

Those things aren't deal breakers for me. He doesn't need to be the life of the party or look like the book covers in the Romance section at Barnes and Noble.

He just needs to be reliable. Stable. Good. Someone with a strong moral compass and limited baggage.

When he reaches the table, I extend a hand. "Eric. I'm Raya. It's nice to meet you."

He slips his hand in mine. Zero sparks. Perfect.

"Nice to meet you too," he says.

"Please, sit." I motion to the booth, and he slides in across from me.

"Thanks for taking the time to respond to my ad," I say.

"I thought it was well written, and I like that you took the initiative to change your circumstances. Honestly, it's a clever approach to a common problem. Most relationships don't work out because there's too much emotion."

I nod and force myself to smile, feeling a little pathetic, though I'm not sure why.

"I agree. It's why I put it out," I say. "I'd rather find someone without the mess."

One quick, decisive nod. "Let's get into it, shall we?"

I pull up his resumé on the iPad so I can refer back to it if needed. "Sure. First, I'd love to get to know a little more about you—"

"As you can imagine, I don't have a lot of free time," he says with a quick look at his watch. "So, while I am open to

46

the occasional social function, there would need to be substantial advanced notice. I'm currently up for a promotion, and if I get it, my time will be even less, which is obviously why dating is so challenging."

I absently wonder if that's the *only* reason dating is challenging for Eric.

He folds his hands on the table, and something in his posture makes me feel like now I'm the one in the hot seat.

I've seen this before—many times—in the office.

I straighten and lean in, countering his body language with my own. "I understand, and that's exactly why I took out the ad. In my experience, dating brings with it a lot of expectations that I simply cannot meet at the moment."

"What do you propose?" he asks.

"An initial two-week period of getting to know each other," I say. "Three dates each week, with an agreed-upon length and location, while we decide if we're compatible."

"Two dates per week," he says. "I'm a good judge of character."

"So am I," I say. "Done."

"Good. What else?"

"Exit strategy. After the trial period ends, we have the option of cutting ties and going our separate ways—or continuing the arrangement, potentially introducing each other to our work circles. Social and professional."

"Agreed," he says. "Drinks twice a week after work."

"One night for drinks. One for dinner."

He nods. "Very good."

I draw in a quick breath. So far, so good.

"What else?" he asks again.

"The only caveat here would be the holidays," I say.

"They'll interrupt our schedule, but I assume you have a function or two, and so do I. I propose two holiday-related work events and one personal."

"Personal meaning—?"

"Thanksgiving," I say. "Christmas. One family dinner for each holiday."

"No family," he says, briskly.

"It's the holidays," I say. "At some point, family will be involved."

He gives his head a quick shake. "I don't do parents."

I frown. "Is that negotiable?"

"No," he says. "Is it negotiable for you?"

"No."

He sticks out a hand. "Well, we tried."

I shake his hand. "I appreciate your time."

"Good luck on your search." He stands, and as he starts for the door, my gaze catches on a familiar face seated at another table.

Of all people.

My shoulders drop, and I blow out a breath. Finn watches Eric as he walks out of the café, then saunters over to my table, like he has a secret he can't wait to tell me.

He doesn't, of course. That's just how he looks. Unbothered. Easygoing. Unruffled. I would be annoyed if I weren't so jealous. I could use a tiny dose of nonchalance every once in a while.

"Well, well, well," he says, sliding into the booth across from me. "I didn't know you liked this place."

I press my lips together and pin him with a look. "I come here almost every day."

"Interesting."

"What are you doing here?" I ask, starting to get a little

48

nervous that Candidate Two is going to show up before I can get rid of him.

"I heard they have good iced chai." He holds up his cup, a rich, caramel brown color swirling with white, but doesn't look away. "Who's the suit?"

"The suit?" Playing dumb might buy me time, but I know it won't matter. I'm a terrible liar. I cannot let Finn—or anyone at work—find out about this plan.

"The stiff guy who looks like he applauds when the plane lands," he says.

I let out a laugh, and do my best to stifle it.

"You've got a pretty smile, Hart," he says. "You should use it more."

At that, I stiffen and look him straight in the face. "Are you always like this?"

"Like what?"

"Happy," I say.

"You say that like it's a disease." He smirks.

"No, I say it like it doesn't feel real," I say. "Nobody is happy *all* the time."

"Well, I'm not happy twenty-four seven." He pauses, then adds, "Only like seventeen seven. The other seven I'm asleep." He pauses, and it's like I can hear the gears turning in his brain. "But I usually have great dreams, so maybe, yeah —like twenty-four seven."

He holds up a pinky as he takes a loud sip of his drink.

"Something is definitely wrong with you," I say.

His eyes narrow slightly, like he's thinking about that, but then he shrugs and nods in agreement. "Eh. You're probably right." His face settles, and I'm struck by how easygoing and self-deprecating he is. It's different.

It's nice.

But I don't want to be thinking nice things about Finn Holbrook, so I say, "Are you still dating the yoga instructor?"

"No," he says, and I admit, I'm surprised.

"You got bored of her already?" I shake my head. "Wow."

"We were never serious," he says.

I smile. "Oh, I know."

His face darkens as he looks away.

Strange.

His gaze drops to the iPad on the table in front of me, and I quickly close the case.

He frowns. "Wait. Are you looking for a new job?"

Is that concern on his face? Why would he care?

"What? No."

"That looked like a resumé." He reaches for the tablet, but I smack his hand away.

"Would you get out of my business?" I say, exasperated. "I'm not looking for a job."

"So, who was that?" He glances back toward the door. "Was it his resumé?"

I scramble to tell a fib that's close enough to the truth that I won't get caught. "Yes, I'm looking to hire someone," I say. "To . . . help out with a few things."

There. Hopefully it's enough to make him go away.

But nope. He's like a puppy who thinks you dropped a peanut in the couch cushions.

"What kind of things?" he asks.

"Finn."

"Because if you need stuff done around your house—you're looking at the wrong demographic."

I frown. "That's very judgmental."

"No way that guy has ever used a drill," he says.

"I don't need someone who can drill," I argue, and I can

50

see the cogs turning in his expression. I immediately cringe at my accidental innuendo.

I shoot him a look.

"What?" He feigns innocence. "I didn't even say anything!"

I pick up my iPad and aimlessly scroll.

"What's the job?" he asks, nodding toward my tablet. "Maybe I can do it? I'll save you some money."

I sigh with a slight laugh. "You can't."

"Says who?"

I level his gaze. "Says me."

He drops his voice. "I have a certain set of skills."

I give an incredulous look, which seems to be my resting face around him, then stiffen when I see the door to the café open.

Thankfully, it's two old women—and not my next candidate—who walk in. Eric was here and gone so quickly that I've got a bit of time before the next one, but if he's at all as punctual as his resumé indicates, he'll be a good twenty minutes early.

"You need to go."

Finn follows my gaze to the door, then back to me. "Oh. You have another person coming in. I could stay, maybe help with the vetting process."

I'm starting to get really antsy.

"Finn," I say, slightly more exasperated.

"I'm a great people person." He smiles and shrugs his shoulders in a give-me-a-shot look.

I know what he's doing, because he's Mr. Nice Guy who wants to help, but in this moment I just need him to go. "You really can't."

"You sure? I'm not bad with—"

I rub my temples and squeeze my eyes shut. "Can't you just leave me alone?" I groan.

I open my eyes and find Finn's smile has vanished. His whole demeanor and body language have changed.

Crap. That was too far. He looks wounded.

My mind races, trying to think of a nice way to backpedal.

And then, like a window opening back up after the winter, he brightens. If he was at all injured, he quickly recovers, painting a broad smile back on his face. "All right, Hart. I get it. I'll go."

I blow out a breath. "I'm—" I start to apologize, but he holds up a hand.

"Say no more. Sometimes I'm a lot." He smiles, and I see no manipulation or insincerity in that smile.

It makes me feel worse.

I'm searching for the right words—as if "I'm sorry" won't suffice—when the door opens again and a man I recognize from a photo in my inbox walks in.

Finn scoots out of the booth, notices the man, stands to his full height, and looks back at me.

"Looks just like the last guy." He holds up his cup like a toast and says, "Good luck, Hart."

He makes his way to the door. I watch him walk through the restaurant, past the next candidate—Justin, who I quickly turn my attention to.

I stand and he greets me with a friendly smile. "Raya?"

He leans for a hug as I go for a handshake.

I recalibrate and wrap an awkward arm around his back, and as I do, Finn turns back and looks right at me, a weird expression on his face.

Our eyes meet, and for a flicker of a moment, I can't look away.

A years-old image I thought I'd erased flashes through my mind—a dark room, his hands on my hips, and a long, lingering gaze that held me captive, just like this one seems to be doing.

Chapter Six

Finn

Who hugs at the beginning of a job interview?

Weirdos. That's who.

Or people not actually there for a job interview.

I don't know what "job" Raya's trying to fill, and I know my experience with interviews outside the food and drink service industry is limited—but a handshake feels way more appropriate.

Unless things have changed.

It did make me wonder where I can sign up for an interview with her, though. She looked amazing.

I didn't go to that place for chai. I went because Raya's assistant, Jill, told me she'd be working there this morning.

I went because I had this stupid idea I was going to get a chai and sit down across from her and what—telepathically change her mind about me? Convince her I'm a good guy with spiced tea and whole milk?

Figure out how to ask her out in a way that finally makes her understand I'm serious?

It went so much better in my head.

I'm starting to think if I'm going to have a shot with her, I'm going to need a personality overhaul, because the one I've got just annoys her.

Maybe Hawke can teach me to be more brooding, or Dallas can give me pointers on how to chisel my jawline.

Unfortunately, I have a feeling that what Raya wants is not the same as what her sisters want.

My phone buzzes with an incoming FaceTime call, the screen lit up with a photo of my parents. I click on the button and accept the call, then wait for my mom to stop walking with the phone at her side.

It's what she does now—hits the button to start the call and then walks to another room in the house.

The dizzying, swinging video fumbles to a stop and she comes into view, face about an inch from the camera. Her forehead is pinched, and I can see straight up her nose. She's clearly trying to sort something out on her phone.

"Hey, Momma," I say.

"Oh! Finneus James!" She tilts her head and looks at me, oblivious to how she looked two seconds ago. "You look tired."

"Momma, leave him alone." My younger sister, Rowena, shoves her face in front of the camera. "Hey, big brother. You playing tonight?"

"Hope to," I say. "You gonna watch?"

"We're *all* gonna watch," Momma says before Rowe can answer.

But my sister shakes her head and moves off-screen. I'm still sitting in my Jeep Cherokee outside Meg's Café, and I start it and flip on the heat. The weather took a turn this week, and Chicago is no joke when it starts to get cold.

"Just called to check in on ya," Momma says. People from here would say she's got an accent, but I didn't notice it until I'd been away from Montana for a few years. "Did ya see Jane's email about the community center?" She asks.

I nod. "I did. Sounds like things are going well."

She moves closer to the screen. "Yep, those free ranch hands got a great thing in that community center."

I laugh. "They're called 'kids,' Momma."

"Well, you're doing an amazing thing for our little community, Skip."

My mind trips on the silly nickname, but I wave her off. "Nah, I'm just trying to give back a little."

She shakes her head. "So modest." She points at the camera. "One of your best qualities." Her expression shifts. "Are you gonna make it home for Thanksgiving? There are a few things about the community center we should talk about . . ."

I shake my head. "We've got a game the day before and the day after, so I don't think I can."

She tuts. "They really should give you time off to spend with your family. It's a crying shame—" She passes the phone to my dad, but I hear her mutter something about "family values" in the background.

"Hey there, Skipper," Dad says. "You keeping your nose clean?"

"No time for anything but hockey," I say, even though that's not exactly true.

"So that's a yes?"

"That's a yes." I chuckle.

"Get any of 'em to try Rocky Mountain oysters yet?" He chuckles.

I laugh. "Not yet, but I guarantee they ain't gonna know what they are until *after* they eat 'em."

I feel my mouth loosen, sliding back into familiar speak.

"Ha! You betcha!" He laughs big. Makes me miss home.

"How's things there? You good?" I ask.

"Oh, you know how your momma gets—" he shakes his head— "wants you to make a big noise out there and wants you home at the same time."

From elsewhere in the house I hear her shout, "They should give him time off to see his family on Thanksgiving!"

We both laugh. Momma is a force. The kind of woman who'd do anything for anyone but who is also a little bit off her rocker.

"Still trying to save the world?" He isn't looking into the screen when he says this. And I know what he's talking about.

"When I can," I say.

"It's noble, Skip, the way you're always watchin' out for everyone—but you know it won't bring him back." Pop looks at me now.

"I know." I watch the oncoming traffic for a few seconds. "Hey, Pop, can I ask you something?"

"You want me to go outside so the prying ears can't hear?"

"Oh, I can't know whatever this question is?" Momma shouts in the background.

"I swear, that woman is two rooms over and she can still hear every word I say," my dad whisper-shouts into the phone.

At that, I laugh.

He leans closer to the screen and raises his eyebrows in a question.

I nod, and he gets up and walks outside as Momma's voice calls out, "He's just gonna tell me when he gets off the phone!" —her voice fading as my dad gets further away.

Dad closes the door and steps outside. "Hang on a sec." He double taps the screen.

The video flips around, and I can see the wide wrap-around porch and, then, the view.

Big sky. Open air.

It's as if "freedom" were a place.

My eyes fix on the snow-capped mountains in the distance, a view I grew up with, and my heart aches for home.

I let out a low whistle. "Miss that."

Moses, one of the many dogs on the ranch, lazes in the yard, and I see my brother Quent's truck parked down by one of the outbuildings.

My dad turns the camera back around and sits in one of the rocking chairs he made for the front porch. "What's on your mind, son?"

I groan and look out the window, back in the direction of the restaurant.

"Uh-oh," Pop says. "It's a woman."

I shake my head, mostly at myself. "That obvious?"

"I've gotten pretty good at recognizing that look." He smirks.

I let out a breath. "How'd you convince Momma to give you a shot?"

He shrugs. "I'm pretty irresistible, Skip."

I chuckle to myself. "Does Momma know that?"

He laughs lightly, then takes a sip from that same old, cream-colored coffee mug he's been using since I was a kid. "When we met, your momma wouldn't give me the time of day." He leans back and shakes his head. "She's so stubborn she couldn't see a good thing—the best thing—right in front of her face."

He pauses, and I pause with him, then crack, "Oh! You mean you! Got it. Go on."

He quirks a brow, mock-unamused. This is the relationship we've got—a healthy dose of banter mixed with the utmost respect.

I wish every kid had a dad like mine.

"To her, I was just a stupid neighbor kid who used to tip her daddy's cows when he wasn't lookin'."

I muse. "Can't imagine why that didn't make her fall in love at first sight."

He exhales softly, lost in a memory for a moment.

"So, how'd you show her you . . . you know. You grew up?" I ask.

"Not sure I did," he says. "Not till later anyway. She helped with that. We're a team that way."

In the best sense of the word.

"I did get my act together, though." He takes a drink, then looks at me. "Had to if I was ever going to get your momma to look twice in my direction." He leans back in the chair. "And I didn't quit. I was determined to win her over. Kept finding ways t' be around her. Anything to remind her that I was put on this earth to admire her."

"You're such a sap," I say, shaking my head.

"There's nothing like the love of a good woman, son." He leans in. "And your momma is a good woman."

I know exactly what he's insinuating, and he's been doing it to embarrass us kids since I was a teenager. "Dad. Too much information, seriously."

He lets out a single, hearty laugh.

"Now listen, Skip." He turns a bit more serious. "I kid around sometimes, but your momma is the best thing that's happened to me. Put aside how she's still the most beautiful woman I've ever seen, and how most days I can't go but five minutes without thinking about her—she's stubborn, driven, but has a heart big enough for all of us in this house."

I go still. I could say the same about Raya. On the surface, she's nothing like my mom, but there are striking similarities. They're both stubborn. They're both driven. And they both have big hearts. Just not the kind you'll ever find on their sleeve.

Maybe that's part of why I'm drawn to her. My momma demonstrated strength, and I saw all the ways she filled in my dad's gaps. But I also saw the way he loved her. They're a team. Different strengths to attack every problem. Partners in the truest sense of the word.

I never paid much attention before, but the older I get, the more I realize that's what I want. *Not* meaningless flings with fitness influencers.

Dad holds the phone up higher and lifts his chin. "Does this woman know how you feel about her?"

I lean forward, forearms on the steering wheel, and shake my head. "No. Not really."

"Hmmph."

"I mean, I joke around with her. Take her mind off work when I can. I, you know, try to make her laugh and stuff," I say.

"All good things—but maybe not the most important thing, yeah?"

I nod. He's not telling me anything I don't already know.

"I guess my *unique personality* makes me hard to take seriously."

My dad busts out laughing. "Well, that's your first hurdle. She doesn't even know how you feel."

"She thinks I'm a joke, Dad," I say miserably. "I don't know, maybe I'm just carrying a torch. She's kind of like . . . the one who got away." I shrug. "Reminds me a little bit of Momma. The stubborn side, anyway."

Dad purses his lips. "Well, I say go for it, kiddo."

"Easy for you to say," I groan. "You're not the one who could make a fool of himself."

"Son, if you're not willing to fall flat on your face, then you don't deserve a woman like your momma." His eyebrows are raised, and then he asks, "Is she worth it?"

Without hesitation I say, "One hundred percent."

He shrugs like he's just made his point and the case is closed, then takes another sip. "You coming home for Christmas?"

I nod. "Just for a couple of days. I get some time off, not a lot, but yeah. I'll be there."

"Good," he says. "I think the whole family will be home for the first time in . . . a while."

The words hang there, feeling wrong somehow. Because the "whole family" will never be home again.

I know Pop hasn't forgotten—sometimes it's just easier not to say the hard things out loud.

My eyes drift to the glove box. It's still in there.

"Let me know how it goes with the girl," my dad says, pulling me back to the present. "And take good care of yourself."

"I will."

"And live it—"

"Like it matters," I say, finishing the thought.

He grabs the brim of his hat, tips it in a nod, and the

screen goes dark, but my dad's words don't disappear so quickly.

Raya

"It sounds like you and I want the same things," Justin says after we get the initial pleasantries out of the way. "I have to say, your approach to taking matters into your own hands is different. And clever."

I give him a quick smile. "I think it's important to be honest about what you want."

"And you want a partner," he says without any judgment.

"That's right," I say. "I don't need the flowers and the chocolates and the boombox over your head outside my window."

"The what?" He looks puzzled.

Hmm. Not knowing the *Say Anything* reference could be a red flag or a green one. I make a mental note to make a real note about that later.

"Just not all of the"—I wave my hand around, looking for the words—"romance. Just another person to shoulder the responsibilities. That may or may not be you. That's what I'd like to find out."

"I'm open to this experiment," he says.

"There's one other thing." I take a quick drink of my latte. "You can't tell anyone that this is how we met. I have a nosy, albeit wonderful, family, and I don't want them to think I'm—"

"Settling?"

"No, not settling. Cutting corners, more like," I say.

"They don't quite understand. Both of my sisters are hopelessly in love. My parents too, come to think of it."

His eyebrows pinch. "You—don't want to hold out for that?"

I shrug. "I think love comes in many different forms, including a well-matched pair who respect each other and have similar goals."

He smiles. "I think you might be right."

I smile back. "So, you're up for the two-week trial period?"

"I'm up for it," he says. "Let's do dinner? Tomorrow?"

"Perfect."

"I'll have my assistant email you the details."

We stand, and Justin helps me with my coat, then motions for me to go in front of him as we walk toward the door. Outside, I stop and look at him, satisfied with this choice and anxious to see where it leads.

"It was great to meet you," I say.

He takes my hand, then leans in and kisses my cheek. "Great to meet you too."

I smile and walk away, aware that there wasn't a single butterfly awakened in my rib cage by Justin's nearness.

And that's exactly how I want it.

Chapter Seven

Finn

"I thought about what you said."

After four days on the road, we're on the plane on the way back home. I purposely sit across from Dallas because I've wanted to talk to him about this for days.

"I say a lot of things," he smirks. "Hopefully it was something useful."

I realize that he has no idea what I'm talking about because the conversation I'm referring to happened over a week ago.

"About this thing. With Raya," I admit without looking at him.

"Ah," he says. "That."

"Yeah. That." I don't let on, but it's *all* I've been thinking about. On the ice. Off the ice. When I'm by myself or with a bunch of other people. I've spent the last week trying to figure out what I want and how to get it.

Throw in my dad's sage advice, and this whole thing has really gotten into my head.

"Okay." He pushes the button on the side of his seat, moving it to an upright position. "What did I say now?"

"That she doesn't think I'm serious," I say.

"Well," he sits, "you're not."

I shift, my seat suddenly uncomfortable. "But I really want to be. I mean, I want to be, for her."

He sizes me up for a beat too long. "So you want to change who you are."

"Well, no." I make a face. "I mean, yeah. I mean—" I sigh, at a loss.

He looks at me. "Do you know what you're getting into here?"

I go still. "Yeah, I do."

There's a lull, and in it, I start to wonder what he's thinking. It's like he said before—Raya is about to be his sister. I know Dallas, and I know how seriously he takes that.

I inhale. "I've had a thing for her for—" I almost say it, but stop myself.

Seven years.

It's not accurate, exactly, because there were a lot of years in between where I assumed I'd never see her again. But the second our circles intersected at my Halloween party —that was it. Flame reignited.

I just haven't let myself admit it because she clearly does not feel the same.

But the night she walked into the bar, looking lost and a little beat down—it was like a switch flipped. Like something inside me woke up at the sight of her. She was icy at first, cold even. A statue chiseled from stone. And I couldn't get enough of her.

She was with a friend who ordered her a drink. They talked for about a half an hour, and I picked up bits and pieces of the conversation—something about an engagement announcement posted on social media and a work crisis. Judging by the small box in front of her, I figured she'd been fired.

And she wasn't taking it well.

The drink went straight to her head, and her friend didn't stick around, leaving this beautiful woman a little tipsy and alone.

I knew it wasn't my job, but I kept an eye on her anyway. She gave me her credit card and opened a tab, then asked if she could stash the box behind the bar. After one more drink, she moved beyond tipsy, and more than one guy in the bar noticed.

Including me. But at that point, my only concern was her safety.

Over the next hour, I watched as this raven-haired beauty danced and laughed and sang with perfect strangers, and after watching her rebuff more than one advance, I stepped in. I felt protective.

The images start to blend together. The stories that poured out of her. The tears. The other guy. The dark hallway. The moment she went up on her tiptoes to try to kiss me, and the absolute pain of having to push her away.

Burke snaps his fingers in front of my face. "Where'd you go?"

"Sorry—" I lean back in my chair and prop my ankle on the opposite knee. "I think I'm just nervous."

He laughs. "Dude, you've got it bad."

I push a hand through my hair and let out a heavy sigh. "You could say that."

"Did you end it with the yoga instructor?" Dallas leans over to zip up a pocket on his bag.

"Never really started," I say. "But yeah, I told her it was nice to hang out a few times, but I'm going to focus on other things. I think she just wanted access to—" I motion to the general vicinity— "all of this."

"Yeah, I've known my share of those."

There's a lull, then Burke raises a brow. He takes a drink of his water, watching me. "Just ask."

"Do you think Poppy and Eloise would help me?" It feels ridiculous to ask this—like I'm getting my friend to find out if a girl likes me. In middle school.

He starts to say something, then stops. "Actually, that's pretty smart."

"I just think if anyone is going to be able to help me crack the Raya code, it's them."

"Tell you what," he says. "Poppy loves having people over. We don't have a game tomorrow, so—we'll have people over. Game night, or whatever. You'll come early, talk through your strategy, and we'll get Raya there."

"Yeah. Yeah, that sounds good, because so far my normal moves don't work on her," I say. "That's why I need help."

He pushes the cup aside and leans in, like he has something serious to say.

He's my captain, so I'm programmed to listen when he speaks. Even about personal stuff.

"Look, Finn," he says. "Raya doesn't do 'moves.' She doesn't do fake, and she absolutely doesn't suffer fools."

"What does that mean?"

He tilts his head, as if trying to find the gentlest way to say it. "She doesn't waste her time on foolish people."

"Ouch."

He leans back. "I'm not saying you're a fool, but you *are*

a little foolish sometimes. And I think it's your best—and your worst—quality."

"So, I'll change."

He shakes his head. "You're not hearing me. You're amazing. You're hilarious. You're easygoing and fun to be around. You have a great family, and you look out for literally everyone else. *You don't need to change that.* Plus, you can't change yourself into the guy you think she wants. You know that, right?"

I chew the inside of my lip. Because part of me hoped to do just that.

"You two are either right or you're not. Doesn't make any sense to pull a bait and switch." He turns the cup around in his hands. "She's too smart for that anyway."

"So I have to figure out a way to win her over without changing my whole personality, which she absolutely loathes," I say. "Got it."

"She doesn't loathe you." He laughs and looks out the window, as if he's considering something, then turns back. "We just have to sell her on your many excellent qualities." He claps me on the shoulder. "I think she'd be lucky to have you."

"You mean that?"

"I do," he says. "You're one of the best people I know. We just need Raya to get on board."

I nod. "Thanks, Burke."

"You got it," he says. "I'll text you details once Poppy gives them to me."

I smile. "You're a lucky guy. She—"

"Yeah, I know," he says, cutting me off. "She's pretty special."

"I was going to say that she doesn't put up with your crap, but yeah, we'll go with special." I crack a smile.

He moves quickly, reaches over, and puts me in a head-lock. He's way stronger than I thought, and I literally can't get free.

"Sorry, what? What was that? I can't hear you, buddy," he says, sticking his free hand in my ribs, making me squirm. I jab him in the side and he finally lets me go, laughing.

Feels like going a round with my older brothers—and it's one of the things I really love about this team.

I go quiet, resting my head on the back of the seat, thinking about what Burke said, about Raya, and about a small, dark hallway that still begs the question—*What if . . .?*

Chapter Eight

Finn

The next night, I show up at Burke's house in Loveland with a bag of chips and a ball of energy in my stomach. Burke's text didn't say who they'd invited tonight, but the prospect of seeing Raya has me nervous.

Because after tonight, I'm hoping to unveil Finn Holbrook 2.0. Still me, just a little more serious. A little more grown-up.

Hopefully, it's what she's looking for.

Poppy opens the door, and I hand her the chips. "I know you're a fancy chef and everything, but my momma said to never show up empty-handed."

Her smile is wide. "Well, I already love your momma. Thank you for this. They'll go perfect with the dips I made."

I follow her into the kitchen and see a spread of food out on the counter, set up buffet style. Poppy empties the chips into a bowl and sets them on the counter next to the dip. It's kind of her since there's already another bowl of chips out.

"Dallas is in the living room with Gray," Poppy says.

"But we think we'll keep you in here with us." Eloise walks in and looks at me. "Just for a second."

"Don't freak him out!" Burke calls from the other room.

Both women face me—Eloise with her arms crossed, eyebrows raised, and Poppy with the hint of a smile on her face.

"Ah, shoot. They told you," I say.

"Of course they told us," Poppy says. "The real question is—what the heck have you been waiting for this whole time?"

"So this really was all real—you *actually* have a thing for her?" Eloise throws her arms up in the air.

I wince and shrug at the same time.

"She thinks you're teasing her," Eloise says.

Poppy looks at me. "She thinks it's all a joke."

"Correction—she thinks *I'm* a joke," I say. "I just . . . let her."

"Aw, Finn," Poppy says, a tinge of pity in her voice. She reaches over and puts a hand on my arm. "You're an idiot."

I frown. "I—"

They both shake their heads in a long, slow movement, like two choreographed disappointed parents.

"You've come to the right place, my friend." Eloise claps a hand on my shoulder.

"Guys?!" I call out to the other room. "You wanna come help me in here?"

"No, no, no," Eloise holds up a finger at me. "They will not come to your rescue."

"Sit." Poppy points to the stool on the other side of the counter. "When did your infatuation with our very cranky but very beautiful older sister begin?"

Again, my mind conjures images of Raya—walking

straight to the bar, then tipsy on the dance floor, then with her arms up around my neck in the dimly lit room . . .

But I can't go there. I've been sworn to secrecy.

"Halloween party two years ago," I say, which is not exactly a lie. Because before that night, I assumed I'd never see Raya again. "You were both there."

"Ah," Eloise says. "Morticia." She grins. "I told her she looked hot."

I laugh, and even though I don't say so, I silently agree.

"So this whole time—" Eloise picks up a chip, scoops up some dip, and pops it in her mouth— "all those flirty little comments—it was real."

"Of course it was real," I say.

"I knew it." Eloise smacks Poppy across the arm. "What have I been saying this whole time? I knew it!"

"You know *why* she doesn't take you seriously," Poppy says.

"Because I'm not serious?" I ask, even though this is really not a question that needs to be answered.

Poppy shrugs.

"That's why I'm here," I say. "I need you to tell me how to prove to her that I may not be a serious guy, but I *am* serious about her."

There's a pause, and then they look at each other and do this weird thing that girls do where it looks like their faces are melting into pouty expressions and they both let out a long "awwww."

I only stare.

"Okay, well, first . . . you flirt with everyone," Eloise says. "So, flirting with her isn't unique or special, you know?"

"I don't flirt—"

She holds up a hand. "You do."

I snap my jaw shut.

"Then there's your little act." Poppy picks up a wooden spoon that seems more like a prop than an actual utensil.

"My act?"

"Where you tease her, and it gets under her skin, then you push a bit farther, and she ignores you and acts like you're super annoying." Poppy shrugs.

I'm chagrined. "That's not an act."

"And if you're going to ask her out—" Eloise picks up another chip, pops it in her mouth, then finishes her thought as she chews— "you need a plan. An actual date. You can't say, 'Hey you, uh, you wanna do something sometime, baby?'" She uses a deep, weird voice when she says this, and I laugh.

"Don't talk with your mouth full," Poppy says. Eloise picks up a chip and tosses it at her. It lands in Poppy's hair.

"El!"

Eloise crunches another chip and grins.

"You two would fit right in with my family," I say.

"Ooh, I like them already." Eloise wags her eyebrows.

Poppy walks over to the fridge and pulls out a bottle of water, then hands it to me. "You have to say, 'Hey, Raya, I've got two tickets to the museum this Thursday night. Do you want to come with me?'"

I make a mental note. "To a museum? You think that's the kind of place she'll want to go?"

"I was just using that as an example," she says. "But you can't take her to a sports bar."

"Or axe throwing."

"Or Top Golf."

"Got it," I say, miming writing out a list. "No . . . fun . . . places."

"How about a nice restaurant?" Poppy says.

I nod. "Like a steakhouse?"

"Or somewhere you'd, you know, dress up. Wear a shirt with a collar. Make an effort."

I nod. "Okay. I'm not—do you know where I grew up?"

They share a look. "Somewhere out west?" Poppy says.

"A ranch. In Montana. A formal dinner was if we all actually wore pants to the table."

They stare at me.

"I'm kidding," I say, then add, "pants were always optional anyway."

Gray walks into the kitchen. "You know, there is another way."

He picks up a bottle of fancy cream soda—the same kind Raya and I both drank at the engagement party—and unscrews the top. He takes a long, slow drink, and my eyes dart to Eloise.

"Anytime, Hawke," she says. "We're just kind of all waiting for—"

"Show up for her," he says. "Like that one—" he points the bottle in Eloise's direction— "did for me."

"Aw," Eloise says.

"How do I do that?" I ask. "The woman literally will not accept help. From anyone. Ever."

"True," Poppy says. "But that doesn't mean she doesn't need it."

"Maybe start small," Eloise says. "Bring her coffee once in a while."

"Or that fancy gourmet chocolate." Poppy sets a bowl of freshly popped popcorn on the counter. "I think paying attention to the little things will go a long way."

"Yes! She works nonstop," Eloise says. "She needs a break. Or an enema."

Poppy bursts out laughing. "Oh my *gosh*, Eloise!"

I'm getting a very clear picture of how Raya's sisters see her. And I get it, but also—I've already seen a completely different side of her.

"Does she take days off?" I ask.

They both shake their heads.

"Figure out what she needs and show up for her," Gray says. "Pay attention. Be a friend. You don't need a collared shirt to prove you're a good guy."

There's a pause, all of us a little stunned that Grayson Hawke is doling out the most sensible wisdom in the room.

"I am so in love with you right now." Eloise walks over to Gray, takes his hand, and pulls him out of the kitchen. "We'll be right back."

Gray sets his bottle down on the counter as he leaves the room, a surprised smile on his face. "I should speak up more often."

I reach over and pick up a chip, but I set it back down. Poppy looks at me, pity in her eyes. "You look like a lovesick puppy."

"Pathetic, right?" I smile, but it's half-hearted. "You think we're a bad match?"

She shakes her head. "Exactly the opposite. I think she'd be lucky to have a guy as kind and good as you, Finn."

The compliment throws me. I'm used to my parents saying nice things, but they're my parents—they're practically contracted required to say nice things.

She pauses, then adds, "It's just sometimes hard to convince Raya to see things differently than she sees them."

"And she sees me as—"

"As a flirty, hockey-playing, not-so-serious guy who is just looking for a good time," Poppy says. She adds, a bit more gently, "Because that's kind of who you've been up to this point."

Yeah. I have. For good reasons too.

Heaviness sucks. I don't like thinking about it. Plus, isn't life much better when you find silver linings everywhere? Isn't it easier if you're not bogged down by the crap life throws at you?

I look at Poppy, realizing something. "You know I'm not some womanizing party guy, right?"

Her eyebrows shoot up like she doesn't believe me. "Do I?"

"Well, I'm not."

"Finn, you've brought a different woman to every team function we've been to. You're famous for your epic parties. Aren't you the reigning beer pong champion?"

I blow out a breath. "I got out of that game without taking a single drink."

She shoots me a look.

I lose the smirk.

I hear what she's saying, and she's right. Don't change me, change my behavior. It makes me feel stupid, but I take the words to heart. I'll be her friend—her *real* friend. Showing up for people is easy for me, and Gray's right—that goes a long way.

"Hey, uh, is she coming tonight? Raya, I mean?" I ask, mentally preparing myself.

"Let me check." Poppy picks up her phone as Eloise returns to the kitchen.

"Sorry, had to make out with my hot boyfriend for a minute."

"Well, thank you for not doing it in the kitchen again," Poppy says smartly, scrolling on her phone. Her face falls. "Oh."

Eloise and I glance at each other, then Eloise says, "What?"

"I'm so sorry, Finn. Raya's not coming." Poppy clicks the phone off, sets it down, and looks at me.

"She's on a date."

Chapter Nine

Raya

It's all going according to plan.

The preliminary interview was above average, his resumé had no typos, and a few well-crafted sentences stood out. Our first meeting for coffee checked the boxes.

So now, I'm halfway through my second trial date with Justin.

After about a half hour, he excuses himself to take a call. On a normal date that would bother me, but because he and I have this understanding—I'm fine with it.

It's exactly the way I want it. It feels like this could happen here, in the restaurant, or at the office in one of the meeting rooms.

Zero feelings activated. It's perfect.

I use the time he's gone to send a few work emails. While this date is semi-important, it is cutting into my Denim and Diamonds work time. With the event coming up next month, there are a ton of details to manage.

I stifle a yawn as I scan an email from Jill with a list of tasks.

In addition to the fundraiser and holiday preparations, our team is also interviewing for three different positions in the HR and PR departments, which means the stack in my inbox is reaching new heights.

Once I get through this season—once we finish just a few of these projects—I'll be able to breathe again.

Maybe if I keep repeating that to myself, it will become true.

But I thrive on this, right? Stress is my love language.

My last job as a corporate headhunter was a *lot* more cutthroat than this job. I thought I'd run that company one day. But the thought of seeing Rich every day after his move to the Chicago office was just too much.

When I met Rich, he lived and worked in our Seattle office. He'd fly into Chicago once a month, and we hit it off. I swore I'd never get swept up in romance after my only other serious relationship ended in disaster, but Rich had his charms.

I'm embarrassed to admit I fell for them.

And him. Hard.

We dated for months. I started thinking about words like *forever* and *I do*. We looked at engagement rings and dreamed about the day when we weren't long distance anymore.

And then, one night, we were out to dinner, and a woman walked up to the table, glared at him, and called him by name.

Then, she looked at me and asked who I was. I fumbled a reply, my brain not really computing what was happening.

Rich muttered something like, "I can explain," but I'm not sure which one of us he was talking to.

Then, she showed me a picture of their children.

They had children.

The crazy thing is she wasn't mad at me. She felt sorry for me, knowing this man had betrayed us both.

Ugh, the number of times I've replayed that moment. The look on her face as her fears were confirmed. I wonder what she saw on my face when I realized the truth.

It was humiliating. And Rich had the nerve to try and talk his way out of it.

How could he do that? How could he turn *me* into a cheater?

Me.

Someone who never even used the answer key for the even-numbered questions in the back of the math book.

I've never told anyone about that day. Not even when Eloise fell for her boss, who was dating one of my friends. I should've been more understanding, but I couldn't say any of it out loud. I was too embarrassed.

Or too proud.

I reported him to HR, and as these things sometimes go in male-dominated businesses, all he got was a slap on the wrist and a "write-up" in his file, whatever that meant.

And later, a promotion.

Which is one of the myriad reasons I'm not working there anymore.

Just thinking about it makes me break out in hives, so I force myself to think of something—anything—else.

I glance down at my text messages and see I've missed on from Poppy:

POPPY

Hey! Come over! Impromptu game night!
I'm making those little meatballs you love
so much!

> Ray, you coming?
>
> RAYA! PLEASE CONFIRM RECEIPT!
>
> I don't know why I think all caps would be louder over a text.

I smile. I can see her and Eloise in the kitchen, bantering back and forth.

RAYA

> So sorry, just seeing this. I won't be able to make it because I'm on a date.

I quickly turn off my phone and put it in my bag because I know the barrage of incoming texts that are coming my way.

In the past, new relationships have always garnered the same reactions from my sisters. Excitement. Giggling. Then, the questions. Assumptions. Googling. Date ideas.

I have a theory that it's this exact kind of reaction that contributes to heartache. Because if I buy into it, everything is heightened. The relationship is made into a bigger deal than it actually is. The only approach worth taking is a level-headed one. Clean, clinical, and planned. Unfortunately, it's going to take some time to convince my sisters of that.

Justin returns to the table and takes his seat. "I'm so sorry —that was work."

"You have to go?"

He nods. "Unfortunately, yes. It's not how I wanted our second date—

I think —*meeting*—

"—to go. But I can make it up to you. Maybe an extra date next week. I can have my—"

"Assistant reach out," I say, finishing the sentence at the

same time he does. I smile. "That's fine with me, but it's okay if it doesn't happen next week. I'm buried at work too."

He smiles. He has a nice smile, but something about it doesn't quite feel genuine.

My first trial date at the coffee shop with Justin had gone well. I'd give it a solid B.

We talked about work and our frustrations with dating. I explained that I'm not looking for anything out of the ordinary. I just want someone to make functions more bearable—but also, it's more than that. More than just a perpetual plus-one. I'm looking for someone to share my life with—just not romantically.

It felt risky to say it out loud, but Justin seemed to understand.

Tonight, we met at the restaurant after work for our second "date" this week. The plan is to spend this trial period getting to know each other, to see if our goals align. But regardless, he's agreed to come to Thanksgiving dinner with me, which is maybe more of a relief than it should be—it gets really old showing up to all these holiday events by myself.

So far, we seem like we could work together.

It's not the "wrong way" to date, I tell myself. It's just a different way. A new way. Or maybe a really old way.

"We'll get something on the books, I'm sure." He waves to the waiter and makes a writing motion to indicate we're ready for the check. Then, he turns his attention back to me. "One more thing, Raya, if you don't mind me asking—"

I lean back. "Of course."

"What happens—" He seems to be considering something— "if you fall in love with someone for real?"

"Or if you do," I say, reminding him that if we do this, we're in it together.

"Oh, I don't think I'm made for romantic love," he says, flatly. "I've tried it a few times. It doesn't work for me. I like your approach much better. No feelings, just clear expectations. I don't want to be put upon to fabricate emotions when, frankly, I don't have many, and the ones I do have I'm not sure what to do with."

"I have emotions," I say. "I just—have distracting ones." And ones I don't want to have.

He nods, thoughtfully. "Hmm. So, there *is* a chance you'll fall in love. It's not that you're incapable."

"I'm *choosing* not to," I correct. "I don't want to fall in love. It never ends well."

I think about Rich. I have no interest in going through that again.

A cordial, respectful partnership can bring me all the things I want and need. And I can't be certain, but Justin might be the perfect person to fill that role.

"I think we need to have an out clause," he says. "Because even though I don't have the need for love and romance, you might."

I start to argue, but he holds up a silencing hand.

"I know, I know, you're choosing not to. But if this is going to have any chance of working the way you want, we need to put it on the table," he says, addressing all of our expectations.

At that, I nod because it makes sense. "You're right."

"So, if in the future you decide that maybe this isn't what you want after all, we'll part ways with no hard feelings."

"And the same goes for you," I say.

He drums his fingers on the table. "I like you, Raya."

I check my stomach for butterflies and again, nope. All cocooned.

"I think you're smart and beautiful, and I could see this working out very nicely." He tilts his head and looks at me. "But I don't think you're quite as emotionally closed-off as you want to be."

"I am," I say, firmly. "You'll see."

The waiter returns with our check. Justin hands over his credit card and I Venmo him the money for my half. That's the deal. Fifty-fifty across the board.

I'm not in this for chivalry, either.

After we square the bill, he walks me outside and waits until my Uber shows up to drive me back to the stadium, where my car is still parked. There's no awkward goodnight kiss. Just a reminder for me to send him my schedule, a polite handshake, and I'm on my way back to work.

It's all going according to plan.

Chapter Ten

Raya

Forty-eight unread messages.

Frankly, I expected more.

I start my car, ignoring the four missed calls, and go straight to the text thread, which is still buzzing with activity.

Hart Sisters Group Chat

POPPY

I'm sorry . . . you're on a WHAT?

ELOISE

A WHAT, Raya? Why were we not informed?

POPPY

You know she silenced her phone.

ELOISE

She's not coming back till after the date.

POPPY

El, we're standing in the kitchen together. I can see you sending me these texts.

ELOISE

I know but this is more fun.

POPPY

You have guacamole on your cheek.

ELOISE

😊😊😊

POPPY

Ray, who's the guy? Who are you dating? Where did you meet him?

ELOISE

Is there a photo? How'd he ask you out? When do WE meet him?

POPPY

Game night is still going on if you want to swing by on your way home!

Tiny meatballs and girl talk!

There's a short break from texting, then they pick it back up again.

ELOISE

Let's just keep texting until the buzzing of her phone gets too annoying.

Ray.

Raya.

Ray-Ban.

X-Ray.

Tell us about the guy.

POPPY

EL. She's going to hate us!

ELOISE

Tell us.

Psst.

POPPY

Just answer so she'll stop.

And we are going to need details

ELOISE

Can't stop, won't stop

And we won't sleep till we get them deets.

POPPY

Text when you're on your way!

I click the phone off, knowing full well they're not kidding. If I don't answer their questions immediately, they *will* show up at my house tonight.

I start my drive and weigh my options. I have so much work to do—but it's not quite 8:00 p.m. I can stop by Dallas's house, explain to my sisters that I met Justin—where? What am I going to say? I can't tell them about my experiment. And I don't want to lie. I'm a terrible liar.

I click my phone open, find Justin's name, and hit the call button.

"Raya?" he says when he answers. "This is a nice surprise."

The cocoons in my chest don't even budge.

"Sorry to disturb you," I say, tone short. "Just a quick question. How should we say we met?"

There's a half-a-breath of a pause before he comes back with, "How about this: I saw your photo on a reply you posted on the app, and I reached out. I was very forthcoming and not creepy at all, stating in gentlemen's terms that I think you're lovely, and I'd like to take you out for dinner."

I laugh at his formal response, but decide it's perfect. "I don't want to make it sound too clinical, but my sisters are known for turning everything into a fairytale."

They tend to forget that not all love stories have a happy ending.

"Embellish as you see fit," he says. "Just let me know if you change any details."

"Okay, thanks," I say.

"Have a good night."

I hang up, realizing it's already starting. We're already a team. A united front. Two partners with a common goal.

Good plan, Raya.

I pull into Dallas's driveway behind Eloise's car, get out, and walk to the door. I ring the doorbell and wait for the inevitable barrage, like Hobbes tackling Calvin when he gets home from school.

I'm also trying not to freak out about all the work waiting for me when I get home. I'm behind, and I hate being behind.

I pull out my phone and check my to-do list, noticing the start of a headache in my temples. Maybe Dallas can spare two Advil.

The door opens and both Poppy and Eloise grab my arms and pull me inside. "You have a *lot* of explaining to do!"

"You didn't even text us back," Eloise says.

"Well, I'm here now," I say. "But I can't stay. Just figured it would be easier to, you know, get this over with."

They both stare at me. "I'm sorry—'get this over with'?" Eloise crosses her arms over her chest. "You have two adoring sisters who are merely asking for every single detail of your love life as it unfolds, and you act like this is a *chore*? I'm offended."

I roll my eyes and look at Poppy. "I was promised tiny meatballs."

She giggles and motions for me to follow her.

I slip my coat off and hang it on a hook by the door. I'm not dressed for game night. While my sisters are both wearing sweatpants and hoodies, I'm wearing an off-the-shoulder black top with flowy, wide-leg white pants and pointy black heels. This realization makes me even more excited to get home and change. These shoes are killing me.

I walk into the kitchen just as Finn walks in from the other side. We both stop. His eyes meet mine, widening as his gaze quickly scans my body, lingering on my bare shoulders. He doesn't say a word.

Eloise looks at him, then at me, then back at him. "You good, buddy?"

I've made eye contact with him dozens of times, but there's something different about the way he's looking at me now. Something I can't quite place.

And even though I want to look away—I can't.

The butterflies burst out of their cocoons and are flapping around inside my entire body.

"You look—" He nods, and I brace myself for some ridiculous and embarrassing flirty comment, surprised when he says, "You look really pretty, Raya."

For a second, the rest of the room goes quiet, almost like we're the only two in here.

Oh.

"Thank you . . ." I say quietly, only slightly aware of the little knowing glances between my sisters.

"You should wear your hair down more often," Finn looks at me seriously, no trace of his usual casual smile. "It's really nice."

I absently reach up and tug on a strand of my hair, skin electric and feeling weird and goose-bumpy, unsure what to do with what sounded like a genuine compliment.

Then I come to my senses and frown. "Finn, did you hit your head? What is wrong with you?"

"Let's go, uh, into the guest room." Eloise grabs my hand and pulls me out the door. Then to Finn, "We'll be right back."

On my way out, I catch a glimpse of him turned to Poppy, with a questioning look on his face. It almost reads, *Was that okay?*

What is happening?

I march down the hallway behind Eloise, waving at Dallas and Gray who are both lounging on the couch, playing a video game.

"I'm wearing heels, could you slow down?" I struggle to keep up with my youngest sister, who is being really, really forceful.

She closes the door of the guest room once we're inside, and I close my eyes, trying to remember everything Justin and I planned before I face the interrogation.

But when I finally look at her, it's not Justin she asks about.

"*What* was that?" Eloise hisses.

I frown. "What was what?"

"That—" she flails her hands around, like she's trying to pluck the perfect word from the air— "*tension* between you and Finn." Her eyes practically bug out.

My frown deepens. "What are you *talking* about?" But

the words sound hollow, even to me. Because I felt it. Every second of it. The nerve endings in my body are zapping around like live wires. If I wanted to, I could close my eyes and feel it all over again.

But I do *not* want to.

There's a sharp *knock-knock* at the door, and Poppy slips in.

"Raya, what the heck?"

I hold up my hands in a *what?* gesture.

"Don't pretend with us," Poppy says. "We were just there, two seconds ago. You stopped him dead in his tracks."

"Oh, come on," I defend. "That's just how he is. He's— you know, flirty."

"That was *not* flirty," Eloise says. "That was—" she shudders. "That was hot."

I drop onto the edge of the bed and take off my shoes, mentally praising the Lord to finally get them off my feet. "If you say so."

Who am I kidding? It really *was* hot.

What am I supposed to do with that?

Eloise jumps onto the other side of the bed, and Poppy sits in a big chair in the corner.

"The way he looked at you stopped you dead in *your* tracks too." Eloise has that smug *I dare you to disagree* look on her face.

"In case you've forgotten—I was on a date tonight," I say. "And I'm so tired. And I still have a ton of work to do. I just came here to answer all your questions about Justin."

"Whoa!" Eloise exclaims. "Justin?"

"Who is Justin?!" Poppy asks.

"The guy I went out with," I say, like, *duh.*

"Okay, but what about Finn?" Eloise asks. "Because if

some hot guy was looking at me the way that man just looked at you—"

I turn and give her an incredulous look. "Eloise. You're dating Grayson Hawke. And in case you didn't know it—he looks at you like that every time you're in a room together."

"Ha! So you admit there was a look!" Eloise points at me, like she's caught me in a lie.

"I have to go." I stand, but Poppy pushes me back down onto the bed, then lies down so I'm sandwiched between them.

"We're sorry. We know we can be a lot." She pauses. "And by we, I mean Eloise."

Eloise reaches over me and smacks Poppy, but also smacks me at the same time.

"Okay," I move to sit up again, "I'm not about to be in the middle of—

"Tell us about Justin." Poppy gently puts a hand on my shoulder and pushes me back down.

"Yeah, and work can wait," Eloise says. "Do you ever sleep?"

"I think I could sleep right now," I say, laying my head back on the pillow.

For a brief moment, I flash back to a memory: the three of us, up late. We're *maybe* middle school age, laying on an air mattress just like we are now. Eloise wanted an air mattress because she thought it would be like a bounce house, and the first night we got it, we lay shoulder to shoulder, looking up at the ceiling where we had stuck glow-in-the-dark stars.

It was us three. Always us three. Poppy and Eloise, being their goofy selves, and me, the center, the glue, holding everything together.

"*After* you tell us about this guy," Poppy says, snapping me out of the memory. "We really are excited for you. It was just, you know, that whole display out there threw us for a loop."

"I don't know who this Justin guy is," Eloise says, "but does he look at you like *that?*"

"Finn is a flirt," I say, a bit exasperated. "And he's too young."

"He's only like three years younger than you," Poppy says.

"Four."

"Three-and-a-half," she corrects me, squeezing my arm. "And that's nothing. It doesn't matter at all."

"He's a really good guy," Eloise says.

"Guys. Stop. You know how I feel about hockey players," I say.

"Dallas and Gray haven't changed your mind?" Poppy asks.

I sigh. "Justin is more . . . my type."

"Boring?" Eloise snorts.

"Smart, successful, and self-made," I say. "We have the same priorities. We want the same things. He . . . gets me."

My eyelids are heavy as my sisters discuss the "priorities" that should matter, and then they begin to debate the kind of guy they each think I need.

It all starts to fade into the background until everything goes quiet, and soon I don't hear anything at all.

Chapter Eleven

Raya

Voices swim in and out.

"Do we wake her?"

"She looks so peaceful."

"A little less scary like this, for sure."

"She can't drive home if she's this tired."

"She needs to take a day off. A sick day. A mental health day. Something."

I crack open my eyes and squint.

There are five shapes standing in the room. Hovering.

I frown. "What the...?"

"You fell asleep," Poppy says. "You didn't even budge when we got up."

"You were mid-sentence," Eloise giggles. "You were about to tell us about your date."

I open my eyes wider and see Finn standing in the doorway.

I sit up, feeling embarrassed and not at all rested. "I fell asleep?" I chew through the cotton mouth and push a hand through my hair, immediately thinking about how much work I didn't get done tonight.

I'd accounted for the time away for dinner, but not this. Not a random nap before 9:00 p.m.

I want to move out of this bed, but someone put a big, chunky blanket on me. It's insanely cozy.

"When was the last time you took a day off?" Poppy asks.

"I went to dinner tonight," I say, struggling with the blanket, finally managing to push it off me.

The five are still standing, looking at me, and I'm not a fan of feeling like I'm on display.

"Let me guess. You worked late, changed clothes in the bathroom, went to dinner, picked at a salad, then forty-five minutes later you were back in your car driving here." Poppy glares at me.

She's shockingly accurate, but I don't admit it.

"It was at least fifty minutes at dinner," I say, trying to lighten the mood.

"You need to take better care of yourself." This from Eloise, who is not an authority on anything except stray dogs.

"Raya, why don't you sleep here tonight?" Dallas says. "We can get you a change of clothes, and you can sleep in tomorrow."

I laugh, pushing my way to a standing position. "You guys, seriously. I fell asleep early. I didn't pass out. I'm not sick. I'm perfectly healthy." I pat Dallas on the arm. "But thank you. Your concern—all of your concern—is greatly appreciated." I grab my shoes and walk out of the room, my sisters following close behind.

"Okay, but Raya, what about taking tomorrow off?" Poppy says, a thread of worry laced across her forehead.

I hold up a hand over my shoulder as I make my way to the front door. "I'm fine. And I really can't." I grab my coat from the hook and drop my heels onto the floor in front of me. "You know you don't need to worry about me. Ever. I'm always fine."

They're both frowning.

"We also know you've never randomly fallen asleep at someone else's house," Eloise says. "You work way too hard," she says, genuinely.

It almost gives me pause—but then I think of my to-do list, and that slams my brain out of Neutral and into Drive.

I slip on my shoes while shoving my arms into the sleeves of my coat, trying not to let any of this attention get to me. It's not only unwarranted, it's unwanted. I pride myself on not being a person anyone needs to worry about.

They know this. Or at least they should.

Finn walks into the entryway, keys in hand.

I stare at him. "What are you doing?"

"Following you home," he says.

I shake my head. "No, you're not. I'm fine."

"I know. I just need to see for myself." He shrugs. "For your sisters' sake."

"Finn. I'll be—"

He leans in and, under his breath, out of earshot of anyone else, he says, "It's kind of what I do."

I open my eyes wide, shaking my head, silently telling him not to broach this subject in this company.

He leans back and, with kind eyes, just smiles and nods.

I huff out an annoyed breath. "Fine."

I want to argue, but honestly, I'm too tired. The exhaustion really is unlike anything I've felt before. My eyelids are so heavy it's almost painful, my muscles feel like they're hanging on for dear life, and I never did take that Advil, so my head is still pounding.

I open the door and walk out onto the porch, wishing I'd gone home after I left dinner instead of stopping here. I really don't feel like driving at all.

"Thanks, Finn," Eloise says as he steps out onto the porch.

"I'll text when she's home safe, promise," he says, then pulls the door closed.

I roll my eyes again. "So dramatic," I mutter under my breath.

"Even you have to admit—that was weird." He stands in front of me, staring at me. "Are you actually okay?"

I reach up to pat him on the shoulder, but instead, I place a hand on his cheek. It's a strangely intimate gesture I hadn't intended, and I'm instantly struck by a memory. It hits me like a flash—images scrolling like a slideshow.

The dark room. His hands on my hips. The long, lingering gaze.

I pull my hand back, trying to ignore the stunned expression on his face. "Sorry, I didn't—" I gather myself. "I'm fine."

He nods and motions toward the stairs. I walk to my car, hyperaware of his presence right beside me.

"How was your date?" he asks.

I frown at him. "You really want to know?"

"Sure," he shrugs.

"It was fine."

He nods. "You like him?"

"I do, yeah," I say. "He's in real estate. Very successful. Kind. Good teeth." I smile.

"Ah," he says in a wistful tone. "Just what everyone is

looking for—good teeth. It must be love." He pulls open my car door before I can get to it.

I glare at him.

"Don't give me that look," he says. "I know you don't need a man to open your door, but my momma brought me up to be a gentleman." He doesn't budge. "And I believe a gentleman can take care of a woman at the same time that that woman takes care of everything else."

"I really don't need anyone to take care of me," I say.

"No, you sure don't." He levels my gaze. "But every once in a while, wouldn't it be nice if someone did?"

Something deep down in my bones answers his question with a loud and resounding, "Yes!"

I shake the thought away and get into my car. "You don't have to follow me."

"I know, but I'm going to anyway." He closes the door, then walks over to his Jeep, and as I round the circle drive and head back out to the road, I can't even pretend his headlights in my rearview mirror are anything but comforting.

Because for whatever reason—it's nice to know I'm not alone.

The drive is only about ten minutes, but I take it slow because something still feels a little off, like I could fall asleep at the wheel. When I pull into my driveway, I exhale a slow sigh of relief, expecting Finn to honk and drive back to the city.

He doesn't.

Instead, he pulls in behind me, gets out of his Jeep, and walks right inside my garage. I push my door open before he can touch it. "I'm home now. Look, I can even open my own door," I say.

He chuckles at that, and I add, "Your services are no longer required."

He pulls out his phone and makes a call, I assume to somebody back at Dallas's house. "Yeah, she's home."

I roll my eyes as I grab my bag and get out of the car, closing the door behind me.

"Yep. All right, I'll tell her." He looks at me, and I shake my head, hoping to convey that I'm not going to listen to whatever they tell me to do.

But after he hangs up, he says, "That was Poppy. She said to tell you they love you and they hope you get a good night's sleep."

My shoulders drop. Oh. I wasn't expecting that. It shouldn't affect me—I mean, of course they love me. I'm their sister. But it catches me off guard. The simple reminder that I'm not alone.

I start fishing in my purse for my house keys, just to avoid letting him see my glassy eyes. The door isn't even locked.

"They're good people," he says. "Makes me miss my family."

I pull my keys out and lift my eyes to his. "You have siblings?"

He nods, and a slight chuckle escapes. "*Oh*, yeah. I have a big family. Five brothers and two sisters."

My eyebrows raise in surprise. "Seriously?" I think about it for a second. "I can totally see that, actually."

He laughs. "Buncha crazy ranchers in—"

"Montana," I say. "I remember."

He nods. "I'll see them at Christmas, so—"

I go still. "Are you the youngest?"

"Youngest brother," he says. "Rowe's the baby, though."

99

"I feel sorry for your sisters," I say, shaking my head. "So many brothers."

"Be sorry for the guys who try to date them," he says.

"Believe me, dating is worse when you have sisters," I bemoan.

He laughs. "I bet."

All at once, I want to know more. "I don't know anyone else from Montana."

"Have you been before?"

I shake my head. The overhead light of the garage door clicks off, leaving us standing in the dark.

Dark room, hands on my hips, long, lingering look—my mind is at it again. I push the memory away, but the feeling from the kitchen returns—light, heightened senses, nerves on edge.

"Well, you've got an open invitation," he says. "Anytime you want to see it for yourself."

"I'm not sure I'd know what to do with myself in Montana," I say.

"I can think of a few things."

The air turns thick, and I try incredibly hard to ignore the flutter in my chest.

"That sounded—" Even in the darkness, I see him wince, laughing gently as he looks away. "Ah, shoot. I didn't mean . . ."

A nervous laugh escapes, and I hear myself say, "Oh, sure you didn't. . ."

He laughs. "Honest! For once, I wasn't . . ."

Flirting? I think.

He shakes his head, cutting himself off. "I was thinking of my favorite hike—this great place in Glacier. Everyone should do it at least once. And there's kayaking in the moun-

100

tains and a really quiet part of the ranch with a hidden lake I think my brothers still haven't found." He smiles.

"It sounds pretty amazing," I say, wondering how hard it is for him to be here, in the city, when he's so clearly built to be somewhere else.

"I'll show you someday." He smiles, backlit by a street-light dimly shining into the garage. "But for now—get inside and put yourself to bed. You need rest."

"Yeah, yeah."

He's about to go, but I stop him.

"Finn?"

He turns back. "Yeah?"

"Thanks," I say, turning my keys over in my hands. "For making sure I got home safe." I meet his eyes and laugh lightly. "Again."

He smirks, and for the first time all night, I see a trace of the playful Finn Holbrook I know. "Sometimes I think it's my calling to make sure you're safe, Hart." He backs out onto the driveway, holding his hands out to his sides. "Lucky me."

I smile, watching as he gets into the Jeep Cherokee. He starts the engine, then rolls down the window, pokes his head out, and shouts. "I can't go until I know you're *inside* the house!"

I shake my head and wave both arms, hoping that will shush him. He flashes his brights at me, and I give one last wave, escaping through the side door into the house.

My phone buzzes in my bag, so I reach in and pull it out to find a text:

FINN

Sweet dreams, Hart.

I stare at the words, not sure how to respond. I walk into

the living room and stand in the darkness, watching as his Jeep backs out into the street, then slowly drives away.

And the butterflies in my stomach finally start to land.

Chapter Twelve

Raya

"You wanted to see me?"

I don't have to look up to know that Finn is making his daily appearance at the door of my office. It's been almost a week of home games and practices since the night he followed me home from Dallas's, and every day, he's shown up here. At my door.

I was used to the occasional drop by, but there's been a definite uptick since that night—almost like he feels responsible for me.

Which is weird, considering how self-sufficient I am.

Another feeling I'm wrestling with is that I've come to expect—and slightly enjoy—these daily check-ins.

Each day he shows up with that same lazy smile.

Most of the older women in the administrative offices enjoy his visits too—though they show it more openly than I do, if the hushed chatter in the office is any indication. I pick up pieces of conversation, and it usually involves the word *charming,* and occasionally, *adorable.*

I glance up, barely, and find him leaning against the

doorjamb, dressed in black Nike joggers and a Chicago Comets hoodie, his stick bag slung over his shoulder.

"No, Finn." I look away, suddenly unable to focus on what I was doing, unsure where I left off.

It's like reading a book and having to reread the same paragraph because the words don't make sense.

He takes a step into my office. "Oh, you sure? I thought I got an email about it."

I look up. "I didn't send an email."

"Weird. Are you sure? I could've sworn . . ." There's a playful glint in his eyes, and I see him daring me to take the bait.

I never take the bait.

"You look nice," he says. "Red is definitely your color."

"Yesterday, you said blue was my color."

He shrugs. "It was. Today it's red."

My gaze drops to my desk, and I keep my face down, just in case the heat I feel in my cheeks is showing.

Because in the days since that night in my garage, I've been actively working to push Finn out of my mind.

Never mind that everything seems back to normal on his end. The compliments. The flirting. The showing up unannounced. He's settled right back into the role I'm used to. But somehow, he's figured out how to compliment me without sounding completely disingenuous.

It's . . . different.

Still, it's Finn. Nothing will ever change the image I have of him.

Never mind that my sisters seem to have joined Finn's fan club. More than once, I've reminded them I'm seeing Justin, but since they haven't met him, he's like an apparition. Finn is very real, and they've jumped on his bandwagon without looking both ways first.

What changed?

My computer dings three times in quick succession. Three new emails.

"Whoa, someone's popular." He shifts the bag on his shoulder. "You good? You need anything?"

"More time would be nice," I breathe.

"I'd help, but . . ." he points at himself. "I'm not the office type. If you need me to hit someone with a stick, though, I might be able to—"

He keeps talking, but I'm struggling to keep my focus on what he's saying along with the emails I'm trying to read.

"I'm busy, Finn, so if you don't need anything—" Having him here is too distracting, and I'm buried right now.

I'm calculating the amount of work I have to do—plus all the details for the numerous projects I'm handling—each one important enough that I can't really prioritize—and I keep coming up with more hours needed to finish them than there are in a day.

That's only if I don't sleep.

Not only is Denim and Diamonds just a few weeks away, but the PR team hired and fired the same person just this past week, which has been a bit of a nightmare for my department.

I type a few lines in reply to the first email when my cell phone buzzes with a new text from Justin. Miraculously, we found time for lunch earlier this week, and we've spoken on the phone twice. So far, we're compatible, and I've started to wonder if this plan really is genius.

It'll be nice to have someone to bring to Thanksgiving dinner next week, even if we are still fairly new.

Ugh. Thanksgiving. I barely have time to think that far into the future.

I flip my phone over and pinch the bridge of my nose, rubbing the spot that usually helps alleviate some of the pressure built up in my head.

Finn moves a bit further into my office and gently sets something down on my desk. It's a small box.

"What's this?"

He shrugs, almost looking embarrassed. "Open it."

I take the small white box and flip it open to find my favorite kind of dark chocolate sea salt caramels.

I look up at him, and he's smiling like, *Eh? You like it?* I start to say something, but there's a soft knock on my open door.

I look past Finn to see one of the interns. She almost looks afraid to come in.

Finn plops down in the chair on the other side of my desk.

"What is it?" I ask with a quick nod to the intern.

Landyn is new. Fresh out of college, and most likely not cut out for this job. She'll have a formal evaluation later this month, but odds are, she's toast. She's too slow and struggles to remember details. Not great for someone in her position.

She can probably sense her impending demise, which is maybe why she looks like she just swallowed a horse. Her face tightens.

"Hey, Landyn," Finn says in that casual, cool tone. "It is Landyn, right?"

She double-takes a bit, probably because he knows her name. "Landyn, yes."

Finn knows everyone's name.

"How do you like working here so far?"

106

Her eyes dart to me, almost like she's asking for permission to respond. I shrug, because this is what Finn does. It's impossible for him to meet someone new and not have a full-on conversation with them. It's like everyone else disappears when he talks to you, making you feel like you're the only one in the room he cares about at that moment.

This is just how he is. His curiosity about me—and his conversations with me—aren't special or unique. He is genuinely curious. About everyone. Once, he did a press conference and ended up asking more questions than he answered. Never mind that there does seem to be something a little more purposeful about him lately.

Landyn shifts her weight uncomfortably, then answers Finn's question. "I love this job," she says. "But . . . it's . . . a lot." She winces. "I'm trying to keep everything straight."

I should be more sympathetic. At this exact moment, I'm also trying to keep everything straight. Working in human resources for a professional hockey team is no joke. And while I am more than qualified to manage teams of people, and I have the organizational skills to keep everything running smoothly, lately I've fallen behind. I'm not keeping everything in order.

And I hate when things aren't in order.

"Yeah, I can imagine," Finn says. "Where did you go to school? I mean, I assume you went to school for this. Like, what's the major for this kind of job?"

Genuine. Conversational. I can see Landyn's shoulders relax, and her face brightens as she talks about college.

I turn back to finish the email I started when two more come in, one a follow-up from yesterday I haven't gotten to yet. I frown, and it's the kind of frown I can feel in my whole face—stressed and tight.

I look back at Finn and Landyn, now fully in conversation, like I'm not even here.

Unfortunately for Landyn, she's part of the problem right now. If the support staff isn't doing their job, that makes it hard for me to do my job. Things fall through the cracks, and I don't want to have to hold her hand to get her where she needs to be.

I can't hold her hand. I don't have time.

"Have you been to a game yet?" Finn asks and the question irks me because, honestly, why are they having this conversation in my office? I am *working!*

Before she answers, I cut in. "What was it you needed, Landyn?" I keep my tone polite but firm, hoping that she—and Finn—get the point. I've got things to do.

"Brian was wondering if you had those new contracts," she says, straightening up like the principal just walked into the classroom. "He sent me here to pick them up."

My brain scrambles. For a few seconds, I have no idea what she's talking about. I look down at my desk when I'm struck with a sharp pain at my temple. "Uhh, yes, I do—" I close my eyes for a second, willing away a stress headache. "Yes. The contracts. They're almost ready. I'll bring them down in just a bit."

Landyn gives me a terse nod, smiles at Finn, and before she walks away, he says, "Ah, don't let her boss you around too hard." He turns back to me. "She's just got a lot on her plate."

Landyn looks at me and says, "Is there anything else I can do? To you know, help? I've got some space to—"

I cut her off with, "No. Thanks, Landyn."

With that, she gives a small smile and nod, then turns to

Finn and says, "It was nice to finally meet you in person," to which he replies, "Likewise," and she leaves.

I turn back to my screen. The image is blurred, and I squint to make it out.

"You know she's terrified of you, right?"

"She's terrified of losing her job, and she should be." I frown, forcing my eyes and my brain to get with the program. They are not cooperating. If anything, it's getting worse. I almost feel crowded.

He slaps his lap and stands. "I get it. You're busy. I thought I'd say hi, drop that off—" He nods at the chocolate. "Try not to work too hard, okay, Hart?"

He feels sincere. I feel terrible.

And his question—*wouldn't it be nice if someone took care of me every once in a while*—keeps spinning in my throbbing brain like a website trying to load. I've tried to convince myself that no, it absolutely wouldn't. I can pull my own weight. I can handle my own work.

But that loud voice—the one that shouted its silent "YES!" in the back of my mind that night—throws me off-balance again.

I look at my computer, then down at my desk, then up at Finn.

He's watching me strangely, and I realize I haven't said anything back to him for a few moments.

I shake my head to try and clear things. "Sorry. Sorry. I've just . . ."

"Got a lot on your plate. Totally understand." He smiles and nods at the box in front of me. "Just find room for a few of those chocolates on your plate, huh?"

I look at the box, and that's when the room starts to close in.

Not emotionally, but *visually*.

There's a strange darkness creeping in at the edges of my vision. I blink a few times, then pull my gaze away, pressing into my eyes with my thumb and forefinger. When I open my eyes, my vision is still distorted, like I'm looking through a tube.

Somewhere, my phone buzzes. I think I should answer it, but I can't.

"Raya?"

I look up, trying to follow Finn's voice, but it feels like it's coming from somewhere else, outside my perception.

My mind swirls, then I'm slammed with an excruciating pain. I whip my hand to the side of my head and shut my eyes tight, trying to alleviate the sharp, crackling pain.

Am I getting sick? I never get sick. I don't have time to get sick.

As if on cue, my computer dings again. Twice. The sound is faint.

I open my eyes, and my gaze falls to the desktop, and I stare at a paperclip that moves in and out of focus. The dark edges at the corners of my eyes are creeping closer to the middle.

What is happening?

I hear a voice at my door, but I don't look up. "Hey, Finn. You're back!"

It's Jill. My assistant. I register her presence like someone trying to make out a face in a dream.

My top lip starts to tingle.

"Raya," she says. "I'm heading out for coffee! Be back in twenty!"

I lift a hand to let her know I heard her, but I don't respond. I can't respond. I'm too busy trying to understand

110

what's happening to my face. I reach up and touch my cheek. It's numb.

The right side of my face is numb.

The headache comes in full force now, and the nausea is so strong that I let out a little moan. I drop my head into my hands.

"Raya?"

Finn's voice is stronger now, panicked.

The fingers on my right hand prickle with numbness, like they fell asleep. I shake my arm, but I can't get the blood to come back.

"I can't feel my face." My voice sounds funny and I touch my cheek. I drag my gaze to Finn's and find a worried expression on his usually nonchalant face. "My face. My face is numb."

In the hazy darkness of my vision, I see him drop his bag and immediately come around to me, taking me in his arms as I sag to the floor.

He holds me with one strong hand, pulling me into his chest while using the other to find out his phone.

"What are you doing?" I ask. Am I slurring my words? Am I dying? My vision is black, only a pinprick of light at the center of my eyes. "I can't see." I hear the fear in my own voice.

Finn puts the phone to his ear and holds me closer. "It's okay, Hart. I got you." He repeats this until he starts talking into the phone.

"I don't have time to lie down," I say, my brain feeling like every neuron is firing at once. My vision goes dark as sparks shoot across it, causing a wave of nausea that I can't contain.

I push against him with the one arm that works and

manage to grab the garbage can just in time to empty the contents of my stomach.

My whole body contracts as heat rushes through me, and in the haze I notice Finn doesn't let go. He doesn't even flinch.

My head throbs, and somewhere in the inky, sparkling blackness I hear his voice.

"Doc, I need you in the executive offices—" Finn says into the phone.

"I think Raya Hart is having a stroke."

Chapter Thirteen

Raya

I hear Finn hang up the call, and he moves back to study me but doesn't let go. "You still feel sick?" He presses a hand against my forehead like a dutiful nurse.

I open my eyes and see that he tied up the garbage bag and set it by the door to my office. I feel instantly ashamed and embarrassed. "I'm sorry about—"

"I've birthed cows, Hart. I can handle a little puke."

That makes me smile, but smiling hurts. I reach up and touch my face to find that my smile only half works.

I push on my cheek. I press on my lip.

Nothing. I feel nothing. It's like leaving the dentist's office after getting a tooth pulled.

I'm terrified.

"I feel better," I say. But my head. My vision. The numbness. I look at him.

"Finn."

He looks down, still holding me.

"Am I having a stroke?" The crack in my voice betrays

me. I'm stronger than this. I don't need Finn or anyone else to see me looking weak.

I'm *not* weak.

"I don't know. Doc is on the way up. He called 911." Finn brushes my hair off of my face, a line of worry knit into his forehead—nothing romantic in his touch, just genuine, honest care.

I feel tears pooling at the corners of my eyes, so I close them. A few spill out, tracing a line to my ears.

"Hey," he says, voice low. "I got you."

I let out a small whimper. At this point, I don't care that it's Finn, I'm just glad he's here.

Doctor Marshall, the team doctor, rushes into the room. "Miss Hart?"

I blow out a breath and try to sit up, but only half succeed. "You don't have to make a big deal out of this. I'm sure I'm fine."

Finn puts a hand under my arm and helps me to a more stable position. "Just try to be still." His tone is firm.

I frown. "Don't boss me around." I sound like a cranky toddler.

"Then don't be so stubborn."

I scoot back against the wall and stop trying to move, but not because Finn told me to. My head hurts again.

"Tell me what happened," Dr. Marshall says, moving toward me. Finn lets me go, and I instantly feel cold. He backs out of the way, giving the doctor space to check my vitals.

I'm starting to feel sick again. I clench, then unclench my hand. Still numb.

"Is my face drooping?" I look at Dr. Marshall.

He gives nothing away as he shines a light in my eyes,

moving it out, then back in, and it makes my head swim. He glances at Finn. "Go downstairs and make sure the paramedics know where to find us."

I press my palm against my forehead. "I don't feel well." I close my eyes again and a tear slips out.

Stupid tear.

Finn picks up the garbage can and moves it closer. "She threw up once."

The doctor nods, and Finn leaves—but not before pausing at the doorway to look back at me.

His face is concerned, and I raise the arm that works and wave him off.

"Can you tell me your symptoms? What happened, Miss Hart?" Dr. Marshall asks once Finn's gone.

I explain what happened—the weird vision, the headache, the numbness—and I start to hear commotion in the hallway. "Am I having a stroke?"

"We'll get you to the ER, where they can do some tests to evaluate, but the important thing is whatever is happening, we're getting you help right away."

The paramedics rush in, followed by Finn, and I start to understand the gravity of this situation. I see Landyn and a few of the other interns through the wall of windows in my office. A crowd is starting to gather, and I'm the center of attention.

The last thing in the world I want to be.

And then, as if he's read my mind, Finn snaps all the blinds closed, and the room gets a little darker.

The darkness is nice.

I tilt my head at him and mouth a *thank you.*

He winks and gives a slight nod, then mouths, *I got you.*

He steps out of my line of sight, presumably to get out of

the way, and I realize focusing on him had been keeping me calm.

I zone out as Dr. Marshall tells the EMT what he knows in clipped, short sentences.

I draw in a slow, deep breath.

"Raya, we're going to move you onto the stretcher," Doctor Marshall says.

I nod. "Where's Finn?"

"I'm still here," he says from somewhere in the room.

"My family . . ." I say this as they help me onto the stretcher, and once I'm settled, they move me out into the hallway like a wedding cake being wheeled into a dance hall. I feel ridiculous.

I'm sure this is an overreaction. I didn't sleep well last night. I'm exhausted. It's been a long couple of months and a lot of long hours. I just need—

Finn is beside me again. He takes my hand and walks with the stretcher as they push me out the door and down the hall. "I called your sister."

"Which one?" I say, my voice a whisper.

He smirks. "Poppy."

I nod. He's been around enough to know that Eloise is the dramatic one. Poppy is much more level-headed. Situations like this call for a level head.

We're in the elevator.

I press on my lip. I felt that—kind of like feeling something through four sets of gloves. "It feels a little better now."

The EMT nods. "That's good. How's the vision?"

I look at him, then at the other EMT. "Darkness is still there, but more of a dull gray now. It's weird." I look at Finn, whose gaze is still fixed on me.

The EMT nods. His nametag says "Barnes," and I absently wonder what his first name is.

"You're going to be okay," Finn says, but I can see that he's putting on a brave face. I see the concern in his eyes.

I close mine, and it feels good to not have to use them for a minute.

I think about the little white box of chocolate. His teasing is harmless. I can handle that and brush it off.

His kindness, though, is much more difficult to ignore.

We reach the ground floor, and they wheel me out to the ambulance. I hate it. I hate that I'm being carted around on a bed with wheels. I drag my gaze over to Finn, who's walking beside the stretcher, looking a little unsure.

"You don't have to ride to the hospital with me," I say, assuming he's looking for an out. After all, it wasn't his fault he happened to be there for my "episode" or whatever this is.

I look at Finn. "I'm already feeling better." I want to erase that line of worry etched across his forehead.

Never mind the tingling in the tips of my fingers. Or the tipsy vision. Or the dull, persistent, thick ache behind my eyes. Or the fact that I currently feel like someone is scraping out my eye sockets with a fork.

"I know," he says. "But I'm going to anyway."

This is becoming a trend.

"Finn, seriously, I'm—"

"Do you have a sedative?" he asks the EMT. "Anything to shut her up?"

Barnes chuckles to himself as he and the other EMT move the stretcher into position to lift me up into the ambulance. Before they do, I level my gaze at Finn. "You really don't have to come. It'll be such a waste of your time."

Why am I pushing this? I don't know how long it'll take my family to get there.

Barnes opens the back door to the ambulance, and Finn meets my eyes. "I'm not letting you go alone."

The words settle something inside me.

Something that's been unsettled for a long time.

A piece of me argues against the calm. *Doesn't he know I go everywhere alone? I like to be alone. I'm better off alone.*

He slides into the ambulance and sits on the bench beside me.

"The emails. The contracts Landyn needs—" I say absently.

"It can wait," Finn says.

"But—"

"*Raya,*" he says gently. "It can wait."

Fine, bossy.

We drive in silence for a few minutes. The hospital isn't far, thankfully, but traffic's heavy, and it's bumpy back here. I wince, my head still pounding as the nausea returns.

Finn takes my hand.

I look at him for a second and decide I'm not in a place to analyze why I don't pull away. Instead, I close my eyes, squeeze his hand, and try to slow my breaths.

"How are you feeling right now, Miss Hart?" Barnes asks, after a few more minutes. "Any better?"

"Still nauseous," I say. "But my vision is way better."

"That's good." Finn looks at Barnes. "That's good, right?"

"Seems promising," Barnes says. "But they'll do some tests to find out what's going on."

I go still. "Promising" isn't the same as "fine" or "all clear."

My stomach clenches. What if something is really wrong? What if this is like, a warning shot?

What if I have a brain tumor?

Oh, stop it, I think to myself. *It's not a brain tumor.*

Something more realistic drops into my head, though.

What if I can't get back to work today?

My entire body tenses, and the nausea comes back on a wave. Finn must sense it, because he squeezes my hand, then rests his other one over it.

My heart races. There are people counting on me. I have new employee packets for two players who just got called up —we had a meeting this afternoon to go over them. There's also a game tomorrow, and I need to be on hand to help entertain one of our major sponsors. I have to be there.

Not to mention the fundraiser. I don't want to think about what will happen to that if I fall further behind.

The EMT looks at me. "Miss Hart? You doing okay?"

I close my eyes and channel every ounce of willpower into calming down—which, predictably, doesn't help.

I open my eyes and look at Finn, who smiles at me and says, "Blue is still your color, even if there's puke on it."

I give a small smile. I wonder how, even in this situation, he can still remain Finn.

"Maybe I'm just dehydrated," I say, hearing the hope in my voice because I need to believe there's a simple explanation for this. "This is all starting to feel like a lot."

"The tests will say for sure," Barnes says as the ambulance bounces over a dip in the road, then comes to a stop.

"We're here," the female paramedic calls from the driver's seat.

Barnes starts to shift. This is real. They're going to take me inside and draw my blood and do tests and scan my insides and God-knows-what else, and what if something is really wrong?

The inevitability of it scares me. This is all out of my control, and I hate it.

"I don't think the tests are necessary," I say, starting to get a bit of my energy back. "My headache is practically gone."

It's not, but do they really need to know that?

"Raya," Finn says. "You're not getting out of this."

"I can refuse treatment."

"No," he says. "You can't. I know you're used to being in charge, but please, for once in your life, you're going to have to listen to someone else."

I snap my jaw shut.

It's not like Finn to be decisive and bossy, but it's not a side of him I've never seen. It reminds me of the day after we met, when he showed up at my apartment with the credit card I'd left behind.

He took care of me that day too.

I didn't remember everything that had happened at the bar, but I remembered enough. My big screw-up at work. Getting fired for the first, and only, time in my life. And then the nail in the proverbial coffin—finding out my longtime ex had gotten engaged. To my sister's high school bully. It was a perfect storm of awful, and I didn't respond well.

And Finn had a front-row seat to it all.

All at once, a wave of fear rolls through me.

I look at him, panicked. "What if something is really wrong?" The shaky question leaves me feeling more vulnerable than I'm ever comfortable being.

He squeezes my hand in both of his. "What if it's all okay?"

I don't respond, but the mental shift calms my worry.

The back door opens, and the EMTs pull me out and wheel me into the emergency room. Finn follows, but we're intercepted by my parents, who rush out of the waiting area the second they see me.

"How did you get here so fast?" I ask, signing the words, as the nausea worsens.

"We were in the city," Mom says, signing the words to draw my father into the conversation. "Early Christmas shopping."

"I'm sorry, folks, we've got to get her back to do some tests. We'll let you know as soon as you can come back."

My mom grabs my hand. There's panic in her eyes.

I squeeze her hand. "I'm okay, Mom. Don't worry."

Her expression holds, and I hate it. I'm the one who doesn't cause trouble. I never want that to change. She doesn't need to be worrying about me.

As they wheel me away, my last image is of my parents standing with Finn, all looking worried. As the doors behind me begin to swing shut, I see Finn reach up and place a hand on my mom's shoulder.

Nobody needs to worry about me.

I can take care of myself.

I always take care of myself.

Chapter Fourteen

Finn

I'm not a patient guy.

I lean forward, elbows on my knees, staring at the floor, trying to get the image of Raya's face out of my mind.

I've never seen her look so scared.

I stand, clenching and unclenching my hands.

I sit back down.

I stand up and pace, wondering if anyone is ever going to come to the waiting room and give her parents an update.

She thinks she can handle everything on her own, but she obviously kept one too many tabs open for too long. Do her parents know what I know—that Raya isn't nearly as strong as she wants everyone to think she is?

She puts up a great front. Half the guys on the team are terrified of her. And I get it. She's blunt. Forward. Smart. She says what she thinks, and most people aren't used to that.

I clench my teeth. I hate that this happened to her. I want her back in her office, rolling her eyes at me, secretly eating the chocolate I gave her after I leave, doing everything she can to pretend she doesn't love it.

A stiff, protective feeling forces a deep breath. I just want to make sure she's okay.

She needs to be okay.

I remind myself to slow down. I've been looking for ways to keep people safe since I was in high school. Always the designated driver. The one who made sure my friends got home safe. Heck, I took that job at the bar in college just so I could keep an eye out. I took keys away from people who'd had too much to drink more times than I could count. And I always paid attention when a guy tried to follow a drunk woman out.

Guys can be real jerks sometimes.

So I started doing what I could. Calling a guy back in, claiming he hadn't settled his tab, stalling him while another bartender called a ride for the girl. I perfected the art of the diversion—usually "accidentally" spilling a drink on a guy to divert his attention away from a woman who didn't want it. I'd follow the spill with a bunch of apologies and an open tab for the next hour, and most of the time, the guy would forget all about the woman he'd been bothering.

I look down the hallway, trying to see any sign, and walk over to the nurse behind the glass.

"Any news yet?"

She shakes her head, "No, I'm sorry, hon. As soon as we get word, someone will come out or we'll let you know."

I tap the glass softly with a closed fist, nodding. "Okay." I cross my arms and straighten, staring at the door where they wheeled her.

In my mind, I imagine her walking through the doors of

the bar—the first time I saw her. From the second she walked in, she had my full attention.

After her friend left, she looked a bit out of her element, and unsure what to do. She asked for the same drink she'd just had—a Long Island iced tea. As I slid it over, she just . . . started talking.

I hadn't been a bartender long, but I could tell when someone needed to talk.

"Did you know I got fired today?" she said, and not quietly. "Me! Fired! Do you believe *that*?!"

I filled a tall glass with beer and handed it to one of the servers. "What happened?"

"I screwed up." She blew a raspberry, and it was pretty obvious this woman was not a drinker. Those two drinks had gone straight to her head. "Plus!" She pulled out her phone, tapped a few buttons, and held it up, showing me the engagement announcement of two strangers. "Look at that."

I'm not sure what kind of look I gave her, but a woman waved at me and ordered a Moscow mule.

I made the drink, half-listening to the dark-headed woman who'd had too much to drink.

"That's Jeremy." She pinched the image and enlarged the man's face. "My ex." Then, she swiped the photo over. "And that's Margot. She's the devil." She went on a mini-tirade about Margot, then the conversation wound back to work, and she actually started to cry.

Alcohol, a poor man's truth serum.

I didn't know for sure, but it seemed like I was the only person who knew about any of this. I was trying to figure out how to respond to her when a guy slid onto the stool next to her and asked her to dance.

"I don't dance," she said.

"Oh, it's not hard. I'll show you all the steps." It was clear she didn't want to, but he eventually convinced her to follow him out onto the dance floor.

Different night, different guy, same old scene.

The other bartender, Mandy, watched me watching Raya, and when the guy started to get a little too handsy, Mandy nodded at me. "I got this, you go."

I moved out from behind the bar and onto the floor, making my way through swaying, sweaty bodies. When I reached Raya, I pulled the guy away from her. "Hey, so sorry, she's with me."

"Get lost, man." He tried to shove me, but I held my ground, and he stumbled back a few steps. He shrank and his expression shifted.

I took Raya's hand and pulled her off the dance floor and into the back room, where it was quiet and cool.

Her eyes were wide. "Where are—what just happened?"

"It's okay," I said. "I got you."

"But—" she started to protest.

"He's not a good guy," I said. "Are you okay?"

The room was dark, but I could see her nod, a quiet "mmm-hmm" escaping her lips. She stumbled a bit, and I reached out to stop her from falling. She grabbed onto me, hands resting on my chest as we both went still in the small, dark space. My fingers splayed across her waist, thumbs pressing gently at her hips.

My chest tightened at her nearness. My pulse raced as my eyes searched hers, and all I could think was—*this is the most beautiful woman I've ever seen.*

Slowly, she wound her hands up around my neck, pressing herself into my chest. "Thank you." She lifted her chin, eyes latching onto mine, and her expression changed.

She looked at me like she wanted me.

And yeah, I wanted her too. My breath hitched. It would be so easy to lean in and kiss her. To inhale the scent of her. To let my mouth explore hers. I could maybe even convince myself that she needed something to take her mind off of the day she'd had.

She moved closer, drawing my lips toward hers. I closed my eyes for a flicker of a moment, but then reality snapped me back. I took her by the arms, firm but soft, and held her off. "I can't—" I closed my eyes again for a quick second, hands still wrapped around her arms. "You've been drinking."

Her body went rigid, and I watched as the horror of humiliation washed over her face, breaking whatever spell she'd been under. "Oh my gosh, I—" She shook her head, then rushed off, out of the room, and back into the bar.

The double doors that lead to the hospital parking lot slide open, and the paramedics wheel in another person on a stretcher, talking fast. It snaps me back to the present, and I'm still staring at the doors that closed when they took Raya back to get her checked out.

I wanted to protect her seven years ago—and all I want to do is protect her now.

So much for just being her friend.

I turn around, feeling trapped and frustrated. I need to *do* something.

I hate the emergency room. The sounds. The smells. The waiting. I shift my weight back and forth. I need air.

I walk back to where Raya's parents are sitting, quietly signing back and forth. I don't know American Sign Language, but I don't need to in order to read their worried expressions.

126

Mr. Hart notices me watching them, and his wife glances my way. "Thank you for getting her here, Finn," she says, signing. "Mick and I really appreciate it."

I nod. "What's the sign for 'no problem'?"

She smiles, and shows me, partially closed hands moving apart from one another, then second and third fingers of each hand bent, twisting and crashing gently into each other like toy cars. I do my best to repeat the motion, and Raya's dad nods.

"Did they say anything in the ambulance? Any other information about what might've happened?" Mrs. Hart asks, signing.

I shake my head. "No, but she already seemed a lot better when we got here, so I really think she's going to be okay."

Mrs. Hart signs this, looks at her husband, who nods at her and then at me, and takes her hand as they retreat with their mutual worry. I wish there was something I could say to ease their minds.

I wish there was something I could say to ease my own mind.

This emergency room is an unwanted reminder that not every story has a happy ending.

The exterior door opens again, and Raya's sisters rush in. They rush toward us in silence, and confronting the "what ifs" no one wants to voice aloud.

There's overlapping commotion, a series of questions from both Poppy and Eloise, all directed at me.

What happened?

Is she going to be okay?

Do you really think she had a stroke?

There were signs. Why didn't we see the signs?

127

Finally, Eloise puts her hands up in front of her, as if to take the floor. "This *has* to be because she never takes a day off. I told her to get out and touch grass once in a while, but *why* would brilliant Raya Hart listen to her stupid little sister?" She rolls her eyes.

"Don't call yourself stupid, Eloise," Poppy says, signing. "We should've known when she fell asleep at Dallas's the other night. That is *not* like Raya."

Eloise waves her off. "Finn, what happened?"

I explain what I know, which sadly isn't much. Black spots. Tingling face, numb lips and hand. Bad headache. Nausea. They'd already gotten the SparkNotes version of all of this, but as I lay it out for them, their expressions go from worried to panicked.

And I know what they're thinking. It sounds like a stroke.

"The good thing is, by the time we got here, she was much better," I say, hoping to reassure them. Poppy signs my words for their father.

"Shouldn't one of us be back there?" their mom asks. "I hate that she's alone."

"You know Raya," Eloise says on a sigh. "She probably prefers it that way. You know she's back there, right now, trying to tell the doctors how to do their jobs."

The phone in my pocket starts vibrating, but when I pull it out, I see it's not mine. "Oh, shoot. I've got Raya's phone."

"She let you have her phone?" Eloise asks, back to signing the words. "That's crazy. Her whole life is on that thing."

"No, I grabbed it when they wheeled her out," I say, dumbly. "I thought she might need it. You know, once she was feeling better." I flip it around and show her the incoming call.

"It's Justin," Poppy says.

I try not to make a face.

Eloise snatches it out of my hand and answers. "Hello?"

Pause.

"No, it's her sister, Eloise, sorry. Raya had a sort of . . ." She looks at Poppy like she has no idea how much to say, and I wonder if she regrets answering the call.

Poppy mouths the word *episode*.

"Episode," Eloise says. "We're in the emergency room waiting to find out. Someone mentioned maybe it was a—" She pauses again. I wish she'd put the guy on speaker. I want to make up my own mind about him. "Oh. Right. Yeah, we don't know yet, but we hope so." Pause. "Right, okay, I'll let her know." She looks up. "Okay, bye." She pulls a face.

"What did he say?" I ask, trying to sound nonchalant.

"He said to tell her to text him when she's better," Eloise says.

Poppy and I look at one another.

"That's it?" Poppy says.

Eloise shrugs.

"Did he even ask what was wrong with her?" Poppy asks.

Eloise shakes her head. "He sounded very . . . busy."

I huff out a breath, irritated. I already don't like this guy.

"I mean, they *are* new, I guess?" Poppy says, like she's trying to give the guy the benefit of the doubt, but seriously, the guy should at least want to make sure she's okay.

The doors to the hallway open and a nurse in blue scrubs walks toward us.

We all stand—and I'm not sure how I'll react if the news is—

"Are you here for Raya Hart?" he asks.

Mrs. Hart signs the question, then continues signing as she says, "Yes, we are."

"She asked me to come out and give you an update," he says. "I'm Matt." As if sensing the question hanging in the air, he holds up a hand. "It wasn't a stroke."

I exhale—we all do—as a huge weight seems to be lifted out of the room.

"So what—she's faking it?" Eloise cracks, and Poppy hits her on the arm.

"I'm guessing you're Eloise," Matt says. "Raya told me not to listen to anything you say."

Eloise's laugh sounds accidental, and it makes the rest of us laugh too. Relieved laughter, tinged with gratitude, ripples through the room.

I immediately like this nurse. He's diffused the tension and made the whole family—and me—feel better in three sentences.

"So what was it?" Raya's mom asks. "If it wasn't a stroke?"

"Hemiplegic migraine," he says, as Poppy signs. "It's a big word that means a really, *really* bad headache."

"Oh, thank the Lord," Raya's mom says softly.

"Good news is that she'll be totally fine. Hemiplegic migraines caused her exact symptoms: numbness, tingling, clouded vision, and it is often mistaken for a stroke, but it's not." He scans our small circle. "We've got a few more things to check on, but you should be able to head back and see her pretty soon. She's in great hands, and she's going to be just fine."

Mr. Hart stands and holds out a hand, face stoic. Matt takes it in a firm handshake. They nod at each other—a silent, respectful thank-you—then he says, "We'll see you in a bit," and turns to leave.

Raya's parents sit back down, and there's a moment where we all just look at each other. Then her dad smiles in relief as the sisters hug, and her parents hold hands.

I feel like I shouldn't be here. The moment is private, and I'm not family. But I don't want to go—not yet.

Eloise pulls back from the four-way hug and frowns at me. "Wait a second." She cocks her head to the side, slowly, like she's shifting gears. "What were you doing in her office? Please tell me you've proven yourself and are now having an illicit affair."

"Eloise!" Poppy pushes her. "Time and place!"

"What?" Eloise pushes her back, playfully. "Raya could use a little shake-up." She shoots me a look. "And we're pulling for you."

I shake my head. "Sorry to disappoint you, but no. No illicit affair."

Eloise pouts, but their dad gives me a firm nod, like I've passed some sort of test I didn't know I was taking. If he knew how much I think about his daughter, he might not feel that way.

I lean forward. "I did bring her chocolate, though." I say this quietly, because I don't want my humiliation broadcast to the entire hospital, but Eloise lets out a sound that can only be described as a squeal.

"You did?"

"The dark chocolate ones, like I told you?" Poppy says, leaning in.

I nod. "She didn't get to eat them, though. All this happened before she could."

"It's the thought that counts?" Poppy says.

I nod. "I'm trying to do what you guys said—show up for her. Be her friend."

Eloise sucks in a breath. "I'd say you got more than you bargained for today."

Maybe, but I'm glad I was there. If I hadn't been, would Raya have come to the hospital at all? I feel bothered. I'm glad the nurse gave us the update, but I need to see her for myself. It's the only way I can know for sure she really *is* okay.

I stand and brush my hands down my thighs, mostly because I'm a ball of nervous energy and need to send it somewhere. "I'll go find us something to drink." I want to be useful, but also I need a change of scenery. "Anyone want anything?"

They give me their orders, and I start down one of the halls, walking aimlessly, hoping the movement quells my fidgeting the way it usually does.

Hockey helps. Plus, you get to hit things and people.

As I walk, I think about my family, my brothers, and the homemade rink in the backyard at the ranch. Oh, the knock-down, drag-out brawls we would have there, skating until the sun went down, parking the trucks in a row to shine the headlights on the rink so we could play in the dark.

My oldest brother, Quent, could never beat Hunter, and that always ticked him off. The oldest was supposed to be the best—but none of us were a match for Hunter. I smile to myself. I can't count how many sticks he snapped, swinging it at the fence after the game, or how many fights broke out on that rink.

We played something fierce—but we loved each other something fierce too.

The dull ache of grief that always comes attached to

these memories pings its way around my chest, and I have to distract myself so it doesn't get a hold on me.

After a few minutes of aimless walking, I locate a vending machine. I buy three bottles of water, a Dr Pepper for Eloise, and an Orange Crush for me. I'm not in a hurry to get back to the waiting area, so I go a different way, and when I round a corner, I hear a man's voice say Raya's name.

"Yes, that's me," she says.

"I'm Dr. Gilroy," he says. "Feeling better now that you've got some fluids?"

"Yeah, but honestly, I'm itching to get out of here. I'm not the best in hospitals."

I stop moving. I shouldn't eavesdrop. It's rude. And probably illegal, since this is a hospital and there are HIPAA laws and all that.

But here I am, not walking away.

Because I need to see for myself that she's okay.

"Great," the doctor says. "We've gone over the MRI results already, and the echo just came back, and that looks clear too."

My shoulders relax. She's fine. She's going to be fine. I know they told us that already, but hearing it again doubles my confidence. I turn to go when the doctor says, "But I'd like you to seriously consider taking some time off."

I hear Raya's sardonic laugh. "You're kidding, right?"

"No, I'm not," he says tersely.

"I thought you said things are clear," she says. "Don't you think we're overreacting to a headache?"

"These headaches—they can be brought on by massive amounts of stress, disrupted sleep patterns, anxiety." A pause. "They can even cause issues for people who don't have good outlets for bottled-up emotion. This is no small thing, Miss Hart."

My stomach drops. I silently pray that Raya will bend. That she'll stop defending her position, and let someone else take the reins. Just once.

"Stress is a legitimate issue that can be incredibly hard on your body—physically and mentally. If you don't make some changes, this could happen again, and next time, it could be an actual stroke—or worse."

"So, what are you saying?"

"You need to take some time off," he says. "No stressful situations, no adverse conversations, nothing that will spike your cortisol or adrenaline levels."

"Time off?" I can hear the look on her face without even seeing it. "Dr. Gilroy, no offense, but that's just —impractical."

"I understand," he says. "But it is something you need to explore. This isn't something you can just ignore."

I realize I've been holding my breath, probably because I should *not* still be standing here. I start back the way I came, exhaling a long, slow breath as I go.

Raya, take time off? Right.

I know she needs it.

I also know there's absolutely no way she's going to let that happen.

Chapter Fifteen

Raya

N o. Way.

All I heard was "time off."

Correction. I heard other things, too. Phrases like "extreme stress" and "significant changes" weave around in my mind, along with another phrase—

No way.

There is no way I can back off. There is too much to do. Besides, my job is my life. I wouldn't even know what to do with free time.

I can hear my family coming down the hall before I see them. They're loud, and they have a way of making their presence known.

It's embarrassing sometimes, but not right now. Right now I'm just glad they're here.

I inhale a sharp breath and put my brave face on. Twice the staff asked if I wanted someone back here with me, but I said no, half out of embarrassment and half because I know they're going to make this into a much bigger deal than it is, especially Mom. The scene the paramedics made at work was humiliating enough.

Besides, I'm *fine*.

Eloise snaps the curtain back with extreme force, revealing my entire family. She and Poppy rush toward me, coming around each side of the bed, wrapping their arms around me and squeezing.

"Are you okay? What happened?" The questions from my sisters overlap.

Mom is signing for my dad, and when I meet her eyes, I see deep concern. I hate being the reason for it.

We have a silent agreement that I will never give her cause to worry. That she can always count on me to jump in when anyone in the family needs me.

That's my role as the oldest daughter. And I'm good at it.

"I'm okay," I say, looking at my mother. "I'm okay, Mom."

She nods, and I see a wave of relief wash over her. My dad wraps his arm around her, and she moves a little closer to him—and a pang of sadness hits me in the chest.

I've accepted the fact that the kind of love they have isn't in the cards for me.

It's a classic kind of love. Untarnished by modern things. A deep adoration for one another that's so simple, yet so complex that it becomes almost an anomaly.

Maybe it's because they had to learn to communicate in a way that was innately intimate—one that most people often don't know what they're saying. There's a frustration in that, I'm sure, but also a privacy that keeps their love pure.

It stings to be reminded that I'll never have that. My sisters have both found great guys, and I'm *so* happy for them. But sometimes—when I see the way my people are paired off in such perfect ways, it makes me feel sad.

And left out.

Great. Now I'm feeling sorry for myself on top of everything else.

I close my eyes for a quick moment, squeeze my sisters back, and assure everyone that I'm okay. When I open them, I see Finn standing in the doorway, looking slightly out of place and a little unsure.

But also—why didn't he leave? And more importantly, why am I glad he's still here?

When I make eye contact, he smiles, but there are several emotions on his face. Relief, pity, and—

Care.

The faint, seven-year-old memory skitters through my mind. One that's proven impossible to forget despite many efforts. I remember how he came to my house the next day to return my card and how he ended up making me cinnamon toast because, as he said, "my momma used to make this for us when we were sick."

He cared then. He cares now.

I shake the memory off and focus on my family and the big job ahead of me—convincing them I'm fine.

"Okay, okay, you can all go home now," I tell them. "The doctor said all my tests are clear."

"So, it was a migraine," Poppy says, signing.

"Yeah, the mother of all headaches," I say with a nonchalance that I absolutely do not feel. My eyes catch on Finn's, and his narrow ever so slightly. I look at my parents, signing as I say, "They did an MRI and an echo to check my heart. They want me to follow up with my doctor, but otherwise, they've prescribed some migraine meds and are sending me home."

I hope that proves I'm good. I've got all my faculties. My

numb hand is working again.

"Do they want you to do anything else?" Finn asks. "To make sure it doesn't happen again?"

I hold eye contact for a three-count, jaw slack, then look at my parents. "No. That's pretty much it. I told them I'm exercising daily, and I eat well. I'm going to be better about my multivitamin and try to sleep more, but—" I shrug— "that's it."

Again, I notice Finn watching me, almost like he's trying to sort something out.

"What about work?" he asks.

I shrug. "Good to go. Might take a day, you know, to let things calm down, but yeah. Everything's fine."

He makes a face.

"Okay, well, can we take you home?" Mom asks.

"Actually, my car is back at the office," I say.

"Well, you can't drive yourself," Poppy says. "You need to rest. Raya, this was a major episode."

"It wasn't," I say, even though it felt just south of "major" to me. "I'm fine. I don't even really have a headache anymore."

"Okay, but still," Eloise says. "You need rest. Do you want to come to my place?"

I shake my head, trying not to let on that I still have work to do. My brain starts running through the list. *Contracts for Brian. Details for press seminar. Coordinate with venue for Denim and Diamonds, then report back to caterer.*

Poppy takes a step closer to my bed. "Oh my gosh."

I frown. "What?"

"You're going to go back to work."

"No, I'm not," I lie.

"You're a terrible liar," Mom says, signing. Dad points at

me enthusiastically and shakes his head slowly back and forth.

"Okay, so, I have a couple of things that have to get done today," I argue, signing. "But it's not even work, it's like emails."

"Raya!"

They all start chattering over each other, hands moving as they also sign their objections. Finn looks unfazed, watching the chaos, eyes steady, landing on me. There's a question there, but I don't know what it is.

I want to tell them to take their opinions right out the door, but we Harts are passionate about getting in each others' business.

To be fair, I'm the worst offender. I take my big sister role very seriously, and I sometimes stick my nose where it doesn't belong.

Not sometimes. Often.

I have strong opinions, and I'm not afraid to voice them, which is probably why everyone feels like they should have a say in what happens to me.

Payback. How fun.

A nurse walks into the room. "Whoa, whoa, whoa!" she says. "What is going on in here?" She scans the room. "Everyone needs to vacate this room."

"Can we really call it a room when the walls are made of fabric?" Finn grabs onto the curtain as the nurse peers at him, brow quirked. He quickly turns sheepish and flashes her that smile—the one he uses like a Get Out of Jail Free card.

She is not impressed and turns to me. "Would you like any of these people to stay with you until we get your paper-work finished?"

I look around. "I'm fine, you guys. I promise. I just need someone to take me back to the office to get my car."

"You're not driving yourself home, though, right?" Finn asks.

My dad shifts, then signs, "No, I'll drive her. Mom can follow us."

Before he leaves, Dad hugs me. When he pulls back, he signs, "You don't have to be a hero. Take care of yourself." He places a well-worn hand on my forehead.

"I know," I say quietly, signing. "I will." I then hold up a pinky, and he takes it with his. A silly childhood thing that's stuck all our lives.

Poppy and Eloise both hug me, their moods melancholy and somber.

"Hey. It's not my funeral," I say.

Eloise turns over her shoulder and sticks her tongue out at me, making a face. Poppy starts to push her out of the room, and gives me a weak smile.

"Oh, Justin called." Eloise stops and pulls my phone from her pocket. "He said he hopes you're okay and to call him when you feel better."

My eyes dart from her to Poppy to Finn and then to my hands, folded over my stomach. "Thanks."

"Raya, he didn't even ask what happened," Eloise says.

I take the phone. "It's—really new. And we're still figuring things out."

Note to self: Explain to Justin that he needs to crank up the concern if I end up in the emergency room again.

Eloise draws in a breath, and I can practically hear the words she's not saying. Thankfully, she must think better of launching into her speech on why this man is all wrong for me.

"Okay, Ray," she says. "Go home and rest."

Before she walks out, she looks at Finn, who is still standing in the same spot in the corner. "Coming?"

He nods. "Yeah, I'll be there in a second. Maybe you could drive me back?"

She looks at me, then back to Finn, a strange expression on her face. "Okay, lover boy."

He rolls his eyes as they leave, then looks at me, throws a thumb in her direction, and makes a face like *getta load of her, huh?*

I try to sit a little straighter in the bed.

"So . . .?" He moves into the space where my parents had been standing moments before.

"So . . .?" I look at him. "What?"

He cocks his head. "You're not seriously going to pretend that everything's fine."

"Everything *is* fine," I say. "It was a really bad migraine. It started off ocular, then, you know—did what it did."

"Because of stress."

"I mean, yeah, but that's normal."

"Raya." He scoffs. "That is not normal."

"Are you a doctor now?"

"I'm quoting him."

"They blow things out of proportion all the time."

"No, they don't. Your doctor wasn't exaggerating. But I have a feeling you're not going to listen to him either." He huffs out a frustrated breath.

I go still. "What are you talking about?"

"I heard the doctor tell you that you need to, you know, make some changes."

"You *heard* the doctor . . .?" I'm confused. I cock my head and look at him. "Like, you were eavesdropping?"

"Yes, okay." He straightens. "I know it was a crap thing to do, but I was in the hall, and I heard him say your name, and . . . it's not like the curtains keep the noise out." He says this quickly, like he knows it's a lame excuse. But then he says, "I did it because I was worried about you." He puts his hands on his hips and glares at me.

My chest is a gong and someone just hit it square in the center.

"You don't worry about anything," I say. "You're the guy who doesn't have a care in the world."

His eyes narrow like he wants to object, but when he doesn't, he validates my assessment.

Still, he's not backing down. "He said you need some time off."

"Yeah, well, doesn't everybody?"

"*Everybody* didn't just have a severe . . . health . . . episode—" he stumbles over the words, like he's not sure what to call it.

"It wasn't a 'severe health—'"

"Stop being so stubborn! You know what I mean." He moves closer. "You need to go easy on yourself."

Ha. Like I have time.

"Raya. Please. It was . . . scary seeing that happen."

Tears prick my eyes, and I'm horrified they might give me away. Because the idea of "going easy on myself" is so tempting and so foreign, it starts a battle in my brain.

I draw in a slow breath, then bring my eyes to his. The concern is so clear, it catches me off-guard. What is happening? This is *Finn*.

"Why do you even care?" I ask. "It's not like we're friends."

It isn't until I see the words register on his face that I

realize how cold they sound. This man just rode in the back of an ambulance through Chicago traffic, then sat in the waiting room for almost two hours to make sure I'm okay—if we're not friends, then what are we?

I want to apologize, but the words stick in my throat.

"I . . . Finn, I didn't—"

"Yeah, no. You're right." He cuts me off. "That's a fair point. We're not, really. I'm sure your real estate boyfriend will make sure you do what you need to do for yourself." He stuffs his hands in his pockets.

"If he ever shows up."

And with that, he walks out of the room.

Chapter Sixteen

Raya

"I'm fine, Mom, I promise. You don't have to stay."

It's later that night, and I'm home, but as I predicted—Mom is hovering. And I hate the line of worry etched in her forehead.

"I do have to stay because if I don't, you won't take it easy." Mom puts her hands on my shoulders, turns me around, and walks me over to the couch. "Sit, will you?" She gives me a little push, and I plop onto the sofa.

She sits down next to me. "Poppy is almost here with the food. You look tired."

"It's the migraine. It wiped me out," I say. "I'll be fine after a good night's sleep."

"And a few days off," she says. "You're taking tomorrow off, right?"

"I wish I could, but I can't," I say. "The team just got two new players. There are contracts to go over, and I'm going over paperwork with them tomorrow. Intake packets and—"

"Someone else can do that," she says, with more authority than she has.

"Denim and Diamonds is next month," I say. "It's a huge event—and I'm practically in charge of the whole thing."

"Raya." She reaches over and rests a hand on my shoulder. "It's okay to slow down a little."

"This is my job," I say firmly. "And I haven't been with the team for that long, I can't—"

I'm cut off mid-sentence when the door flings open, and both Poppy and Eloise barrel their way into my house, followed by our dad. They're each carrying a box.

"I hope you like soup," Poppy says. "Because I have enough here to feed a small country."

I stand, and Mom grabs my hand and pulls me back down.

I glare at her.

I'm not going to like this one little bit.

Stop worrying about me. Stop holding my hand. Stop with all of this "making sure" and "are you okay" and "let me get that for you."

I just want to lie down, but for some reason I cannot let them know for a single second that I'm exhausted.

I love that my family loves me. But the attention is too much. I'm much more comfortable being the one taking care of everyone else. This role reversal has me on edge—and I can still feel the dull ache of this afternoon's events weighing on my head like I'm balancing a sandbag there.

Poppy looks at my parents and asks them to help set the table and serve the food. Dad signs a quick, "Yes, please, put me to work," and takes a stack of bowls to my small kitchen table.

I pick up my phone and see that I missed a text from Finn.

FINN

I'm still annoyed with you, but I'm checking in anyway.

Are you okay?

RAYA

Yes. I'm good.

FINN

Are you resting?

RAYA

My family won't go home, so no...

FINN

Good. I'm glad you're not alone.

The day after my "episode," I wake up feeling tired.

Which is weird, because I slept almost ten hours. Half a bowl of Poppy's soup, and I was out. My head is still foggy, and I feel like I went ten rounds with a heavyweight fighter, but my body is just going to have to get on board. I've got stuff to do.

I force myself out of bed and go through my normal routine. I move slowly and feel sluggish. And I'm not happy about it.

Shower. Helps a little.

Clothes. Make-up. Hair. Coffee. Protein bar.

By the time I walk to the door, I'm ready for a nap.

I almost feel unable—no, un*willing*—to push through.

Regardless, I get in my car, start the engine, and put the car in reverse. I catch a glimpse of myself in the rearview mirror. I look about as good as I feel, which is to say—terrible.

I have *got* to figure out a way to get over this.

I reach into my bag, pull out a compact, and apply more powder under my eyes, but it doesn't help. I look in the mirror and there's a zombie looking back at me.

I let out a frustrated groan, but underneath, I feel the buzz of panic that I've been trying to shake since the second they put me on that stretcher.

I reach the office, a little zoned out and trying to mentally assemble some sort of to-do list as I head into the building. But my mind feels blank, like searching it produces no results. It's hard to think, and I don't like it. This isn't me. I'm clear-headed and sharp. I'm the quick one. The one you go to when you need something done.

Right now, I feel like I'm operating at half of my normal processing power.

I step into the elevator as a text comes in.

> **JUSTIN**
> Sorry I didn't get to touch base with you last night. I hope you're feeling better this morning? Sounds brutal.

I don't text back. I'm not annoyed that Justin didn't track me down yesterday. We've been out three times, and while that's enough for some people to start planning a future—it's not to me. We're still new.

Still, if the roles were reversed, I'd like to think I'd care enough to at least check in.

This is what you signed up for, Raya.

It's unfair to move the goalpost on him now.

The doors open, and as I step out onto the third floor, I try to keep my head down and stay focused on the path to my office. I rush even faster than usual, trying to avoid the curious stares. I can't blame my co-workers—I was carried out of here on a stretcher yesterday. But I also don't have it in me to tell the story a hundred times or convince anyone else that I'm okay.

Maybe I should send a mass "*I promise I'm fine*" email to the entire team.

Tonight, I'll go to the game to sit in a VIP box with execs from The Alabaster Group. Entertaining major sponsors is something my boss, Brian, asked me to do once a few months ago. Apparently, I was good at it, because I've done it three times since. If I'm honest, I like making those VIPs feel special, and I especially love it when they tell my boss I've done well.

I might need some extra caffeine to get through tonight, though.

Jill intercepts me in the hallway. "Raya?" She looks confused. "We didn't know you were coming in today."

I don't look at her. "Of course I am. Why wouldn't I?

"Oh, just because, you know . . ."

I shuffle past her, flip on my office light, hang up my bag on the hook by the door, and sit down in my chair. I turn away from Jill, trying to slow my breathing.

Why am I out of breath?

I turn back as she hugs a stack of folders to her chest. "Brian said you were taking a leave? Told us we need to look for ways to fill in the gaps until you're healthy enough to come back."

I stare at her, trying to process this. "He said what?"

Jill winces, giving me a half-hearted shrug.

I stand, but the movement makes me feel a little light-headed, and I have to pause for a second before I move.

What is happening? Why is my body being so uncooperative?

The doctor's words rush back: *"If you don't make some changes, this could happen again, and next time, it could be an actual stroke—or worse."*

The low-level anxiety is back, just beneath the surface. I shove it aside.

"Raya, are you okay?" Jill moves toward me, but I stop her with an upheld hand.

"I'm fine." I get my bearings and walk down the hall, past Landyn's cubicle and into Brian's office. He looks up and frowns at me.

"What are you doing here?" he asks. "Didn't you get my email?"

"No," I say. "I just got in."

He clucks his tongue and squeezes the knot of his tie. "I should've called. Could've saved you a trip."

"I don't need time off, Brian," I say. "I can't take it, anyway. We have The Alabaster Group tonight. You asked me to oversee their visit."

"I put Hoff on that," he says.

I glance through the glass of Brian's office wall and see Hoff, whose name is actually Douglas Hoffmann. He's the newest addition to the team, and I have no idea if he can handle this. I refuse to have office drama with a guy who graduated from college a few months ago, but I'm annoyed. It feels like I'm being punished.

I sit in the chair opposite Brian's desk. "Why would you do that? I've been coordinating it for two weeks."

"Jill gave him all the notes yesterday while you were out," Brian says.

I raise my eyebrows. "She gave him my notes?"

"Raya, we're a team here. We all have the same goal. Doesn't matter who gets the credit for getting us there."

"Did I do something wrong?" I frown. "I thought I was handling things well."

He leans back in his chair. "You've done nothing wrong. In fact, you're pretty amazing."

"Thank you."

"But—" he says, and I feel like that just erased everything he just said. "After yesterday—" His eyes go wide, like he's remembering. "We can't work you into the ground, Raya."

"You're not. I don't understand," I say. "I need to be here. I need to be working."

"And you will be," he says. "After you give yourself a break."

I squeeze my folded hands tight in my lap, memories of sitting in another boss's office seven years ago running through my mind.

"We take the health and wellness of our employees very seriously," he continues. "You know that. We have a whole initiative that you yourself have worked on."

"For the players," I say. "The health and wellness *of the players*."

He shakes his head. "You know that's not true. This organization has worked hard—more than any other professional team—to prioritize *people* over *profit*. We'd be hypocrites if that didn't extend to our executive staff."

I sigh. I hate everything about this conversation. My clothes feel too tight all of the sudden, and I want to walk out of here and pretend I have no idea he's trying to send me home. I just want to do my job.

"Look, this is not a demotion. This is not a replacement.

150

This isn't even a punishment or a write up or a slap on the wrist. *This is self-care.*"

I hear him. I know, somewhere deep down, that he's right. I just don't know how to *not* do things.

"You know I'd much rather have you here—you're one of the best in this entire building. But you're no good to us if you run yourself so ragged you fall apart. You need a break, Raya," he says. "There's no shame in that."

And that's when I start to understand where this is all coming from. Because there's only one person who knows what Dr. Gilroy said to me before I left the hospital yesterday, and I'm about to give him a piece of my mind.

I sigh and look away. "I hear you."

"Good."

"But I don't like it."

He chuckles. "I know you don't. It's one of the things I admire about you. Your dedication to do things right. But Raya—" he looks at me— "your health comes first. Period."

I grit my teeth and nod. "Okay."

"Look at it as a well-deserved vacation. Paid time off."

Right. Vacation. That thing I never take.

"For how long?" I ask, thinking for a few days, four at the most, I'd rest a bit, and—

"Four weeks," he says.

I only stare. I'm not sure I heard him right. "Did you say—"

"Yep," he nods. "Four weeks. It's not up for debate."

"You can't be serious." My mind spins. "I'm not taking four weeks off."

Brian shrugs. "It wasn't all my decision, though I did have a say in it. This one came from the higher-ups, Raya.

Plus, you're going to have to see a doctor before they'll let you come back."

"Four weeks is a whole month," I say, mostly to myself. My mind tries to work out the math. That's practically the end of December before I can even come back. Then you add the holidays, and it's even more time off, and—I huff out a breath. "What about my projects? The contracts? The holidays . . .?" It's a week before Thanksgiving—are they really going to make me miss the holidays in the stadium? "What about Denim and Diamonds?"

He holds up both hands to stop me. "We're already working on all of this, and there's a whole team of people working on that fundraiser—they'll be okay," he says. "And as far as the games, you can still come *as a fan*. But now? Go home and rest. Take care of yourself. You're no good to anyone if you're getting carried out of here on a stretcher." He levels my gaze. "Like I said, this isn't a punishment."

"It sure feels like it," I say.

"Your job is safe," he says. "Heck, most people would be grateful for the time. A whole month to do whatever you want right before the holidays? Sign me up."

Brian is about a decade older than me—a husband and a dad. His life outside of here is full, so he doesn't understand what it's like to go home to an empty house every night.

I shake my head and stand to go, but before I do, I turn back, square his gaze and say, "What I want to do is work."

Chapter Seventeen

Finn

G ame day.

I love game days. Sleep in. Good food. Morning skate. Huge crowd.

And with Gray and Dallas, it usually means a win.

My happy place.

I'm trying to focus, but I keep thinking about Raya.

The look on her face when they wheeled her out of her office is burned in my mind. With the exception of the first day we met, I've never seen her be anything other than strong and confident. No trace of vulnerability.

Nothing to suggest she's ever been anything but fierce.

Until yesterday.

Yesterday, I saw vulnerability. A reminder of that night seven years ago. A reminder that she's not Superwoman.

Like Poppy and Eloise, I've been kicking myself thinking we should've seen this coming. She's clearly running herself ragged—we should've stepped in.

Well, someone should've. She wouldn't have listened to me.

"It's not like we're friends."

The words felt like a kick to the gut, but she's right—we aren't friends.

Yet.

If Gray's right, I need to show up for her. Be her friend first. Someone she can count on—not someone who's going to annoy her incessantly. I'm determined to win her over, no matter how different we are.

After yesterday, that goal pales in comparison to my new goal—help her figure out how to relax. If anyone can do that, it's me. I'm the king of doing nothing. Apart from hockey, it's my favorite pastime.

There's a wooden *chunk* sound to my right.

"Brookie!" I turn and find Crosby looking at me. "What are you doin', man?!"

We're at a morning skills and drills practice, and this particular drill, 10-Pass Chaos, requires you to actually pay attention.

"Shoot! Sorry!" I call out, swing around, snag the puck, and pass it to coach so he can start the drill back up.

It's supposed to be fast—hence the name. Three defenders—me, Crosby, and Jericho, get the puck right next to the opponent's goal. We take the shot, and if we score, it starts over. If we don't, the offense takes it and starts down the length of the ice.

The catch is—they've got six guys to our three, and they need to make ten passes before taking a shot. 10-Pass Chaos.

Their job is to make clean passes and score. Our job, as defense, is to get a stick on the puck and stop them.

I love this drill. *Let's GO.*

Crosby takes the pass from Coach, slings it to me, and I jack a shot toward the goal, but the puck lifts wide. I swing around as Esposito gathers it up and starts up the ice.

Let's go, Brook. Move it.

We're up against the first line, so it's Gray, Krush, Esposito, Kemp, Fritz—the rookie, who is out of his mind fast—and Myers. They're all skilled.

I take the left as Crosby takes center by the blue line and Jericho locks down the right. I look over to him and think, *Man, I'm glad he's on our team. I wouldn't want to get hit by him.*

A pass skirts under my stick and is taken by Kemp, then swung over across the ice to Krush, who handles it for a second, sizing up Jericho. That's the fifth pass already—geez.

How am I going to get her to relax? It's not like I can just go to her house and make her. She doesn't like to be told what to—*CRAP!*

Gray and Fritz are now both on my side.

And Fritz has the puck.

Pay attention!

Fritz skates hard right, and he's by me, open lane right to the goal. There's a split second where I see an angle to tattoo him into the boards, so I take off. I launch, but just as I'm about to hit him, he cuts his skates *hard* and stops on a dime, ice spraying, and I fly right past him—shoulder first into the plexiglass.

I completely whiffed.

I turn around just in time to see him look me dead in the face, drop off a no-look pass to Gray, who skates in and one-times it in the goal. He looked at me the whole time, that chump.

The six offensive guys gather in a tight circle, whooping, while I'm sitting there in a pile.

Crosby makes a loop and stops in front of me. I see Dallas watching me from the other side of the rink. "Where's your mind at? You let a rookie do that to you?"

I dig my stick into the ice and use it to push myself back to my feet.

"Gettin' slow, *Brookie*," Fritz says to the *ooh*s of the rest of the guys.

"Yeah, yeah, I might be getting slow, but you'll always be ugly," I crack back at him. He doesn't even respond—he just skates away to set up the next line to come in, dancing his rear end at me.

Pssh. Rookies. Grow some hair in your armpits and get back to me.

In the years since the Comets picked me up, I don't think I've ever let myself get distracted out on the ice. Ever.

For a guy who doesn't seem to care about anything, the one thing I do care about is hockey.

For starters, I never thought I'd be here. I didn't plan on it. Being a pro hockey player was not on my Bingo card. I played in college because I loved the game—and because it was the only reason I went to school. A lot of guys entered the NHL draft, but I didn't. I knew I wasn't good enough. I'm not the star. I never was.

I just loved it. For me, this sport was always about hanging out with my brothers and my friends.

Most guys in the league are *hockey players*.

And I'm a guy who plays hockey.

My college coach talked me into going to the combine with a buddy of mine—said he could use the support. I figured if I could help him, then I should go. Never expected to be picked up. And by the Comets? Are you kidding me?

It was the GM who said he saw something in me, apparently after Burke put a bug in his ear. Said I was good for morale—a team player—and that his team needed a selfless player like me. I don't start every game, but I train like I do. I know my role out here is to support people like Grayson Hawke and Dallas Burke.

I'm good with that, and in a lot of ways, I prefer it. I'm not about to miss a single opportunity to play with these guys.

But today? Good grief, I'm distracted. And my teammates can tell.

"Sorry, man," I say to Crosby. "Just a little out of it today."

And a little wrecked knowing I shouldn't have confronted Raya yesterday because I shouldn't have been eavesdropping. That's not going to make her feel closer to me. If anything, it's going to annoy her, and she's going to push me away. Which means we'll go right back to the dumb little game we play—I'll keep teasing her, and she'll keep rolling her eyes, with no idea that my feelings for her are real.

I skate back into the line, and when it's my turn to do the drill, I get a stick on a pass and break it up.

The next time though? I'm mentally listing things I could take to Raya to help her relax, and we get scored on again.

I skate off the ice, drop onto a bench, and start unlacing my skates when Dallas sits next to me. "You good?"

"Yeah, man," I say, brighter than I feel. "All good."

Dallas pulls a baseball cap out of his bag and sticks it on his head. "Your mind wasn't on what was going on out there."

I look over at him, and I know he can read on my face that he's right.

"That was a lot yesterday."

"Yeah, it was," I say.

"If you hadn't been up there annoying her, that might've ended up differently," he says. "Least that's what Poppy said."

I chuckle as we stand and walk toward the gym. "I'm glad I was there, even if she's not."

"I'm sure she is," he says.

"Then you don't know her as well as you think you do." I shoot him a wry look.

"She'll come around," he says. "She's just stubborn."

We hang our bags up and head over to the stationary bikes. Most of the guys on the team end up here, getting in a session before tonight, keeping things loose. Everyone has their own regimen.

"Do you know how she's doing?" I ask. "Did Poppy say anything?"

"Only that she brought her some food last night, and she fell asleep after about forty-five minutes. Have you talked to her today?"

I shake my head. I'd love to, but I don't want to make it weird. She's dating someone else, and like she said, we aren't friends. "Do you think it's better if I just, you know, leave her alone?"

I don't have to look at him to know he's watching me. "Is that what you want?"

I pedal faster. "No. I mean, I want to help, you know? Actually prove I'm not useless." I blow out a frustrated breath. "I think I can help her figure out how to slow down."

"That sounds smart," he says.

Smart. Right. If I can get close enough to actually do it.

Raya probably wants someone to come alongside her and

conquer the world, to have huge goals, accomplish a ton of stuff, and that's just not me. I'd be perfectly happy with a piece of land, a family I love, a couple of dogs, and a home-made ice rink in the backyard.

Throw in a job where I can help people, and that's a good life.

That's the life I want.

We really are too different.

I'm ten minutes into my ride when the door of the gym opens and Raya walks in. Her eyes lock onto mine, and the rest of the room goes quiet, like someone hit the mute button.

Then Jericho lets out a low whistle, like we're back in high school.

She's tall and graceful and carries herself like a freaking Greek goddess. But today, that goddess is Athena.

And she looks like she's ready for war.

Chapter Eighteen

Finn

"**W**hat did you do?" Dallas asks, his voice low. I don't take my eyes off of her, but I manage a quiet, "I have no idea."

Should I take cover?

She walks over and stops right in front of us. "Hey, Dallas." She gives him a quick nod.

"Hey, Raya. How are you feeling?" Dallas asks.

She makes a point of looking at me when she says, "I'm *fine*, actually."

I slowly stop pedaling. I'm in trouble but I have no idea why.

"Hey, Finn."

"Hey, Raya." My tone is cautious, like I'm about to poke a crocodile.

"Can I talk to you?" Her expression is clear—she's ticked.

I hold my hands up. "I feel like you're mad at me."

"Nope," she says, coolly, but there's something behind her eyes that I don't trust. "Just a little chat. Promise it won't take long."

160

Crap. She's definitely mad at me.

By now, most of the guys are watching this. From behind me, someone says, "Don't go, man, she's gonna kill you!"

I frown at Raya.

She narrows her eyes.

I lean toward her, keeping the bike between us for protection. "What did I do?"

She scoffs. "Don't pretend you don't know." Her tone cuts.

"I have no idea," I say. "Clue me in?"

"Hallway," she says firmly. "Now." She turns on her heel and marches out of the gym to a chorus of "Oohhhs" from the guys.

"Dang, Brookie, you're in trouble!" Jericho says as I get off the bike.

I grab a towel and look at Dallas. "I should be terrified, right?"

"Hope you have your affairs in order." His grin makes light of it, but there's a pit in my stomach.

"Hey, maybe now's a good time to tell her you're in love with her," Jericho calls out.

I throw the towel at him, grateful Raya's already in the hallway and doesn't hear this.

"Hey, get Coach—tell him we're gonna need a new lineman," Krush calls out from the bench. "Brookie's going on the Injured Reserve."

I'm pretty sure he's right.

I walk into the hallway and find Raya waiting, arms folded, tapping her fingers like she's had too much caffeine. And even though she's never not looked beautiful, she doesn't look like herself right now. She's pale, and I could pack for the weekend in the bags under her eyes.

"What's going on?" I ask. "Why are you even here? Shouldn't you be home?"

She lets out a sardonic laugh. "I. Can*not*. *Believe* you."

Her eyes drift past me, back into the gym, which is basically a big room with four walls of windows. I follow her gaze and see a whole lot of hockey players watching us. She grabs my arm and pulls me around the corner.

"Look, Hart, if you wanted to get me alone, all you had to do was ask," I say. "There's no need for violence."

She glares at me, and I instantly regret trying to lighten the mood. Apparently, now is not the time for jokes.

I hold up my hands in surrender. "Sorry. Really, I didn't mean—You're clearly upset about something."

"Yeah, and I have every right to be." She looks trapped, like she's not sure where to go.

I rest a hand on her arm. "Tell me what I did. Whatever it is, I'll apolog—"

"Who did you talk to about what the doctor said?" she cuts in, moving out of my grasp.

"What? When?"

"When you were *eavesdropping* on a private medical conversation."

I press my teeth together. "I didn't mean to do that. I was just in the wrong place at the right time, I guess. I'm sorry about that. It wasn't on purpose. I was getting drinks for your family, and I heard him say your name. I—I don't know, I listened." I replay the moment in my mind. It *was* a shady thing to do. "I didn't mean to, Hart, I swear. I was just . . . really worried."

She waves me off like my apology isn't important. "Who did you tell?"

I'm confused. "I didn't tell anyone."

"Then why did Brian just put me on a four-week leave?" As she says this, her voice breaks slightly, and I can see the tired, raw emotion in her whole face—her whole body.

"He did?"

"Yes!" She raises her voice. "Because of you!"

"Raya, I didn't say anything. I don't know anything about that," I say honestly.

She stops for a minute. "Then why did he do it? You were the only one who heard what the doctor said." It's an accusation, not a question.

"Well, I'm not the only one who thinks you should take some time off after what happened." I cross my arms. "If you remember, half the building watched them take you away in an ambulance."

She seems to accept that as a fair point, but she's still bothered. "But you were the only one who knew!"

I soften my tone. "I didn't say anything to anyone."

I can see she's fighting back tears. She turns away from me, arms crossed, but one hand rubbing her forehead.

"What am I going to do?" Her tone sounds defeated. Desperate. Lonely.

I shift my weight. I want to pull her close, tell her everything's going to be okay, prove to her that she's not alone. I want to be the guy she can count on, but how do I do that when she's intent on not letting me?

She turns back to me. "Four weeks? What the heck am I supposed to do with four weeks off?"

I lean against the wall. "Rest."

"Ha. Okay. Like *that's* easy to do. Just 'rest,'" she says, as if it's a made-up word.

"I'm guessing work will still be there when you get back," I say.

She rolls her eyes. She's in a defensive stance, worked up, but something is off. The image of her terrified face flashes through my mind. She needs to lie down.

The elevator down the hall opens, and Dr. Marshall walks out. When he sees us, he turns in our direction.

"Miss Hart!" he says. "Good to see you upright."

Raya is still flustered, but she forces a smile. "Yes! Thank you for your help yesterday. I'm feeling much better."

If I had to guess, that's a half-truth. She's better than she was, but she's still not one-hundred percent. If she'd just slow down for five minutes, she'd realize it too.

"Slow" is not in Raya's DNA.

"I'm actually surprised to see you here," Dr. Marshall says. "You need to be home, resting."

"Oh, no," she says. "I'm doing so much better. And I've got a few projects that are time-sensitive."

Doc's bushy eyebrows pull together. "Oh. Has something changed? I thought you were on leave."

"I'm actually trying to sort that out now," she says, relaxing her arms. "I think there's been a mistake. Maybe you could help me?"

"Help you how?"

"I just need someone to pass the message up the chain that I'm good to go back to work."

Doc looks confused. His eyes dart briefly to me, then he smiles warmly at Raya. "Did you get the email about your time off?"

"Not yet," she says. "I spoke with Brian, and I came straight down here to, uh—" She looks at me, and I barely resist finishing her sentence with *rip this innocent man a new one, even though he did nothing wrong.*

164

"The email came from me, Miss Hart," Doc says. "I'm the one who put you on leave."

She doesn't seem to understand for a few seconds. "I'm sorry. You—?"

"I talked to Dr. Gilroy yesterday," he says. "I called to get an update, check up on you, make sure everything was okay. Since I was with you when the paramedics got here, they looped me in. We discussed your condition, and he told me his recommendations."

I see comprehension spread over Raya's face like honey dripping down the outside of a jar. She turns her head slightly, her eyes darting to me and then back to Dr. Marshall.

"If you want to come into my office, we can discuss this in private." He motions down the hall toward his office, presumably because he's not accustomed to discussing medical issues in the hallway.

She ignores that, and even though I'm feeling slightly vindicated, I don't relish it. Raya is spinning out.

"Dr. Marshall," she says after a pause. "I . . . I'm not sure what I'm supposed to do with that. I have to work." The desperation seeps through her words.

"Miss Hart." Doc puts a hand on her shoulder, and I hope the tension in her starts to ease. "Your body is trying to get your attention. From what I understand, you came from a high-stress environment to this job, which can also be pretty high stress. And you're a great employee. The best, according to Brian. But he also said you look for ways to take on work that's not yours, that you go above and beyond what is required, and that you will not accept anything but perfection."

I bite my tongue. He's just completely read her mail.

"You're running yourself ragged. It's unhealthy. If you don't slow down, your body is going to make you slow down."

Her gaze falls to the floor. I really hope these words are sinking in and not sliding off.

"Think of this like a warning shot," he says.

"Plus, you've earned some time off, I think." He squeezes her arm. "And just in time for the holidays. It's great timing."

Even though she's still looking at the floor, I can see that she doesn't agree.

"After a few weeks, come back in, and we'll do a quick assessment to make sure you're good to get back at it, okay?" Dr. Marshall says. "I promise the place won't burn down without you."

"Thanks, Dr. Marshall," Raya says quietly. "Honestly. Thank you. Have a good Thanksgiving."

"You too, Miss Hart." He looks at me. "Have a great game tonight, Finn."

Once he's gone, I look at Raya. She's completely deflated, her bravado evaporated into the ether. She looks up at me, and there's just a little bit of fight left in there.

"Fine. It wasn't you," she says.

I can't help myself. "I tried to tell you . . ."

She scoffs, rolls her eyes, and storms off down the hall.

And I watch until she disappears around the corner, wondering how to help someone who doesn't think they need it.

Chapter Nineteen

Raya

By the next morning, I'm more convinced than ever that this is a huge mistake.

The doctor told me to go home, so I did, and it was miserable. I was so restless and didn't know what to do with myself. I tried to heat up some of the leftover soup Poppy brought over, but for some reason the smell made me nauseous, so I ended up putting it back in the refrigerator.

I showered, but even that made me antsy, wishing I was self-cleaning so I didn't have to waste time washing myself.

I almost went to Poppy's restaurant and volunteered to wash dishes just to get myself out of the house and keep my hands busy.

What Brian said is true—most people would love paid time off, but I am not most people. Work is more than what I do. Without it, I don't even know who I am.

On the bright side, my pantry has never been more organized.

Even though I'm jittery, irritated, and unable to quiet my mind, I'm thoroughly exhausted.

Not exhausted. Wrung out.

Last night, I fell asleep before 8:00 p.m., and slept a full twelve hours, and I don't even feel rested this morning. I'm sure that has less to do with some medical condition and more to do with the fact that my mind knows if I'm awake, I'm going to feel edgy and restless all over again.

It just feels so weird, almost illegal, to not be doing anything. And "not doing anything" means there's too much time to think. More than once, I've had to push memories of those moments in my office out of my mind. It's the only way to keep from spiraling.

I'm awake now, staring at the ceiling, daunted by the prospect of a whole day with nothing on the calendar. What am I going to do with myself?

I force myself to get up and brush my teeth, then grab my phone and walk into the kitchen to make some coffee.

I stand there, soaking in the silence, convinced I will never get used to it. On a normal workday, I have a plan. A system. I would've left an hour ago.

But here I am. Home on a weekday with absolutely no plans. I hate it.

I pick up my phone. "Hey, Siri, what do I do with a month off?"

After a pause, the female voice says, "I found this on the web for 'what do I do with a month off.'"

The answers are, as expected, not appealing.

Travel. Learn a new skill. Focus on self-care. Staycation. Spend time with loved ones. Catch up on projects you've been putting off.

Ha. Catch up on projects. That's what I *should* be doing.

I immediately think of ten reasons none of these things will work for me. And as soon as I do, I feel a dull ache at the base of my skull. There's a dizzy feeling, followed by the fear I've been forcing myself to ignore. Because hearing "You have to make some changes" is one thing—doing it is something else entirely.

Where do I even begin?

I have to sit down—so I do. My body is making its case loud and clear. I need to figure this out. I need to find a way to calm everything down.

But I don't know how.

A realization slowly makes its way from the basement of my mind to the main floor: I constantly feel pressure to do something other than the thing I'm currently doing. I always feel like I'm not doing enough, and time is against me. Even after a full day of accomplishing everything on my list, all I think about are the things I didn't get done.

My inbox is always full.

I open the chat with my sisters and see their unanswered texts from this morning.

POPPY

> Just making sure you're resting, Ray.
> Feeling better today?

> I hope you took the day off. You need to take it easy.

ELOISE

> You know she doesn't know how to do that.

POPPY

> You never know.

> Text back when you get a chance!

I sit there, feeling a little paralyzed, staring at the phone in my hands. What do I say that won't lead to more concern? More worry. More fussing. They'll want to tell me how to spend the next four weeks. They'll check up on me.

Why do I bristle at that? Why is it so hard for me to have others take care of me—or at the very least, be concerned about me?

What did Siri say—catch up on a project you've been putting off? That's what I need—a project. Just a little one, one that I can do from my laptop. I promise myself I'll drink tea and take breaks. It'll be totally fine.

I open my computer and click on the Remote Desktop icon, and it auto-fills my work email. After I click Connect, I'm met with an error message.

Username and Password Do Not Match.

Weird. I try typing it out but get the same notification.

I call Jill. She answers on the first ring. "Yes!" Not a question, but almost a cheer.

"That's the way you answer the phone?"

"Sorry, I just won the bet that you wouldn't last twenty-four hours before checking in!"

"There's a bet?!"

"Yep." She calls out—I'm guessing to the rest of the people in the office—"It's Raya! Pay up, losers!"

I hear a smattering of voices in the background, groans and yelling.

She comes back. "Sorry about that, I just had to gloat a bit."

"Funny," I say, unamused. "Why can't I get into my work email?"

"Because you're on leave," she says.

"Right, but I have to be able to at least check in." My pulse quickens.

"Sorry, I think they've pretty much banned you," she says.

My pulse quickens. "What? Why?"

"I'm guessing because they knew you'd try to work from home," she says. "Also, I think Brian wanted to make a point that you should listen to your boss."

"So I don't even have access?"

I can practically hear the shrug through the phone. "You're not supposed to work."

I roll my eyes. "This is so obnoxious."

"I would be way more sympathetic if I didn't just win a hundred and ten dollars in the pool."

I'm simultaneously flattered that the pool is that much and angry that they bet on this at all.

"Okay, but can you get me into my email? You must have a work-around." A wave of fatigue crashes over me. I trade the stool in favor of the oversized armchair in my living room. How am I still this tired? I slept twelve hours!

"No. I like my job, and I want to keep it," she says. "Also, I'm under strict orders." A pause. "They're taking your health very seriously. New wellness initiatives and everything."

"What am I supposed to do if I can't check in?" I ask. "There are actual projects I'm right in the middle of."

"Trust the team?"

I push a hand through my hair and sigh. I don't trust the team. Not to do it the way I would, nor the way it needs to be done.

"I can practically *hear* you spiraling," Jill says. "You have four whole weeks to do whatever you want to do! Paid! Good grief, I would *kill* for that. Take a trip. Find a beach. Something! Enjoy it."

Right. Easy for her to say. "I gotta go. I have another closet to organize."

"Lucky," she says.

I roll my eyes.

"Have a great Thanksgiving, boss."

I click my phone off. I hate this, and yet, as I sink deeper into the armchair, there's a tiny part of me that knows it might be something I need. Maybe what I really hate is that —I feel like I'm at war with my own body.

I open Justin's last text and stare at it—then type:

RAYA

You're not going to believe this, but they sent me home. I can't work for four weeks.

JUSTIN

Whoa. Why?

RAYA

For "my health." <eyeroll emoji> It's worse for my health to be stuck at home.

JUSTIN

I thought you just had a headache.

I stare at the words. They seem cold.

But . . . that's what I want, right? No emotion. It bothers me a little that he said it that way.

RAYA

More involved than that, but yeah. The prescription is rest.

JUSTIN

Yikes. Sounds brutal.

172

RAYA

> Yeah, I'm not one to sit on the sidelines.
> Do you want meet for lunch this week?

JUSTIN

I'll have to see how the calendar looks.

Right. Because *he* still has a job.

RAYA

> No pressure. Just let me know.

> Also I realized with all the health stuff I
> never sent you the details for Thanksgiving
> dinner

JUSTIN

Oh, right. Text the details to Andrew?

RAYA

> I'll send it now.

I stare at the text I just sent. He doesn't respond. No thumbs up, no "thanks, have a great day," nothing.

A business transaction, just like I wanted.

I can't get upset when that's exactly what I get.

I send Justin's assistant, Andrew, a quick email with the details for the Hart family Thanksgiving dinner, then drop my head back against the chair and close my eyes, a low mixture of itchy electricity and dull heaviness churning inside me.

I sit like that for a few moments, and I can feel myself drifting off when there's a knock on my door. My eyes pop open. Probably Poppy. Or my mom. This is what happens when texts go unanswered. They show up.

It's nice, but I don't need anyone to take care of me.

"But every once in a while, wouldn't it be nice if someone did?"

Finn. Back in my head.

Another knock.

I think about hiding in the bathroom, but everyone in my family knows where I keep the spare key. I'm a little surprised they haven't used it yet.

I stand, toss my phone on the chair, shuffle to the entryway, and open the door, not even all that surprised it's not one of my sisters standing on my porch.

It's Finn.

Chapter Twenty

Raya

"Finn."

Do I bother asking what he's doing here?

He's wearing a Comets hoodie, black sweats, and a baseball cap. No coat, even though it's late November. And that trademark grin.

My head is jumbled. He's constantly around. Insufferably chipper. Always in my business and not serious about anything.

But he took care of me the other day, the same way he did seven years ago. He seems to genuinely care about how I'm doing.

And he wasn't the one who told Brian what Dr. Gilroy said.

I start to sort through this mix of emotions but quickly get overwhelmed. I'm too tired to figure anything out right now.

"It's not enough for you to bug me at my office, now you're coming to my house?"

"Good morning to you too." He's holding two cups of

coffee, and after a beat, he offers one to me. "Poppy said you like a plain oat milk latte, so I got you a white chocolate mocha." His smile holds. "Tastes better."

I quirk a brow and stare at the cup. When I don't take it immediately, he gives it a little shake.

I roll my eyes and take the cup. "Where is your coat?" I try not to sound like his mom, but I'm pretty sure I fail.

"Back home, this is T-shirt weather. Chicago's got nothing on Montana."

I think of wide-open spaces versus shoulder-to-shoulder buildings. He might be on to something there, but when he shoves his hands in his pockets and shivers a little, I realize he was blustering.

The coffee warms my hands, and I feel a twinge of thankfulness. Without even thinking about it, I say, "Do you want to come in?"

"Uh, sure." He steps inside. I walk back into the house, taking a discreet sip of the drink when my back is turned to him.

I hear him come inside and close the door behind him. "It's good, right?"

Not as discreet as I thought, I guess.

"It's sweet," I say, because it is. But also, yes. It's *really* good.

Why can't I just say that?

He follows me into the kitchen, and the room feels instantly smaller, though he doesn't seem to notice. I suppose he's used to his broad 6'2" body and the space it takes up.

I'm used to being the only one in my house.

He takes a drink of his coffee, then sets the cup on the table. "Oh! Did you see the game? I played thirteen minutes in the second half. Had a block that showed up on ESPN."

For some reason, this makes me happy. And oddly, proud. Finn might be overbearing, but it's easy to root for him. He's the player whose name nobody really knows. The one who makes the other guys look like stars.

I want to ask if that bugs him, but it feels too personal. And the last thing I need is to open that door. Because why am I wondering so many things about Finn?

"I missed it," I say, aware that he's still looking at me.

"That's right," he says. "You hate hockey."

I lean against the counter and cross my arms over my chest. "What are you doing here?" I ask, and when I realize it sounds like an accusation, I add, "I assume your visit is about more than coffee."

He leans on the counter opposite me. "Well, you owe me something."

I frown. "What do I owe you?"

"An apology," he says. "A heartfelt one. Like you mean it. Has to be at least ten words long."

I press my lips together. I don't particularly *like* apologizing, but we both know he's right. I do owe him an apology. I chew the inside of my lip.

The corner of his mouth turns up in a smile. "This is killing you, isn't it?"

"I can admit when I'm wrong." I straighten. "I'm very sorry I jumped to conclusions."

"And . . . ?"

I fold my arms. "And accused you of something you didn't do."

"Great!" He holds out his hands. "Apology accepted."

"Good, because—" I'm suddenly light-headed. I'm hoping I can mask it, because I really don't want this to be the norm from now on. "I'm going to sit . . ."

"Are you okay?" he asks. "Did you sleep last night?"

I make my way to the oversized chair again and fold myself into it. "I slept for twelve hours, but I still feel completely wiped out. I hate it."

He crosses to the ottoman in front of the chair and sits on the edge of it. "When was the last time you ate?"

"Poppy brought me soup," I say, trying to remember. "But I fell asleep before I ate it." My eyes flick to his. It's been a day and a half since I've really eaten anything substantial, and even then, it was only a salad at my desk.

He points at me and jumps up. "Come on." He holds a hand out to me. "I'm buying you breakfast."

"No, you don't have to—"

He turns. "You need to eat, Raya."

I reach for the white chocolate mocha and take another drink, my head starting to clear a bit. I'm keenly aware that Finn is doing Finn things. He's constantly trying to help, even when no one asks. Most of the time, it's intrusive.

But sometimes, it's not.

He pulls out his keys and swings them around his finger, catching them. "You know what I don't get about you?"

"Tell me."

"It seems like you don't let yourself indulge in anything. It's almost like you don't have space for fun."

I chuckle to myself. "Because I don't. *Some* of us can't play a game for a living."

He drops his hands to his sides. "Ooh, low blow there, Hart—keep the gloves up."

"I mean, I know you're a professional and everything, but it's still a game." I keep my tone light, needing the levity right now. "It's not like a nine-to-five job in an office at a desk."

He whistles. "Yeah, that's *not* for me." Then, after a beat, he says, "So are you coming?"

"Coming where?"

He makes a face. "To breakfast. We'll go see your sister— I hear she makes the best pancakes."

I don't respond.

"*You* need to eat, *I* know a great place, and I'm *pretty* sure your schedule is wide open, so . . ." He motions toward the door, lifting a hand at it to indicate we should go.

I get the sense that this is how he lives his life. On impulse. He has an impulse and he follows it. Wash. Rinse. Repeat. Amazing that his impulses have landed him on a professional hockey team. For some reason, this makes me wonder how he *did* end up on a professional hockey team, but I decide not to ask.

"I don't eat breakfast," I say.

"Riiiight," he says. "Because breakfast is *fun*." The words taunt. "And Raya Hart doesn't have time to do anything just for fun."

"That's not true," I say, though I'm pretty sure it is.

"What was the last *just for fun* thing you did?"

I press my lips together, trying to think of something— anything—that will pass this "fun test," just so I can prove him wrong.

Finally, I say, "I went to the Comets' Trick-or-Treat Day and handed out candy for two hours."

"Did you break out the Morticia dress?"

"No."

"Bah. Missed opportunity." He's still watching me. Is it weird I want to know what he's thinking? It is. Since when do I care what Finn Holbrook thinks about anything—especially me?

"See, this is why you're so stressed out all the time."

"I think I'm stressed out because I have a lot on my plate," I say.

"And I think you don't have to fill up your plate like the buffet is closing."

I frown. I have no idea what that means.

He smirks. "Are we going, or do I have to go get you frozen waffles?"

"I'm pretty sure whatever you're planning isn't something I'll want to do."

He frowns. "What makes you say that?"

I gesture between us, like it's obvious. After all, we're very different.

"You misjudge me, Hart." He shakes his head. "One of these days you're going to realize I'm an actual grown-up now." He holds a hand out toward the door again, and I stare at it like it belongs to an alien.

The comment takes me back to the first time I found him at my door—the day after he and his co-worker walked me home, saving me from making even more mistakes.

Drinking alcohol is not something I do. I don't like to lose control. But when my entire life imploded in a single day seven years ago, Finn was there.

And he's here, again, at another pivotal moment.

I hadn't intended to spill all my secrets to Finn back then. I hadn't planned to tell anyone that I'd messed up so badly I'd gotten fired. And the fact that I was mourning the engagement of my high school boyfriend? Pathetic.

That next morning, after the drinks and the dance floor and hazy bits I still can't quite piece together, I woke up in a fog, hungover from two drinks and full of regret. I was trying to stitch the memories together when Finn showed up at my door with the credit card I'd left behind. He said he wanted to check on me. Make sure I was okay.

Not sure how ethical it was for the bartender to return a credit card to a patron at her home—but it didn't take long to realize he had no ill intentions.

"It seemed like you had a terrible day," he'd said, standing in my doorway. He brought me Advil and Gatorade and made me cinnamon toast, turning my apartment into a hangover recovery zone.

The flirty bartender with a heart of gold.

If I'm honest with myself, I liked him immediately. He was kind and funny, and he made me laugh. But more than that? He was a *good* guy. The kind who would be nice to have in my life.

Then I remembered the almost kiss. The humiliation. The embarrassment. It all turned to absolute horror when I discovered that Finn was actually a twenty-two-year-old college senior who was heading to Montana for *Christmas break*.

I'd tried to kiss a college kid. And he'd pushed me away.

Even now, heat floods my body at the memory—not the kind that warms you from the inside, but the kind that breaks you out in a cold sweat.

How embarrassing.

Worse, I never thanked him for being such a stand-up guy that night. After all, he could've really taken advantage of the state I was in.

I look at him now. He looks more like Chris Pratt the superhero and less like Chris Pratt in *Parks and Rec*, but Finn is still kind. Success didn't steal his personality.

"You're not going away, are you?" I ask, playing my part.

"Nope." He wags his eyebrows.

I groan. "Fine. I'm going to go change." I stand up, waiting for the dizziness or the light-headedness or the nausea but none comes. "Don't go through my stuff while I'm gone."

"Totally going to," he calls after me as I walk upstairs to change into real clothes.

And I have absolutely no doubt that he will.

She looks at me for a beat, but it's long enough for me to catch her frown.

"I'm cool with it," I say. "I don't mind being an NHL stepping stone. Pretty people pay attention to me, plus I can weed out the crazy ones before introducing them to the other guys on the team."

"So why do you go out with these women if you know they're just using you?"

I shrug. "I don't know. I just like people, I guess."

She flips on her blinker and makes a turn. "It's really shady for anyone to go out with you just to get to someone else. You don't deserve that."

"Raya." I bring a hand to my chest, mock-serious. I nod my head slowly. "This is a moment. It's almost like you care about me."

"Funny." She grips the steering wheel with both hands and sighs. "I'm not as heartless as everyone thinks."

"People think you're heartless?"

She slowly turns to me. "I know how I am. People walk on the other side of the hallway when I'm coming."

"You'd be great as one of those people in Costco with a clipboard," I joke. "You're like a hot version of an extended warranty phone call."

"I'm not—!" She stops mid-sentence.

"—employed by Costco?" I jump in. "Yeah, I know, but if you were, you'd be *great*."

She frowns at me, and I shrug at her. "Just sayin'."

She heaves a big sigh, but I can see the corners of her mouth turn up a bit.

"Plus," I add, "I know the real you, remember?"

"Will you stop bringing that up?" She shoots me a look, but I see the smile in her eyes.

"I can't. It was one of the best nights of my life." I smirk.

"Well, it was one of the worst nights of mine." Her expression shifts. "A close second to what happened a few days ago."

I can tell she's upset. Still bothered by what happened in her office. Maybe the best thing I can do is keep things light.

"Yeah, but now you get a vacation, free breakfast with someone who's not even a friend . . . " I say, lightly. "Win-win."

She smiles weakly but looks conflicted, and I let the subject drop. We drive in silence for a few minutes, just the sounds of the road.

I'm not a huge fan of silence.

"So, in my current position as non-friend, is there any upward mobility? Any goals I can hit to move up the ranks?" I ask. "If I'm going to stay with this company, I need to know there's a chance for promotion."

She chuckles to herself, a good sign, and says, "I'll consider advancement if—*if*—you show some kind of growth in maturity."

"Uh-oh," I say. "Thaaat's gonna be a problem."

She takes a deep breath. "Yeah, I figured. Might have to just stay acquaintances, then."

"Might have to."

"I'm glad we're clear. Expectations are important."

"Right," I say. "No chance of anything romantic. Totally off the table."

She side-eyes me. "Only executives get that perk," she quips.

At least she's playing along. That's a step in the right direction, I guess.

"And for the record, I never thought that was ever—"

"Good," she says. "I mean, you *are* completely wrong for me."

I frown. "Okay, wait. How do you even know?"

She comes to a stop at a red light and turns to me. "Oh, come on, Finn. First of all, I already told you, you're a professional hockey player. Which is a big red flag."

"Feels judgy, but okay."

"Second of all, you're like a big kid!" She shudders. "You don't take anything seriously. You joke about everything, and the real world isn't like that—"

"Some would call that a *perk*, but you know," I mutter over the sound of her still talking.

"Plus! You're *so flirty* with everyone. It's like you can't help yourself. I think I saw you flirting with Mara Mitchell one day last week after a game."

"Mara *loves* me," I say, thinking of the old woman who funds one of the team's largest outreach programs.

"She's eighty years old."

"She thinks I'm cute." I grin at her.

She shakes her head, smiling. "You are maddening."

The light changes and she accelerates into the business district of her small hometown.

"Listen," she takes on a slightly more serious tone. "If we're going to be friends—and I'm not saying we are—but if we were, I'd love to offer you some advice. Friend to friend."

I turn in my seat toward her. "Bring it on."

"For the right woman, these will be strengths," she says, eyes back on the road. "Your joking around, your outlook on life, your whole"—she waves a hand in my direction—"thing. They're just not right for me."

"Don't check your boxes, huh?" I say, with more lightness than I feel.

She initially doesn't say anything, but then winces and shrugs.

"Youch. Like, none of them? Do you have a 'he's a nice guy' box?"

"You smell good," she says. "That's a box."

I laugh loud at that one, though I can't shake the feeling that my plan to win her over is a fool's errand.

"I'm sure I don't check any of your boxes either." She slows down in front of a parking space.

"Eh, I don't put people in boxes," I say.

The car jerks, and she looks at me. "That's not what—"

"No, I'm sure you're right," I interrupt. "You're way too uptight for me. I need a woman who knows how to go with the flow."

A honk sounds behind us, and she goes back to parking the car, sandwiching it between two others like a pro. She puts it in park and turns off the engine. "I can go with the flow."

"No, you *literally* can't."

She frowns, a quiet pout crossing her lips.

"Are you *offended*?" I ask, laughing. "You spent the whole ride telling me things that are wrong with me, but *you're* the one who's offended?"

"I'm not offended," she says, then changes her expression. "Wait, are you offended? I didn't mean—"

I hold up a hand. "I'm not. I'm just messing with you. Lighten up." I get out of the car and close the door. Through the closed window, I cup my hands to the glass and shout, "You're so serious all the time."

Chapter Twenty-Two

Finn

It's only been about a half hour, and I've counted at least eleven eye rolls.

But they haven't been irritated eye rolls. That's a good thing. Progress, maybe?

That entire car ride should've served as a reminder that Raya Hart will never look at me as anything other than an annoyance—but all it did was make me like her more.

She sees straight through me. Most people don't even bother to look that hard.

I walk around and meet her on the street. "So this is your town."

"You've been here before," she says.

"Yeah, but I haven't been downtown." I look around as we cross the street. It's the kind of town you might see in one of those cheesy Christmas movies. Buildings line both sides of the quaint little main street—businesses and restaurants, most with awnings and decorated windows.

"After Thanksgiving, there's a big Christmas kickoff. All the businesses down here will be decked out for the holidays.

There's a carnival and a Gingerbread Walk—the official start to the Christmas season." She avoids looking my way. "Not the kind of place you're used to, I'm sure."

"You *really* have to stop assuming things about me," I say. "You don't actually know that much."

She stops moving. "You're right. Sorry about that."

"Two apologies in one day? Look to the east! Is Jesus coming back on a cloud?"

"You bring out the worst in me." She bites back a smile and starts walking again.

"I actually prefer this sort of small-town Christmas celebration," I say.

She looks at me. "And you live in Chicago?"

"Only because of the team." I stuff my hands in my pockets. I move around her so I'm on the street side as we stroll down the sidewalk. "When hockey's done with me, I'm pretty sure I'll end up back in a small town. I'm not built for city life."

"I love the city," she says.

"But you bought a house in Loveland." I look at her. "Why?"

She pulls a pair of gloves from her pocket and puts them on. "To be close to my family. In case they need me." She quickens her pace, and I have to jog a few steps to catch up to her.

I put a hand on her arm.

She looks at it, then at me.

"We're not in a hurry," I say, dropping my hand.

She looks a little embarrassed. "Sorry. I'm used to—"

"Yeah, I know. But today we're taking it easy." *This* is how I can help her, right? Help her slow down?

"I don't need to—"

"It's for me," I lie. "My body is a perfect specimen that requires a full nine hours of sleep each night, and I didn't get it."

Her eyes go wide. "Nine hours? That's insane! I usually shoot for four." She starts walking again, toward the end of the block.

"Four? What are you, a giraffe?"

She half-laughs, "I have no idea what that means or if I should be insulted."

"Giraffes sleep like five hours a day, sometimes standing up." I shrug. "I'm not sure how I know that, but it's true."

"You're so weird." She stops under the sign for Poppy's Kitchen. "Whoa, it's busy," Raya says as she pulls open the door.

We step inside, and I look around the space. Every table is full, and people wait in a small alcove by the door.

A young woman at the hostess stand looks up and smiles. Her expression quickly turns confused. "Raya? Poppy didn't say you were coming in! We never see you on weekdays."

Raya looks unsure. "Hi, Bella. Yeah, I'm, uh—taking the day off."

Bella's eyes widen. "Wow." Then, she looks at me. "Well done." She grins, like she's just slid two puzzle pieces together.

If Raya wants to correct her, she doesn't.

"Poppy will be so happy you're here," Bella says. "But you might have to wait a little bit. I'd move you to the front of the line, but there's nowhere to put you."

Raya looks around. "Should we come back for lunch?"

Bella shakes her head. "It'll be the same at lunch. Poppy's kind of freaking out. She thought it would be slow today, and she didn't call in a third cook."

Raya turns to me. "By the time we're seated, our meal won't be *fun* anymore."

"Do you think we could help in the kitchen?" I ask, ignoring her sarcasm and flashing Bella my most charming smile.

"I think I'll lose my job if I let you back there," Bella says.

"Ah, we'll just go say hi," I say with a nonchalant wave.

"We'll be in the way," Raya says.

"I've worked in kitchens," I tell her. "You said you live close so you can jump in when your family needs you, right?" I look around. "Seems like your sister could use the help."

She presses her lips together, uncharacteristically unsure, but she must not be able to think of a reason to object because a few seconds later, we're walking back to the kitchen while Bella pretends not to notice.

I slowly push the kitchen door open and see what can only be described as chaos.

"Holy. Cow!" Raya says.

Poppy looks up from the griddle, her eyes widening, almost like she needs a second to place us. "What are you guys doing here?" She looks at me. "Together?"

"Came to help." I pull off my hoodie, hang it on a hook by the back door, grab an apron, and turn my baseball cap around. "Put us to work."

Poppy flips a pancake and lets out an amused laugh, but then she looks at me and seems to realize she's drowning and I'm holding out the life preserver. "Have you worked in a kitchen before?"

"Yes," I say, though even if I hadn't, my family's big enough to need a short-order cook.

Her eyes jump from me to her sister and back. "Fine.

Wash your hands." She looks at Raya. "You can sit right there, because I know *you* haven't worked in a kitchen. Plus, shouldn't you be home? Resting?" She nods to a stool nearby, and Raya sits.

"If I do any more resting, you'll have to order me a headstone," she says, irritated.

"Well, I'm glad you took the day off," Poppy says. "Shocked, but glad."

I catch Raya's sheepish expression and realize she hasn't told her family about her leave. I dry my hands and tuck the towel into the belt of my apron.

Poppy looks at me. "Do you know how to make pancakes?"

"My hockey team in high school hosted a pancake breakfast fundraiser every year."

"All that tells me is that you've been around people who made pancakes," Poppy says.

"Flour, eggs, salt, sugar, baking soda, baking powder, oil, and buttermilk," I rattle off, spinning the spatula on my palm and catching it. "Just tell me if you want them fluffy or *ultra-fluffy*."

Poppy's eyebrows go up, and I grin.

I turn to give Raya a wink, and she props her chin on her fist and watches, amused.

"Okay." Poppy pushes a bowl of batter into my gut. "Get on pancakes." She rushes off.

I look at Raya. "I guess bossiness runs in your family."

"She's only like this in the kitchen." Her eyes follow Poppy as she moves around the kitchen. "Impressive, right?"

"It's awesome."

Raya drags her gaze back to me. "Do you really know what you're doing?"

I hold up a hand. "I got this, Hart." I know she thinks I'm a joke, but I'm a lot more capable than she gives me credit for.

The other cook waves at Raya. "Your sister told me about what happened. You good?"

Raya smiles, but it looks forced. "I'm good, thanks for asking."

He looks at me. "I'm Miguel."

"Finn," I say.

"We're lucky you're here," he says. "Maybe Chef will listen to me and hire a new cook!" He leans toward me. "She's dragging her feet."

"I heard that!" Poppy calls from somewhere in the kitchen.

"I wanted you to hear it!" Miguel calls back, then mutters, "She's so stubborn."

I look at Raya. "Runs in the family."

Miguel chuckles, and I get to work. After only one botched attempt, I learn the heat of the stovetop griddle and get the hang of their system. Miguel calls out the orders, and I stay focused on doing the one thing I know I won't mess up.

I've made pancakes so many times for so many people it's like second nature—and it feels awesome to help out.

"Is there anything I can do?" Raya asks after a few minutes.

Poppy's eyes dart to me, and I give my head a little shake. Because even though Raya could probably figure out how to run a commercial kitchen in eight and a half minutes with zero training, what she really needs to do right now is sit still.

"Uh, no," Poppy says. "We'll get you some breakfast. Guys, when you have a minute—" She points at her sister, and Miguel picks up on the shorthand.

"Coming up!"

I take some of the batter and pour two heart-shaped pancakes on the griddle. Four and a half minutes later, I flip them onto a plate and slide it over to Raya.

"Hearts for Hart! Order up!" I call out, like I'm a line cook.

She *almost* smiles.

Miguel adds a side of eggs, and Poppy makes her a coffee. "We'll catch up when this all slows down," Poppy says. "I had two servers call in sick, and Miguel's wife, who sometimes fills in back here, is out of town." She winces. "It's not usually like this."

"It's great that it's so busy," Raya says. "Good for business."

A server walks in with a new order, stealing Poppy's attention.

Raya picks up a fork and pushes the food around on the plate. I'll be shocked if she eats any of it.

After about forty minutes straight—constant orders and directed chaos—we start to sense a little break in the madness.

Raya stands and refills her coffee cup, then—shockingly —grabs a water out of the standing cooler and brings it over to me.

She holds it out to me with a soft, uncharacteristic smile.

I look at her, a little confused. "Thanks?"

She nods, and walks back to the counter. I catch Poppy, watching us.

She gives me a look like, *What was that?* and I return her look with a half-shrug, shaking my head like, *Yeah, weird.* Poppy looks as surprised as I feel by Raya's unexpected kindness. Maybe setting her platonic boundary made her feel safe treating me as something other than a nuisance. She made herself clear, so kindness won't encourage me.

Or so she thinks.

Poppy wipes the sweat from her brow in the lull and looks at me. "First of all, thank you. I don't think we would've gotten through that without you."

I give her a little bow. "Always happy to help a friend."

Her eyes narrow. "Second of all—what are you guys doing here? Together? On a Friday?" There's an expectancy on her face that's more hopeful than accusatory.

"We came in for breakfast," I say.

"Together," Poppy repeats. "On a Friday." She moves closer to her sister. "What is going on?"

Raya reaches up and smooths her hair. "I'm taking some time off work."

Poppy frowns. "Are you okay? Did something else happen?"

Raya holds up a hand. "I'm fine. But my doctor insists that I need time off. If you need some extra help, maybe you could give me a job here for a few weeks?"

"Absolutely not," Poppy says without hesitation. "I would never let you work here."

"Thanks." Raya's eyebrows pinch together.

"Sorry, Ray, but this is not your wheelhouse." Poppy walks over to the sink and washes her hands. "Besides, if the doctor is saying you need to rest, don't you think you should —I don't know—rest?"

"I tried to tell her," I say, folding my arms like I'm a parent with a disobedient teen.

Raya shoots me a look.

Poppy dries her hands, stopping in front of her sister. "I assume this means you lied about what they said before you left the ER the other day?" She crosses her arms and stares at Raya.

"I didn't lie," Raya says, but when she meets my eyes, she adds, "I just didn't tell you the whole truth."

Poppy shifts. "What's going on, Ray?"

Raya looks at me, almost like she's lost.

And that's my cue to walk away.

Raya

I tell Poppy the whole story. The doctor, Brian telling me to take a month off, even the part about me falsely blaming Finn for this unwanted time out.

I don't tell her, though, that I'm worried. I don't tell her that the whole ordeal has me on edge because at the back of my mind, the low-level fear from the day of my episode is still hovering.

"Everyone wants me to relax. To take time off." I meet her eyes. "But I don't know how."

"Why didn't you say something sooner?" she asks. "I would've brought you dinner last night. We could've hung out, watched the game."

"I didn't want to watch the game. You know I hate hockey," I mutter with a quick glimpse at Finn, who is now cooking bacon with Miguel, joking and laughing like they're best friends.

How does he do that? It looks so easy.

"What is going on with you two?" Poppy asks, voice low.

I sigh. "Absolutely nothing. He showed up at my door this morning, and I can't get him to leave."

"Aw." She smiles. "That's really sweet."

"It's really not."

I can tell by her expression she disagrees.

"I made sure he knows this is all very platonic." I take a drink, then look at Finn. "I think he felt obligated to check in, since, you know, my brain shut off in his arms the other day." The words sting a little, a reminder of something still tender.

"Okay, Ray, if that's what you think," she stands. "Kind of nice for someone to show up for you, though."

Poppy picks up a kitchen rag and tucks it into the belt of her apron.

And then she walks away.

Chapter Twenty-Three

Raya

I feel a little like a toddler, stomping my foot and throwing a tantrum.

"I'm not getting in the car unless you tell me where we're going."

After breakfast—where Finn was, dare I say, pretty amazing for jumping in the way he did—we're standing on the sidewalk in front of my house. He insisted that he needs to be the one to drive.

"I bet you've never just gone along with someone else's plan, have you?" he asks.

I don't answer, because I'm pretty sure it's a rhetorical question.

He holds up a finger in a knowing point. "*I bet* that if I did tell you where we're going, you'd map out the quickest, most practical route to get there, and if I went a different way, you'd think we're wasting time." He pauses, but he's not finished. "*And!* I bet you never, ever take the back roads." He cocks his head and looks at me. "Did you shake your Christmas presents too?"

When my eyes dart away, he lets out an "Ah-ha! You did! You're a *shaker*!" He says it like it's *criminal*.

"I told you. I don't like surprises."

"Even good ones?"

I fold my arms. "How am I supposed to know if it's a good one if I don't know what it is ahead of time?"

He looks at me like I've got an arm growing out of my forehead.

"I've got my work cut out for me." He walks around to the driver's side of his Jeep.

I stand there, arms still crossed, really not wanting to admit that after all my protestations, I actually *want* to go wherever it is we're going. My curiosity is piqued.

Maybe I don't hate surprises as much as I let on.

I hear a *whirrr* as the sunroof opens on his SUV. He kneels on his seat, sticking his head out of the roof.

"Last chance."

I fidget. Most people give in by this point.

After a few seconds of hesitation, he says, "Okay, well, I'll see you later then." He plops down and starts to slowly pull away.

"No! Wait!" Before I can talk myself out of it, I quick run to the passenger side door and bang on the window. He slows to a stop, and I get in.

I don't have to look to know he's smirking at me.

"Just drive," I say, eyes focused on the dashboard.

A few minutes later, we're on a highway, behind a car driving five miles under the speed limit. It's making my skin crawl.

Finn doesn't seem to be bothered at all. He's not even looking for a way to pass it.

"This is why I don't take back roads," I say.

He chuckles to himself, but still makes no move to pass the car.

I let my head rest on the seat and close my eyes, feeling suddenly tired again. If Finn notices, he doesn't say anything, but mercifully stays quiet, allowing me to rest my eyes and, more importantly, my mind.

Maybe I'm just worn out, but I notice that even though I don't know where we're going—and Finn is the one in control—I don't feel tense right now. The seats are big and comfortable, and the ride is smooth. It smells woodsy, like him, and for the moment, I'm not thinking about what I need to do or where else I need to be.

He finds an eighties station, but keeps the volume low enough that I can still hear the rhythmic sound of the tires on the road. And soon, I'm drifting—not asleep, but not awake either. It's not until he pulls into the parking lot of a nondescript brick building and stops the car that I open my eyes.

He turns off the engine and looks at me. I spot the hint of concern in his eyes, but he must think better of saying anything because his face shifts and he brightens. "Ready?"

"How can I be ready? I have no idea where we are."

"Right. Good point." He opens the door and walks to the back of the car. I get out as he opens the hatch, and inside, I see six neatly stacked bins. He pulls one down and hands it to me, then grabs two more. He presses a button to close the back of the car, locks it, and motions for me to follow him into the building.

"Since it's you, I thought it would be smart to start with *productive* fun before we move on to *mindless* fun," he says.

"Since this is a one-time thing, I don't see that happening," I say, walking alongside him.

"Oh, ye of little faith." He holds the door open for me,

and inside, we're met by the sound of voices—overlapping chatter from a group of people. I'm not sure I have the energy for strangers, but I follow Finn down a flight of stairs.

The noise picks up as we get closer to the bottom, and he peers over his shoulder. "Get ready."

I respond with wide eyes. "For what?"

At that, he smiles and opens the door to a large room with tall ceilings. The sound of voices and laughter swells as we step inside, and I pause in the doorway to look around. On one side, there are kids and adults seated at round tables. Most of the kids are writing or coloring, some of them are reading or drawing. One little girl is knitting, which instantly makes me like her. A few of the adults are talking quietly—teaching, maybe?

On the opposite side of the room, there are couches and armchairs situated on top of a brightly colored rug and, off to the side, an open window to what looks like an industrial kitchen.

"What is this place?" I ask, as Finn takes the bin from me and stacks it on top of the two he set down against the wall.

"Tutoring club," he says, leading me further into the room. "There's no school today, so they opened early this morning. Parents still work, so kids need somewhere to go. For some of these kids it's the only meal they'll get all day."

I'm struck by the lightness of the mood, the smatterings of laughter, the engaged adults who kneel or sit with the kids.

"They'll feed them, help with homework if they've got it, and once they're caught up, the kids can go down the hall to the game room to hang out."

"Mr. Finn!" A little girl rushes toward him.

"Hey, Amalia!" Finn kneels down so he's at her eye level.

She holds up a piece of paper with a big 10/10 written in red ink. "Look!"

"Spelling test?" he asks.

She nods. "I got them all."

"Did that boy you have a crush on give you the answers?"

She shakes her head, her pigtails flopping from side to side, and laughs out a loud, "NO!"

"Okay, okay, just checking," he says, feigning exasperation.

She's missing her two front teeth, and there's a trail of freckles across the pale skin of her cheeks and nose. Her eyes are bright, and she looks so proud. My heart squeezes when I realize she now has Finn's undivided attention.

"Did you get a prize out of the cupboard?" he asks.

She shakes her head again. "I was waiting for you."

"Well, let's go! Why are we standing around here?" He stands and says, "See, now I'm waiting for you, just standing here, lollygagging—" She laughs and grabs his hand, starting to pull him away. He glances at me. "Be right back."

I nod, but as he's tugged across the room, I move back toward the wall, watching the chaos and commotion of a space that feels like it's meant to be a safe haven for these kids.

An older woman walks over, her eyes kind. "Hi there, welcome!"

I feel a little on display. "Hi . . ."

"Haven't seen you around here before," she says.

"Oh, I came with Finn—" I point in his general direction, but she doesn't look away.

"Oh . . .?" She smiles. "He doesn't usually bring friends."

My gaze snags on him, across the room. "He comes here a lot?"

The woman laughs. "You could say that. I'm Tasha." She points to another woman who is sitting at a table with three kids but looking our way. "That's my sister, Toya."

When I make eye contact with her, she frowns at me and looks away.

Tasha notices and gives me a sheepish smile. "She has a little crush on Finn."

Toya has to be in her sixties.

"She's probably a little jealous." Tasha puts a hand on my arm and leads me around the room.

"Of me?" I laugh. "Unnecessary. Finn and I aren't even really friends." But as I say the words, they don't feel true.

"Well, that's a shame," Tasha says. "He's a great one to have." She peers over at the area with the couches, where Finn lies on his stomach on the floor, reading a book with four young kids, including Amalia, who sits on his back reading over his shoulder.

I think I understand what she means.

"Wow. He's good with them, huh?" I ask, even though the question doesn't need an answer.

"The best." She squeezes my arm. "These kids adore him."

I wonder if this is the result of growing up in a big family. Not for the first time, I want to know more about him, his family, his house, his brothers and sisters. I wonder if it was anything like mine.

A little girl walks out from the kitchen. "Miss Tasha, the sandwiches are ready whenever you want to serve lunch."

"Thank you, Grace," Tasha says with a smile. Then to me, she adds, "Grace is our best helper. She always shows up with all her homework done and helps tutor the younger kids or get meals and snacks ready to serve." She leans toward me. "She likes to be busy."

Ooh. A kindred spirit. I smile at the girl. She gives me a stern look.

"Have you seen my brothers?" Grace asks. "Brady has a math test Monday, and he needs Miss Toya to explain fractions—" She looks at Tasha. "If he's playing that stupid Nintendo—" She walks off, pushing through the door and out into the hall.

"She's a little intense." Tasha motions for me to follow her into the kitchen, where we see a tin of perfectly made sandwiches next to a basket of individually packaged chips and a tray of cookies. "Carries the weight of the world on her shoulders, that one."

"What's her story?" I ask.

Tasha walks over to an industrial-sized refrigerator. "Their dad is deployed right now, and Grace knows it's hard on her mom. I think she's trying to do whatever she can to lighten the load." She pulls out a big metal tray with juice boxes neatly stacked inside. "She's a good girl, but no one that age should have to feel that kind of responsibility."

This hits me with a pang of nostalgia. I understand, maybe more than most, the weight that girl is carrying.

Tasha nods at the sandwiches. "Grab that?"

I pick up the tray, follow her to the counter behind the open window, and help as Tasha lays everything out. I go back for the cookies while she grabs the chips, then see Grace return with a dejected-looking dark-haired boy who looks a few years younger than her.

Grace walks the boy over to Toya, says something to her, then nods at a backpack sitting on the table. The boy sits and pulls a textbook from the bag. His sister straightens, looking around the space. When she spots another boy who looks younger but otherwise identical to the one at the table, she walks over to him, sits down and wraps an arm around him.

"Is that her other brother?" I ask as Tasha lays out a stack of napkins.

Tasha follows my gaze over to the kids and stands up straighter. "Yes, that's Bodie. He's taking it pretty hard that their dad is away again so soon." She smiles. "They're lucky to have Grace. She's such a good girl."

"I wonder who takes care of her," I say absently.

Tasha laughs. "We do, when we can—although Grace is perfectly capable of taking care of herself. You good?" I nod as she walks away, leaving me standing there to watch Grace and Bodie.

It's all I need to see to understand this little girl. Because once upon a time, I was her. In a lot of ways, I still am.

Grace talks to Bodie, who sits and looks up at her. I can see his love for her on his face, but she looks like she's still lecturing him. An eldest daughter with all the traits that eldest daughters have. Strong leader. High achiever. Responsible. A good role model. Conscientious. Organized.

Perfectly capable of taking care of herself.

But just because Grace is capable doesn't mean she should always have to. Once in a while, it would be nice if someone took care of her.

"Wouldn't it be nice if someone took care of you for a while?"

I grew up with people who would've definitely taken care of me . . . but I gave them no opportunity. I wouldn't even know how to let them. And I haven't been letting them ever since.

Chapter Twenty-Four

Finn

Raya is quiet on the way back to her house.

Not that I expect her to open up to me, but I do wish I knew what she was thinking. She helped serve the kids lunch, then sat in the stands for an epic game of dodgeball. I took one to the side of the head and one between the legs (which the boys thought was *hilarious*), but thankfully the kids don't throw that hard.

She sat. She watched. She smiled sometimes, but mostly she seemed lost in thought. Given her state a few days ago, it's likely going to take her body—and her mind—more than a couple of days to heal.

"Thanks for playing along today. You were a good sport." I don't want to force conversation, but the silence is killing me. Is she okay? Does she need electrolytes? Has she eaten enough?

Is there anyone else in her life asking her these things?

"It was nice," she says. "Thanks for distracting me."

"Anytime, *friend*." I put a bit more emphasis on that last word.

Her smile is soft, but I see it.

"You're really great with kids, too," she says. "They love you."

I smile. "Kids under ten and women over sixty-five, I'm telling ya. That's my real fan base."

Her phone buzzes. She checks it, then tucks it in her bag without responding. I'd love to ask about it, but I don't.

And then I do.

"Real Estate King?"

She shakes her head at me, but amusement lines her brow. "You shouldn't call him that."

"You're right," I say. "He's probably more of a duke."

She looks out the window, but I catch her smile.

I keep my eyes on the road but decide to test the waters a bit. "Are you guys . . . serious?"

"No, it's new," she says.

"Exclusive?"

She looks at me. "Why?"

I hold up a hand. "Just being a nosy friend—I know this is"—I flick a pointed finger from her to me and back again—"you know—platonic."

She watches me for a beat. "We haven't labeled anything. It's all new. Like . . . a trial phase." She goes back to staring out the window. Subject closed.

But it's a reminder that pursuing her right now isn't a good idea. My goal is just to be her friend. I can do that, right?

I notice she's discreetly wringing her hands. Not sure what that's about. "You okay?"

Her gaze falls to her folded hands, then she shakes her head. "Yeah. Yes. Just tired."

"Tired," I repeat.

She nods. "More than just tired—I feel drained."

I want to talk, to get her mind off it, to joke around, lighten things up, but instead I take Gray's advice and just listen.

"I don't know how long I'm supposed to wait until things go back to normal. I'm so used to"—she stops, trying to find the right word—"*doing*, to working on things, being busy—and this whole taking it easy thing is . . . it's just hard."

"You ever hear the saying 'it's okay to not be okay'?"

She scoffs. "So cliché."

"Being cliché doesn't mean it's not true," I say.

She goes still.

I tap my thumb on the steering wheel. We're back on the highway, driving to Loveland, and I have a feeling there's more going on in her mind, and I really wish I knew what it was.

"Okay," I say, trying to keep my tone light. "I know you don't like to share, so I can take the hint."

"Just because I don't share with you doesn't mean I don't share with anyone."

"Oof, point taken." When she turns to me, I say, "I'm just playing. I don't expect you to spill your guts to me." Then, after a beat, I add, "Except in the garbage can in your office."

I'm glad when she laughs. Feels like a win. But then she says, "I think it's pointless to talk about my feelings."

"Probably why you're so tightly wound." I come to a four-way stop with a blinking red light and a semi turns in front of me, out of turn.

Raya practically growls.

"We're not in a hurry," I remind her. "You've got nowhere to be, remember?"

She rolls her eyes. "How can I forget?"

I hit the gas, but behind this truck, I'm stuck at thirty-five miles per hour. I purposely don't pass it because the longer it takes to get back to her house, the more time I get to spend with her.

"Okay, so if you were around someone who you *would* talk to about your feelings, if you didn't think it was pointless or stupid . . . what would you say?"

For a long moment, she doesn't respond.

"Come on, Hart, you already know I can keep a secret."

I expect her to ignore me or tell me to shut up or something dismissive like that, but instead, she says, "I was thinking about Grace."

Oh. That's unexpected. "What about her?"

"She reminds me of me."

Raya

I'm not sure what it is—the quiet in the car, the fact that we're driving at a snail's pace, or simply that Finn cared enough to ask how I'm doing. Something most people don't bother to do. Something Justin definitely doesn't do.

I get it. I mean, my answer will always be the same— *"Fine."*

I'm always "fine."

And if I'm not, I make myself. It's in my DNA.

If I had to guess, it's in Grace's too. But seeing her take care of her brothers—so competent, but so young—has me feeling out of sorts.

If I had to guess, her mom has no idea she's putting all this pressure on herself. She's probably just thankful to have the help.

I'm not a person who analyzes why I am the way I am, but watching Grace, all I could think was—*What does she do for fun?*

Followed by—*What do I do for fun?*

Stupid Finn is getting in my head.

"I can see the similarities," Finn says. "You're both cranky little perfectionists."

I laugh out loud. "Yeah, that. But also—she's just a kid. She shouldn't have to take care of anyone."

"I don't think she has to," he says. "I think she just does."

That lands. Because the same could've been said of me when I was her age. Nobody asked me to help with my sisters. Nobody told me I needed to be perfect and follow the rules. The pressure I've put on myself to achieve—that's mine to own.

I don't know when it started, I only know it's been there for as long as I can remember.

I became the person who watched out for everyone, the person on high alert in case there was a crisis. I became independent and strong. The girl who didn't need anyone for anything ever. And once that's who I was, I owned that identity.

And now I'm not sure how to soften it.

"She's like an adult in a tiny body," Finn says. "Which is probably how you were, right? You were a full-fledged adult at age ten, and my maturity peaked when I was twelve."

I bark out a laugh.

He grins. "Someday I'll tell you the story of how me and my brothers flipped our dad's tractor during a midnight joyride across the creek."

I laugh again, probably because I need to. "Do you think you'll ever have a day where you grow up?"

"I hope not," he says, then smiles again.

And I think, *it's a nice smile.*

He goes back to watching the road.

I want to ask him how it feels to be the only person who's seen the vulnerable side of me, but I wouldn't dare give him the satisfaction. Instead, I let out a dramatic sigh and say, "Can you go around this truck?"

He shakes his head. "You're so impatient."

"And you drive like a grandma who just took a Benadryl."

He chuckles. "Do other people know that you can be funny?"

I narrow my eyes. "Only my friends," I say.

He holds up a fist in celebration and shouts, "Promotion! Yes!"

I look out the window and hide a smile.

Chapter Twenty-Five

Raya

Over the next several days, I spend a whole lot of time doing a whole lot of nothing.

After Finn and I went to the tutoring club, the team went on the road. I'd expected him to drop me off and go, but in true Finn fashion, he walked me into the house and made me cinnamon toast for the second time since I've known him.

Only this time, I ate it, then went and laid down, surprised to discover that I wanted to rest.

The next day, the team went on the road. I told him I was glad I'd finally get a little peace and quiet without him bugging me every day, to which he responded that he would FaceTime me every day, to which I responded that I wouldn't answer.

Like everything else, he took that in stride.

Surprisingly, it only took a few hours of being awake today for me to rethink the "peace and quiet" claim, because if Finn showed up at my door, at least I'd have something to *do*.

Thankfully, albeit predictably, my family has been hovering.

And it's actually been kind of nice.

On Saturday, my mom showed up late morning with bagels and cream cheese—two of my favorite things. I tried to tell her I didn't need a babysitter and I didn't want her to give up her entire day for me. Her response? "Raya, I'm your mother, and this is what mothers do. You'd know that if you ever let anyone help you with anything." And with that, she pushed her way into my house, leaving me standing in the doorway, pondering her comment.

I don't let her help with anything because I can take care of things myself—not because I'm trying to rob her of the chance to be my mom. She knows that, right?

We ended up sitting on the couch watching Christmas movies the entire day. I've never spent an entire day watching television! By the third movie, our commentary had become the real entertainment, and it took three-and-a-half hours to get through *Santa Clues* because we kept pausing to laugh at the ridiculous premise.

The heroine—forced back to her small, Midwestern hometown because of a family emergency— is putting her true crime podcasting skills to good use by trying to figure out who's been going around the town answering all the letters written to Santa.

We figured out after the second scene that it was her old flame from high school, the "one that got away," mainly because he was the only character with any lines and the only one wearing red and green checkered flannel.

On Sunday, after our usual Hart family dinner, I reached out to two work colleagues to check on the Denim and Diamonds event, but both of my texts went unanswered.

That night, I went to a Loveland Town Meeting and tried to volunteer to chair three different Christmas events, but every single time I raised my hand, Poppy grabbed it and pulled it down.

"You can *attend* the events," she hissed. "But you're not going to be the one in charge of them."

"I could plan these things in my sleep," I said. "And it's important to volunteer."

"Fine, I'll sign you up to work the kissing booth," Poppy whispered.

I glared at her, and then—"There isn't really a kissing booth, is there?"

She widened her eyes and nodded slowly, wagging her eyebrows. "The Mistletoe Bungalow."

I shuddered. She giggled.

"I'm so bored," I'd told her miserably, then went back to listening, but when Margot, Jeremy's wife, took the stage, I gave myself permission to zone out. I'm not harboring ill will toward Jeremy and Margot, but she's genuinely not a very nice person. Most of my feelings about her have less to do with Jeremy and more to do with the fact that she bullied Poppy right up until Dallas entered the picture.

Now, she sort of kisses up to my sister, which would be hilarious to watch if Poppy wasn't so nice in return.

Inwardly, I groan. I should be more like Poppy. I don't need to be carrying grudges over here. Especially on my sister's behalf when she's clearly moved on.

Do better, Raya.

I pull out my phone and see I have a new text. From Finn. I try to be discreet when I open it because I don't want Poppy to see it. I also silence notifications because, knowing Finn, there will be a *lot* of incoming texts.

I was right. Four right in a row.

FINN

Hey

Sorry to bug you

Actually not sorry because we're
FRIENDS now

Did you know your hometown has a big
kick-off Christmas celebration?

RAYA

I'm at a town meeting listening to them talk
about it right now.

FINN

No way! Do they need someone to play
Santa? I'll totally volunteer.

I smirk at my phone because I can see it. And he'd probably be great at it. Heck, if he stuck around longer than a month, the mayor would probably name a day in his honor. Finn has a way of winning people over.

Not me, of course, but *other* people seem to gravitate to him.

RAYA

I'll be sure to ask.

FINN

We should go. It looks like they have tons
of events. A parade? Sleigh rides? Tree
lighting?

RAYA

Do they not have Christmas in Montana?

218

FINN

Of course they do! And I love it. There's something every weekend starting the Friday after Thanksgiving. Dang. I'm making a list of the things I want to do. Do you do all these events?

RAYA

I do some things.

FINN

Uh huh

RAYA

We go to Pine Creek Tree Farm to get our tree every Thanksgiving weekend. That's always an adventure.

FINN

Do you get one of your own? For your house?

RAYA

No.

FINN

We'll fix that. What else do you do?

I think back on the past few Christmas seasons and realize it's been a while since I've done anything to celebrate the holidays beyond the actual day. When I don't respond right away, Finn texts again.

FINN

Don't tell me . . . you don't do any of this stuff.

RAYA

The holidays are busy enough.

FINN

<sends gif of Scrooge McDuck>

RAYA

<eyeroll emoji>

FINN

Did you know they have holiday fireworks?

Do you think those are different from regular fireworks?

He can't seriously be this awestruck over Christmas, can he? Maybe this is just how he is about everything.

RAYA

I think they're pretty much the same.

FINN

Still cool. The ice rink looks decent too. Do you skate? Dallas said he took Poppy once and she was terrible.

RAYA

She is. And so am I. Nobody in our family skates.

FINN

Great! I'll teach you.

RAYA

I'm good.

FINN

Nah, I got you. <winking emoji>

The Monday before Thanksgiving, Poppy and Eloise take pity on me with a sisters' night. It was Eloise's idea, and once she had it in her head, there was no talking her out of it.

She also said she didn't want me to leave my house, so they were coming to me.

I told her to stop babying me, and she said she wanted to give me a dose of my own medicine. There was no laughing emoji or "LOL" attached to that text.

She meant it.

Secretly, I'm glad they're coming. Not only have I been struggling to stay *not* busy, but it's been a long time since we've hung out, just the three of us.

They show up together, armed with snacks and drinks, both wearing Comets hoodies I assume belong to their significant others. They storm into my house, Hurricane Harts, and Poppy sets up a spread of snacks that looks like it could feed a small army.

Eloise pulls a bottle of Dr Pepper from her bag, opens it, and takes a drink. "I thought we were going to be late. Poppy insisted on stopping at the grocery store, and we ran into Jan Potter, and you know how she talks." She turns toward my living room. "Why isn't the TV on?"

I frown. "Because you guys just got here."

She rushes into the room, picks up the remote, and clicks on the television. "But the game"—she stops flipping channels and sets the clicker back on the table—"is starting." She grins. "Look, there's Gray!"

"I thought we were going to watch a rom-com," I say. "I think 27 *Dresses* is streaming. We love that one.'"

Eloise turns to Poppy. "Didn't you tell her about the game?"

Poppy waves a hand over the spread of food. "No, El, I was a little busy."

Eloise looks at me. "Do you want us to leave? We could go watch at Poppy's, or—"

"No, it's fine." I glance at the screen just as they pan across the team warming up out on the ice. I squint, searching the jerseys for the one that says "Holbrook."

What am I doing?

I look away, but not in time for my curiosity to go unnoticed. Eloise quirks a brow, but I ignore her and walk into the kitchen. "Can I help?"

Poppy shakes her head. "Just go sit."

"I'm so tired of sitting."

She eyes me.

"Please? Something little. I can handle bringing a bowl from the kitchen to the living room."

She smiles, capitulates, and slides a tray of veggies over to me.

"Thank you. I hate not being at least somewhat useful."

"I know," Poppy says. "But it really is the best thing for you right now."

Eloise grabs a handful of nuts from the charcuterie board Poppy is arranging, messing up the neatly stacked arrangement and eliciting an "El!" from Poppy.

Eloise is oblivious. "How many times have you called work?"

"Only a few." I pull a bottle of water from the fridge, hold it up with raised brows, and Poppy nods. I hand it to her then grab one for myself. "It's pointless, though. Nobody will take my calls, and they locked me out of my email."

Poppy laughs out loud. "Epic."

"It's awful," I say. "I know they care about my mental health, but good grief." I pause. "Also, I think my boss is

222

trying to make a point about me taking direction. Apparently, I have a tendency to do things my own way."

They both stare at me.

"What?"

"Do not pretend you don't know this about yourself," Poppy says.

I only shrug, because yes, I do know this.

We load up plates, and once again, they try to convince me that this time off is doing wonders for my nervous system, which I mostly ignore. Poppy goes on a little tangent about something called "adrenal fatigue," which sounds totally made up—another buzzword—and a way for wellness influencers to convince you something else is wrong with you. But during a commercial break, I Google it, scan a few articles, and start to change my mind.

It's not that I don't believe the doctors when they say stress can wreak havoc on your body. I know this—in theory.

That's just something that happens to *other* people.

And if these articles and doctors are right, and I'm reacting this poorly to stress, then how am I supposed to fix it? It's not like I can quit my job. Even if I were independently wealthy, I have zero interest in sitting around and not being productive. The source of my stress is still going to be there whether I take a day off or not. In fact, taking a day off makes me even *more* stressed because it's one less day to chip away at the very long list of things to do.

But I'm not thinking about that tonight.

Tonight, apparently, I'm watching a hockey game.

To my utter horror, every time Finn shows up on the screen, my stomach does a little somersault. I never got that "Oh my gosh, I *know* that guy" feeling when seeing the team on TV. I mean, I've watched a handful of games. It never registered with me before.

Now it's registering. And it's unfamiliar and exciting and annoying all at once.

The whole reason for dating Justin is to prevent these kinds of emotional gymnastics.

I turn my attention back to my phone because I need something else to occupy myself with, but then one of the announcers mentions Finn's name, and it draws my eyes up to the screen.

"Before the game, Dallas Burke told me that Holbrook is an absolutely crucial piece to the health of this team."

"That may surprise some of our viewers since Holbrook isn't one of the Comets' big stars," the other announcer says. "But he is well-loved among his teammates and the Comets' fans."

"He's a rare kind of player who makes everyone else better every time he's on the ice."

There's a close-up of Finn, who is focused in a way I don't think I've ever seen before. He moves around on the ice, completely engrossed in the job he's there to do. I watch as he glides so effortlessly, and it's—stunning, really. Surprisingly so.

"You see something you like there, Raya?" Eloise cracks.

I look up and find both of my sisters watching me watch Finn.

I clear my throat and look away. "Nope."

The game starts, and they both disappear into it the way our dad does when he watches. It's hilarious because once upon a time, they both disliked—and didn't understand—this sport as much as I do. Now, there's a lot of gasping and hollering at the TV.

I pull out my phone and scroll, thinking maybe I should text Justin. Only . . . I'm not sure what I would say.

I already sent him the details for Thanksgiving.

We're getting together Wednesday, so I can explain to him who everyone is, and really, what else is there? We'll never be two people who need to know what the other is doing at all times.

And that's the point. I don't want to miss him when we're apart.

"And Holbrook takes an elbow to the jaw!" the voice blares from the television.

I glance up in time to catch a replay of Finn getting in between a player from the other team and Gray.

"That's what he does," Eloise says, more to herself than anyone else. "He keeps the path clean."

I frown. "What does that mean?"

"He protects the other guys," Poppy says. "Dallas says he's their most selfless player."

I can see that, actually. He might be all wrong for me, but it's not hard to believe this about Finn.

"So . . . tell us about this new guy," Eloise says. She picks up a chocolate cream puff and shoves the entire thing in her mouth. She almost instantly realizes this was a two-bite snack and covers her mouth with her hand as she chews.

"What do you want to know?" I ask, hoping they ask softball questions.

She shrugs, still chewing.

"We know he's in real estate," Poppy says. "What else?"

"He runs," I say. "He's doing the Turkey Trot on Thanksgiving morning before he comes to dinner. He's an only child. Never been married. His parents live in . . .

Naperville, I think? No, Barrington? Work is really important to him, so we have that in common."

Poppy looks away.

"We both believe in direct communication, so we've laid out clear expectations," I say.

"Wow. Sounds swoony." Eloise's tone drips sarcasm.

"I don't need or want swoony," I say. "Sensible suits me just fine."

Eloise does a robot motion with her arms, a blank look on her face, but I ignore her.

I take another cracker and load it up, wishing I could convince my sisters that this really is the best thing for me.

There's a collective "Ooh!" from the crowd, a huge reaction from the announcers, followed by a series of loud whistles on the television that draws our attention back to the game.

"And Holbrook is down! A *huge* hit on a wind-up by Pendleton!" one of the announcers shouts.

The cameras cut and swing around to Finn, sprawled out on the ice.

"Oh my gosh," the words escape before I can stop them. The crowd is going crazy. "Why are they still cheering?!"

"It's an away game," I hear Poppy say, but my eyes are glued to the screen.

"Holbrook just got absolutely destroyed, and it looks like —yeah, on the replay—it looks like he saved Hawke from a hit of his own," the play-by-play announcer says.

They switch to a zoomed-in shot, and on the replay, there's a player from the other team who lowers his shoulder to hit Gray, but at the last second Finn skates in from the left and blocks the hit.

"And now that hit has drawn a crowd—a scrum with

several of the Comets. It looks like the gloves are off. Stevens and Pendleton are locked up, with—*OH!*" Both the announcers react to Jericho, who rears back and levels the guy who hit Finn. "Jericho Stevens lands a shot, sending Pendleton to the ice! Other players are starting to jump in—"

"—Yeah, I wouldn't want to mess with Stevens, he's got forty pounds and five inches on Pendleton—"

"—And Finn Holbrook is still down—either knocked the wind out of him or knocked him clean out—but he is not getting up."

My eyes are glued to the screen.

The referees manage to separate the players, pulling them away from one another and sending them off, but Finn is still down.

They replay the moment of impact in slow motion, and I see the guy lower his shoulder, launch a bit off the ice as Finn takes the brunt of the hit on his chest—but he's sent flying backward, out of control, and lands in an awkward position.

I gasp as I watch Finn land on his back, his head snapping back and bouncing off the ice.

"Oh no." Eloise stands. "That looked bad."

"The trainers are out on the ice, tending to Holbrook, who still hasn't moved—we'll be right back."

It cuts to commercial.

I'm holding my breath. I didn't know I was doing that.

I look over at my sisters, who wear the same expression I feel on my own face.

After about a minute, the game pops back on. The trainers have Finn upright and help him to his feet. He looks dazed, but he's up. There's lackluster applause in the stadium from the opposing fans, peppered with boos and whistles, and I realize I'm standing, eyes glued to the screen.

"That'll most likely be the last we see of Finn Holbrook today, I'm afraid," one announcer says. "Let's hope the Comets can get by without him."

I know I'm not supposed to care, but there's no hiding the shock of watching someone you know get hurt on such a public stage.

"How do we find out if he's okay?" I ask.

"I think we just have to wait," Poppy says. "They usually give an update."

I turn my attention back to the TV, willing someone to tell us something. "They're just going to go on with the game?"

"They can't stop every time someone gets hurt, Ray," Poppy says. "It's hockey."

"But . . ." I hold my hand out at the screen, like *he's hurt!*

I pick up my phone and open my text thread with Finn, but quickly realize I have no idea what to say.

My fingers hover over the tiny keyboard, and I type the only thing I can think of.

RAYA
Please tell me you're okay.

I pause, then delete it.

And I realize I care a whole lot more than I thought.

Chapter Twenty-Six

Finn

Mario is mid-jump when there's a knock at my door.

I pause the game and stand—achy—and walk into the entryway to answer it, shocked when I pull it open and find Raya standing in the hallway.

Her face is tight, brows knit, like she's here against her will.

My eyebrows shoot up and I give her a quick once-over. "Wait a second."

I shut the door. Then I open it again. She's still there.

"Is that actually you or have you been cloned?" I stick my head out the door, looking up and down the hallway. "Are you being held at gunpoint? Is there a bomb strapped to your chest? Blink twice if you're in trouble!"

She stares at me. "I see the knock on your head didn't make you any less insufferable. I guess that's all I need to know." She turns to go.

"Hold up, I'm just kidding—" I step out into the hallway, and she stops. "Did you come here . . ."

She almost turns around, but only halfway.

I narrow my gaze. ". . . to check on me?"

She straightens and turns away from me. "No."

"You came here to check on me." I don't even try to hide the smile. "Ha! You were *worried* about me."

She turns to me. "I wasn't," she says, tone dry, face straight.

I quirk a brow, studying her. "Then what are you doing here?"

She sighs, like she's owning up to something. "I thought it was the decent thing to do. To check in. Since—you know . . ."

"I *don't* know," I say.

"Since you checked on me." She avoids my eyes, but I see her jaw clench.

"So. This is payback," I say.

She shrugs. "I guess."

"Well, I came to your house to check on you because I was *worried* about you." I watch her. "Because I *care*."

Her eyes flick to mine, and even though I have no proof—and it might be wishful thinking—I swear I see relief there.

I move out of the way of the door. "Do you want to come in?"

She stands there awkwardly, like a kid on the first day of class. "I don't want to impose."

I walk away, leaving the door open. "If it's really gonna be payback, then you have to impose."

"That's true." She steps inside and closes the door behind her.

"How'd you get past the doorman?" I ask.

"Oh," she says like she's just remembered something. "Right. He asked me to give you this. I think he assumed you and I were . . . whatever. Anyway." She holds a plain white envelope in my direction. "Montana stamp. Maybe someone from home?"

I take the letter and turn it over, trying not to linger on the return address. "Thanks," I say, then tuck it in my back pocket.

"You okay?"

"Always," I say. It's not exactly true, but I don't want to get into it. I turn toward the living room, searching my mind for a way to change the subject. "You haven't been here since that Halloween party," I say. "You didn't come this year."

"I was working." She's standing there like she's not sure where to go, but then her eyes drift to the paused screen on my TV. "Are you playing video games?"

I pick up the controller and shake it. "You want a turn?"

"You have a concussion," she says. "You're not supposed to play video games. Or be on the computer or the phone. No screens at all."

"Okay, first of all, it's a *mild* concussion," I say. "And I think those are more like guidelines than rules."

"They're not."

"And second of all," I say, ignoring her, "did you look up the treatment for a concussion?"

She scoffs a no, but wow, is she a bad poker player.

"You sure?" I ask. "Because I'm gonna go out on a limb here and guess that you looked up treatment for a concussion."

"Whatever. Everyone knows that you can't be on a screen if you have a concussion."

"Uh-huh." I toss the controller on the couch. "Fine. I don't have to play. But I get bored really easy."

She rolls her eyes, then lets out a sigh. "How is it . . . really? Your concussion?"

It's a sincere question. She's really asking. "It's good. I mean, not *good* good, but manageable. Could've been worse."

"It looked . . . *not* good."

"It looked gnarly." I shouldn't have watched it, but I did. "Seeing my head bounce like that was wild. Looked worse than it was, though." Every hockey player knows they're one collision away from the end of their career, which makes me grateful for every second I have on the ice.

We stand there for a long few seconds, then she says, "Your place looks different during the day." She walks over to the entertainment center and picks up a framed photo I put away when I have people over. She turns. "Is this you?"

"Uh, yeah." I take the photo and put it back on the shelf, staring at Hunter's face a beat too long.

"I'm sorry, I didn't mean to—" She frowns, and I know she's seen on my face what I don't usually show.

I shake my head. "Nah, it's all good." I pick up a different photo, this one of my whole family, and hand it to her. "My people."

She takes it. "I don't know anyone who actually wears a cowboy hat." She grins. "Quite the crew. Is that your parents' house? The porch is amazing."

"Yep," I say, suddenly aware of the ache of missing home. "Grew up there." I pull out my phone, open the photo app, and scroll until I find the photos I'm looking for. I turn it around and show her the screen. "That's the view."

Her eyes go wide. "Oh my gosh."

"Yeah, it's pretty spectacular." I scroll to a drone shot of the house and stables.

"Your family owns all of this land?" She looks at me.

"And more," I say. "It's one of the biggest ranches in the state."

"But here you are in the heart of a city." She studies me. "You must miss it."

I nod. "I do. One day I'll get back home. I just . . . like to seize the day and all that crap."

She laughs. "'Seize the day and all that crap.' You should put that on a T-shirt."

I smile and put the photo back, the one of me and Hunter catching my eye. "That's my older brother, uh, Hunter." I'm surprised I say this. I don't talk about him. Ever.

"One of the four?" she asks with a smile.

"Uh, no," I say. "He was the fifth." I look at her.

The second she understands, her smile fades.

In the photo, we're out on the homemade ice rink Pop built after a hockey scout sought him out to talk about my brother. Said Hunter had real potential, and that encouragement lit a fire under him like I'd never seen before. Hockey became his whole life.

Our dad said he wanted to support this big dream, so he built the rink as a way to do that. And I became his practice buddy, not because I loved hockey, but because I loved my brother.

Raya puts a hand on my arm, and I realize I zoned out for a second. I pull my hand back from the frame. "Sorry—I don't really . . ."

"It's okay," she says. "You don't have to talk about it." A pause. "Unless you want to."

I nod. "Yeah. Thanks."

She presses her lips together, and we stand there, silent, for a long moment.

I look around the apartment, searching for something—anything—to say. "Do you want to go walk around the city? Some of the Christmas decorations are already up. Have you seen the Macy's windows?"

She shakes her head.

"Of course, you haven't because you don't do fun things." I grin, aware that I'm forcing a lightness I absolutely do not feel. It shouldn't be this difficult to talk about Hunter after all these years, but it is. I don't like dredging it up—it makes me angry. And helpless. "We could go check them out? Or that German market is open—we could get hot chocolate."

She hesitates for a beat, then relents. "Fine."

"Fine?" I exaggerate, blinking in disbelief. "We really are friends now, aren't we?"

She levels my gaze. "Don't make me regret it."

As I grab my shoes, Raya walks over to the wall of windows overlooking the lake. "They said on TV that you make your teammates better."

I chuckle. "Yeah, they love to say that."

"Is it true?"

I finish tying one shoe and pull on the other. "I mean, that's the goal, right? We're a team, and I can set up the other guys, keep things clean, and apparently get in the way of an oncoming freight train just so your sister's boyfriend doesn't get his teeth knocked out"

"Does it bother you?" She turns and looks at me.

I stand. "Does what bother me?"

She shrugs. "Not being the star."

"Pssh. No," I say, chuckling. "Believe me, I just feel lucky to be here. I'm never going to be a Burke or a Hawke, but how many people get to say they played with those guys?"

She watches me and, for a second, I feel almost naked, like she's solving a puzzle about me that I haven't even started.

"You're probably wondering why I'm not wanting more, huh?"

She shifts. "Well, kind of, yeah. What's the point of doing something if you're not trying to be the best at it?"

With that, I see right into what drives Raya Hart.

And I'm the complete opposite.

"I don't need to be the best to be happy," I say.

She doesn't move.

"Foreign concept to you, right?" I say.

"Yeah, kind of. It seems like a waste of time to do something at the level you do it at, spend all of that time and energy and money, and not want to be the best."

"My dad always says 'Perfect is the enemy of great.' When you take away the need to be perfect, you can be happy with whatever's left."

Her eyes go wide. "Wow, that was almost . . . deep."

"Don't be so surprised," I say. "There's a lot you don't know about me."

"Oh yeah? What other secrets are you hiding?" Her tone is different now, almost playful.

Without hesitation, I turn and say the first thing that pops in my head, "I'm an excellent kisser."

She doesn't look away.

I didn't mean to say that. It was too forward, especially since I meant to keep things light and flirty, and we're finally on common ground here—but . . .

She doesn't look away.

I keep my face neutral, a little shocked she isn't blustering at the comment, but now that I've said it out loud, I can't reel the words back in.

I *want* to kiss her.

I've wanted to kiss her for a very long time.

"I'm really glad you came to check on me, Hart." The air between us shifts, and I pray I'm not misreading it. I take a step closer and reach up to brush her hair away from her face. She goes completely still, but I know Raya—she'll let me know if she wants me to back away.

I let my fingers trail down her neck, resting on her collarbone. I rub a thumb over the warm skin there. I want to bring my lips down to that exact spot, to press kisses into her soft skin, along her chin until I reach her lips.

Instinctively, my eyes dip down, not that I need a visual reminder of what her lips look like—I think I've got them memorized.

What am I doing? This is *Raya*.

And yet—she's not pulling away.

My free hand skims down her back to her hip, my touch so light I bet it doesn't even register. She doesn't move. Almost like she's waiting to see what happens next.

I shift my hand behind her neck as my gaze sweeps up from her mouth to her eyes, and I stare at her. Quiet as she searches my eyes. Does she feel this—whatever it is that's happening?

Or am I stuck in a daydream?

I draw in a slow breath as she inches closer, our faces only a breath apart. My mind spins. I'm going to kiss Raya.

But then, almost like a flipped switch, she blinks and steps back, hands dropping to her sides. "Wait."

I freeze, the air tight in my chest.

Crap.

Her breath hitches, and she avoids my eyes. "We should... I, um...I should go." She brushes past me, moving toward the entryway.

You idiot! I mentally beat myself up. *What was I thinking?*

The goal was to become her friend. *Her friend, you idiot!* And the second I make an inch of progress, this is what I do? She's seeing someone! Yes, it's new, and no, they're not exclusive, but still.

I sigh into my hand, then drag it through my hair, knowing I just screwed everything up.

I turn and find her standing near the door, looking lost. That freaked her out. *I* freaked her out.

"Raya, I—"

"We should go," she cuts in, tone nervous.

I scrub a hand down my face—I can't believe what I'm about to say. "Maybe it's better if I stay here. For now."

Her face falters for a second, but then she nods. "Right. You should probably rest."

"Yeah." I point to my head. "Concussion."

She nods. "No screens."

I hold my hands up in front of me. "Promise. And hey, thanks for coming by."

"Of course." She nods and turns to leave. She opens the door, but before she walks out, she turns back and looks right into my eyes. "That's what friends are for, right?"

Right. Friends.

Raya

I shut the door behind me, rush down the hall, and bang on the elevator button, like hitting it a hundred times will make it move faster. I'm holding my breath out of sheer panic.

What. Was. That?

Finn was going to kiss me—and in a horrifying twist I did *not* see coming—I wanted him to. This doesn't make sense.

The elevator doors open, and I step inside, frantically pressing the button for the ground floor. Finally, the doors close, and I blow out a slow breath, grateful for the solitude. I lean against the wall and rub circles into my temples, mind spinning.

Okay. Let's be logical. Finn is a good-looking guy, and he's been nice to me. And I was worried about his injury. That's all. There are no emotions here. No *feelings*.

A momentary lapse in judgment, sparked by the superficial attraction happening between us.

It means nothing.

"It means nothing." But even as I speak the words aloud, another word creeps into the back of my mind.

Liar.

This is ridiculous. This is *Finn*. He's *all wrong* for me.

I close my eyes, trying to remember all the reasons why that is . . . but the image of his face, watching me with a kind of quiet desperation, appears in my mind.

I open my eyes and drag in a giant, deep breath.

Okay. Enough nonsense. I need to do what I always do and put these ridiculous feelings in a little box and move on. They'll only get messy.

"Nothing good can come from this, Raya." I breathe the sentence out loud just as the elevator dings.

And I use the sound as a signal. The end of the round. Closing off whatever this was and shifting back to common sense.

Chapter Twenty-Seven

Raya

I f there's one area where I'll never take charge, it's in
the kitchen.

Which is why, when I show up to Thanksgiving
dinner two days later, I know I'm going to feel useless.

I hate feeling useless.

It's been a week without work, and I'm ready to go back.
I feel good. My body feels good.

My heart? Different story. I desperately need a
distraction.

Yesterday, I'd hoped to see Justin. I want things to progress
with him because how else am I going to get Finn out of my
head? He'd asked if Justin and I were exclusive, and once I can
answer "yes" to that question, I think he'll stop flirting with me.

Right?

It doesn't really matter because Justin had to cancel our
plans to show a luxury property to an investor.

"He's the kind of guy you don't put off," he'd told me,
and I assured him it was fine. Understanding things like this

—last minute changes and having work take priority over social things—was the deal.

But when I hung up the phone, for the first time since this thing began, I started to question whether or not it's working. Our arrangement is only effective if he shows up, and in the nearly three weeks since we first agreed to try this, most of our dates have been cut short or outright canceled. As a result, I feel a little like I'm walking half-blind into Thanksgiving dinner with my family.

Really, how well do I know this guy?

More to the point, how well can I pretend to know him in front of my family?

The Comets had a home game last night, which they won, a fact I know because I watched the whole thing. Finn didn't play—he's still in the concussion protocol—but he sat on the bench with the team, and every so often they'd show him on the screen, reminding viewers what had happened to put him there.

Every time, my breath caught in my throat at the memory of his nearness, something that's been happening regularly since I left his apartment Tuesday. My brain has been pretty much replaying the almost-kiss on repeat every hour.

On a continuous loop.

I'm really conflicted about it—and my straightforward, clinical, logical side is having trouble reconciling this new, heated, emotional side.

Maybe the trick here is to kiss someone else. Interrupt the mind stream. Disrupt the desire to unlock the box where I stashed my feelings for Finn. Seems plausible. Justin and I haven't had the opportunity to explore what attraction there might be between us, and I'm thinking maybe today is a good time.

The thought of kissing Justin does absolutely nothing for me.

I don't really *want* to kiss Justin.

What does that say about our future? Or more to the point, our present?

I huff out a breath like that's going to clear my head and pull into Dallas's long driveway. There, inconspicuously parked, is a familiar Jeep Cherokee.

Nobody told me Finn was coming.

A burst of nerves shoots through me. *Nobody told me Finn was coming!*

My pulse quickens. I hadn't planned on seeing him today. Like *planning* on seeing him would help. I don't know if I can pretend I'm not wrestling with all these emotions that I really, really do not want right now.

Not when he's in the same room.

No. It's fine. I have years of practice locking out every single thing I feel. I'm a fortress.

I go over the plan in my head, and it's as ridiculous as it is futile. Not only do I have to pretend I'm smitten with a man I don't really know, but I have to do it while simultaneously pretending I'm not thinking about Finn.

Piece of cake. Not stress-inducing at all.

I park the car, steel my nerves, and grab the bottles of sparkling cider—Poppy's request—from the back seat. I walk to the front door, surprised when it opens before I knock.

But not surprised to find Finn standing on the other side. He's wearing jeans and a sweater, and it throws me for a second. I'm not used to seeing him in anything but gym clothes or hockey gear.

"Saw you pull in," he says, nonchalant and easy. "Your hands were full, figured I'd, you know . . ."

I force myself not to react, tamping down the little flutter in my stomach. I straighten—like I'm locking my armor into place.

Impenetrable. Except for that gaping hole in my breast-plate where my heart sits.

He smiles, moves aside, and I step into the house, our arms brushing as he takes the bottles from me and sets them down.

"Coats in the guest room." He motions for me to follow him like this is his house and I'm the guest.

"Are you on door duty?" I ask as I slip my coat off and trail down the hallway behind him.

"I wanted to help," he says, because of course he did.

"I didn't know you were going to be here." I keep my tone clipped. Just stating facts.

"That okay?" He smirks, and I can feel him working extra hard to be normal with me.

"Fine," I feign nonchalance.

"Dallas invited a few of us who didn't have plans." He opens the door to a bedroom, then nods toward the bed where there's a whole pile of coats. I drop mine on top.

I turn to go, avoiding his eyes, but he gently catches me by the elbow. I look at him and he squints, like he's trying to decipher a secret code hidden underneath my skin.

"You good?"

"Yep," I lie.

"You know, it doesn't have to be like this," he says.

"Like what?"

"Weird. Tense. Whatever your face is doing right now."

I try to change my expression, but it defaults to chin out, eyebrows up, *come at me.*

"Don't get me wrong, it's a beautiful face." He says this like he is also stating a fact.

Heat crawls up my neck, and I look away before it shows on my face, aware that his hand is still resting on my arm.

This is not going well.

"This is because of Tuesday," he says.

I scan behind me, on lookout for family members, then hiss, "Nothing happened Tuesday."

"Did you *want* something to happen Tuesday?" he asks.

I think *YES*, but say, "No, and don't bring it up around my sisters. They'll turn it into something it's not."

"It doesn't have to be a big deal," he says lightly. "We almost kissed. It happens."

I look at him. "It doesn't *happen*. Not to me."

He faces me, studying. "So it meant something."

I scoff, but my heart could give Secretariat a run for his money. "You wish."

"Actually, you're right." He leans in. "I do."

He walks away, and my fortress of pretending that moment in his apartment never happened falls under siege.

I take a second to get my head back in the game, then walk down the hall just in time to see Finn open the door for Justin. "Welcome to the Hart fam—"

I reach the entryway and push Finn out of the way. "I got it!" I look at Justin, brushing my hands down the front of my outfit. "Hey!"

He's wearing a long, dark coat, gray dress pants, a white button-down and a maroon tie. I should've included the casual dress code in the details I sent his assistant. Shoot.

"Come in." I grab his arm and pull him inside the house,

then see Finn, studying him. "Finn, Justin, Justin, um . . . Finn." I awkwardly hold out a hand between them.

Finn settles into Finn mode. "The famous Justin!" He extends a hand, but then gets a quizzical look on his face.

Justin reaches out and takes it, "Nice to meet you."

Finn holds his hand for a second too long. "Man, you look familiar. Have we met?"

Justin smiles awkwardly, looks at me, then back at Finn. "Uh, no, I don't think so, unless I showed you a house recently."

Finn shakes his head, "Nah, that's not it. But welcome! Glad you're here!"

This feels *so* surreal. It's like I'm watching this happen on a screen and not in Dallas's house.

"Uh, how was the race," I ask, doing my best to snap out of it.

"Good," he says. "Guess I made it on time after all."

I smile, then take the bottle of wine Justin's holding and hand it to Finn. "Hey, do you mind taking this into the kitchen?" I widen my eyes at him, trying to silently tell him to stop being weird.

I move to take Justin's coat, heart pounding a mile a minute.

"I can put this in the guest room," I say. "Be right back."

Justin nods, and I shoot Finn a *Be nice* look. He raises an eyebrow, like *Who, me?* and I walk away, wracked with guilt I'm not even sure I should feel.

Do I owe Justin my emotional loyalty if our relationship has barely started and isn't exactly real? This is a conundrum I don't want and didn't predict, and there's nobody to ask because nobody knows the truth about how we started dating.

I open the door to the guest room, but instead of dropping Justin's coat on the pile, I lay it neatly over the back of an armchair in the corner. I'm about to leave when Finn walks in, his expression smug despite the confusion lacing his brow.

"What is this, Hart?" he hisses.

I slowly look around. "What is *what*?"

"That's the guy? That's Justin?"

I roll my eyes. "Don't come in here and start talking trash about him. You don't even know him."

"Actually, I do."

I frown. "What are you talking about?"

"That's the guy from the café," he says. "I *knew* I recognized him. You said you were interviewing him, remember?"

My stomach drops. I'm a notoriously bad liar, and I'd forgotten he was there that day. Another thing I didn't plan for.

"You said you were looking for someone to help out with a few tasks," he says. "And now he's here? At your family's Thanksgiving dinner?"

"That's how we met," I say, and it's true, to an extent. "I didn't want to tell you it turned into a date."

"Wait. Your interview turned into a date? That's . . . isn't that totally against the rules?"

Notoriously. Bad. Liar.

"No, the interview didn't turn into a date, the interview" —it's out before I can stop it—"*was* the date."

Wait. That's not how I meant to say it. Because that's not exactly true, either.

Finn stops. He has three distinct faces in a row—confusion, realization, then suspicion.

"You had back-to-back dates?" he asks. "Because the other guy was there first."

I frantically look down the hallway, knowing we're not exactly being quiet. "Can you keep your voice down?" I whisper at him. "And no, I didn't have—"

"The resume on your tablet," he says, piecing things together. "Don't tell me he brought a resume to a date."

"No, I mean—" I sigh. "Just stop."

He inhales a sharp breath, then stands, listening. But I am not telling Finn the truth about this. It's personal. And it makes me sound pathetic.

"Look. It doesn't matter how we met, we just did. We've been out a few times, and he's nice. I invited him to Thanksgiving, end of story."

His eyes narrow. "What tasks did you hire him to do?"

"What do you mean?"

"I mean, what was the job you were hiring for?"

My mind goes blank. I don't have an answer that sounds plausible other than the truth.

And I can't tell him the truth—because now, thinking about it in this panicked moment, it feels utterly ridiculous.

I let out a groan of frustration. "Will you just get out of my business?" I push past him into the hallway and rush back to the front door, but Justin's not there. I walk into the kitchen and look around, but he's not there either.

Poppy is at the stove and Eloise is arranging pickles on a platter.

"Did you guys see Justin?"

"Justin's here?" Eloise stands. "Where?"

I walk back toward the front door, look outside, and there he is, on the porch, on his phone. "Never mind. I found him."

I open the door and he turns to look at me, holding up a

finger to signal *one second.* "Yes, you're right about that," he says into the phone. "No problem. Yep. Yep. We'll talk soon." He hangs up. "Sorry about that."

"It's okay," I say. "Work doesn't respect holidays."

"A truth universally acknowledged," he says, and I admire the *Pride and Prejudice* reference.

"Sorry I disappeared for a second," I say, feeling off. Guilty. Conflicted. Do I need to tell Justin that I almost let Finn kiss me?

"No problem." He smiles. It's a kind smile. A safe smile. Not the kind of smile that releases a flock of geese in my rib cage.

Maybe I just need to recommit to the plan. A plan that seemed so good, so *right* at the beginning. It made total sense on paper. The perfect solution to my loneliness. No emotion, just business.

But even as the thought enters my mind, I imagine that a life with Justin wouldn't look a whole lot different from my life these past several years.

Maybe you can't cure loneliness without actual connection.

That thought stops me in my tracks. Because if it's true, then all of this has been for nothing. Because I'm not willing to risk an actual connection.

I can't.

"Are you ready to go back inside?" he asks.

"Yes, of course." I lead him back into the house, straight to the kitchen, thankful Finn has apparently parked himself elsewhere.

"Uh, guys, this is Justin." I look at him. "Justin, these are my sisters, Poppy and Eloise, and our mom, Tammy."

They all smile and exchange pleasantries.

"Do you like football, Justin?" my mom asks.

"Not Chicago football," he says. "I'm a Patriots fan, I'm afraid."

"Well, we won't hold it against you." Mom smiles. "Is your family nearby?"

"Yes, they live in Barrington," he says.

Mom looks at me, then back to Justin. "Will you both be seeing them later?"

"I will be," Justin says. "We do a quiet, formal meal for Thanksgiving, just my parents and me."

"Oh," Mom says with a quick glance at me. "That'll be nice."

If she's worried I'm offended not to be included, she doesn't have to be. After my episode, he let me off the hook, said he didn't want to add any unnecessary stress. It was thoughtful.

There's a shout from the other room, and Justin has a visible reaction. He quickly recovers, laughing at himself. "Sorry, I'm not used to big families."

"Do you have siblings?" Poppy asks.

He shakes his head. "I don't."

"Aw, how sad," Eloise says, a little pout on her lips.

"I think it suited me, being an only child," he says. "I like the quiet. I think better when I'm by myself."

Another raucous cheer from the next room. If Justin weren't here, I don't think any of us would've noticed it, we're all so used to the noise when everyone's together. It's its own kind of comfort, a reminder that I'm not alone.

Justin's phone buzzes, and he pulls it out of his pocket. He looks at it, then at me. "Do you mind if I . . .?"

"Of course," I say.

"Is there somewhere quiet I can go?" he asks, wincing.

I look at Poppy, who grabs a towel and wipes her hands. "Follow me."

She leads him down the hall, and I pick up a carrot—not because I want it but because I need something to do with my hands.

"He seems nice," Mom finally says.

"He is," I say.

Eloise shoves a cucumber sandwich into her mouth.

"Where'd you meet?" Mom asks.

I don't get a chance to answer, though, because Finn comes into the room, holding his phone up, clearly on a FaceTime call. "Oh, I have to show you what I made." He walks over to the counter and picks up a wonky-looking cake. "It's pumpkin with cream cheese frosting."

"You made that?" I hear a voice say, along with several other voices overlapping in the background.

"That looks terrible!" the voice on the phone says.

"I know!" Finn grins. "But I tested it, and it still tastes amazing."

It strikes me in that moment that Finn meant it when he said he doesn't care about being the best—that perfect is the enemy of great. If I'd made that ridiculous-looking cake, I would've thrown it in the garbage. He put it on a plate and brought it to Thanksgiving.

And he's proud of it. Joyful, even.

I can't remember the last time I felt that kind of happiness. Even when I accomplish something important or finish a big project I've been working on, there's no pausing to celebrate. No moment of reflection. Done? Great. On to the next.

I'll start to work on things even before a project is finished.

250

Finn doesn't suffer from that particular malady. He takes it all in stride, celebrating every success, being in the moment, not worrying about what's coming next.

Even if it's a cake that isn't baked all the way through.

"Uncle Finn, I saw you hit your head!" a tiny voice says.

Eloise makes an *awww* face.

Finn sets the cake down and shifts his grip on the phone. "You saw that?"

"Uh-huh," the voice says. "Are you okay?"

"That must've been scary for you to watch," he says. "But yes, I'm okay. I promise. Oh wait . . . there's . . . something . . . happening . . ." He crosses his eyes, then uncrosses one of them, making it look like he has a lazy eye. "Wait. Is something wrong with my eyes? How do I look?" He tilts his head back and forth, turns the phone sideways, and makes a weird face. The voice on the other end bursts into laughter.

The oven timer goes off, and Finn looks up, like he's just realized for the first time there are other people in the room. He fixes his face and the phone and looks back at the screen. "Oh, hey, Momma—"

Eloise grins when he says this, probably because she thinks it's adorable.

I force myself not to agree.

"I want to introduce you to the beautiful Hart women." He turns the phone around. A woman on the screen smiles and waves.

Finn walks over to my mom, holding the phone up so they're both in the frame. "This is Mrs. Hart—"

Mom puts a hand on his arm. "Tammy."

"Nope. It's Mrs. Hart. Momma won't like me calling you by your first name," he says.

"It's lovely to meet you," Mom says into the phone.

Why are my palms sweating?

"Thank you for taking in our boy," Finn's mom says. "He's a lot," she adds, laughing.

"Oh, we know," my mom says, "but we *love* it. We'll take good care of him here!"

"Thank the Lord. I was worried he was going to end up with KFC on the couch again."

"That was college, Momma," Finn says with a good-natured eyeroll.

"We're happy to have him," Mom says with a smile. "And we can't wait to try the cake."

"Have the Pepto-Bismol handy," his mom says with a laugh, a not-so-subtle dig at Finn's attempt at baking.

"Hey! I can hear you," Finn says in mock-offense.

He moves to Eloise as Poppy reenters the room, then introduces them one at a time, explaining who they are, who they're dating, and why they're "so cool."

When he looks at me, his expression changes. "And this is Raya."

Finn doesn't say my name very often. Usually, he just calls me "Hart," like I'm one of the guys. It shouldn't have any effect on me, but it does.

I smile into the phone camera as Finn moves into the space next to me, his nearness a reminder of the moment I'm desperately trying to forget. The moment *we almost kissed*. Pretending it didn't happen isn't going to make it go away.

"Oh," his mom says. "*This* is Raya—"

"It's nice to meet you, Mrs. Holbrook," I say.

"You too," she says. "My son was not kidding about how beautiful you are."

"Momma!" Finn laughs, but he whips the phone away.

"Oh, was that a secret?" she asks loudly.

"I gotta go, Momma." Finn's cheeks are red, and I'm pretty sure it's the first time I've ever seen him embarrassed. "Tell Pops I'll call him after dinner."

"Okay, Skip," she says. "Live like—"

"It matters," he says, finishing her sentence. And then together, they say, "because it does." He nods at her, like they've just made a silent pact. "I will."

He clicks the phone off, and we all stare at him.

Mom smiles. "You're close with your family."

"I am," he says. "They're a lot, but they're the best."

"You must miss them." Mom pulls a pan from the oven and sets it on a trivet on the counter.

"I do, especially on holidays." He nods. "But I'm really thankful to be with you all."

"Why'd she call you 'Skip'?" Eloise asks.

"Eh. It's a stupid nickname," he says. "I don't even know where it came from. You'd think they'd want to use all of our real names since there are so many of us."

"So it's a big family," Mom says.

"Yeah," he says. "I've got four brothers and two sisters."

"Those poor sisters!" Eloise laughs. "Five brothers!"

Finn's eyes flick to mine, and I hold his gaze, wondering if he's thinking about Hunter, and realizing there's pain behind that smile that he never shows. I never would've guessed Finn Holbrook had ever experienced grief.

He either hides it well or he's made his peace with it. All at once, my own problems seem silly by comparison.

There's a cheer from the other room, and Finn's eyebrows shoot up. "Sorry, ladies, the less attractive side of the house is calling . . ." One more quick look at me, then he walks out.

Before anyone can comment on that, Justin walks back

into the kitchen. "Sorry about that. Work has been crazy lately."

The mood shifts from talk of misshapen cake to something that feels like a library or a museum.

"Justin, Raya tells us you're in real estate?" Mom asks.

He nods. "I am. I also have a few investment properties, and I'm looking to buy a few more."

"Wow," Mom says. "Impressive."

I smile at him, and she offers to take him into the other room and introduce him to the guys. But as she leads him out of the kitchen, I have the horrible realization that Justin doesn't fit in with my people.

It's like the chess club meeting the football team.

And I'm not sure there's a way to change that.

Chapter Twenty-Eight

Raya

Dinner is a little like a nightmare.

First of all, I can't stop thinking about what Finn's mom said, and that distraction is making me sweat. Because seriously—he told his mom about me?

Secondly, Finn is sitting right across from me, and the way he's studying Justin and me is unnerving—and a little uncomfortable.

Third, Justin gets up from the table three times during the meal to deal with phone calls. If this continues, he's going to turn Dallas's guest room into his own personal office.

The third time he gets up, Dallas's grandma, Sylvia, looks me straight in the face and says, "What are you doing with that man?"

Poppy almost spits her water out, and neither Finn nor Eloise even try to hide their laughter at Sylvia's bluntness.

I would be offended if I weren't wondering the same exact thing.

"Gram," Dallas says, putting a hand on her arm, "Raya

can date whoever she wants. She doesn't need all of us weighing in."

Mom signs this, and I catch the look that passes between her and my dad.

"Raya is an intelligent, beautiful, and successful woman," Sylvia says. "All I want to know is why she would ever think about settling with such a dolt."

"I love you like crazy," Eloise says to her. "Can I be you when I grow up?"

I shake my head. "Not everyone wants the same things out of a relationship," I say, though the words sound weak coming out of my mouth.

"That's true." Poppy nods. Always the peacemaker. "There's someone for everyone, it doesn't have to all . . . make sense, you know, to . . . everyone." Her positivity trails off, grasping at verbal straws.

"But Raya, come on—" Eloise points to the door, as if to say *This guy?*

And I watch my plans crash and burn. Because they're right. Sitting through a Thanksgiving meal without checking your phone every three seconds is sort of a no-brainer. Even I know that.

Justin walks back into the room to the sound of clinking silverware against plates.

"Sorry about that." He sits back down and squeezes my arm. "Demanding client."

I smile as if to tell him I understand, but I'm starting not to. Even if I weren't on a hiatus from work right now, my phone would not be on this table.

Maybe he and I have different priorities after all.

"So, Justin, what is it you like about our sister?" Eloise breaks a roll in half and shoves a very large chunk of it into her mouth.

He looks at me, and my face flushes.

"You don't have to answer that," I say, then shoot daggers at my youngest sister.

"Oh, I don't mind." Justin lays his napkin over his lap and picks up his fork. His food has to be cold by now. "I think I'm most drawn to her strong work ethic."

Finn coughs, and I glare at him. He ignores me.

Mom signs for Dad, and I can feel his eyes on me, like he knows something is off. Dallas and Gray stay heads down, focused on their food.

"Her work ethic," Sylvia says, her tone dripping.

Justin nods, like he's just gotten the answer correct on *Jeopardy*. "It's hard to find someone who understands my own ambition like Raya does. We're alike that way."

"And that's an important similarity?" Mom says out loud as Dad signs the question.

"I think so, Sir, yes." Justin says this a little louder than he should, as if speaking up will make my father suddenly able to hear him.

I can practically feel everyone in my family cringe.

"What else do you do?" Poppy asks, signing the words. "Besides work. Like for fun?"

Justin finishes chewing the bite of food in his mouth. "Hmm. Honestly, that's pretty much it. I run, but I'm training for a marathon, so that's more of a goal than a hobby. I'm pretty boring, I'm afraid."

There's a quiet lull.

"I've been working with this new trainer—she's amazing. I feel like I hit a whole new level." He looks at me. "Have you tried running? You might love it."

Poppy laughs. "Raya doesn't do anything she can't win."

Finn's eyes flick over to me, the memory of our conversation fresh in my mind.

"Okay, family!" My laugh is nervous. "How about we change the subject?"

Justin's phone buzzes on the table. He picks it up, and I can feel the irritation pinballing around the table.

"Oh, wow, sorry," he says, pushing back from the table. "I need to get this."

He leaves the room, and my gaze falls to the nearly empty plate in front of me.

It's a visual representation of how I feel right now.

Mom changes the subject, and the rest of them join in the conversation, eager to relieve the tension in the room.

When I finally dare to look up from the table, I find Finn watching me, a question behind his eyes. It reads, *You okay?* And I can't explain why, but I feel like I've let him down.

It's silly, I know, but there it is.

"I'm going to just—" I stand and walk down the hallway, following the sound of Justin's voice. I'm about to open the guest room door when I hear him say, "I know, I can't stop thinking about you either."

I freeze.

"It's hard to explain, but yes, I'm ending it today." A pause. "Because I already gave my word." Another pause. "I know, and I'll be there soon. Are you wearing the dress I bought you?"

My stomach sinks as my mind reels back to the day I found out the truth about Rich.

"Did you know this man is my husband?"

I force myself not to dwell there, in the muck of old memories. This is not that. I made sure of it. Thankfully, I never gave Justin the power to hurt me in that way.

I push the door open and meet his eyes.

"I'm going to call you back." He hangs up, and I give him a sad smile.

I'm not emotionally wounded, though my pride might've taken a hit. I went to such great lengths to protect myself, and here I am again. Abandoned for something better. The similarities hit a little too close.

"I wanted to tell you," he says, looking guilty.

"You should've," I say quietly. "You could be with her today." I pause. "We agreed there would be no hard feelings."

He nods. "I wasn't looking—I just—"

"You don't have to explain," I say, holding up a hand. "I don't blame you. I can't fault you for wanting something real, even if I don't."

He half-laughs. "Kind of took me by surprise, really. Who knows, maybe the same thing will happen for you."

"Maybe," I say, but in my mind I'm more resigned than ever that it won't.

Because clearly, I'm easy to walk away from. Even with a business agreement, even with things thought-out and planned, even with clear expectations—Justin still chose someone else.

It's difficult for me to think that any other situation would end differently.

We stand in silence for a long moment, and the weight of this failure settles on my shoulders. I tried to orchestrate the perfect relationship, the one that would keep my heart safe, and I couldn't even do that.

Maybe I really am better off alone.

"I met her on a run," he says, eyes more alive than

they've been all day. "We started training together, and I don't know. The rest is history."

"That's really great, Justin," I say, and I mean it, because he's a decent guy to show up here and go through with this dinner, even if he spent more time on his phone than at the table. The least I can do is be happy for him.

"Do you think—" he motions toward the door.

"Of course," I say. "Go"

He nods, grabs his coat, and leans in to kiss my cheek.

It's the most emotion I've felt for him—apathy.

"Good luck, Raya," he says.

"You too." I smile, not sure how I'm going to explain this to my family.

On his way out, I hear him thank them for the hospitality as he claims to have a work emergency to deal with. I drop into the armchair and let out a sigh.

A few minutes later, there's a quiet knock on the door, and I look up to see my mom standing in the doorway. "Are you okay?"

She walks over and sits on the ottoman, facing me.

"I'm fine," I say, unsure why tears sting the corners of my eyes. "I don't think it's going to work out with Justin."

Mom's smile is sad.

"I'm really not upset about that," I say. "It's just—" I meet her eyes. "Do you think some people are just meant to be alone?"

She watches me for a few seconds. "I imagine some people might be."

I nod.

"But I don't think you are."

"It's starting to feel that way."

"I'm sorry, hon," she says. "You're so strong, I think it's

260

easy to forget sometimes that being strong can be exhausting."

I look at her, thinking about all the ways she modeled strength for us over the years. All the ways I tried to do the same for her. I wanted to be strong so it would give her one less thing to worry about it. I still do.

"You know it's okay to *not* have everything all figured out, right?" she asks, her eyes kind. "You have such specific ideas about what it is you think you need," she says. "And usually you're right about everything, so I understand why it's difficult to change your mind."

I frown. "You think I'm wrong?"

She shrugs. "Not wrong, exactly. Stubborn, maybe?"

I give her a knowing look, and she smiles.

"You've always been strong-willed. You get an idea in your head and it stays there." Her eyes go wide. "Forever." She squeezes my hand. "You know I don't like to get in your business, and I rarely have opinions on your life because you really don't need my advice."

My frown deepens because it's not the first time she's alluded to this. "Is that what you think?"

"Oh, Raya, you haven't needed anyone else's opinion since you were eight years old. You know your own mind. Always have."

"But that doesn't mean I don't care what you think," I say.

"Do you?" she asks.

I nod. "Of course I do." And it breaks my heart to think that I somehow sent her the message that I didn't.

"Okay." She leans in. "When I think of the kind of man I want you to end up with," she says, almost wistfully, as if Prince Charming really does exist, "I think of someone good and kind, who looks at you like you hung the moon. Someone who champions the things you accomplish . . . and values some of the things you don't."

"What do you mean?"

"When I heard Justin talking about your work ethic, I wanted to scream," she says. "Because your job is not who you are."

My eyes cloud over with fresh tears. "It kind of is, Mom."

She clasps both of my hands in her own. "No, it's not. That's what you *do*, Raya, it's not who you *are*. And sometimes you get so wrapped up in it that you forget to live. You forget there's a whole big world out there just waiting for you to explore. Not to conquer. Just to explore. Because you get to be here on this earth right now, and that is a beautiful thing.

"Sometimes it feels like you're working so hard to earn your place here. Like if you don't work for it, you have no right to it."

My gaze drops, but hers remains on me. I can feel it.

"For the right person, you won't have to do a single thing to earn their love," she says. "You have it simply because you exist."

A tear streams down my cheek. I swipe it away.

"I don't think the right person exists, Mom," I say, my voice wobbling.

"You have such impossibly high standards for yourself," she says. "So you have impossibly high standards for everyone else too. Maybe it's time to try something new. To challenge your own way of doing things."

I think about Justin and the way I'd epically botched that. My way hadn't worked out so well, had it?

"What if, over the next few weeks, you didn't try to find

ways to work?" she says. "What if you simply let yourself off the hook? Rest doesn't always mean lying around on the couch. And taking a break doesn't have to mean sleeping in until noon. You can relieve your stress by doing things that fill you up. Just for fun."

Fun. There's that word again. I look at her. "I don't really know how to do that."

"Oh, I know," she laughs. "But I think I know a few people who can help." She smiles at me. "We'll start this weekend with the Christmas carnival. Finn told me he wants to buy you your own tree."

I half-laugh and shake my head. "I don't understand why he's so invested in my life."

Her expression shifts. "Because he's in love with you, sweetheart."

Her words land. It's like what she just said lifted a veil, or cleared my vision.

And for the first time, I don't argue. Not because I believe her, but because . . . what if he is?

I don't even know how to feel about that.

I think about the other things she said too—about not earning my place. About letting myself rest. About wanting a break.

I want to believe her. The truth is, I *am* tired.

And it would be nice if someone took care of things for a while.

It dawns on me that's kind of why I tried collecting resumes in the first place. To share the load. To take the pressure off. To take my one and plus it.

So far, everything romantic for me has been a negative.

I don't actually *want* to be alone. I'm okay admitting that now.

But I also don't want to get my heart broken again, so where does that leave me?

The door flings open, and my sisters burst in. "Finn's cake is *amazing*." Eloise is carrying a plate with a giant slab of the wonky cake on it. "Raya, you have to try it!"

My eyes drift over to my mom, and I can practically hear her daring me to eat the cake.

Eloise holds the fork out to me.

"That is a huge bite," I say. "You know not everyone eats like you do."

"I know," she says. "But everyone should."

I laugh, shovel the bite into my mouth, and . . . it's good. I cautiously step over that mental line that's been holding me back for so long.

And I enjoy this moment.

There's a tiny twinge challenging me to think about some things differently.

Maybe that starts with a big bite of cake.

Chapter Twenty-Nine

Raya

Normally, I would be announcing to everyone that I'm here against my will.

But my mom's words are still ringing in my ears, so contrary to tradition, I'm going to try and enjoy things.

We'll see how *that* goes. I'm bucking twenty years of crankiness here.

My family is cozied up on my parents' front porch, drinking hot drinks, and acting like they have nothing to do but be here.

Which, I suppose, is exactly what they should do today, since everyone cleared their schedules to keep our Hart family Saturday-after-Thanksgiving tradition alive.

Mom fills a mug with hot cider from the carafe she's brought out onto the porch, and hands it to me with a gentle pat. "Just try and go with the flow today, okay?"

Behind me, Eloise laughs.

I shoot her a look, and she widens her eyes.

It's late morning, after the breakfast rush at Poppy's

restaurant, after the Comets' morning practice, after my exciting few hours of trying not to dwell on all the annoying thoughts piercing my mind.

"'Go with the flow' is my new motto," I say, signing with expression to convey my sarcasm. I sit down on the porch swing next to Poppy.

"I, for one, am glad you're here," Poppy says. "Last year you didn't get to do this with us." She's wearing black leggings, an oversized, cozy sweater, a puffer vest, and a stocking cap with a ball on top. She looks adorable.

By contrast, I'm in jeans, a not-cozy green sweater, my boring winter coat, and boots. My outfit screams urban, while hers whispers rural. I don't even think I remembered to bring gloves.

I think back to last Christmas and realize she's right. Our own Hart Family Christmas kickoff is a holiday tradition, and I didn't go. I can't remember why.

"You were working," Eloise says.

"But at least I wasn't a seventh wheel like I'm going to be today," I groan, then take a drink of the cider. I look up and find them all watching me.

My eyes jump from Poppy to Eloise to my mom, then my dad. "What?" I say, signing.

"It's not a setup," Mom says, in a tone meant to calm small children.

Dad smacks a hand on his knee and hoots. "Sure, Tam," he signs.

Neither of my sisters is looking at me, but they don't need to for me to know that whatever they've done, I'm not going to like it.

Just then, Finn's Jeep ambles up the driveway, followed by Dallas's shiny new SUV.

I toss my mom a look. "Not a setup?" I sign this, then look at my dad. "You let her do this?"

He holds up his hands in surrender, as if that absolves him from blame.

"You guys, I just ended things with someone—"

"Nope!" Eloise cuts me off with an upheld hand. "To end something, you have to have started something. None of us is buying that you ever had feelings for that guy."

She's right, of course, but I don't say so. Maybe one day I'll tell my sisters the truth about Justin, but for now, I'm keeping it to myself.

Finn and Dallas pull off to the side, parking in the yard where people always park when we have company.

"Regardless of how I feel—or felt—about Justin," I say, voice firm, "I cannot stress enough how this is just not going to work with Finn."

"Is this one of those times when you think if you say something often enough you'll actually start to believe it?" Eloise grins at me.

"I'm not making this up," I argue. "You have to stop pushing this. I think he's starting to—" I look at Mom, her words ringing through my mind.

"Because he's in love with you."

I thought about those words all day yesterday, turning them over and over in my mind, trying to make them make sense. I can brush off the almost-kiss as a heated, confused moment of attraction. But if those words are true, it's going to come up at some point. I'm going to have to deal with it. And when I do, he's not going to come around anymore.

Isn't that what I've been saying I want?

When did everything change?

"Starting to what, Ray?" Eloise says. "Starting to be an

incredibly excellent guy with a whole lot to offer someone who's uptight and in desperate need of a good time?"

I frown and look over at Dad just in time to see him secretly sign something to Mom. I catch the last of it—something like, "I'll show you a good time."

"Dad!" I shout at him, "I saw that!"

He fakes innocence, shaking his hands in front of him as my mom swats him on the arm.

They did this stuff constantly when we still lived here, thinking we couldn't see them silently flirting in ASL.

He turns to my mom and pumps his eyebrows twice. Eloise laughs.

Finn and Dallas get out of their cars as another one shows up at the end of the driveway.

"So. Who exactly do I have to blame for inviting him today?" I ask. "To join in our *family* tradition?"

As if on cue, everyone points right at my mom.

She holds her hands up in front of her. "After dinner on Thursday, Finn got another call from his folks. I got to talking with his mom—who is just lovely, by the way—and I promised her I'd invite him to all of the holiday festivities."

"You're friends with his mom now," I say dryly.

"Yes, I have her number. We were just texting this morning. We have so much in common! She invited us to stay at their ranch—have you seen the view?" Mom stands and waves as Gray parks next to Dallas. "She hates that he's alone for the holidays, and I would too if one of you were far away."

Leave it to my mother to make it impossible to stay annoyed.

"They really should've carpooled," I mutter. "It's better for the environment."

My sisters exchange a look. That's when I see Gray's daughter, Scarlett, is with him. Eloise rushes off the porch and pulls her into a giant hug, and that's when I notice Finn is not alone.

I stand when I see a thin, dark-headed girl and her two brothers exit his Jeep.

Grace.

I'd thought about her a lot since the day Finn took me to the tutoring club. Twice, I'd wanted to go back—to reach out to Tasha and see if there was something I could do to help out over the next couple of weeks—but both times, I chickened out.

I'm not sure I'd be good at tutoring kids. Or talking to kids. Or being around kids.

Mom raises a hand. "Welcome, everyone! And Merry Christmas!"

Yesterday, we decorated our parents' house for Christmas—another Hart tradition. Staying in pajamas, heating up leftovers, unpacking all of the binned-up decorations, and dousing the entire house in holiday cheer. I still remember how us girls would fight over who got to hang this one ugly, orange handmade shell ornament.

I did not inherit my Scrooge-ish tendencies, that's for sure. They came to me all on their own.

Every year, my parents try to outdo what they did the year before. Swaths of greenery thread through the porch railings and hang from the eaves of the roof. How my dad got up there, I don't even want to know. When the sun goes down, that greenery will twinkle with white lights. Big, beautiful wreaths are hung from every window, tied with thick, red ribbon, and there's a huge Nutcracker standing guard by the door. Inside, they cleared space in the alcove of the front windows for what is certain to be "the best Christmas tree we've ever had."

And it will be. Because it always is.

I stand back and watch my family for a few seconds, charmed by the spirit and simplicity of it all, and I wish that Christmas feeling was the kind of thing you could purchase. Or at least bottle up. It would be easier than trying to manufacture it when I feel so out of sorts.

I haven't gotten into the holidays for a long time. Partly because I was always alone, but also because I was just so busy. The holidays almost felt like an unwanted interruption in my work week.

The pressure I put on myself to do more, to get more done, drove out the holiday spirit. While my family found ways to stretch the holidays out, I kept mine short and sweet, relishing the time alone while everyone else was distracted.

At least, that's what I told myself.

The truth is, once again, I was heading disappointment off at the pass. The build-up of Christmas never paid off for me.

Maybe I just wasn't looking hard enough for the wonder.

But yesterday, being back home with my sisters and my parents, watching our childhood home transform into a Christmas wonderland, I saw hints of it. I started to understand.

I don't want time with my family to be the casualty of my ambition anymore.

I stand and zip my coat, watching as Finn introduces Grace and her brothers to Scarlett. Then he walks over to my parents, and to my surprise, signs, "Thank you for the invitation" as he says the words aloud.

Dad's face beams. He hits my mom on the arm, and points at Finn, then signs, "You're welcome here anytime."

Finn turns to my mom with a questioning look. "I'm still getting the hang of it."

She smiles and says my father's words aloud.

Finn says and signs, "We are glad to be here."

Dad pats him on the shoulder and signs, "Glad to have you, Finn." But when he signs Finn's name he uses the sign for *kind*, using the first letter of Finn's name.

I go still.

My father gave Finn a name sign. And the adjective he chose to describe him was "kind."

A few weeks ago, there were other adjectives I would've used to describe him—goofy, silly, unserious—but the one my dad chose is so appropriate that I have to look away because there's a stupid lump at the back of my throat.

I doubt Finn even realizes what's just happened. But I do. Only a member of the deaf community can give someone a name sign. It's a sign of inclusion in my dad's community.

And when Finn introduces Grace and her brothers to my parents, I catch my dad's eye.

He nods at Finn then quickly signs, "good guy." I watch Finn for a second, as he drops down on one knee and says something to Bodie.

My dad's right. He is a good guy. But that still doesn't mean he's right for me. I can't let myself go there even if there's a part of me that's ready to admit I'm curious.

I just can't see it ending well. And it will end. Because it always does—even when it's meticulously planned out, right down to the schedule and resume.

"All right, who's ready to go?" Mom calls out. "We're not going to find the perfect tree just standing around!" She

271

makes a circular motion over her head, like she's rallying troops, and everyone starts to move toward their cars.

I head down the front stairs and into the yard, unsure who I'm supposed to ride with when Finn walks up, Grace trailing behind.

Her brow is knit so tightly, that I recognize her expression immediately—a first line of defense that matches my own. It's the stubborn streak that keeps my feelings safely locked away behind a strong façade.

The one I keep in place because, for whatever reason, I can't let on when I'm happy. Or having fun.

Why do I do that? Why can't I let other people know when I'm enjoying myself, or that things are actually great?

"Morning, Hart," he says. "You remember Grace and her brothers, Bonkers and Booper."

The boys immediately laugh and protest. "Bodie and Brady!" they yell at him.

"Oh! Shoot. Yeah, I keep forgetting." Finn smacks the side of his head with a playful grin.

I smile and nod at the boys, then look at Grace. "I'm glad you're here."

"Mr. Finn is going to get us a tree!" the youngest brother shouts.

"Talk softer, Bodie," Grace says, firmly.

"I'm going to get Miss Raya one too," Finn leans over and whispers to them, "but only if she's been good this year."

He looks at me, winks, and then picks up the kid and tosses him over his shoulder. Bodie lets out a gleeful scream, but Grace rolls her eyes.

Finn bounces Bodie. "Come on, crew! Hop in."

I do a quick scan of the driveway and see that everyone in my family is already loaded up into vehicles. Engines are started. Cars are moving. And I'm still standing here. With Finn.

Not a setup, my eye.

I look at Grace, whose brow is still furrowed. "Are you okay?"

She looks at me, then gives me a quick nod. "I'm glad the boys will have a tree this year."

"What about you?" I ask. "Are you glad you'll have a tree?"

She shrugs. "I don't really care about those things." She starts toward the Jeep. "I just need to figure out how to help with the presents." She looks at me. "For my mom."

I nod, knowing how hard it is to carry the kind of weight she's carrying. I took on the weight of watching over my sisters and being my mom's second-in-command even though she never asked me to.

When I look at this little girl, though, I see how misguided that was. How do I steer her in a different direction when I'm struggling to find the oars myself?

I watch as Grace gets into the backseat and helps Bodie buckle in, pushing his hands out of the way when he tries to help. She just does it herself. She doesn't need help.

That's familiar.

"Hey, Hart?"

I glance over and find Finn watching me. When our eyes meet, his brow knits in concern.

"All good?"

I pull my sunglasses off my head and put them on my face with a nod. But no, I'm not good. Not really. Because if all of these revelations are the truth, then I've got some soul-searching to do.

And I have no idea what comes next.

Chapter Thirty

Raya

This is going to be an uphill climb.

I sit like a statue in the passenger seat of Finn's Jeep, listening to Bodie rattle off the list of things he's going to tell Santa he wants for Christmas. I look at Grace and find her watching him intently—and I know she's taking notes, probably so she can try to make some of these wishes come true.

In a lull, Finn tosses me a look. "No Justin today?"

"Uh, no." My muscles tense. "We're not really a thing anymore. My sisters didn't tell you?"

His forehead creases. "No, they didn't. Are you okay?"

I smile. "I'm fine. It wasn't serious." *Or real.*

Whatever Finn thinks about this, he doesn't say, and after a beat, he's back to his usual antics.

"Attention, passengers! I have an idea!" he announces—loudly. "Today you all have a mission." He shoots me a look, as if to make sure I know I'm not exempt from whatever it is he's about to say.

"Like spies?" Brady asks.

274

"Eh. Sort of." Finn pulls a face. "More like explorers. Today, the only thing on our to-do list is"—he drums his hands on the steering wheel—"fun!"

The boys let out a whooping cheer. Neither Grace nor I respond.

"None of us have ever done a Loveland Christmas kick-off, Hart," he says, nodding at me. "So you are going to be the Master of Fun for the day."

"Me?"

"Yep."

"I think it's pretty obvious that I'm wrong for that job," I say.

"But you have the insider info."

"I really don't."

He frowns, then shakes his head. "Oh, Hart, you really need to hang around me more often. I can show you how to have a good time. Lesson starts now."

He flips on the music and an upbeat rendition of "Jingle Bell Rock" comes on. He starts singing, even though he only knows about half the words, and soon both boys join in.

I catch a snippet of Grace's I'm-so-over-it face in the side mirror, then look back at Finn.

He's actively trying to bring joy to these kids' lives. Just because he can.

The least I can do is try to go along with it.

Finn glances at me as he starts the chorus, bellowing loudly (and very off-key) about the bright time being the right time, and I make the conscious choice to set aside my awkward insecurity and start singing along.

I'm quiet at first, but then I realize I might be the only person in this car who A. knows all the words and B. can actually match pitch, so I start singing a little louder. When

Finn notices, he cheers, and instead of letting it embarrass me, I let it fuel me, and pretty soon, we're all singing. Everyone except Grace.

The song ends right as we reach downtown Loveland, all decked out for Christmas. Finn flips off the music and flashes me a smile.

I do my best to hide a smile of my own, but I fail. "I did it for the kids," I say as he parks the car in a lot near the bank.

He shrugs. "Whatever you need to tell yourself, chief."

After he turns off the engine, the kids scramble out, the boys clambering over one another until they fall out in a pile, then Grace, leaving me alone with Finn.

"I had no idea you could sing," he says, smiling.

I laugh. "You also have no idea that you can't."

"No, I do know." He chuckles and gets out of the car, watching as Scarlett runs over to the kids.

"Thanks for letting me bring them," he says.

"I didn't even know you were coming, so you're thanking the wrong person." I smile so my words don't come out harsh. "But I am glad you brought them. I've been thinking about Grace."

"She thinks you're beautiful, by the way." We start walking toward our group.

"Aw, she does?"

He smiles. "Yeah. She asked why I'm not married, and I told her I haven't found the right person yet. She said, 'What about the beautiful lady with the black hair'?"

This makes me smile as I turn my attention back to the kids, who are all now in line for roasted chestnuts. "And what did you say?"

"I said that the beautiful lady with the black hair"—he looks at me—"is *way* out of my league."

And then he walks away.

Finn

Being with the Hart family takes away the sting of not being with my own family.

We spend a full day downtown, taking in all the sights of the Loveland Christmas Carnival. We stop to eat giant, decorated Christmas cookies, admire the handmade decorations, and shop at the countless booths and displays that are set up throughout downtown.

Streets are blocked off for this carnival, with an entire section just for kids—bounce houses, a hot chocolate train car straight out of *The Polar Express*, and soft, climbable presents in an open playground area.

I might've spent some time in there with Bodie and Brady.

The boys are a whirlwind, and every new thing is an adventure, something they're seeing for the very first time. By contrast, Grace is quiet and keeps to herself.

I understand why she reminds Raya of herself.

Though, to her credit, Raya actually seems to enjoy herself. She's more relaxed. She smiles more than she frowns. And she even tells us about the times she spent here as a kid.

"The Christmas Carnival," she says, "is a Loveland *and* a Hart tradition," and to prove it, each member of her family takes turns sharing what they claim is "the best part of the whole carnival."

These "best parts" range from the Holiday House Walk —a tour of four historic homes, all ornately decorated for

Christmas—to the outdoor market featuring local vendors selling handmade goods like candles, caramels, or chocolates.

I bought a dark chocolate covered caramel topped with sea salt and gave it to Raya. "You never got to eat the other one I bought you because I think you were puking or something," I joke.

Her eyes go wide, and she gives my shoulder a little push. "That's not funny!" But her laugh tells me I didn't go too far.

"Eh . . . I mean, it kind of is." I grin.

"You're the worst." She shakes her head, but takes the chocolate.

I pop one in my mouth and wince. "*Ew.* This is your favorite candy?"

She takes a bite. "It's so good."

"Why is there salt on it?" I shudder, making a show of trying to brush it off.

"You have no taste at all," she says, taking another one.

"No, I know a good thing when I see it." I hold her gaze a beat longer than I probably should, then follow Bodie and Brady to the petting zoo where they have "real live reindeer."

Which is hilarious to me, because what's the alternative, "fake live reindeer?"

They're *huge.* And I'm not sure who's more excited—the boys or me.

Grace isn't interested, but when one of the reindeer gets close and licks her face, even she can't keep from laughing.

Mr. Hart shows off the living windows, his favorite holiday tradition, and we vote on which ones we like best. After that, we loop around and take a turn in line with Santa.

I pick up a pamphlet with the details for the other Christmas events in town, thinking if Raya plans to attend the luminary walk or the fireworks, maybe she'll let me tag along.

I've spent more than a few holiday seasons in Illinois now, most of them in Chicago. And even though I've seen almost everything the city has to offer, there's something sort of magical about being here, with a family, even if they aren't my own. Covers the ache of homesickness just a little.

And even though there are no mountains, Loveland reminds me a bit of my own hometown. I talked to my parents this morning, got the update on the community center Thanksgiving dinner and Silverwood's own Christmas kickoff, which isn't a whole lot different from this one.

I absently think that someday, I'd like to show it to Raya. The divide between us has closed a little, but I remind myself not to risk widening it again by being stupid or impatient.

Just be her friend.

After we get our fill of the carnival and the cookies, we all pile back into our cars and drive to the Pine Creek Tree Farm, way out in the country between Loveland and its nearest neighbor, a town called Pleasant Valley.

We do a hay ride and get hot chocolate, then as we trudge out to the field lined with rows and rows of trees, I start a sing-along of Christmas carols, and we take turns picking which songs to sing.

Even Gray hums along. Which is shocking. I'm guessing he's doing it for Scarlett, who has been tugging on him to join in. The entire scene feels like something straight out of a Christmas movie.

At the end of the night, I place a blanket down on the roof of my SUV and strap the kids' and Raya's trees down on top of it. We head back to the Hart family farmhouse, enjoying the silent, satisfied car ride that only comes after a full day. I'd love to stay and help decorate the Harts' tree, drink more hot chocolate, and watch a Christmas movie, but I know I need to get the kids home to their mom.

I thank everyone for letting us tag along, and just as I'm about to leave, Raya shocks me when she asks if she can come along to bring the kids home. She bought each of them an ornament, picking ones out that fit them perfectly. Bodie's ornament is a Tasmanian Devil holding a present over his head, Brady's is a hand-carved motorcycle with the back of it packed with gifts, and Grace's is a curvy bookworm, with glasses and a Santa hat, holding a book that says "Frankincense and Sensibility."

I think she might be trying to find an opening to talk to Grace, too, her prickly little twin.

After we drop them off, their mom, who isn't a whole lot older than we are, sends us home with a fresh batch of homemade cinnamon rolls and her heartfelt thanks. And it's nice. A genuinely relaxing, restful day.

Once it's just Raya and me in the Jeep, I let out a tired— but happy—sigh.

"It was really nice of you to bring the kids," she says. "I think I saw Grace smile at least twice."

My eyebrows shoot up. "A Christmas miracle." A pause. "Saw you smile a few times too."

She nods. "Yeah, it was . . . fun."

"Did you just say the F-word?"

She giggles. "You're such a dork."

"I'm starving," I say, realizing. "I didn't eat enough today."

"You had two hot dogs and a brat like two hours ago," she says.

"I'm thinking pizza," I say, not letting her facts get in the way of my perfectly good argument. "You up for pizza?"

She pauses, like she's thinking about it, then finally says, "Sure."

"Really?" I don't bother to hide my surprise, but that one word feels like a golden ticket.

"I'll order it now." She opens her phone, clicks around on it for a few seconds, then tucks it away, leaning back into the seat. "They're going to leave it on my porch."

Even though she hasn't mentioned it, I have a feeling her exhaustion is still bone-deep, and I start to wonder just how long it's actually going to take for her to feel like herself again.

And what happens after the four weeks are up? Back to the grind?

It's not my place to worry. Our friendship is still new, but sometimes I want to protect her—even from herself.

We reach her house, and I see her car sitting in the driveway. Someone in her family must've driven it over so she wouldn't have to go out again.

"Looks like the pizza's already here." She fishes around in her purse for her keys. She stops and looks at me. "Is this weird?"

"Is what weird?"

"You being here?" she says. "Like, socially?"

"I don't think it's weird. We're friends, right?" I'm hopeful that today put us back on the right track. "Is it weird for you?"

She winces. "Kind of."

I laugh. "You never pull any punches, do you?"

"I don't even know how."

"See, that right there, that's one of the things I like about you," I say, my Jeep still idling in her driveway.

She laughs. "It's not my best quality."

"True. Your face is your best quality."

She rolls her eyes at me.

"But speaking your mind is a close second, for sure." I lean back in the seat. "It's hard to find people who do that."

She stares out the windshield. "Most people don't like that I do."

I shrug. "Most people are idiots."

She laughs.

There's a quiet lull, and then I say, "If it's weird, I can bring your tree in, grab a slice, and hit the road. I won't be offended."

She seems to be contemplating this, and I'm kicking myself for suggesting it.

"Or . . . we could go inside, set up your tree, eat some pizza, and watch *The Polar Express*."

She frowns. "You want to watch a cartoon?" She opens the car door and gets out, so I shut off the car and do the same.

"Six of my top ten movies are animated," I say.

She muses. "Why am I not surprised?"

"Okay, but have you seen *Lego Batman*?" I reach up to start untying the twine from around the tree, and once it's loose, I heave it down, then up over my shoulder.

"Absolutely not."

"We need to fix that." I walk up to the porch and find Raya standing there with the door only slightly ajar.

"This doesn't mean anything," she says, pointing at me. "It's just pizza and you know, Christmas . . . things."

"Message received," I say.

"No flirting and no"—she waves her hands around, like she's swatting gnats—"reading into it."

"Got it," I say, shifting the tree. It's not exactly small. "Strictly platonic."

She starts to open the door then freezes, and I stop short. The front of the tree tips forward, and I lose my balance.

I shoot out a hand to the top of the door frame to stop myself from falling and as the tree dips inside the doorway, and my face ends up about an inch from hers.

Her breath hitches. "Strictly platonic."

I nod.

She goes still.

"Hart?" I say.

"Yeah?"

"This is really heavy."

Chapter Thirty-One

Raya

S trictly platonic.

This should be easy.

It's not. Not by a long shot.

While Finn deals with the tree, I walk into the house and set the pizza on the kitchen counter. Thankfully, he had the forethought to convince me to buy a tree stand, but I don't have a single ornament to decorate this thing with.

I never tried to win Christmas, I guess.

Once the tree is stable, I rush into the bathroom where I spend at least three straight minutes telling myself this is a terrible idea. Earlier today I'd decided not to let myself be alone with him, and now here we are—about to eat pizza together.

Very much alone.

But it's fine. My willpower is strong. And I can make and follow rules with the best of them.

Never mind that I spent the day watching him make kids laugh. Or that he learned sign language so he could talk to my dad. Or that I still have memories of that almost-kiss floating around in the back of my mind.

I splash some water on my face and walk out to the kitchen where he's dishing up slices of pizza. There's a crumpled piece of paper on the counter. "What's this?" I pick it up.

"My Christmas checklist," he says.

"You actually made it?" I notice he's crossed out "Get Raya a Christmas tree."

"I said I was going to."

I scan the list:

~~Get Raya a Christmas tree~~
Teach Raya to ice skate
Christmas Carnival
Luminary Walk
Ice Carving Contest
Watch The Polar Express
Tree lighting
Macy's windows
Shop for nieces
Community Center donations
Go to the Christkindl Market
Drive around and look at Christmas lights

"This is ambitious," I say.

"I love Christmas." He looks at me. "Remember the first time we ate pizza together?"

I don't have to think too hard to conjure the image of him leaving his Halloween party to make a frozen pizza because I said I wanted it.

Without responding, I walk over to the refrigerator and pull out two bottles of water. I hand one to him. "Sorry I don't have a beer or anything."

"Oh, it's fine," he says. "I don't actually drink."

"You don't?" I sit down at the island, across from where he's standing.

"Nah." He hands me a plate. "Never really tried it. Even figured out how to win beer pong without ever taking a drink."

I run back through my memory and realize I don't have a single memory of him drinking. "I don't really drink either," I say. "For obvious reasons."

He smirks at me. "Oh, I know," he teases. "I was there."

I wince. "Yeah." I pick up a slice of pizza and take a bite. "I guess I never realized this about you."

"I'm not super strict on it—it's just not something I really enjoy."

"Me neither." I take another bite and watch him. "Can I ask why you don't? Is it just the taste or . . . ?"

"Actually, no, not the taste." He pauses, then, like he's made up his mind about something, he adds, "It's because of my brother."

I stop chewing and look at him, but his eyes are on the counter. He doesn't say anything for a moment, and then he looks up at me. He smiles, but it's one of those smiles that masks another feeling. "He was killed by a drunk driver."

I set my pizza down. "Oh."

"Mood killer, right?" His mouth quirks.

"Finn—"

He holds up a hand. "It's okay. It was a long time ago."

And yet . . . there's still pain there. I can see it in his eyes.

"I've never lost anyone that close to me," I say. "But I imagine there's no statute of limitations on grief."

"Yeah, but I don't like to be a downer," he says, shrugging and acting like he'd rather talk about something else. He piles another piece of pizza on the stack already on his plate. "It kind of wrecked our family for a long time. Everyone dealt with it differently. It's better now."

I think about the way he talked to his mom on the phone. The way this tragedy must've bonded them for life. The way a person's outlook would change after something like that.

"I can't even imagine." I say. "How old were you?"

"Fifteen," he says between bites. "He was seventeen."

I go still, thinking about my own family, knowing that if anything happened to one of my sisters, I wouldn't recover.

He gets a faraway look on his face. "He was that guy everyone loved, you know? The guy who never met a stranger. The one everyone wanted to be friends with. All the girls wanted to date him." He looks at me. "He was that guy."

"So, this runs in the family," I say.

He chuckles, then takes another bite. "He's the reason I play hockey."

"He is?"

"I mean, I play because he can't." He opens his water. "This was always his dream—to play in the NHL one day. He was good too. Definitely would've made it." He picks up his plate and walks into the living room.

I follow him, taking a seat on the end of the couch. "So it's not your dream?"

"I mean, it is *now*. After he passed away, I just kind of put all that on the shelf." He sits. "I know that's a crazy thing to say to someone like you, but I'm not a person who needs to accomplish some big goal. Losing my brother shifted my perspective on that. On everything, really. I'm just happy to be here. Happy for every opportunity I get. Every chance I get to do something incredible—like play professional hockey with the likes of Dallas Burke." He says his name like he's reading a headline. "But every little thing too—like buying you your first Christmas tree."

I wonder if he's cracked some sort of happiness code. I can't imagine feeling as content with a day like today as I would after a day with a huge win on a professional stage.

Maybe that's the problem.

I look at him. "You do know that they're also really lucky they get to play with you, right?"

He shrugs and waves me off. "You have to say that because, like, your whole family is dating the team," he says, mouth half-full of pizza.

"I mean it, Finn," I say. "It's awesome to be content and grateful, but don't sell yourself short. You put a lot of good into the world too." I say it matter-of-factly because I don't want him to see that all of this is affecting me in ways I don't understand.

I'll process it later. I'll process *all of it* later.

He sets his plate down and looks at me. "Hey, do you have a calendar?"

I do a double take, confused. "Yeah, I've got my calendar on my phone." I fumble for it, then open the calendar app.

"Okay, you're going to want to mark the date—" he taps my phone with his finger. "The first time you've ever complimented me."

Slowly, I lower the phone and look up at his stupid grinning face.

I take a bite and look away. "Don't let it go to your head."

Chapter Thirty-Two

Finn

She pulls her legs up under her and watches as I push a slice of pizza around on my plate.

"So, I'm pretty bad with emotions," she says.

"No. You?" I tease.

"Shocking, I know," she muses. "But I've known you for a while, and I've never heard you talk about Hunter."

I nod. "Yeah. Like I said before—it brings the mood down. And I don't want to be the guy who lost a brother. People look at you differently when they know." And it's true. I want to be the guy who leaves every place a little better than how he found it.

What I don't say is that I don't like the way it feels when I talk about it. I don't like to feel the anger that's stirred up, or the way it mixes with grief. I can't change it. I can't go back and fix it.

What I can do is live my life like he would've, and never ever miss an opportunity to be grateful. For the big things and the little things.

But then Raya asks, "Do you . . . need to? Talk about him, I mean."

Do I? Do I want to go there? Do I need to go there?

"No pressure," she says. "I won't be offended if you'd rather not."

I really don't like revisiting this. But part of me wants Raya to know. It's the only way she'll ever know Hunter and how amazing he was—the only way for me to introduce my brother to this incredible woman.

"No, it's okay," I say. "It's hard because—well, it's just hard." I set my plate on the coffee table and think about the brother I lost.

"Hunter was two years older than me," I say, thinking it's best to start with the facts, but also aware that apart from that day she picked up his photo in my apartment, it's been a really long time since I've said his name out loud. "He was obsessed with hockey.

"He'd talk about professional players nonstop. Knew all of their stats, who was getting traded to which team, even who was coming out of high school or college and was going to make a huge noise in the league.

"He was going to enter the draft." I pause. "He would've gotten picked up too—he just had a gift. Dozens of letters and emails telling him he was a 'rare talent.'" "A kid with crazy natural talent paired with the work ethic of a rancher? Unstoppable," I laugh just thinking about it. So many chores. And so early in the morning.

Who would've thought eventually I'd be grateful for it?

I scoot back, settling into the couch, and look at Raya, grateful to find her eyes kind and curious.

"Everyone thought he was crazy, you know, because he was such a loudmouth, even at age twelve, about the fact that one day he was going to play pro hockey. He talked about it like he had no doubt he could do it. Nobody from our small town had ever done anything like that. He may as well've told people he was going to be an astronaut," I laugh, remembering how the guys would tease him. He never backed down.

"My pop isn't the best with words—he thinks actions are louder, so he built an ice rink in the backyard. His way of showing support, I think." I pull out my phone and scroll through my photos until I find one of me on the rink with my brothers, taken last Christmas. "This is it." I hand it to her, and she looks at it, pinching the screen to make it bigger.

"You all look so much alike," she says.

"Right?" I take the phone back and scan my brothers' faces. "Bunch of knuckleheads." I laugh.

I pull in a slow, deep breath. This is the hard part. The part I don't like to remember. I've found that if I say it quick, it hurts less. But only a little bit.

"So, one night," I say, "on the way home from a game, Hunter came up over a hill and there was a car on his side of the road. In his lane. Head-on collision. The woman driving walked away without a scratch. Hunter didn't . . . uh . . . he didn't . . ." A ball of anger forms in my chest, replacing the sadness that's always there when I think about the life my brother didn't get to live.

"Hunter didn't walk away at all."

Raya goes still. She knew the ending, but it's still jarring. The kind of tragedy that should never, ever happen. "I'm so sorry," she whispers.

Somehow, her words don't sound empty. Or pitying. They just sound honest and heartfelt.

"You know, as awful as it was, I do think losing Hunter

taught me—my whole family, really—a lot about living in the moment," he says. "I know better than to waste a single day."

"Says the guy who spends his days off playing video games." She shoots me a look.

It breaks the tension a bit, and I'm grateful. I turn mock-serious. "Hey. That is not a waste. That—is a very fun distraction."

"I'll never understand it," she says, shaking her head.

"Well, don't knock it until you try it," I grin at her, and the weight of the conversation settles back in a bit, but not as heavy.

"I just want to make him proud." I shrug. "Live like it matters. Because it does. Gotta make it count for something."

Curiosity washes over her face. "'Live like it matters.' You said that to your mom when you got off the phone."

I nod. "Yeah, we say it for Hunter." A soft shrug. "Easier than saying his name."

I'm glad I told her, but talking about it always comes with a price. I go back to my food, trying to put all the feelings back in the right boxes.

We eat in a comfortable silence for a minute or so, and then she looks at me, brow knit with concern. "What happened to the driver?"

I don't know what my face does, but it must be something because she frowns.

"Oh. I'm . . .sorry, is that a bad question?" she asks.

I look at her. I want to be honest, but I'm not sure I want to talk about the woman who killed my brother. Not tonight. Not when we have a tree to set up. And Christmas to celebrate. Not when I know that the anger is always directed at her.

"I don't really know where she is now," I say, which isn't a lie.

It's just not a whole truth either.

"But she's in prison, right?"

I look away. "Not anymore."

She goes still. "Wow."

"Yeah." I look at her, and without thinking, I add, "She, uh, sends me letters sometimes."

She hugs her legs a little tighter. "She what?"

"Yeah, I don't know if it's a step in a program she's in or what, but . . ." I trail off.

"What does she say?"

"I'm not sure." I shake my head. "I've never opened one."

"Oh." She watches me.

I haven't opened one because I know she's going to say how sorry she is. Or worse, ask for forgiveness. I'm not exactly ready to read the former or grant the latter.

"I don't know if I'd be able to read those either," she says. "I can't even begin to imagine what a mess I'd be if something happened to Poppy or Eloise."

"I know, somewhere, there has to be some kind of, I don't know, closure, or forgiveness, or whatever, but—"

She finishes my thought, "—But you aren't there yet."

I nod, a little embarrassed, because aren't I supposed to forgive? I'm pretty sure that's written in a very important book somewhere. But nobody explains how to do it. It's hard to hand out forgiveness when the person you're supposed to forgive stole something priceless.

Man, I miss him.

Raya studies me, almost like she's seeing me for the first time. "Did you know that my dad gave you a name sign?"

I shake my head, thankful for the change of subject. "A name sign? What does that mean?"

"In the deaf community, only a deaf person can give you a name sign. It's usually the first letter of your name mixed with a sign that describes you."

"What was mine?" I ask, because I really had no idea.

She does the motion with her hands, then says, "It means kind. My dad has only been around you a few times, but he knew that about you."

"Show me again?"

She does, and I repeat the movement with my own hands. "How do I say your name?"

She shows me—hands in an "X" over her heart, then opened out to the sides, fingers crossed on both hands.

I do the sign back to her, then meet her eyes.

"Independent," she says, without me asking.

I smile. "Ha. That tracks."

She rolls her eyes and smiles, then her gaze settles back on me, and the mood shifts again.

"Forgiveness isn't for her, Finn," she says. "It's for you."

I nod. This is the part that's head knowledge, not heart knowledge. I know this already. I've known for years. Makes sense, right? Just forgive, no big deal, get on with your day—but my heart's not willing to do that. "My pop has said that exact same thing."

"I also think kind people," she indicates to me, "have a hard time when their emotions don't feel kind," she says.

"Like independent people," I indicate to her, "have a hard time when they need help," I volley back.

Her eyebrow lifts so slightly I almost miss it. "Touché. But we aren't talking about me." She pauses, then adds, "My point is—you get to feel all of that. It's all valid."

I blow out a breath. "I know."

"And—" she shrugs, "if you did decide to forgive her, maybe some of that anger would go away."

"My dad says holding onto it only hurts me."

"You disagree?"

I scoff. "No, I know he's right. I guess that's the point. I don't know how to let it go." I look up and find her watching me, but there's no judgment there. Only concern. Or interest.

Or . . .

I remind myself to stop reading into things, blow out a breath, and shake the thoughts away. "Okay. Let's move on. That was a lot." I shake my head. "I don't really talk about this stuff with anyone. And I've never told anyone about the letters."

Her face softens. "But you told me . . . ?"

I nod.

"Why?"

I shrug. "Maybe I wanted you to know there's more to me than you think." I meant for that to come off as light-hearted, but it doesn't land that way.

I look at her. The air between us shifts, and that pang of desire is back so strong I have to look away.

"So since you shared all of that about you," she says, "it's only fair that I share something about me. Something no one knows."

"My back's about to break from keeping so many of your secrets," I say with a smile.

"Yeah, about that—" She twists the end of her napkin. "Thank you. I'm shocked you never let it slip."

"What can I say?" I shrug. "I'm a lockbox."

She goes still. "Which is why I think I can tell you how

Justin and I started dating."

Finn

I leave Raya's house a little dazed, not only because I now know the truth about Justin, but also because I dragged out the memories of Hunter, and now they're sitting right at the forefront of my mind.

I walk to my car, snow crunching under my shoes, air brisk and cold, replaying my conversation with Raya.

Hearing her talk about Justin, about the resumes and this crazy plan she came up with to try to manufacture the perfect mate, makes me realize that Raya's scared.

She's scared of her own feelings. Scared of getting hurt. Scared of not being in control. She'd never admit it—not out loud—but I can see it clear as day.

Which is why I need to concentrate on just being her friend. And stop giving in to every impulse to reach out to her.

I can be patient, right?

The conversation stirred up more than my feelings for Raya. It stirred up my feelings about everything. Things I haven't dealt with and don't want to, even if I probably should.

I shove my hands in my pockets and rub my fingers together to get them warm.

Maybe that was the point.

I try not to think about it. But now, apart from Raya, it seems like it's *all* I think about. Like, those letters I've hidden in my glove box are alive, still pulling my attention.

It's annoying. And I'm pretty sure there's only one way to silence them.

This is what I'm thinking as I park my Jeep in the parking garage. Tomorrow we leave for Canada for a week, with games in Toronto, Montreal, and Ottawa. I should go inside and pack, but instead of getting out of the car, I just sit.

I stare at the glove box.

I think about what Raya said. About what my dad has said.

I reach over, pop the glove box open, and pull out the letters.

And for the first time, I actually ask myself if forgiving that woman is even an option.

The thought makes me react like I tasted something rotten.

I lean forward on the steering wheel, remembering the night I found out Hunter was gone. The way losing him tore our family into pieces. How hard it was to work our way back from that. How each one of my siblings processed the loss differently, and how I never processed it at all.

How our family's story now has a "before" and an "after."

I grit my teeth at the injustice of it.

So I set out to live a life that would make my brother proud. To do the things I thought he'd do and take every chance I got because anything less than that would be like kicking sand in his face.

I play the way I do because he can't. I live the way I live because he can't. And I love the way I love because he can't.

I shouldn't have to do that. I shouldn't have had to go through what I went through.

And I wouldn't have if it weren't for her.

How am I supposed to forgive *that*?

I suck in a sharp breath and look at the return address on the top envelope. Eileen Tierney.

I take the envelopes and shove them in the pocket of my coat, not caring whether or not they get crumpled.

I get out of the Jeep and close the door, anger bubbling down deep, and Raya's words are back, an unwanted reminder.

"If you did decide to forgive her, maybe some of that anger would go away."

If I decide. Like it's a switch I can flip.

Should it be that easy? Should it be a simple decision that happens overnight?

I don't know. And I can't think about it now. I have a trip to pack for. And even though it's not perfect timing, I'm glad to be going out of town because distraction is good right now.

But the next day, as I walk out to the chartered jet, I slip my hand into the pocket of my coat and feel the balled-up letters—an unwelcome memory that none of this is going away.

Chapter Thirty-Three

Raya

I've gotten more comfortable sleeping in.

So much so that it's probably going to be hard to return to my normal schedule. But I think the extra hours of sleep are helping me feel stronger. I'm a little less rundown than I was even two days ago.

Despite what everyone thinks, I *have* gotten on board with slowing down.

Sort of.

Fine. It's a process. But I'm trying.

It's been days since I told Finn the truth about Justin. The whole truth—from the second I got the idea to the second he walked out the door.

And Finn didn't laugh. At first, he didn't respond. Just sort of looked at me, almost like he was calculating something —which was weird. I couldn't read him, but I wondered if I'd shared more than I should've.

I changed the subject, desperate to focus on anything other than my utter humiliation, and Finn went right along with it. If he thought I was a complete moron for concocting this plan in the first place, he didn't let on. He was back to his easygoing self, and while I haven't seen him since, he's been actively texting me nonsense while he's on the road, which has been kind of nice.

Last night, I went over to my parents' house and watched the game with my family. Hockey Finn is different from the real-life teddy bear I've gotten to know. He's focused and fierce and . . . hot.

He's hot.

It's very distracting.

Now, it's Friday, a day with no plans, so I treat myself to a slow morning. I stay in my pajamas. I drink my coffee slowly. I read a chapter of a crime novel I started two years ago and never found time to finish. And I purpose to savor every second of it.

A little before noon, there's a knock on my door, and I open it to find Finn, arms loaded with shopping bags. He takes one look at me and says, "You look cute."

I absently touch the messy bun on top of my head, wondering why I don't feel more put off by his impromptu visit. Normally, I don't answer the door unless I'm presentable, which I am definitely not. For some reason, I don't really care if Finn sees that I'm a mess.

More than anyone, he already knows.

I frown, but I'm smiling on the inside, still not quite able to wear all my emotions on my face. "What are you doing here?"

"You have a naked tree." He holds his arms up. "I'm here to fix that." Then, after a beat he says, "Do you care if I come in?"

The butterflies in my stomach are doing gymnastics, but

I move aside and let him in, closing the door behind him. "You're wearing a coat."

He groans. "I didn't want you to yell at me again."

I giggle to myself because, for no reason at all, I find this amusing.

"Okay, anything you hate, I'll take back," he says, excited. "But I brought options."

He starts pulling all kinds of things from the bags—tinsel and ornaments and bows and an angel for the top of the tree. "Oh, and this one is special because it reminded me of you —" He hands me a small box.

I turn it over and find a Scrooge McDuck ornament. I laugh. "I'm highly offended."

"Nailed it, right? Took me all week to find that." He grins at me, then takes the box. He rips it open and pulls out the ornament. "Here, hang him up. The first ornament of the season."

So I do.

We spend the next hour adding all kinds of decorations to the tree, and by the time we're done, it looks like a group of preschoolers went to town on it. There's no clear color scheme, the ornaments pull some of the lower branches almost to the floor, but Finn is clearly proud of the mess he's made, so I decide—for once—to go with it.

To his credit, he added so many white lights I'm pretty sure it'll look beautiful at night.

We finish with the tree, and Finn picks up the only bag we haven't opened. "Okay, I know you don't like surprises, but . . . I have one." The look on his face is slightly adorable, even I can admit, because it's obvious this man loves surprises. And he's right. Normally, I hate them. Right at this moment, though, I feel a little giddy wondering what's in that bag.

"I promise it's good." He hands the bag over.

Inside, I find one of the ugliest Christmas sweaters I've ever seen. It's a putrid lime green and has a giant Grinch on it, plastered in front of rows of Christmas trees. Before I can even register a reaction, I turn to find Finn holding up what looks like a video game Christmas sweater in front of his torso, goofy grin on his face.

It has the words "IT'S ON LIKE" above a big chunky gorilla standing on a bunch of orange platforms. And is that a barrel? The colors are hideous.

I don't ask the question, but he must see it on my face because his smile widens. "I booked an ugly sweater food tour." Before I can respond, he pulls on the sweater over his shirt. "It starts in half an hour though, so we have to hurry."

"You're serious."

He holds up one hand and puts the other one over his heart. "I never joke about food."

I frown. "I'm not even close to being ready to go anywhere."

"Who cares?" he says. "You don't have to look perfect." A shrug. "You look cute anyway."

"I'm not trying to look cute," I argue. "Just like a person with a pulse."

"Come on, you need to eat, *I* need to eat—" he shoos me away from the tree. "Go do whatever you need to do, and let's go."

I sigh. I know all about this ugly sweater food tour. Poppy participates sometimes, and it really does seem like fun, but he's springing this on me, and I wasn't ready. He knows I don't like to be caught off guard.

And yet, maybe that's the point.

"Don't do that Raya thing and overthink it. Let's just go have fun." He looks at me. "It's an adventure." He says "adventure" on a whisper, as if he's going for "mysterious."

I press my lips together, trying to figure out why everything inside me is protesting this idea, and then I remember I have no job, no plans, and no reason not to go.

And I realize I really do *want* to. "Fine, but give me a second." I start to rush off to change when Finn makes an *eh-eh-eh* sound. I turn and find him holding up the sweater.

"You forgot something."

I hesitate for a three-count, and he shakes it at me, pumping his eyebrows at the same time.

I snag the sweater and rush off to my room. I pull my hair from the messy bun and shake it out while simultaneously searching for a pair of jeans. I pull them on, then hold the sweater up in front of me, studying myself in the mirror with a groan. "Ridiculous," I mutter under my breath, but I tug it over my head anyway.

I leave my face mostly bare, opting for a little blush and lip gloss, then I join Finn in the living room. He takes one look at me and his whole face brightens. "Dang, you even make that ugly sweater look good."

He doesn't give me time to respond, choosing instead to hold up my bag and coat, open the door, and rush me straight outside.

"Tell me you haven't done this before," he says as we drive toward downtown Loveland.

"Do you really need to ask that question?" I try to glower, but I feel . . . excited?

"But you've probably eaten at most of these places," he says.

"Not really," I say. "I usually eat at Poppy's or some-where in the city. This will be new for me too."

He looks pleased. "I was hoping for that. I just want you to have fun."

"This isn't like, a pity outing, is it?" I ask. "Because of my humiliating confession? About Justin?"

He looks at me, face serious, and says, "Of course it is."

I hold eye contact for a couple of seconds, then his face brightens with a wide smile, and I burst out laughing. I shove him in the shoulder, and he grins at me. "You're obviously a hopeless case, so *someone* had to take pity on you."

I roll my eyes, and he parks in front of a Loveland pub a few blocks away from Poppy's Kitchen.

We meet up with about ten other people in ugly sweaters, and the tour organizer hands out lanyards that show we're all together. We spend the afternoon sampling food from bakeries, and restaurants, and coffee shops in and around downtown Loveland. It's more food than I've ever eaten in the span of two and a half hours, but it's all *so good*. Finn makes fast friends with the other people in our group, including three college guys who are—no surprise—huge Comets fans. He's gracious and funny and kind, and never once does he leave my side. Instead, he looks for ways to draw me into the conversation, sometimes in very clunky, but endearing ways.

He takes tons of pictures and sends them to his family. His mom sends back photos of his two nieces, Libby and Jordy, both wearing tiny Christmas aprons and making cookies in her kitchen. The little one holds up both of her flour-covered hands while the older one licks a wooden spoon.

Finn wraps an arm around me and snaps a selfie—which I make him retake because "I was not ready!"—then sends it back.

His mom responds, but he doesn't show me what she says.

As the tour comes to an end, we leave our final stop, stuffed to the gills, but somehow—I don't feel tired.

I haven't felt this *not tired* in months.

It's nearly dark out, and as I look around, I see several luminaries are already glowing for The Luminaria, a night when the entire town is shines with candlelight in celebration of the season.

"Okay, this next part is up to you. No more surprises. Do you want to get home or . . .?"

I zip my coat and shove my hands in my pockets. "We could walk for a little bit? I've come to The Luminaria before. I think you'll like it."

"Yes! I was hoping you'd say that."

We start to walk, and I tell him what I know about Loveland's Christmas traditions. "The Christmas Carnival kicks it all off, but Loveland really knows how to do holidays. Tonight, as part of The Luminaria, they've brought back the" —I stop in front of a storefront—"living windows."

We watch as three girls dressed as ballerinas spin in unison. "Tourism has really been up over the last few years, so they go all out."

We move on, weaving through the slow-moving crowd, pausing to look at the windows, smile at neighbors, and marvel at how beautiful this town is, glowing from the candles inside the luminaries. In the middle of the block, in the town square, live musicians play in front of a huge

Christmas tree—which is impressive to me because they must be freezing.

The foot traffic picks up, and at one point, I end up boxed in on one side of the sidewalk. Finn moves to the other side and waits until I can make my way over to him.

When we reenter the fray, he takes my hand, then looks at me. "Just so we can stay together."

I don't say anything, even as the alarm bells go off in my mind. I should pull away. I should reinstate the "strictly platonic" boundary. But I don't. Instead, I let him lead me around my little hometown, soaking in the quiet glow of Christmas, letting myself experience everything without overthinking it for once.

At the end of the night, he drives me back to my house. We pull into the driveway, and I smile at the sight of the tree glowing in my window.

"Looks cool, right?" Finn puts the SUV in park.

"Festive," I say.

"Did you have a good time?"

I nod. "I did. Christmas is growing on me."

He smiles. "Then my work here is done."

There's a lull, the kind I've never known how to fill, so I open the door. "Thank you for hanging out with me today." I turn back and find him watching me.

"Thank *you* for showing me around."

I smile and step onto the pavement, lingering, I realize, because—I don't want to say goodnight.

"We're going on the road again," he says. "But I'll check in. Someone has to make sure you're taking it easy."

"You've taught me well," I say. "I think I'm actually getting the hang of it."

"Sleep well, Hart," he says, eyes locked onto mine.

I nod. "You too."

Once I'm inside, Finn drives off, leaving me standing in my dimly lit house, watching my resolve crumble to pieces around me.

Chapter Thirty-Four

Raya

Over the next week, I do anything I can to stay busy, grateful to have some space away from Finn. I need to think. Sort my feelings. Talk some sense into myself.

So far, I'm not doing a very good job.

It doesn't help that, thanks to my sisters, I watch every one of the four away games. Or that Finn texts me while they're traveling, "just to check in."

It's hard to forget him when he keeps sending me goofy selfies, or photos of Gray dead asleep on the plane, or a series of questions making sure I'm still taking it easy.

My reasons for staying away from him are thin, and even I know it. Yes, we're friends, but I'm not an idiot. I feel what's happening between us.

And it scares me. Because all the things about him that felt so wrong—all the reasons it was easy to keep him in the "just friends" box—are getting harder to focus on.

Distance and space are my friends right now.

I'm not someone who has ever been ruled by my feelings,

and I won't start now. I need to get my head on straight and let logic prevail.

Just like always.

The Sunday after the food tour, I go to family dinner at my parents' house, which proves a great distraction. We bake and decorate Christmas cookies, and I can't remember the last time I laughed that hard. It's nice to laugh.

The next afternoon, I take the cookies to Tasha at the tutoring club, and while I'm there, help Grace get dinner ready. All the kids want to know why Finn didn't come with me, and when I explain he's playing hockey out of town, there's palpable disappointment in the room.

I gather them all together and snap a photo, then send it to him with a text:

RAYA

They miss you!

FINN

That's great, but . . . do you miss me?

I smile and tuck the phone away without responding because once again, it's not my brain leading the charge.

Every morning, I drink my coffee under the soft glow of the Christmas tree and read. For fun. It's a quiet hobby, but it suits me, and I'm starting to realize that forcing myself to be productive twenty-four hours a day might not be the best way to "live like it matters."

I've even adopted his family's saying as my own.

This revelation leads to a harsher one. If I'm really going to live that way, I have to make some changes. Stop volunteering for everything. Stop filling every waking hour with work to avoid having a real life outside of the office—something I once convinced myself I didn't want. In reality, maybe I've just been afraid to admit that I do in case I couldn't figure out how to make it happen.

Which is why, the day I return to work, after a checkup with Dr. Marshall, who gives me the all clear to return, I bypass my office and go straight to Brian's. He has a decorated tree in the corner, wrapped gifts underneath, and colorful string lights hanging around the perimeter. A Santa hat tops his desk lamp, with a snowman right next to it.

He looks up from his computer and smiles. "You're back!"

I nod. "It's like Santa threw up in here."

He stands and holds out his hands. "It's Christmas!"

"So I'm told."

His whole face frowns. "Don't tell me you're a Scrooge."

"Maybe an ex-Scrooge." I think of my cozy little armchair right next to my Christmas tree and how much I love my new morning ritual. Then I think of my Scrooge McDuck ornament and smile to myself. I think the real Ebenezer is pretty much gone.

"You look good, Raya. Rested. Brighter, even," he says. "How are you feeling?"

"Good," I say. "Really, really good."

"That's amazing to hear," he says. "Truly."

"But I need to discuss something with you." I close the door, aware that my entrance has garnered a few nosy looks.

"Oh, boy," he says. "You're not quitting, are you?"

I laugh and take a seat on the opposite side of his desk. "No, not quitting."

"Good. If you were, my entire plan would've backfired."

"No, I think you were right to insist on the time off." I cross one leg over the other. "It was good for me."

"See? I know what I'm doing." He smiles, folding his hands on his desk. "So, what's on your mind?"

"My work schedule." I meet his eyes. "I need to work less."

He nods. "I was hoping you'd say that."

"Really?" I ask. "I'm not looking to shirk responsibilities or anything—my job *is* still important to me." I pause. "But my life is *more* important. Or at least, I want it to be."

"I think we can find a balance," he says, and it dawns on me how lucky I am to work here. The last company I worked for would not have been this accommodating. Brian meant it when he said the Comets organization prioritizes the health of their employees and their athletes. I've seen it in action.

We talk through ways to dial back my hours, starting with the extra tasks I've been taking on. He has a lot of great advice on sticking to this plan, and I listen when he warns me that it would be really easy to end up right back in the same spot if I'm not careful.

"You have to protect your time off. Diligently," he says. "Whatever that looks like for you."

I'm not sure what it looks like for me, but I want to find out. I want to leave some margin for time that isn't structured or planned.

This makes me think of Finn, who is the undisputed king of unplanned time.

As his face appears in my mind, I realize something.

I miss him.

He's been back for a few days, but I've been putting him off, purposely trying to maintain the distance I'm sure I need to quash this little crush I have.

But I can't deny that all it's done is make me miss him more.

After my meeting with Brian, I walk down to my office and, when I flip on the light, I see a "Welcome Back" banner hanging on the wall behind my desk.

Jill appears in the hallway behind me, Landyn and Hoff close behind.

"We've been waiting for you to get out of your meeting," Jill says. "Are you feeling better?"

There was a time I would've hated this attention, but now I see it for what it is—kindness.

"I am, thank you." I smile and hang my coat on a hook near the door, then walk to my desk. I look at the three of them, standing just past the threshold of my office, and I think about what Finn said about Landyn being terrified of me.

I smile and point to the banner. "Did you do this?"

"I did," Landyn says. "If it's not okay, I can take it down."

"It's really nice," I say. "Thank you."

"We also got donuts," Jill says as Hoff steps forward with a box.

"We didn't want to eat them till you were officially back," Hoff says. "But—"

I can see he's been counting the seconds before he can break open the box. "Don't hold out on my account." I clear a spot on my desk and motion for him to set the box down.

He does, then flips it open. "You pick first, Miss Hart."

Normally, my internal alarm clock would be signaling for them to get out of here because I have things to do, but as I look at the assortment of pastries, I realize *this* is what I have to do right now, and it's the most important thing.

I reach in, grab a long john, then sit, motioning for them to pull up chairs around my desk. "Tell me everything I've missed."

After about a half an hour and a full debrief of all the important things that happened while I was away, the impromptu meeting breaks up, and they all stand to go. Hoff and Jill walk out as Landyn picks up the empty donut box, that timid look on her face.

"Has it gotten better for you this past month?" I ask.

She looks at me, wide-eyed, like she was just caught shoplifting. "Uh, yeah. I'm getting the hang of it, but it's still a lot. I don't want to let anyone down."

I smile, trying to summon the warmth that doesn't come easily to me. "I get that."

She turns to go, but I stop her.

"Would you want to meet once a week, just to check in?" I ask. "See how we can take care of some of the overwhelm you've been feeling?"

"With you?" She stares at me, unblinking.

"Yes," I say. "I've been at this a while, and I think I can help."

"I'd love that," she says. "I really want to do a good job."

"I'll ask Jill to set it up."

"Thank you, Miss Hart." She smiles, then walks out, leaving me sitting in the quiet, realizing that I can help her acclimate instead of dismissing her before I even give her a chance.

I think Finn would be proud.

I pull out my phone to text him when he shows up at my door. The second our eyes meet, I realize that space, distance, and time away from him did absolutely nothing to ease my crush.

I smile.

He smiles.

And two words pop into my head: *Oh, crap.*

Chapter Thirty-Five

Raya

I wake up on Saturday and force myself to take the morning slow. For reasons I can't explain, I snap a selfie with my coffee mug, the white lights of the tree twinkling in the background, and I send it to Finn. Like I *want* him in on this ritual.

I instantly regret it. Because *what am I doing?*

My feelings are overtaking my logic, and I don't like it.

But he returns the text with a selfie of his own. He's holding the video game controller and looking like he just got out of bed.

I tuck the phone away before I text back something stupid like, "Hey, I think I like you."

His visit yesterday was brief, and while I don't want to read into it, he almost felt distant. Like maybe he's letting me get my sea legs back at work. A check-in without lingering.

I should be grateful, but I missed the lingering.

I shake that thought away because *who am I right now?*

The Comets had a game last night, and even though my sisters asked me to go, I opted out. My resolve is so shaky, I couldn't let myself get caught up in the hockey hype. On that stage, those guys are larger than life, and I don't need to get sucked in.

I watched the whole thing alone in my living room.

Poppy and Eloise let me off the hook, but only if I promised to go to the Christkindlmarket Wrigleyville with them today. This makes me think of Finn because he's mentioned this market to me before. I pull out my phone to ask if he's been yet, but I delete the text before sending it.

Space is good.

After a two-stop train ride into the city, I get to Wrigleyville and reach the spot where my sisters and I agreed to meet, and find I'm the first one here. I don't know much about the Christkindlmarket other than it's a German-style outdoor market, and judging by the number of people milling around, it's wildly popular. There are vendors and booths lined up around a large ice rink, just outside Wrigley Field. Each booth is lit from the inside with swaths of greenery along the edges of the red-and-white striped roofs. The smell of roasted nuts fills the air, and tall heating stations line the brick sidewalk that winds all the way around the ice rink. The vendors are selling all kinds of handmade goods, fresh pretzels, and hot spiced drinks.

I pull out my phone to check for a "sorry we're running late" text from Eloise or Poppy when I hear someone call my name. I look up to see a whole group of people walking toward me, and I realize that one or both of my very social siblings has turned this into a Chicago Comets outing.

Dallas and Gray are there, of course, along with Jericho and his wife Monica, Krush and his wife Lisa, Junior and his wife Kari, Crosby, Kemp, and a rookie they call Fritz, who still has outstanding paperwork he seems to be avoiding.

Trailing behind, hands in pockets with a huge smile plastered on his face like he's a kid at Disney World, is Finn.

"Hey, we invited some friends," Eloise says. "None of these jokers have ever been to the Christkindlmarket."

"Neither have I," I say, as Finn catches my eye and holds his hands over his head like, "*Do you see all of this?!*"

"Hart! Did you see the size of the pretzels?!" He shouts this so loudly that more than a few passersby turn and look.

Jericho grabs him from behind and tries to pull his arms down, but Finn fights him for a second.

"Oh, good grief. I thought I left the kids at home," Monica says, as Finn breaks free and pushes Jericho, fake-boxing him for a second.

She falls into step beside me as we start walking along the brick sidewalk. "Jericho told me about your health scare," she says. "How are you feeling?"

"I'm better, thanks for asking," I say. "They forced me to take some time off, and as much as I hate to admit it, it helped. Gave me some much-needed perspective."

"We're trying to keep her busy." Poppy bumps my shoulder with her own. "But in a restful way." She loops an arm through mine, as we stop in front of a vendor selling handmade glass ornaments. Kari and Lisa move into the booth while a small crowd gathers on the sidewalk around the hockey players, asking for photos and autographs.

Monica looks on. "Nights like this always puff my husband up like a marshmallow. That man lives for the fans." She shakes her head, amused, and Poppy watches Dallas, lovestruck as always. I know she can't wait to marry that man and start a family, and while I want that for her too, I won't pretend there isn't a part of me—a newly discovered part—that also wants that for myself.

My gaze drifts to Finn, who is currently on one knee, surrounded by several young kids taking a photo, while he makes a crazy face and stuffs half a German-style pretzel in his mouth.

He's fun. And happy. And good. But the scene is a stark reminder that he is the opposite of my ideal. It's a reminder I need, one that's definitely not been at the forefront of my mind lately.

I pull away from my sister because I need a second to compose myself.

I'm not the girl who believes in fairytales. I'm the realist. The pragmatist. And I need to figure out something—anything—to quell the illogical feelings I have for Finn.

Stupid feelings.

I press my lips together and draw in a slow, deep breath, then let it out just as slowly. We would never, ever work—

"There you are!"

I turn and find Eloise standing in an aisle of the booth I wandered into.

"We're going to skate. Do you want to come?" she asks.

I scrunch my nose. "I don't know how."

"So?" She grabs my arm and pulls me out onto the side-walk, then physically pushes me toward the entrance of the rink. "It'll be fun!"

"I'll make a complete fool of myself," I say, knowing that protesting with her is pointless. She's not really listening. And she has no qualms about making a fool of herself, so she won't understand.

"I don't care if I suck, and I'm going to try it so my hot boyfriend has to put his hands all over me to make sure I don't fall down." She wags her eyebrows and runs off, and I resist the urge to remind her that I don't have a "hot boyfriend" to steady me.

I find a spot on a bench near the edge of the rink and watch as the hockey players take the ice like it's their home rink. People in the crowd start to notice them, and they feed right into the excitement over their presence there.

Finn waves at me, motioning for me to join him. I wince lightly, shrugging a *maybe?* He holds up both hands like *no pressure*, and then points at me, holds up two fingers and flicks them down against his chin twice.

I quickly look around to make sure no one in my family just saw him tell me I'm cute in sign language. Who is teaching him this stuff?!

I point at him and make a claw with my hand at the side of my head, rotating it slightly. "You're crazy!"

He laughs and skates off.

I see Eloise take one step on the ice and her legs go out from under her, but Gray catches her under her arms. She looks up at him with a giant smile on her face, and I wonder if he knows she's falling on purpose. Monica and Jericho skate hand-in-hand while Lisa breaks loose from the group to show some serious skills, successfully landing an impressive jump.

I scan the rink, and my gaze snags again on Finn, who is gliding so effortlessly he looks like he was born with blades for soles.

Poppy hugs the railing as Dallas coaxes her out onto the ice. She's unsteady on her skates, but she's got a wide smile on her face. And when she almost slips, her laugh echoes through the chilly December air.

It looks . . . fun.

A part of me wants to try.

A month ago, I wouldn't even be here. I'd be in the office. But I'm different now. Or at least, I want to be.

My heart rate kicks up as I stand and walk over to the skate rental, quietly moving to a bench where I take my shoes off and lace up the skates. My hands are shaking, and I try to reconcile the fact that I'm going to fall. I'm going to look silly. I'm not going to be good at this.

And that's okay.

"It's not a big deal, Raya," I mutter to myself as I pull the laces tighter. I'm tired of missing out.

I grab onto the wall and move around to the entrance of the rink. I notice parents with small children and these neat little contraptions that keep them from falling.

I want a contraption.

But I'm a grown woman.

I step out onto the ice as a little kid flies past, falling in a heap right in front of me, exactly where my feet are pointed. The movement is so shocking, and I'm about to collide with the kid when something pulls me upright.

"Whoa, there, Crash."

A strong arm wraps all the way around my waist, lifting me up and over the kid, away from the wall.

Finn sets me down on the ice, like it's nothing. "I got you."

Those words again. This time, they send heat straight through my body.

"I'm all for trying new things, Hart, but let's not die in the process," he jokes, steadying me on my wobbly legs.

"Thank you," I say.

"Saving you is what I do, remember?" He flashes a smile without looking at me, and something inside me settles.

"So, are you here to learn how to skate or what?" he asks, pulling away.

I wobble and cling to him. "Not ready for that yet."

"I'm going to keep doing it if it means you're going to hold onto me like that." He laughs and leads me through the kind of "how to skate" lesson he might give to a toddler. We start by bending our knees, finding our balance, and doing little marches on the ice. Every time I wobble, he's there to make sure I don't fall.

My face is so hot it could melt ice right now, a combination of embarrassment and Finn's nearness, and I give the rink a cursory look to see if anyone's watching me.

They're not.

"Yeah, you look ridiculous, Hart," he says when he notices me looking around. "Own it." Then he leans closer. "Nobody cares."

I start to loosen up, so much that when Finn grabs my waist and leads me around the edge of the rink, I actually feel a breeze in my hair. It makes me feel free, even though I'm basically a stiff ragdoll in his hands. But it's fun—I can't help but laugh out loud, in spite of my feeble protestations.

Finn's right—nobody cares. And more importantly—if I'm having fun, why does it matter what anyone else thinks about it?

I know this ice rink is not the place for philosophical epiphanies about my life, but it almost feels like something inside me cracked open.

Eloise, who looks a little like a baby giraffe, wobbles past us, whips her arms around in circles as she tries to stay upright but tips over and lands on her butt. She laughs and Gray shoots over from who-knows-where to help her up as I go back to my small marches.

"I thought you'd be better by now," I hear Gray say to my sister.

I start to get the hang of it, but I'm still clinging to Finn. Crosby whips past us with a low whistle, followed by Junior and Kari, who pretty much look like a pair of ice dancers at the Olympics.

My skate slips, and I start to fall, but Finn catches me again. I let out a nervous laugh. "I'm terrible at this."

"You're doing great."

"You're just being nice."

He laughs softly, and my brain shifts into high gear again, trying to imagine what an actual relationship with Finn would look like.

I like him. I'm attracted to him.

But enough to act on it? I don't know. For the life of me, I can't see myself with someone who plays video games and watches cartoons. I can't get past the thought of falling for a guy who is the exact opposite of what I've always imagined for myself.

Even someone as kind as Finn.

Chapter Thirty-Six

Raya

By the afternoon, I should be exhausted, but I feel oddly energized.

After skating, we walked around the booths, ate too much food, did a little shopping, and I actually let myself loosen up.

It was nice.

I think I'm going to like having a life.

As the group disbands, I say goodbye to my sisters, then walk over to say goodbye to Finn. "Thanks again—for helping me skate."

"It was fun." He smiles, then looks past me, back to the shrinking group.

"It was." I stand there for a few seconds, then smile back at him. "Well, I'll—"

"Are you tired?" he asks.

I pull my gloves out of my pockets and tug them on. "Shockingly, no. I think I'm going to be up late tonight. Adrenaline rush or something."

I should say goodbye and walk away—any progress I've

322

made convincing my heart to listen to my head will be undone if I don't. And yet, I hear myself say, "I recorded *The Polar Express* last night."

He gasps. "For real?"

"You've probably already watched it—"

"No, I haven't," he says. "I mean, not this year. Have you?"

I shake my head. "Still haven't seen it."

He claps his hands together. "Let's watch it!" Then, as if he's trying to restrain himself, he says, "I mean, if you want to."

I shrug. "Sure."

"Yeah?"

"Why not? I didn't want to ride the train back anyway."

"Let's go!" We walk toward the parking lot, comfortable chatter between us, which carries through the car ride back to my house.

He feels like what he is—a friend. And it's nice. No need for that to change, right?

When we reach Loveland, he navigates to my house without the help of GPS, which says something, but I'm not sure what. He parks in my driveway, turns off the engine and looks at me. "You have hot chocolate, right? Because we can't watch this movie without it."

I shake my head. "Yes, you weirdo. Your obsession with this movie is a little concerning."

"You'll see. And you'll kick yourself you waited so long to watch it." He gets out of the car and marches toward the front door. "Hurry up, Hart!"

I laugh as I join him on the porch. I unlock the door, and we step inside, taking off our boots and our coats, and then I turn to face him.

"Fine, but if we're watching a movie, I'm going to need to change my clothes. Jeans are not comfortable enough for a movie night."

"Fine. Go." He waves me off and moves toward the kitchen. "I'll make popcorn."

"There is no way you're still hungry." I think he sampled something from every food vendor at that market.

"The heck you say."

I shake my head and rush off, and once I'm safe behind my bedroom door, I lean against it and try to slow my breathing. My stomach is doing backflips, my head is spinning, and I am literally the epitome of everything I said I would never be—the giddy schoolgirl with a big, fat crush, and it's starting to get away from me.

"I'm putting butter on this!" Finn calls from the other room, snapping me back to reality.

He's my friend. He's *just* a friend. I will not lose my head over a guy.

"It's already buttered!" I call back, rushing around to find clothes that are comfier than jeans.

"It needs the real stuff!"

Once I'm in sweatpants, I come back into the kitchen to find Finn ruining a bowl of perfectly good popcorn with what has to be a whole stick of butter. He's also making two mugs of hot chocolate, which he douses with whipped cream because "whipped cream makes everything better."

I queue the movie, we plop down onto the couch, and I quickly learn that Finn is a movie-talker. He narrates his favorite scenes, and frankly, I'm surprised he doesn't get up and dance the entire "Hot Chocolate" number. He's engrossed in the entire thing. Watching *him* watch the movie is more entertaining than the movie itself.

As it ends, he clicks the pause button on the credits and turns to face me. "Honest reaction?"

"I really liked it," I say, surprised to realize I'm telling the truth. "Except for the creepy elves."

"They are *so* weird looking. Plus the hobo on the train, what the heck is that doing in a kid's movie?" Finn laughs.

I scrunch my face. "Super weird." The room is lit only by the white lights of the Christmas tree and the dim glow of the TV, and there's something soft and magical and calm about it.

I go still, but notice how content I feel right now. "I really have to thank you," I say, thinking over the whole day.

"For what?"

I shrug. "For hanging out with me again. It was . . . fun."

"Wait. Did you use the F-word again?" He angles toward me, one arm draped along the back of the couch.

"I'll try not to make it a habit."

"You might want to." He goes still. "You know I'd hang out with you anytime, Hart. That's what friends do."

Yes. Friends. *Just friends.* He finally seems to have accepted that, and now I'm the one who's struggling? I have *got* to get a hold of myself.

I nod. And because I desperately need some distance, I stand and pick up the empty popcorn bowl. I walk into the kitchen, but he grabs the mugs and follows me.

"You know, there's something I've been wanting to ask you about," he says.

I glance back. "Oh?" I set the bowl in the sink.

"Justin . . ."

"I wondered if you'd ask about that." I wince. "I can't believe I told you—my sisters don't even know."

"You had to tell someone," he says, like it's no big deal.

"Like I needed to give you more reasons to think I'm a total disaster." I try to match his nonchalance, but I think I fail.

"You're not a *total* disaster," he jokes. "Just a tiny one."

I shoot him a look as I turn on the faucet and rinse the bowl.

"I'm glad you told me. It's nice to see there's a side of you that doesn't have everything all figured out," he says.

I flick the water off, and he motions for me to hand him the bowl.

He picks up a towel, dries it, then hands it back, and I put it away.

"I definitely don't have everything figured out," I say, realizing it's true. I close the cupboard and face him.

He moves an inch closer. "Nobody does."

"Yeah, I'm starting to realize that." I lean back against the counter. I should make an excuse to go back into the living room, but I don't. Instead, I stay still.

"So, what did you want to ask me?" I chew the inside of my lip, suddenly nervous.

"Not a question, really," he says, shaking his head. "More of a clarification."

"Okay."

"It's not that you don't want to be with someone," he says, like he's thought about this. "You just don't want to be in love with the person you're with."

I avoid his eyes. "Pretty much."

"That's weird," he states.

"It wasn't when I thought of it," I say. "Part of me likes the idea of having someone . . ." I press my lips together, suddenly warm.

"And the other part?"

326

"Hates the idea of giving someone else the power to hurt me."

"Ah"—he lifts his chin—"so it's a control issue."

"No, it's—" But I go quiet. Because maybe it was? Maybe it still is. When our eyes meet, and I find his filled with concern and understanding, and I see a future where I don't have control.

And that's terrifying.

He moves closer, looking at me so intently it makes my toes curl. He reaches up and brushes my hair away from my face, fingers skimming softly against my cheek as he does.

"I would never do that," he says.

I drag my gaze to his. "You don't know that."

"Yeah, I do." The words are firm, but his touch is soft. He brings his free hand to my waist, eyes fixed on me as his thumb sweeps across my bottom lip.

I look into his eyes and silently count to three. "What are we doing?" I whisper.

"Nothing," he says, with a smile. "What are *you* doing?"

Trying not to think about how much I liked having your arms around me on that ice rink. Trying not to let myself get swept away in a moment that I know will end badly. Trying to remember all the reasons that you and I don't make sense. Trying to stay in control.

But I don't say any of those things. Instead, I say, "I'm not sure."

Warmth from his hand on my skin radiates through my entire body. The heat of his grasp on my hip makes my pulse quicken. Without letting go, he moves in closer, his feet bracketing mine, and I inhale his familiar, masculine scent.

"This is crazy," I say, desperate to access the part of my brain where the common sense lives.

"Because you don't want to feel anything," he says, still watching me. "Right?"

"Right." My voice is so weak even I don't believe me.

"So you don't want me to do this—" He leans in and presses a kiss to the soft spot under my ear. Then he hesitates, like he's giving me an out.

I don't take it.

"Or this—" He drags his mouth down my neck, pausing at the dip in my collarbone, then looks at me again. Again, I remain still. "And you *really* don't want me to—" His hand tightens around my waist as he reaches up and moves my sweater aside to reveal my bare skin, kissing all the way to my shoulder in long, drawn out movements. He stops and looks at me. "Right?"

I shudder a breath. My face is hot, my palms are sweating, and the only thing I can think is, *do that again.*

Instead, I whisper a quiet, thin, "Right."

One more soft kiss, then Finn carefully shifts my sweater back over my shoulder. "Okay, fair enough." He takes a step back. "You're in control here."

Disappointment floods my entire body, and my muscles tense at the realization that I did not want him to stop. I wanted his lips on mine. I wanted his body even closer.

I want Finn.

Oh my gosh. I want Finn.

He drops his hand from my waist, but before he moves away, I grab his arm. "Wait."

He turns back, and for once, I don't *want* to listen to the voices telling me all the reasons this is a terrible idea. I just want Finn.

I grab onto his sweatshirt and pull him flush against me.

He wraps his arms around me and holds me tight, looking at me like if he blinks, this will all go away.

But it won't go away. I've tried to make it go away.

"I really want to kiss you," he says, breath ragged, like it's taking every ounce of willpower *not* to.

I don't want to think right now. I don't want reason and logic to be a part of the conversation in my mind.

My breath hitches, and I hold his gaze as his eyes search mine, seeing me in a way no one ever has. I reach up and press my hand against the side of his face, then pull him lower until finally our lips meet.

He takes my face in his hands, kissing me so fully, so intently, that I lose my breath.

My head spins. His lips search mine, firm but soft, and I force myself not to think, not to worry what this means, not to let reason get in the way right now. In this moment, there's only Finn and me, and I like it that way. Our bodies are close as he deepens the kiss, my heart racing with desire for this man I shouldn't want but really, really do.

He pulls back and breathes my name on a shaky exhale, still holding my face, eyes searching feverishly for a place to land.

My lips tingle, and reality sets in. "Oh my gosh." I cover my mouth with my hand, eyes wide, searching. "Oh my gosh." My other hand rests on his chest, the remnant of that kiss still hanging in the space between us.

"Don't freak out," he says calmly.

I shake my head and clear my throat.

He steps back from me, and his hands move to my arms. "You're freaking out."

"I think—" I look away.

"Hart," he says. "Talk to me."

"I'm so sorry." I shake my head. "That was a mistake."

Chapter Thirty-Seven

Raya

I am not in control.

I let my emotions take over the reasoning part of my brain, and now that reason has returned, my mind is spiraling. Nobody has ever kissed me so intently, so purposefully. This isn't just me getting caught up in my feelings—it's more than that. Finn has the power to wound me—more than anyone else ever could.

How did I let myself get in so deep?

I push past him into the living room trying to calm my loopy, fluttery, ridiculous feelings—the ones I always avoid. The ones that are exactly why I started my dating experiment in the first place.

And even though that failed, that doesn't change the reason I did it.

How do I undo feelings? I'm usually so good at keeping them in check, at keeping everyone at arm's length, at never getting close enough to risk the real thing.

I'm close now, and I don't know how to back out.

He follows me into the living room. "Raya, I'm sorry if—"

I cut him off. "That can't happen again." I hear the uncertainty in my own voice. Or maybe what I really hear is fear.

He straightens. "We've been dancing around this thing for months."

I take a step back. "See, this is why I knew being friends with you was a bad idea."

"Because you realized you actually want to be more than friends?" He isn't backing down. Why isn't he backing down?

I feel myself get defensive. "No. Because this is what you do. You flirt and turn everything into a game. It's confusing."

"It's not a game," he says, voice tense. "Look, I know you appreciate bluntness, so let me say it plain so there's no confusion." He waits until I dare to meet his eyes. "I have feelings for you. Real ones. And I'm sick of pretending I don't because it might freak you out. I don't care if you're freaked out. Maybe you need to be freaked out if that's what it's going to take to get you to admit there's something here."

I freeze for a split second, turn a circle, then rush over and flip on one of the lamps. It's too *romantic* in here with the white lights of the Christmas tree.

He moves toward me. "Listen, I know you think what you want is someone just like you. But have you ever considered that maybe you need someone who is completely opposite of the guy you have in your head?"

He takes another step toward me, and I turn away, holding up a hand. I'm so conflicted, feelings raw and exposed in a way that makes me feel ashamed.

I've shown him too much. *I want him too much.*

He stops moving, but he doesn't stop talking. "Maybe you need someone who knows that sometimes you fall apart. Someone who gives you permission to not have everything figured out all the time."

I shake my head, but his words burrow straight into my soul because there is a part of me, a quiet part at the back of my mind, silently wanting exactly what he's offering.

"Tell me I'm wrong, and I'll drop it," he says.

Our eyes meet. My heart is racing, and it's hard to catch my breath.

But I don't say anything. Because I can't lie to him when he so obviously knows the truth.

"Raya," he says, voice soft. "I know you don't take me seriously. You think I'm a total screwup, and I get it. I play into that. And I let you believe I treat you the same way I treat everyone, but I don't." He moves around in front of me so we're face-to-face. "This is me throwing my hat in the ring. I'll go head-to-head with any guy who thinks he can love you better than I can if that's what you want me to do." He takes my arms and waits until I look at him. "All I'm asking for is a chance."

There's desperation in his voice. And it scares me because it sounds real. And honest. And I can almost believe it could work.

Almost.

"Finn," I say his name on a sigh. "You know we would be terrible together."

"Are you kidding?" he says. "We'd be awesome. We *are* awesome."

"We are *so* different," I say. "We want different things."

"I think when it comes to what actually matters, our

priorities are pretty much the same." The words are laced with frustration.

I inhale a slow, deep breath, look him straight in the eyes and say, "You should go."

Disappointment spreads across his face, but after a beat, he drops his hands, nods, and takes a step back, then grabs his coat off the back of a nearby chair.

I push my hands through my hair. "You don't want to be with someone like me, Finn."

"You're right. I don't want to be with *someone like you.*" He pauses until I look at him. "I just want to be with *you,* Raya. What are you so afraid of?"

I try to swallow, but my throat is dry, and I can't find the words I want to say.

He stands there for a long moment, then sighs. "Fine. I'll back off—because you asked me to, but it won't change how I feel," he says. "The ball's in your court now."

He shrugs his coat on and slips out the door, and it's only then that I realize I'm holding my breath. I let it out in a long, slow stream and walk over to the window, inching the curtain back slightly, and watch as he gets in his Jeep and slowly pulls away.

Once he's out of sight, I back away from the window and realize that this changes everything. I can't keep pretending that this thing between Finn and me is a playful flirtation. His feelings are real.

And as much as I don't want to admit it, so are mine.

What am I so afraid of?

Chapter Thirty-Eight

Raya

What am I doing here?

I've been to Comets' games before, but I don't usually sit with the girlfriends and wives. Usually, when I'm here, I'm working, and that's how I prefer it. I know how to be professional.

I do not know how to be casual.

It's not my favorite feeling, being out of place, but if this past month has taught me anything, it's that once I get in, the water's usually fine.

Which is why, when Eloise asked me to come, I said yes.

We find our seats in the arena, and I put myself between Poppy and Eloise and try to pretend I'm not searching the ice for a glimpse of Finn—the real reason I agreed to come to this game. As if seeing him will be enough.

Can I microdose a person?

The day after the kiss, I woke up full of regret, not because we kissed but because I pushed him away. It's been two full days of replaying it, and every time I get to the second I told him to go, my stomach wrenches.

I screwed up.

But I can't figure out how to fix it. What would I even say?

I screwed up. I'm sorry. That was the best kiss of my life, and it scared me. Did you still want that chance because—

Some of the women who came to the market file into the row behind us while Monica takes a seat on the other side of Poppy. We all say our hellos, and I listen as the conversation turns to kids and husbands and things that don't involve me. I try to pay attention because I need the distraction, but it's hard.

After a few minutes, Eloise shoots me a look. "Are you okay? You seem tense. I mean, more than usual."

I fold my hands and watch as the Comets take the ice for their warm-up. "I'm just trying to figure things out now that I'm back," I say, which isn't a lie but also not the whole truth. "It's hard not to fall right back into the same schedule."

Poppy squeezes my arm. "I like that you're lightening your load. Sometimes it feels like you think you have to conquer the world instead of just, you know, living in it."

I study the players on the ice, searching for Finn's number—twenty-two. Most of the guys are out there hamming it up with the fans, exactly the kind of thing he'd want to be doing.

So where is he?

Dallas throws a puck up in the air and catches it on the end of his stick. Then he skates to the other end of the ice, serving the puck like it's on a platter to a kid holding a big sign that says, "Can I get a puck, Burke?" The kid takes the puck and holds it over his head, a huge grin on his face. Dallas smiles as he starts back down the ice for some pregame drills.

I squint, scanning the area around the ice, still searching for Finn.

"For someone who hates hockey, you sure are engrossed," Eloise says. "They're not even playing yet."

"What else am I supposed to look at?" I keep my tone light, but I feel caught. I don't want to be teased about this—it feels monumental to me—but they don't know anything about how I feel about Finn and my conflicted emotions. I haven't told them.

Why?

Just tell them you're happy. Tell Finn you're happy. Tell Finn he makes you happy.

Why is that so hard?

Because I'm supposed to be independent? Because I'm supposed to take care of myself?

Is that it—am I afraid of needing someone else?

I go still.

I'm afraid of needing someone else.

I'm afraid of needing someone who might change his mind about me. Someone who might leave. I've always been good on my own—why is Finn messing with that now?

The swirl of thoughts and emotions pinballing around my brain make me feel fidgety from the inside out. I hate when things aren't cut and dry. I hate that none of this makes sense.

Why don't emotions make sense?!

My knee bounces as I watch the guys start to file into the tunnel, a bunch of pucks still on the ice until Dallas shoots them all into the goal. Gray is all business and skates off without looking back, followed by Crosby, Krush, and Kemp, who all wave at the fans as they go.

Jericho and Junior each take off in opposite directions, do

one last lap around the ice, meet in the middle in some sort of strange, testosterone-fueled ritual, and then the ice is clear.

"Raya, since we're all friends here—" Kari leans forward, but it's clear whatever she's about to say is not meant just for me. "Can we ask what's going on with you and Finn?"

There's a collective *"Ohhhh,* and my face lights on fire.

"You guys, you guys," Eloise says, "they're just friends."

A chorus of "Yeah, okay," and "Oh, I bet they are" rings out, and I shift in my seat.

"We really are friends." I say this with conviction, but my skin tingles at the memory of his body pressed against mine, his hands tangled in my hair, and the way his lips moved against my own.

"He's a good friend to have," Lisa says. "Last year, when Krush was injured, he showed up every few days to hang out with him. Rehab is super hard on these guys. It's lonely, and I think Finn saved him from getting really depressed."

"These guys are not themselves when they can't play," Monica says.

"These guys are *huge babies* when they can't play," Kari says, and the others laugh.

I picture Finn showing up the same way for me. Getting me out of the house. Taking me to the tutoring club. Getting the tree, then coming back to decorate it. What was he saving me from by doing that? I doubt I would've made good use of my time off without his help.

"I still can't get over how he saved that tutoring club," Kari says.

"*That* was really sweet," Monica adds.

"Wait, what do you mean?" I turn around.

"Okay," Kari scoots forward in her seat like she has a

story she can't wait to share. "So you know how the guys get fan mail all the time—there was this one kid, a die-hard fan, who wrote almost every day asking for help saving this tutoring club where he went after school. I think he thinks the guys are like superheroes or something—it really was so sweet." She beams, like she loves this story.

"He said that the club helped his family because his dad was sick or deployed or something"—she flicks her hands in the air—"and his mom worked a lot of hours. He was scared they'd have nowhere to go if the club closed."

The image of Grace and her brothers appears in my mind.

"Right, but the club didn't have enough money to keep going," Kari says. "So Finn gets wind of this and decides to fund it. He donates money every month to keep them open."

He . . . what?

"He's also convinced a bunch of the guys to go volunteer there, and he's brought most of those kids to games," Monica says.

"You're kidding," I breathe.

Kari shakes her head. "Nope. That place would no longer exist if not for Finn Holbrook."

"I didn't know about any of that," I say slowly. "I've actually been there."

"Well, Brookie saved it," Lisa says.

"Brookie." Monica giggles. "Everyone's favorite."

I think about the way the people at the tutoring club responded when they saw Finn. Not just the kids, but the adults too. No wonder they all love him so much.

I go still, and Eloise leans in. "See? I told you he was a good guy."

"I knew he was a good guy," I say, mostly to myself.

I just didn't know he might actually be good for me.

His words rush back.

I got you.

And I believe him. My mind is frantic, an overloaded processing system that can't sort through the information fast enough. And then, it's like a switch flips in my head, or a searchlight stops scanning the clouds and lands on one specific spot.

I believe him, and I *want* to take the risk. Even though it's scary. Even though it might end. Because . . .

"I love him." The words are out, barely a whisper, and I can't take them back.

Both Eloise and Poppy look at me like they aren't sure I said anything.

"What did you just say?" Poppy asks, shock in her voice.

I look at her. "I—You guys. I love him."

Poppy's eyes go wide. "You love him? Finn?"

I nod. Tears spring to my eyes. My thoughts are like gates that swing wide open, finally letting the outside world in. I've been trying to reason with myself, but what if I don't have to explain it? What if I just have to accept it?

I love Finn, and if the ball's in my court, I need to take a shot.

"I need to take a shot!" I lean forward and say this so loudly the other women all stare at me, confused.

"What's happening now?" Kari asks, eyebrows drawn downward.

"She loves Finn!" Eloise says, practically squealing.

I feel excited, frantic, and unable to sit still. I start talking fast. "I have to find him. He said I was in control. He said that right after we . . . and then we talked about . . . I have to find him. I have to find him and tell him that I love him." I scoot forward, looking from Eloise to Poppy and back, unsure what to do next. My hand goes to my head. "I'm finally ready. I'm scared, but I'm ready. He makes me happy —I *want* to be happy."

I jump up, and my sisters do the same.

"There's only about twenty minutes before the puck drop," Poppy says.

I stare at her. "I have no idea what that means."

Eloise grabs my arm. "It means we have to hurry!" She starts walking, tripping over two guys at the end of our row.

"Where are we going?" I rush up the stairs of the arena, Poppy close behind.

"We're going to find Finn!" Eloise shouts. "This is huge! We can't risk you chickening out!"

"I won't chicken out!" Not again.

We reach the top of the stairs and start running, then Eloise comes to an abrupt stop. "I don't know how to get there from here."

I laugh. "Follow me."

We push through the crowd, Eloise shouting, "Get out of the way! Move it, people—my sister's in love! Finally!" All three of us are laughing, rushing through the hallways, past the restroom lines, down three flights of stairs. I have to flash my VIP lanyard to get access to a back hallway that leads to the locker rooms.

We're stopped four times, and each time I show my badge, one of my sisters explains that I have fallen head over heels in love, maybe for the first time in my whole life, and a path needs to be cleared so I can tell Finn Holbrook immediately.

Once upon a time, I might've been mortified by this, but

right now, fueled by the kind of delusion that only comes from the heart, I'm okay with it.

We rush around the corner at the end of a hallway and reach the doorway of the locker room, where yet another security guard stands at attention.

We all stop, breathing heavy, and it's Poppy who says, "We have to talk to Finn Holbrook immediately."

I'm bent over, trying to catch my breath, and I hold my badge up so the guy can see it.

"Please, it's an emergency," Poppy says.

"A romantic emergency," Eloise says.

"A what now?" the man says.

"A work emergency," I say. "We need to see him before the game starts."

He looks at his watch. "Ma'am they're about to go out."

"I'll be quick." I stand upright.

He looks at all three of us, suspicion on his face. "Stay here."

He disappears behind the door, and I look at Poppy, then Eloise, fear knotting in my stomach. "Oh my gosh. What am I going to say?"

"Just be honest," Eloise says, smiling.

I cover my face with my hands and let out a loud, hearty laugh. I love Finn. I'm *in love* with Finn. I'm terrified. It could all go up in flames. I might get *really* hurt. But I have to at least try, right? I owe him the chance he asked for.

"I can't believe this," Poppy says. "You finally came to your senses!"

I smile at her, so thankful for these two sisters and how beautifully they've grown up. Two strong, independent women who don't need a big sister to look after them anymore—just a friend to come alongside them.

Which is exactly what they are to me.

The door opens, and my breath catches in my throat. But it's the security guard, not Finn. He looks at me, then at my sisters. "Sorry, ladies, Holbrook isn't back there."

My heart stops. "What?"

"Seems he took off for Christmas a day early," the guard says. "Left for Montana last night."

Wait. What? He didn't tell me.

But then, why would he when he promised to give me space?

"Game's starting in five," the man resumes his post. "Better get back to your seats."

I look at Poppy, then Eloise, still feeling like all of my nerves are firing at the same time, unsure of what to do next.

And then, in a flash—I know.

I see a picture of Finn in my head. It's from the first time I saw him seven years ago, and I realize I never updated that image. I kept him in that box, seeing him as that twenty-two-year-old kid. Goofy and unserious—and in my head, those were always flaws that kept me from looking deeper.

My mind runs through a series of memories with the updated picture of Finn fresh in my mind. Smiling. Laughing. Picking up Bodie and tossing him over his shoulder. Singing Christmas songs at the top of his lungs. Showing up on my porch with a box of Christmas decorations or a white chocolate mocha.

I see him in Poppy's Kitchen, sleeves rolled, apron on, ready to jump in and help.

On the ice, celebrating, cheering, *living*.

I see cinnamon toast and Advil and tiny gourmet chocolates.

I hear the tiny voice on the other end of his FaceTime

call, so worried that he's okay, and the way he spoke to his mother—not like she was a nuisance—but like she mattered.

I see this man, who's shown me the value of fun despite the depth of pain he hides behind that wide smile. And I start to think these little things all add up to big things. These little things all add up to Finn living like it matters.

It's not accidental. He is the way he is and does the things he does on purpose.

Which means making his feelings known was a choice.

The picture of him in my head was so outdated. The realization shocks my heart like a jolt of electricity.

He showed up for me.

And now it's time I showed up for him.

Without saying another word, I pull out my phone and open a browser to a blank webpage.

I type in "Flights from Chicago to Montana" and click Go.

Chapter Thirty-Nine

Raya

This is insane.

But somehow it still makes sense.

It helps that my sisters are cheering me on. They even come with me back to my place to help me pack, and I tell them the entire truth about Finn, starting with the first time we met and ending with that knee-buckling kiss in my kitchen. I don't even mind when they squeal, because if I were a demonstrative person, I'd be squealing too.

Instead, I stand there, embarrassed, trying to be okay with the rush of emotion.

They make me promise to stop keeping things from them, even though Eloise seems a little too pleased to hear I'd been fired from that job. Considering how many times she's been fired, I should've known she would understand.

And yet, for some stupid reason, probably my pride, I couldn't let on that I didn't have everything figured out all the time.

I've been so stupid.

The whole way to the airport, they coach me on what I

should say, and by the time I get out of the car at O'Hare, I have a whole script memorized.

"Finn, you were right," I recite. "I didn't want to admit that there's something between us because I'm stubborn and pigheaded and—"

"Proud," Eloise fills in.

"And proud," I roll my eyes at her. "Can't forget 'proud.'"

"I think you should chuck the speech and just kiss him," Eloise says as Poppy pulls up next to the sidewalk in front of my airline's departure terminal.

"That would work too," Poppy says, a conspiratorial gleam in her eye.

At the mention of kissing Finn, my face gets hot and my fingers go cold. The image of his disappointed face flickers through my mind. Disappointment I caused because I was scared. I hate that my fear hurt him even for a second.

I shove the thoughts out of my brain and focus on a plane landing overhead.

It's dark, and the airport lights spill out onto the sidewalk. I stare at the door, clutching my bag, still fueled by pure adrenaline. It's surreal that I'm even here.

Eloise jumps out and opens the door, then grabs my arm and pulls me out onto the sidewalk.

Poppy joins us, leaving her car door open.

A traffic cop blows a whistle. "Hey! No parking!"

Poppy waves and smiles at her. "We'll just be a minute!"

"Back in your vehicle, ma'am!" The cop starts moving toward us.

"Shoot. We're in trouble," Poppy says. "We have to go, but you're going to be fine. Just be honest. Speak from the heart."

Eloise does a little dance. "Pull him into a closet and grab onto him and—"

The whistle is so loud we all jump, then laugh, then they pull me into a tight hug.

"Okay, I'm going," I say, then I look at them with wide eyes. "I'm doing it." *Oh my gosh, I'm doing a grand gesture. Who even am I?*

"Sleep on the plane," Poppy says.

"Yeah, you're gonna need your energy for Finn." Eloise wags her eyebrows, and I roll my eyes, hugging them both once more before I race off into O'Hare.

Later, after a stereotypically predictable delay, I'm finally looking out the window of a plane headed to Montana.

The drone of the white noise and the darkness of the sky make me drift off, the image of Finn's face filling my mind. And when I wake up to the bump of the landing gear hitting the ground at Billings-Logan International Airport, my nerves ramp right back up.

Time to make a fool of myself for a boy.

Finn

I'm home.

When I wake up on Christmas Eve morning, it takes me a minute to remember where I am. Copper Ridge Ranch. Silverwood. I showed up yesterday to touch base with the board of the community center here.

I knew from emails with Jane, who pretty much runs everything, that the center had grown. By quite a bit. It's now extending beyond families in need to families who want to be part of what's happening.

It's one thing to hear about it over an email—it's a whole other thing to see it in action.

I'm told the way this place has brought our little community together has been an unexpected by-product of the decision to open in the first place.

We have a fundraising team, along with volunteers who work directly with the kids, from after-school programs to tutoring to serving food. There are always ideas for making an impact, and while I can't be here regularly, it's nice to know almost my entire family is involved in some way.

Last month, Rowe brought a group of kids out to the ranch to teach them about horses—which is hilarious because growing up, she was the one who never paid attention. My mom makes all the after-school meals, and I'm pretty sure even my brothers helped with the center's first annual Christmas party. We're expecting a great turnout, and I knew I had to be here to help, even if it meant missing a game.

Yesterday, after a big, family meal at the ranch, I spent a good portion of the rest of the day in meetings discussing a possible expansion of the community center. I never planned to start a nonprofit, but after getting involved in the tutoring club back in Chicago, it felt like something I could do for my hometown.

Maybe I was always meant to find Brady's letter, addressed to "Dear Chicago Comets." Reading it made me realize that while I can't impact the whole world, I can help impact one person . . . and that might mean the whole world to them.

When I visited his tutoring club and met the kids and

people running it, it hit me that I could do more than give money. I could give time. I could get to know these kids. Maybe even make a difference.

That whole experience inspired me to buy this building and start something similar in Silverwood. My parents helped get it up and running, but we realized pretty quickly we needed more help, which is when we hired Jane.

I imagine I'll end up back here one day, maybe working with the community center, maybe working on the ranch. And even though I'm not ready to walk away from hockey just yet, I know that when the time comes, I've got a lot to look forward to.

I stare at the ceiling of my childhood bedroom, which looks a lot like it did before I went away to school. Medals and trophies line shelves and walls, along with newspaper clippings and photos from the good years of growing up here.

My feet still hang off the end of the bed. I'd gotten so used to it that I still scoot down sometimes to fall asleep.

A photo of all of us kids on a hike to Two Medicine Lake in Glacier National Park catches my eye. It's pinned to a bulletin board over a too-small desk, and I wonder if I'll ever look at it without the pang of sadness. The memories are good, but the loss is so great it's hard to think about them.

The letters.

I didn't leave them in the glove box—maybe I should've—but I didn't. They're now shoved in the side pocket of my laptop case. Why did I bring them with me? Why do I keep them at all?

As if it's not hard enough to put it all out of my mind now that I'm back home.

Or maybe I want to show them to my parents, get their

permission to toss them in the fire without ever reading them.

I get up, take a shower, get dressed, and walk out into the kitchen. Momma told me last night she has some things to do in town, then said something about "having a chat when she got back," which was odd since Momma doesn't usually "have chats." When she wants to say something, she just says it. I didn't press her, though, mostly because I was exhausted.

The coffee is made, and there are fresh cinnamon rolls on the stove with a note from Rowena:

Made these for you, Skip. Let me know what you think. —Rowe

I pick one up, take a giant bite, then close my eyes to savor the taste.

Man, that's good.

Rowe inherited Momma's love of baking, and over the summer my brother, West, built her a little "on your honor" farmstand that sits along the road near the Copper Ridge gate. Rowe got the idea from some girl on social media, and last I heard, she's making some money.

Once I've inhaled two cinnamon rolls, I grab another one and pour myself a cup of coffee. I shove my feet in my dad's work boots, shrug on a coat, and step out onto the porch. I pause because this is the view I live for, and I've missed it. I love the energy of Chicago, but there is nothing like the big sky of home. I pull my phone out of my pocket and snap a couple of photos.

Like everything else, this makes me think of Raya. I

should've told her I was leaving, and I feel bad about that now, but I said I'd back off. Give her space. I didn't want to go back on that, but that doesn't mean I've stopped thinking about her since that kiss.

For a flicker of a moment, I actually thought finally my patience had paid off. I let myself believe she realized that what I said was true—we're *great* together.

I should've known she'd get cold feet. The woman is a beautiful, frustrating, amazing pain in the neck.

I wonder what she's doing right now.

I blow out a breath and try to stop thinking about her. I can't fix anything until I get back anyway.

Since everyone's busy this morning, I decide to head over to the community center to see if there's anything I can do to help before the party tonight. When I was there yesterday, I was mostly in meetings, talking with the new volunteers, and touring some of the renovated rooms—now outfitted with more technology to keep up with today's kids.

It's important to me that I connect with the people who are making this all happen, and I know they're going to be decorating and prepping most of the day.

I grab my laptop and keys, then hop in Pop's work truck, and drive toward town, carefully balancing my open mug of coffee.

I take in the big, open views as I drive into downtown Silverwood, struck with a pang of nostalgia when I see the familiar Christmas decorations downtown. Tonight, the entire street will glow from strings of lights hung on lampposts, zigzagging from one side to the other. There's a Santa booth at the end of one block, and all the stores are decorated for the holiday. People rush around, trying to finish last-minute shopping, and I flip on a Christmas station to get in a festive mood, something I just haven't been feeling lately.

I park outside a nondescript brick building a few blocks from downtown and spot Momma's red truck parked a few spots over. I don't understand why she still drives that thing —it's more rust than truck—but I think there's sentimental value she's hanging onto with Ol' Red.

A mom and her two young kids walk into the building. I think Momma said there's childcare all day for working parents or those who don't have uninterrupted Christmas shopping time. This place is making an impact.

Right here where we are.

I get out of the truck and walk toward the building, eyes fixed on the mountain range in front of me. I take my phone out and snap another photo, then tuck it into my pocket and walk inside.

The building has been great, but the community center is already out of space. The expansion is going to require a lot of fundraising and maybe a grant or two. But after yesterday's meetings, we have a solid plan.

When I walk in, I stand in the lobby and get my bearings. There's no one at the front desk, but I hear voices coming from one of the three large activity rooms. I start walking toward the door when I hear someone call my name.

I turn and find my mom marching toward me. She looks . . . worried?

"Hey, Momma." I saunter toward her. She grabs my arm and turns me around. "What's going on?"

"I thought you'd come down later, after lunch," she says. "After our chat."

I frown. "I wanted to see if I could help. Maybe try on the Santa suit." My smile is faltering. Something is wrong.

She glances back toward the open door where the sound of Mariah Carey's "All I Want for Christmas is You" is playing. "Do you remember when I said I wanted to talk to you about the center?"

I shake my head. "No."

She waves a hand in the air. "It was last month. You were distracted, and Dad took the phone from me and probably gave you terrible advice on your love life."

I cross my arms. "He said he was put on the earth to admire you."

She bites back a smile. "That old flirt." She pats my arm. "That's where you get it, you know."

"Oh, I know." I grin. "But I get my good looks from you."

She sighs comically. "Will you go home and wait for me to come talk to you? Go help your dad with the horses."

"Momma, if it's a big deal, why didn't we have the *chat* yesterday?" I emphasize the word *chat* because she keeps using it like it's important.

"It was the first time we'd all been together in months," she says, visibly troubled. "I didn't want to spoil it."

"Okay. What's going on?" I ask. "Just tell me whatever it is."

She works the corner of her mouth between her teeth, then lets out a sigh. "Fine, but just know—"

But before she can say more, a woman with wiry blond hair walks out into the lobby. "Melinda, I wasn't sure if we were wrapping all the—" She sees me and stops short.

I start to introduce myself, but then I realize that I recognize this woman.

She's older now, but I see her face every time one of her stupid letters shows up.

I remember the trial. The way she sat there, stone cold

until it was time for her sentencing. Then, she had plenty of tears. And now she's standing right in front of me, in a place that I helped build.

Just her presence here mocks me and everything this place stands for.

I glare at Eileen. "What is she doing here?" My voice doesn't sound like my own. It's fueled by anger I don't like feeling.

"Finn, let's go outside," Momma says, trying to take me by the arm.

"No, I'll go," Eileen's eyes are glued to mine.

"Yeah, I think you should," I say.

"Finn!" My mom turns to Eileen. "Don't go, Eileen. Let's talk this through."

I look at my mom, feeling stabbed in the back. "How could you let her in here after what she did?" I take a step back, shaking my head, anger seething from a dark place inside. I turn to go.

"Finn, wait," my mom calls after me, but I don't turn around. Because how could she do this? I storm out the door and onto the street. How could she betray our family like this? She knows how we all feel about Eileen.

How can anyone who loved Hunter ever let her walk around here thinking that it's okay?

I get in the truck and slam my hand on the steering wheel, again and again. My palm starts to hurt, and I switch to rearing back and swinging my fist into the passenger seatback.

I hit it. I hit it again.

A group of carolers pass by, singing "Joy to the World." They're dressed in old Victorian costumes, and their happiness feels wrong given the way I feel right now.

Angry.

Frustrated.

Hurt. And more than anything—betrayed.

Chapter Forty

Finn

It's taking everything inside of me not to push the gas pedal all the way to the floor.

I drive out to the farthest edge of my family's property, white knuckles on the steering wheel, and a cloud of dust in my rearview mirror.

I wish that cloud could erase the past.

I'm headed to a small lake with a pristine view of the mountains. Something about it has always calmed me down.

And right now I need to calm down.

My phone keeps buzzing. I have three missed calls from my mom and one from my dad, but I don't want to talk to anyone right now. I don't want to hear explanations of how this happened, excuses about why this was a good idea, none of it. If Eileen was there—having a conversation with my mother about gift wrap—then that must mean they've all moved on.

Do my brothers and sisters know about this? Is everyone just okay with it?

What about Hunter?

I open the truck door, step out into the cold December air, and slam it shut with enough force to knock all of the loose change out of the inside door handle where Pop keeps it. It's cold enough to shock my lungs, but not so much that it stings my skin.

I crunch toward the lake. There's snow on it, but it's not frozen yet. Once I reach the shoreline, I take a second to study the scene in front of me. Hunter's spot. I don't even know if my brothers and sisters know about it, but he showed it to me. Probably because I never left him alone.

I pull out my phone and find Raya's number. I want to hear her voice. She's the smartest person I know, and I need her opinion. I hit the button and hold the phone to my ear, waiting for the call to connect. I get nothing but silence.

I pull the phone down and look at it—no signal.

Normally I'd love that, getting unplugged, away from connectivity, but right now I feel like I need a connection. To her, specifically.

I turn the phone off, open the truck door, and try to toss it onto the seat. It hits the center console and flips down into the space between the console and the driver's seat.

Gritting my teeth because of *course* it doesn't do what I want it to, I bend over and try to fish it out. With my arm crooked under the seat, two fingers pinching the phone, I see the corner of one of those stupid letters sticking out of the case on the floor of the passenger side.

It's there because I threw it there.

Something new rises up. Something other than anger or betrayal. It feels a lot like slamming the truck door.

Closure.

It's time to put a stop to all of this. To rip off the Band-

Aid and deal with it—whatever it is and however it makes me feel.

I won't forgive her. I won't do that to Hunter. But I need to put it behind me once and for all.

I reach inside the bag and pull out the first letter Eileen sent me a few years ago. I stare at it. It's folded in half and crumpled on the edges because I've almost opened it so many times.

I never had the courage.

But today I do.

I tear it open, rip out the plain sheet of white paper, and read.

> Dear Finn,
>
> It's been almost seven years since the day all of our lives changed. Years of regretting the stupid decision I made that day. The decision to drive after I'd had too much to drink. I don't know what I was thinking.
>
> Maybe I thought I didn't have that much. Or maybe I thought I could handle the short drive home. Whatever I thought, I know now it was wrong.
>
> I don't know why I'm writing to you. I'm sure you hate me, and I don't blame you. I hate me too. It's going to be a very long time before I forgive myself for what I've done. Actually, I'm not sure I ever will.

And I don't expect you or anyone in your family to forgive me either.

But I do want to tell you how sorry I am. I want you to know that my whole life is different now. *I'm* different now. And I'm going to dedicate the rest of my life to trying to make amends for what I've done. To figure out how I can help other people.

And I promise I'll never have a drink again.

I know that's no consolation considering what you lost, but I wanted you to know anyway.

When I think of the pain I've caused you and your family, it makes me sick. I go back to that night every time I close my eyes, and I wish I could hand the keys to someone else. I don't have any excuses, only apologies.

A whole world of apologies.

I'm so, so sorry.

I'll say Hunter's name out loud every day until the day I die as a way to always remember him.

Sincerely,
Eileen Tierney

I stare at the last sentence of Eileen's letter.

My first thought is *maybe keep his name out of your mouth.*

I make a point to *not* say Hunter's name out loud. Every time he comes to my mind, I feel the sting of losing him all over again.

Time heals all wounds? Yeah, right.

Before Raya, I can't remember the last time I told someone stories about the brother who was my best friend.

I haven't talked about him in a long, long time.

But then a thought occurs to me. *Why don't I talk about the good things?*

His lifetime of good things was erased by one horrific thing.

Isn't talking about how awesome he was a way to remember him? Isn't telling everyone how supportive, and crazy, and fun, and talented, and mischievous, and loving he was part of carrying on his memory?

Little by little, I've been erasing him from my life. Why? Because it hurts?

I look out at the lake. Have I been wrong?

Have I been wrong this whole time?

Lord. Maybe I have.

In silencing the hard things, I let the good things go quiet too. And there were *so* many good things. The way he stuck up for everyone, whether he knew them or not. The way he spread joy everywhere he went. The loyalty he showed to his friends. The way he'd get up before dawn every day before school to practice because he had a dream he believed in. He was fierce and loyal and good and kind.

All things he taught me to be.

My brother knew how to love with his whole heart. He never held back.

Nobody ever wondered where they stood with him.

He taught me that too.

Even his death taught me to appreciate every single day, every single experience.

A thought slips in without my permission. *Hunter would forgive her.*

I pretend the words aren't there. I try to focus on the lake. The mountains. The sky. But as I do, I hear it again.

Hunter would forgive her. And I know it's true. Because my brother never held grudges. Maybe he still has one more thing to teach me.

I sit with the word—forgiveness. It feels too good for her after what she did.

And then I remember what Raya said—"*Forgiveness isn't for her. It's for you.*"

Forgiving that woman isn't going to bring him back. It's not going to make it okay. But will it help me move on?

My legs stop supporting me, and I fall to my knees in front of the lake and the mountains. I feel small, insignificant.

And for the first time since Hunter's funeral, I break down and cry.

I don't try to stop it. Or hide it. I just let it all come, and I let myself feel the whole tidal wave of emotions. What should've happened years ago all happens now. I fall forward, my hands pressing into the snow to keep me from hitting the ground, and I mourn my brother.

I don't know how long I'm there, or how many tears I have left in my eyes—but I stay, wracked with emotion, until the crying is done. And when it is, I wipe my face dry and sit back up. My hands aren't cold, even though they've been plunged into the snow in front of me.

It's quiet.

Snow has a sound-deadening effect, and there's nothing except a quiet, almost silent crinkle of white noise.

I stand to my feet, brush off the snow, and walk down to the edge of the lake. I start to feel a quiet desire for a change, and I have to believe that's a step in the right direction.

Maybe this is the way it works—in fits and starts. One step at a time.

On the other side of the water, a white-tailed deer walks into a clearing. She freezes, ears fluttering as she looks right at me. I hold my breath for a long moment, not wanting to spook her.

She bends down, looking for grass beneath the snow, and I watch her for another minute. With a huff, she slowly trots back into the trees, disappearing from view.

I know what I need to do.

I'm back at the community center twenty minutes later, years of hurt left on the snowy shore of Hunter's lake. The letters, most still unopened, are in my pocket, except for the first one, which is balled up in my hand.

I pull the door open and walk into the lobby. There's no music playing, but voices are coming from the room, so I walk through the door and look around.

Just like back in Chicago, this tutoring club switches gears on days when there's no school. Instead of coaching kids in math and science, there are coloring pages, art projects, and Christmas crafts on the tables.

Down the hall, I hear the sound of foosball being played. I remember hauling the old table from the ranch's basement, fixing the leg that my brothers and I broke during one specifically heated game, and setting it up in the game room here last year.

I look around, expecting my mother to try and intercept me, but a quick scan of the room comes up empty, and I wonder if she went home thinking she'd find me there.

And then my eyes lock onto Eileen's. She's sitting in a big, oversized armchair with a little girl on her lap, pointing into the pages of a Dr. Seuss book. She stops reading and doesn't move.

I take a breath.

With my head, I motion back toward the door and nod a *Will you come with me?* at her. She catches her breath and stiffens, but then nods, handing the book and the child to another volunteer nearby.

I walk into the lobby first, not waiting for her. I keep my back to the door, but I don't need to turn around to know she's there.

"Finn, I—"

I hold up a hand. "I didn't come here to have some big conversation with you." I turn around, but it's hard for me to look at her. I guess one emotional by-the-lake session isn't enough to let go of years of habitual hatred.

And it's hard to hold onto my hate when there's a real human standing in front of me.

I hold up the balled-up letter. "I just read this today. It's the first one you sent."

Her face falls.

A battle wages inside of me. I want to yell years of pent-up rage at her, like a cannon, but I'm still clinging to the release I felt only a half hour ago.

"I'm not going to read the others, and I want you to stop sending them to me," I say. "Every time I get one, it ruins my day, and it makes me feel like crap. Because I still hate you for what you did."

She nods.

"And when I see your stupid name on the return address. . ." I ball up the letter tighter in my fist, holding it at her, letting the motion finish my sentence.

"I understand."

"But I don't like to be angry," I say, the softer side of me taking the lead momentarily. "It's not who I am."

She doesn't respond.

"It is not who I am." It bears repeating.

I push a hand through my hair, then scratch the back of my head. *What am I doing here?* I turn a circle, not sure what to do next. I want to leave. I don't want to give her the satisfaction of thinking that any of this is okay. It's not.

Nothing about what happened is okay. Nothing about what she did is okay.

But I am on my way to being okay.

I realize that I've been going about this the wrong way—not talking about Hunter. Living like I mean it includes not forgetting the reason why.

I bite the inside of my lip and shove the letter back in my pocket. "I don't like that you're volunteering here, but I assume my mother said it was fine."

"She did," Eileen says. "And in one of the more recent letters, I asked for *your* permission to be here. To help if I can."

"I didn't read it," I say coldly.

Her face falls. "I know."

"This doesn't make up for—"

"I know." Her eyes are wet with unshed tears.

A small, faraway piece of me is moved. My compassion is fighting with my conviction.

"Forgiveness isn't for her. It's for you."

I don't *feel* like forgiving her. I don't *want* to let her off the hook. I don't like that she put me in this position, and I hate that it feels like I'm betraying my brother. But still, I draw in a shaky breath and blow it out slowly. "I . . ."

I look at her. Her eyes are full of hope, and I sense something inside me shift. I'm not cruel. I don't want to become bitter or give my past the power to keep me from moving forward.

I hold the letter up at her once more, in my fisted hand. "I forgive you." I choke the words out. They don't feel honest, so I shove the paper in my pocket, put my hands on my hips, look her straight in the face, and say them again. "I forgive you."

"I—"

I hold up a finger at her, stopping her from saying anything else. "That's all I have to say."

I turn around, walk out into the street, get in my car, and shut the door. I can feel my heart in my chest, and I blow out a nervous breath. I don't feel like some huge weight has been lifted. I don't feel like I just fixed everything. I feel as conflicted as ever.

This is something I'm going to have to do over and over again until those things happen.

Little by little.

One step at a time.

Chapter Forty-One

Finn

Copper Ridge crests into view as I drive up over the rolling hill near my childhood home.

As I pull up I see several pickup trucks and SUVs parked outside. I don't have to walk inside to know that most of my family is in that house. After all, it *is* Christmas Eve.

I stare at the cars, parked this way and that, and I think it's foreshadowing of the craziness that awaits me inside that house. Come as you are, leave your stuff outside, and welcome to the family—thank you very much.

It's a nice thought after the ones I've been fighting with for the past hour.

I get out of the car and walk toward the house, struck by the smell of cinnamon the second I open the door. It's late morning, almost lunchtime, but the overcast skies make the house glow with light from the fireplace, mingling with the white lights of the Christmas tree in the living room. Pop and my brothers, Quent and Boone, are sitting in the leather armchairs, drinking coffee and most likely talking ranch business, but when they see me, they all stop.

It's the first time I've seen my brothers since I've been home.

Immediately, we're all kids again.

They jump up, hollering my welcome. Quent rears his hand back to clap mine, which I do, making that satisfying *pop*, and Boone wraps his arms around my midsection and tries to lift me off the floor.

Unfortunately for him, I've got two inches and twenty pounds on him now, and I sit on him.

"Might want to rethink your tactics, little guy." I feel him squirm beneath me.

"Get off me, you tub a' lard!" He tries pushing me, but I don't budge. He jabs me in my side, and I finally release my grip on him.

Quent shakes his head and sits back down.

"Where's everyone else?" I ask, pushing Boone over one last time.

"West is out back," Pop says. "Hudson and Hattie aren't here yet."

"The girls are here," Quent says. "And they expect piggyback rides and lots of presents from their rich uncle."

I laugh. "Guess I need to go shopping."

"Christmas is tomorrow, dude." Quent shakes his head like the disapproving older brother he is, but I ignore him and walk into the kitchen where Momma is kneading dough.

She looks up at me, caution in her eyes, but I smile and nod at her.

"Buttons and bows?" I ask when I spot the ingredients on the counter.

"Your favorite," she says. Then quietly adds, "The way to your heart was always through your stomach."

I lean against the counter. "You're not wrong there, Momma."

She stops. "I should've told you."

"Yeah. You should've told me," I say.

She nods, going back to the dough. "I was afraid you wouldn't understand."

"I don't." I pour myself a cup of coffee, something I never drink this late in the morning unless I'm home, where there's always a fresh pot on the counter. "That woman—"

She turns and faces me. "Has done her time."

I scoff and look away, thinking the rest of her life wouldn't be enough time. I have to remind myself, again, to forgive. I'm bad at this. I look at my mom. "Did she send you a letter too?"

"She sent us all letters, Skip," Momma says. "Every single person in the family. You think you were the only one she had to apologize to?"

That actually never occurred to me.

"And how each of you kids—and your father and I—responded to her was everyone's own personal decision." She looks at me. "I don't want to live my life angry and bitter. Do you?"

I close my eyes and force air into my lungs, her comment reinforcing my lakeside decision. "No. I don't."

She takes a towel in her hands, cleans them off, and then reaches up and pats my cheek. "I'm sorry I didn't talk to you about it first. I always planned to—" She looks away, puts her hands back on the towel, squeezing and wringing it. "I didn't know how to bring it up, but I should've found a way."

"You're right," I say. "You should've."

Her face changes. "Is this the way it's gonna be? You gonna be mad at me now too?" Her tone has that *Momma-didn't-raise-a-fool* sound to it.

I immediately straighten up. "No, ma'am." Then, after a pause, I add, "I just—"

I shake my head, not knowing how to finish.

She takes my hand and pulls me into a tight hug. "I know, Skip. I know. It's hard . . . but I got you."

I hesitate a long moment, then hug her back.

She holds me the way only she can, and when I exhale, some of today's anger dissipates, if only a bit.

"Uncle Finn!" Quent's oldest, Libby, rushes into the room and attaches herself to my right leg, while her sister Jordy grabs my left. It's a game we play every time I see them, one they never seem to tire of.

I walk around the house like Frankenstein, dragging them behind me until my quads burn or until Momma calls them in for a meal, whichever comes first. On my way through the kitchen, I tousle my little sister's hair.

"Rowena," I say. "Cinnamon rolls were good, for once."

She smacks my hand away. "You been out to the stables yet, lazy?"

"Uncle Finn! Don't stop!" The girls both giggle, and Jordy calls out, "Giddy-up!"

"Not yet," I say to Rowe. "Show me the new mare after lunch?"

She sticks out her chin at me and nods.

The side door opens and West, walks in. "Anyone know whose car that is?"

"Boots off," Momma points at him without looking up.

"Ma'am," West calls out, like a sous-chef acknowledging

he heard the direction from his boss. He kicks one of his shoes off, and it hits the wall.

"Weston Thomas!"

"Sorry, ma'am!" He's mid-kick with the other one and it flings down the hall.

Boone winces and nudges the boot toward the boot mat. He walks over to the front window. "Who do we know with a—" he squints. "What is that? A Taurus? Camry?"

My mom frowns. "Nobody."

"Everyone we know drives a truck or an SUV," Rowe says.

West sees me for the first time and pulls me into a bear hug. He *can* lift me off the ground—and he does. Easily.

"Little bro. Welcome home. Looking a little slow out on the ice last week."

"It's the Chicago pizza, chubs." Boone calls, still staring out the window.

"Let's see you keep up, old man." I pull out of West's grasp and pinch his belly.

He wriggles back and gives me a shove—something that would normally escalate but doesn't, only because West is still trying to figure out why there's a sedan parked outside.

"There's someone in the car," Boone says, peeking out the window. "A woman?" He tips his head toward the front room. "Any one of you knuckleheads ask for a woman for Christmas?"

A throw pillow comes flying into the kitchen, and Boone ducks.

Momma's eyes dart to mine, and I know what she's thinking.

Eileen.

Is she crazy enough to come to our house? On Christmas Eve? I thought I made myself clear.

"I'll take care of it." Momma unties her apron, wipes her hands on a towel, then tosses it aside and pulls on her rubber boots. She grabs a jacket and walks out the back door, probably trudging through the yard like an angry neighbor sick of people tearing up her lawn.

I'm the only one not at the window now, because if it is Eileen, I don't want to risk going back on my decision to forgive her—and if I have to see her right now, I might.

Forgiveness isn't a one-and-done thing, I guess.

"Who the heck is *that*?" Boone asks.

"She's pretty," Libby says dreamily.

"Ooh, she *is* pretty," Rowe says. "Means she's not here for any of *you*," she cracks. "Probably needs directions."

I frown. Eileen is in her late fifties with wiry blond hair and frumpy clothes. I can't imagine my niece and sister would describe her as "pretty."

"Probably Boone's fault." Quent walks away from the window and refills his coffee. "He's left a whole string of broken hearts in this town."

"I can't help it if I'm irresistible," Boone says, wagging his eyebrows.

"You can help being a total *tool*, though," Rowe cracks.

I glance at Pop, who chuckles to himself but doesn't look up from the newspaper.

"But I can safely—and sadly—say I've never met that woman in my life," Boone says. "I could go now—" He tugs his pants up like he's about to make an entrance, but it's all bravado that quickly fades.

"The license plate says—" West squints out the window —"Pennsylvania. Is that a rental car?"

"Maybe you should just wait for Momma to come back in and tell you who it is," I say, trying to figure out if I have time to go Christmas shopping before we head over to the community center for the party.

"Momma doesn't look mad anymore, so I guess that's something," Boone says.

Quent walks back into the living room and sits down on the couch.

I pull my phone out of my pocket and see I've missed two calls and a text from Raya.

RAYA

Hey, not to seem like a crazy stalker but . . . is this your house?

<photo of Copper Ridge Ranch>

I check the timestamp and see that this text was sent fifteen minutes ago, right after I got home.

I jump up and look out the window. "Holy heck!" I rush over to the front closet, grab one of my dad's old work coats, pull on a pair of boots that are at least one size too big and ignore all the questions being hurled my way.

Raya is here. In Montana. At the ranch.

And she's talking to my mother.

Raya

"I'm so sorry to intrude, Mrs. Holbrook," I say, my third apology since Finn's mom walked out of the sprawling house at the end of the long driveway.

When Finn said he lived on a ranch, he failed to explain what that meant. This isn't just a farm with a bunch of cattle.

This is a whole operation. Acres and acres of open land, rolling plains against the most stunning backdrop I've ever seen. Now I understand why he doesn't like living in the city.

God vacations here. If I'd grown up on this ranch, I don't think I ever would've left.

"Don't be silly," his mom says. "And call me Melinda. It's nice to see you off the screen." She smiles.

"It's so nice to meet you in person." I smile, awkwardly, because *what am I doing here?*

"Does Finn know you're coming?" Her brow knits, almost like she thinks he's done something wrong. "I feel like he would've said something, but who knows with him." Her smile is kind.

"He actually *doesn't* know," I say. "It's a—" the words *grand gesture* race through my mind—"surprise?"

A new smile crawls across her lips. "Well, we should get you in—"

The door opens and Finn rushes out. His coat is half on, and judging by the way he's clomping toward me, his boots are too big for his feet. It's comical but endearing, and my heart swells at the sight of him.

The second I meet his eyes, I know I'm doing the right thing.

"Finn!" She lifts a hand and waves at him. "Raya's here!"

I don't take my eyes off him as he rambles up to us, practically skidding to a stop in front of me.

"I was about to warn her what she's in for when she comes inside," his mom says. She looks at me. "Only two of his siblings are missing at the moment, so it's a full house."

"I can't wait to meet them," I say, realizing I mean it. I want to know all of Finn's people.

"I'll give you two a minute out here first." She pats him on the shoulder and adds, "I haven't seen you move that fast on or off the ice in a while, Skip." She grins and walks back toward the house.

We stare at each other for a brief moment, and then start talking at the same time.

"What are you—"

"I should've told you—"

We both stop. I'm nervous, and I hold up a hand to say, *you first.*

"What are you doing here?" he asks. "You look—"

I push a hand through my hair and wince. "I know. I took a late flight, but we were delayed, and I slept on the plane, but not very well, and . . . it's been a long night."

"I was going to say you look beautiful." His eyes gleam, taking me in.

"Oh." I look away, feeling suddenly—shy? "Thanks."

He scrubs a hand over his chin, then says, through his fingers, "I can't believe you're here."

"I know," I fake curtsy. "In the flesh." I instantly regret the move and look around for something—anything—to say. "So this is where you grew up." Still haven't found the courage to give my prepared speech.

"Yeah, this is it," he says. "Do you . . . want me to show you around?"

"Yes," I nod. "I want to see all of it, but—maybe in a little bit . . ." Oh gosh, here it is. The moment of truth. I hate feeling so uncertain. So vulnerable.

If I do what I came here to do, I'm giving him the power to hurt me.

All it takes is one more look at him for my nerves to

settle, his words rushing back. *"I'll never do that."* The promise doesn't feel empty.

He shoves his hands in his pockets and watches me for a long moment, a lazy smile on his face, almost like he knows I'm working up the courage to say something big.

I avoid his eyes and chew the bottom of my lip. "I had a whole speech prepared, but now that I'm here, the only part I remember is"—I look at him, square in the eyes—"I love you."

The words tumble out like bowling pins accidentally knocked over, and I can't get them back. Oddly, I don't want to.

He freezes, and for a second, I'm not sure he heard me. He cocks his head and studies me. "Did you just say . . ." A smile breaks loose on his lips, and the hope I've been holding starts to take root.

"You were right," I say. "We're awesome together."

He looks at me like he's trying to rearrange my facial features because they don't quite make sense. "You actually *meant* to say that you love me . . ."

I wave him off with a quiet smirk. "Let me talk."

He holds up a hand. "Yeah, no, keep going, please."

I close my eyes and breathe deep. "When you kissed me, I got—"

"Freaked out," he interrupts. "Because you're scared of getting hurt."

"Finn." My tone is a mix between amused and exasperated.

"Oh. Sorry. Go ahead." He mimes zipping his mouth shut.

I nod. "Yes. I did freak out a little. But I realized I'm not so much scared of getting hurt as I am scared of letting myself . . . I don't know . . . *need* someone else. I've spent so much of my life moving from crisis to crisis or working to proactively avoid one. Always preparing for the worst . . . and never allowing for the best. The other shoe and all that stuff . . ." My voice trails off, and I wonder if I'm making any sense.

He nods slowly, watching me sort this all out because I still haven't gotten it all straight in my mind.

"I don't have all the answers," I say.

His eyes go comically wide, and I can practically *hear* the quippy gears churning up his response in his head.

"Shocking, right?" I grin. "I'm learning that it's okay not to have everything figured out."

He appears to be holding in a smile. He's failing.

"But I do know that you're kind." I sign the word as I say it. "And you're good. You saved the tutoring club because some kid you didn't know wrote a letter. And now you hang out with that kid and take him to see Santa. You show up for the people you care about—" I look at him. "And you showed up for me too."

"Twice." He grins.

"Twice," I agree. "Both times I was at my absolute lowest." My gaze drops to my shoes, and I kick at a piece of loose gravel. "So. That's it. I'm done being proud and stubborn, and I'm done not admitting when things are good. And fun."

His expression is disbelief, and I get it—part of me can't believe any of this either.

He steps closer, lifts his hand, and his thumb brushes across my cheek. His eyes catch the late morning light, sparkling with the promise of whatever comes next, and he looks at me so fully I wonder if anyone has ever seen me this clearly before.

"You said the ball was in my court," I say. "So, I guess this is me, shooting my shot."

He holds my gaze for three seconds that feel like three years, then says, "Slam dunk." He pulls me into his chest, arms tight around my back. His mouth crashes onto mine, and every ounce of nervous energy inside me melts away. All the true feelings I've held back rise to the surface as one hand rests at the back of my neck, holding my face so gently you'd think it was porcelain.

His kisses aren't tentative or polite—this is a man who knows what he wants. And I'm thrilled when I wrap my head around the idea that what he wants is me.

He pulls back, eyes searching, hands holding my face, thumb brushing softly across my cheeks in one smooth, gentle motion.

"I can't give you absolutes that this is going to go exactly as you planned."

I smile. "I know."

"And last I checked, I can't predict the future."

"I know that too."

"But," he touches his forehead to mine. "No matter what, the one thing I *can* promise is that whatever happens, we'll figure it out together." He leans in and kisses me again, eyes open, like he's afraid if he closes them this will all wash away.

"I believe you," I whisper.

He smiles against my mouth, and I smile right back. Then the front door of the beautiful, sprawling house swings open, and a loud commotion spills out, like a clown car filled with linebackers, onto the quiet lawn.

"Oh no," Finn says with a light laugh. "Are you even ready for this?"

I grin. "I'm so ready."

"You're about to get dropped in the deep end with the nosiest, loudest, most obnoxious—"

"Uncle Finn, what were you *doing* to her? Why were you sucking her face off?" An adorable little girl runs a circle around us, another little girl trailing close behind.

He pulls back, and we both laugh as the questions continue.

"Finn, bring that girl inside," his mom hollers from the porch. "You're both going to freeze out there."

"I dunno, she's keeping me warm because she's so hot," he calls back, followed by a chorus of "*Ohhhhh!!*" from his brothers.

"So, this is what I'm getting myself into with you, huh?" We start walking toward the house.

He shrugs, faux innocence on his face.

His hand slides down my arm and wraps around mine. He tugs me to a stop. "Oh, hey, before I forget . . ."

"Yeah?"

"I love you too."

Chapter Forty-Two

Raya

I can remember, as a child, watching a nature documentary about lionesses and their cubs. The cubs would fake pounce, tackle, wrestle, and roll around with one another, kicking up dust and not caring what they'd knock into, and the lionesses would just look on, making sure they didn't really hurt themselves.

Finn's family is like that.

The house is beautiful and homey, fun and loud, and raucous and lovely. And not at all what I imagined.

I did imagine it sometimes, because I don't know anyone who grew up on a ranch in Montana.

And because I spent a lot of time thinking about him.

I notice the line of shoes right inside the front door, and I quickly slip mine off.

"Oh, Momma's gonna love you." Finn nods at my stocking feet with a smile.

The lower level of the house is open, one room flowing into the next without walls or barriers, yet somehow, the space is cozy and inviting. From where I'm standing, I can see straight into the living room, where a group of guys is watching a football game. A pretty, younger woman is standing in the entryway along with Finn's mom and the two little girls.

"Don't worry, nobody expects you to remember everyone's names," Finn says, closing the door behind us.

But I'm determined to learn them all.

I smile up at him, and when my eyes catch his, a pang of desire rushes through me. What I really want to do is find somewhere quiet with *no* people so I can kiss him again and again until it feels like second nature.

My heart practically short-circuits at the thought.

Finn's mom motions for me to hand over my coat and looks down at my feet. She practically beams and says, "Honey, you are welcome here *any* day of the week. Someone raised you right!"

"She flew here to tell me she loves me," Finn grins.

"Finally wore her down, eh?" A guy sitting on a couch in the living room says.

"Well, come on—come inside. We'll introduce you to everyone," his mom says. "Finn, did you get her bag?" Then, to me, she adds, "We have plenty of room."

"Oh my goodness, no, I can stay at a hotel or—" I really didn't think this through. How very unlike me.

"Don't be silly," she says. "We have two empty cabins on the back of the property. It'll be nice and private."

"Should be more," one of the guys prods.

"Don't you start," their mom says.

"My brother thinks we should host tourists," Finn says, leaning toward me.

"It's a goldmine, but what do I know?" the guy says, hands raised.

"Ignore them, Raya. They're the worst." The younger woman smiles at me. "I'm Rowe. Youngest sister."

I smile. "Nice to meet you."

"We've heard a lot about you," she says.

My eyes find Finn's. "Oh?"

"Mostly that you're out of his league," one of the brothers cracks.

Another calls out, "Too good for him."

The first turns to the second. "Too smart for him too."

The second one turns to me and says, "Did you lose a bet?"

"Hey, shut up?" Finn says, then to me: "Like Momma said, ignore them."

"It's Christmas, boys, be civil." Their mom shakes her head and says, "Boys," with an exasperated eye roll.

I have to laugh because I can only imagine what it was like raising all these people.

"You're pretty." A little girl is standing right in front of me.

"Why, thank you, so are you," I say back to her.

"I know," the girl says with a shrug.

"That's Libby," Finn says. "And this is Jordy." He picks up the smaller girl and tosses her over his shoulder. "Quent's kids."

Finn sets Jordy down, but not before fake-dropping her twice. She giggles, loud and long, and the sound of it makes everyone laugh.

He leads me further into the house, his hand on the small of my back. The ceilings are tall, and there's a wall of windows at the back of the house with a perfect view of the mountains. There's a little bit of snow on the ground, and the scene outside is breathtaking and peaceful. But the view inside is pretty incredible too. The biggest and most beautifully decorated Christmas tree I've ever seen is in the corner. It has to be at least fourteen feet tall. It's massive but also impeccably and rustically decorated. There are dozens of wrapped gifts underneath, and crocheted stockings—nine of them, each with a letter or two on the top—hang from a wooden mantel above a large, stone fireplace.

The entire house looks and smells like Christmas, and I'm starting to understand why Finn has so much holiday spirit.

I turn to him. "How are you not homesick every single day you're not here?"

He smiles. "I *am* homesick every single day I'm not here."

"Boys, manners." Melinda pops one of the guys on the back of the head. He stands, pulls off his ball cap, and holds it in front of him, like a kid brought to apologize to the neighbor for breaking a window.

I *immediately* love her.

He raises a hand in a wave. "Hi. Pleasure."

"That's West," Finn says. "And these are my other brothers, Quent and Boone. Just stay away from them. They're terrible, awful people."

I laugh. "I think you're just scared they'll tell me stories about you."

His brothers laugh, and so do I, instantly loving the connection he has with them.

"Nice to meet you guys," I say.

"You sure you're here for him?" Boone asks, a lazy grin hanging loose on his mouth.

Finn's mom doesn't give me a chance to respond. She

wraps an arm through mine and says, "*That* one is a terrible flirt. Like his dad, but dumber."

"Hey! You said I was the favorite!"

"I lied," she says, leading me into the kitchen, and I'm glad that Finn is close behind, though it would be hard to feel out of place among such friendly people.

This makes me think of my own family—equally as warm and inviting. I have a fleeting vision of our families getting together over the holidays and the madness that would ensue.

I have the overwhelming sense they would fit like puzzle pieces.

An older man walks in from outside through a side door, carrying an armload of firewood. I assume he's Finn's dad. He stomps his boots and takes off his coat, and the little girls run to meet him.

"Pop, did you find the reindeer?"

Finn's hand finds mine, and I glance over at him. He smiles. "I can't believe you're actually here." He says this so quietly only I hear him, and while someday he might tease me for this impulsive decision, today is not that day.

"Who's this?" Finn's dad walks in and smiles at me.

"Boots!" Melinda pats him—hard—on the chest. "Off."

He winces. "I'm getting to it."

"You're tracking snow in. Get to it faster."

He shakes his head and steps on the back of one boot to pull it off with his feet, unsuccessfully.

"Dad, this is Raya," Finn says.

His dad stops and his eyebrows shoot up. "No kidding."

"No kidding," Finn says, beaming.

"Good to meet you, Miss Hart." He tips his cowboy hat, then walks back to the door and fights to get his boots off.

The oven beeps. "Casserole's done!" Melinda calls out—loudly. She looks at Finn. "Buttons and bows are done too."

There's commotion from the other room, loud, like a washing machine getting thrown down a flight of stairs, as Finn's brothers climb over one another to make their way into an area with a huge dining table.

"Hope you're hungry," Melinda says, nodding at the boys. "You can see we don't do anything small around here."

I laugh. "I'm starving, but could I wash up first?"

Melinda looks at Finn, who nods. "Yep. I got you."

I got you. Simple words that mean so much.

I follow him back through the entryway and into a long hallway that leads to several other rooms. I slow my pace, stopping to look at a little cluster of framed family photos, zeroing in on one of their whole family on the ice at what appears to be an important high school hockey game. I point to it.

"The night Hunter scored the winning goal and Silverwood won the state title." Hunter's smile is huge, and the entire family looks so happy. Finn is also in uniform and has his arm wrapped around his brother, the rest of the family surrounding them. I can practically hear the laughter and the shouts of joy.

"I read one of the letters," Finn says, eyes firmly focused on the picture.

I turn and look at him. "You did?"

He nods, but still avoids my eyes. "I mean, it sucked, but I did it."

"Finn. That's huge."

"Yeah," he says, then turns to face me. "It is. I have so much to tell you, but right now I just want to stare at you for a minute because I still can't believe you're here."

I smile. "I honestly can't either."

"Without a plan and everything. Gosh, look at you," he fake-gushes. "Our little Raya is growing up," he jokes.

I laugh at him, and he takes my face in his hands and kisses me so sweetly it makes my head spin. When he pulls back and looks at me, there's longing in his eyes. "You're sure about this."

"Positive," I say.

A smile crawls across his lips, and he kisses me again. "I have a theory that kissing you is never gonna get old, but I'm looking forward to proving it."

I go up on my tiptoes and kiss him again, head a little dizzy as I try to get used to the fact that I'm doing this. I'm going to let myself fall. And I have a feeling Finn is going to make it fun.

"I was worried about showing up here," I say. "Worried you'd maybe gotten tired of waiting for me to figure things out."

"Hart, I would've waited for you till the day I die."

I bite back a smile.

He pulls me into a tight hug, burrowing his face into my neck, and I let out a too-loud laugh. I clap my hand over my mouth and push him back. "Not right now—" I hiss. "We have to go eat." I widen my eyes dramatically. "I'm *starving*."

"Okay, go wash your hands or whatever," he says. "But just know that from now on, I'm going to kiss you every chance I get."

I open the door of the bathroom and step inside, then glance back in his direction and grin. "I'm looking forward to it."

Chapter Forty-Three

Raya

The food, the family, the feelings—I can't find the words to describe how each is more fulfilling than the next.

After we ate, Finn told his family he was taking me to town to "show me off." In reality, he had to do almost all of his Christmas shopping, but the bonus was that I got to see the town he calls home. Silverwood is a lot like Loveland—quaint and charming, all decked out for Christmas—with one distinct difference.

The mountains.

The *mountains*.

They take my breath away. How anyone ever gets used to a view like that I'll never understand.

Our first stop was to see an old friend of Finn's dad, a guy who makes custom signs. Finn said he needed to call in a favor for a last-minute Christmas gift for his parents, and while they talked, I called home to check in with my sisters, who've been texting for updates ever since I landed.

They tell me that my family moved their Christmas celebration to the day after Christmas so I could be there. Even though I'd made my peace with missing it this year, the thought of showing up with a real, live, not-hired plus-one to spend the holiday with the people I love most in the world warms me from the inside out.

Finn held my hand as he led me from shop to shop, picking out gifts for his nieces, his parents, and his brother Hudson, whose name he drew for Secret Santa. Even though he was cramming all of this shopping into the span of a single day, he was thoughtful about what he bought for each person, which didn't surprise me at all. Turns out he's a *great* gift giver.

Twice, he pulled me off the main sidewalk, stealing kisses.

As if I wouldn't have given them freely.

We went back home and watched *How the Grinch Stole Christmas* with his nieces while Finn ate a plateful of frosted sugar cookies. That night, we all went to the community center to help with the big Christmas party. When he showed me around the building and explained the plans to expand, he did it with so much excitement that I could see his purpose goes far beyond hockey.

And part of me wondered if he was starting to see it too.

It's rare to find a person so intent on putting other people first, but Finn does this like it's second nature. It's inspiring me to do the same.

He told me about Eileen and how he was still wrestling with forgiving her. It's obvious he's beating himself up over that, but I agreed that his plan to tackle it in small bits at a time sounded smart. And maybe it was silly, but I told him I was proud of him. Because he did something hard that he really did not want to do.

I think the words landed.

After we leave the community center, his entire family piles into pickup trucks and takes me to my first torchlight parade, a Silverwood Christmas Eve tradition where skiers and snowboarders zigzag down the mountainside, carrying torches that paint swaths of light across the cool, dark air. I watch in complete silence, captivated by the beauty of the tradition and overcome with gratitude that I was finally able to let go of my own rules and allow myself to love, want, and need someone else.

As we watch, Finn wraps an arm around me and whispers, "I still can't believe you're here."

I nestle in the space under his chin, leaning into him and thinking how thankful I am that none of my previous relationships ever worked out. Because I would've missed out on this. On Finn.

After the torchlight parade, we drive out to a big, open spot on the Holbrook land, right in the middle of the field, where Finn's dad has built a huge bonfire. We sing Christmas carols, and the brothers take turns telling loud, rambunctious stories, mostly about Finn, which I love hearing. Later, they play a rousing game of hockey on the home-made ice rink I'd only seen in photos.

No one can agree on what counts as a penalty.

More than once, Hunter's name comes up, and even though it's clear that they all miss their brother, it's also clear that they love telling stories about him, something I think Finn has avoided up until now. As they reminisce, he seems to get more comfortable with the idea of talking about him.

And while those stories are tinged with sadness, they are also *full* of joy, making it feel like a gift to everyone.

One thing is certain—Finn's family lives out loud. In living color.

They don't hold back in their love for each other, the ranch, or simply for being alive. And as I sit and watch them, I think about how many years I've held myself back from everything and everyone.

Even my own sisters.

I've kept a part of myself from them because I thought I needed to live up to certain expectations I'd placed on myself.

I don't want to do that anymore.

Finn's sisters, Rowena and Hattie, want to know what I see in their goofy brother, and I have to stop myself from gushing. Now that the revelation has come, I keep thinking of more things I love about him.

His brothers argue with about ninety percent of what I say, claiming that "I don't know him like they know him," and that he "cries at movies" and "farts in his sleep."

Finn gently tells me to "wait one second" and launches himself, tackling Boone.

I can't wait for my family to meet this family.

Eventually, his parents tuck their granddaughters into bed with promises of Santa Claus and reindeer and gifts and magic, but the rest of us stay huddled under blankets and coats, warming our hands by the fire until we're all too cold to stay outside any longer.

It's a Holbrook Christmas tradition for everyone to sleep at the ranch, so they drag mattresses out into the living room to sleep under the lights of the tree, which might've been awkward for me once upon a time, but not anymore. This family has brought me in like I'm one of them, and it's actually fun. With a capital F. All of it. I can't even try to pretend it isn't.

The brothers and Finn argue about which Christmas movie they should watch—and which one's the best—until they all turn to me for my opinion.

Without pausing, I tell them that it's *A Christmas Story*, with little Ralphie and his Red Ryder BB gun, because that's the one my sisters and I would watch every Christmas growing up. They all agree, rent the movie, and just as Ralphie is getting pushed down the slide, I tell Finn I couldn't remember when I'd ever had a better Christmas Eve, then quietly drift off to sleep.

Now, it's Christmas morning, and I wake to the smell of toothpaste and Finn. He kisses my cheek and whispers, "Good morning."

When I open my eyes, he smiles. "Get up. I want to show you something cool."

I cover my face with my hands, embarrassed that when I agreed to sleep on the couch surrounded by Holbrooks, I didn't think through the morning bedhead and bad breath.

"You have to hurry," he whispers.

"Okay, but if I'm going anywhere with you, I'm brushing my teeth first," I say, inching my way off the couch.

I see him grin, lit only by the light of the Christmas tree. "*Definitely* brush your teeth."

"Ew, Finn, you're gross," one of his sisters says.

We both laugh, and I rush into the guest bathroom where I got ready for bed, brush my teeth, then find him in the kitchen, wearing his coat and boots, holding my coat, along with two stocking caps and mittens.

"What are we doing?" I ask.

"Do you trust me?"

"Yeah, I do." I pull the coat on, shove my feet into my boots, then follow him outside and get in a pickup truck idling in the driveway.

It's warm in the cab of the truck, and before we go anywhere, he stops and looks at me. "Morning."

I smile. "Good morning, you weirdo. What are we doing out here before dawn?"

"I want to show you something cool." He leans over and kisses me. "You're pretty in the morning."

I bite back a smile. "I look like roadkill, but thank you."

He hands me a big, fuzzy blanket, and I move closer to him, spreading it over both of our laps. I loop a hand through his and savor the quiet, easy way it feels to be his.

The peace and calm my life so desperately needed is right here, and I'm more comfortable taking it now than I ever was before. I owe that to him, I think.

We drive through the darkness as the sun becomes a hint in the sky, and after several minutes, Finn slows down near a small, wooded lake at the back of the property.

"Hunter's lake," he says. "The best place to watch the sunrise."

At first, I think that's the actual name of the lake—but then I put two and two together that this place must've been special to his brother. And now it's special to Finn.

By proxy, that means it's special to me.

He shifts into park, pulls two more blankets from behind the seat, and leads me to the bed of the truck, where a big, open sky stretches above us. We're surrounded on all sides by nature, and the peace of the quiet, magical, brisk Christmas morning seeps into my bones.

He spreads a blanket across the bed of the truck, then helps me up. He sits with his back to the cab, and once I'm situated in front of him, he wraps his arms around me, and we tuck the other two blankets around our bodies. We watch in silence as the sun breaks through the clouds, casting its golden, glorious light over the blue-tinged land in front of us, glimmering off the water. I wonder what life on this ranch would be like.

It's a strange thought, and not one I'll entertain, but being here is a reminder that there's beauty everywhere if you slow down long enough to see it.

I don't want to rush anymore. I want to see it all.

"My favorite spot on the ranch," Finn says quietly as the pink and orange meld together behind a few scattered winter clouds.

"This is the quiet place you told me about," I say softly, only now remembering. "The place on the ranch even your brothers haven't found."

"You remember that?" He looks at me.

I keep my eyes on the sky. "I guess I paid attention more than I let on."

"I knew you liked me." I hear the smile in his voice as we both go quiet.

"It's amazing," I say, filled with awe.

"Happy Christmas, Hart."

I look up at him. "Happy Christmas, *Brookie*," I say quietly.

He kisses my forehead so tenderly that I mentally kick myself for waiting so long to let him love me.

"I didn't get your present yet," he says.

I smile as I watch him thread our fingers together, so content I could fall right back to sleep in his arms.

"I *am* your present," I say.

He laughs softly and kisses the top of my head. "So, when can I unwrap it?"

I bark out a laugh, because of *course* he'd go there. I smack him across the arm, and he squeezes me close, his smile fading. "Best gift ever."

As the sun rises on a new day, I feel something inside me shift. Our first full day as a couple.

I'm filled with an overwhelming feeling—a new and different feeling—hope. And while a tiny part of me is still cautious, mostly I'm focusing on everything I have to look forward to.

And I can't wait to see what happens next.

We return to the house and find delicious Christmas chaos. Everyone's awake, still in pajamas, drinking coffee, and helping arrange a big Christmas breakfast. The entire scene makes me imagine my life with Finn—a life that goes against everything I predicted and planned for myself—and what I see isn't even a little bit scary.

It's good. *We're* good.

After breakfast, they exchange gifts, which results in an epic, balled-up wrapping paper war, and in the midst of it all, Finn disappears outside for a few minutes. When he returns, he's carrying what looks like a large wooden sign. At the sight of him, the room falls quiet, and even I'm curious what he's up to.

He clears his throat, his expression turning uncharacteristically serious. "I thought a lot about what I wanted to give you all for Christmas this year."

"A new pony?" Jordy asks.

A quiet laugh ripples around the room.

"No, not a pony," Finn says.

"*Aww*," Jordy says.

"We've all been through a lot. We lost a big part of our family when Hunter died, and we all deal with it in our own way. I've been dealing with it by pretending it never happened, but being home has made me realize that if I pretend it never happened, I might as well pretend he never existed. And I don't want to do that anymore." Finn pauses, then looks at me, and I can almost feel him deciding to forgive Eileen again. I wonder if it feels any easier today than it did yesterday.

Finn pulls in a deep breath and turns the sign around to reveal the words: **The Hunter Holbrook Community Center.** The room falls silent.

"I don't talk about him because I'm afraid it'll bring the mood down, or people will look at me sideways, knowing that I had some big tragedy in my family, or whatever." He shakes his head. "I don't know. It's stupid. I realized it's stupid to hold back when you love somebody—shouldn't we tell everyone about him—to keep him alive?" He scoffs. "I realized that when I was talking to Eileen, of all people." He shakes his head again. "Never thought I'd learn anything from that woman." He stops, almost like he doesn't want this to be about her.

"Last night, when we were all telling stories about him, I didn't feel sad," Finn says. "I felt like a part of him was still here with us. Like he was still schooling Quent on the ice."

A quiet laugh fills the room.

"Still driving Momma crazy, eating spoonfuls of cookie dough before she could bake them."

"He *did* do that, the stinker," Finn's mom says, with a smile.

"Still telling me that I could do anything I set my mind to," Finn says, his voice cracking a little.

"Yep, he did, Skip," his dad says. "And look where you are now."

Finn smiles at him, then carries his smile around the room to the rest of his family.

"When we started helping at the community center, it was always a response to what we'd been through and wanting to make things better for people—something Hunter would've loved, you know? So—we still have to make it official with the board and all that boring stuff, but," he shakes the sign, "when we open in the new building, it'll really be in his honor, and everyone will know it."

Finn's parents stand and hug him, and soon everyone joins in. Jordy crawls into my lap, and Libby sits right next to me, and somehow, instead of feeling out of place, I feel like a part of them. And that has to be the best Christmas present I've ever gotten.

That night, as we sit in the airport after a full day of gifts, food, tradition, and fun, Finn pulls a sheet of paper from his bag. It's handwritten and messy, with chicken scratches and whole words crossed out.

I frown. "What's this?"

"My resumé," he says.

I look down and see his name, in all caps, centered across the top of the page.

Beneath that he has it broken down into Objective, Qualifications, Experience, Special Skills . . . he actually made a real resumé.

I fight a smile. "Okay, when in the world did you . . . ?"

"I wrote it while you learned to make buttons and bows with my mom," he says. "I *might* be a bit overqualified, but you should definitely hire me anyway." He takes a drink of his water but keeps his eyes on me. He taps it. "Read it."

I make a show of holding it up. "Finneus James Holbrook." I chuckle. "I'm definitely calling you Finneus from now on."

"Only when I forget to take off my boots in the house."

I smile and clear my throat, start with Objective, and read the whole thing.

When I finish, I look at him.

His eyebrows shoot up. "So?"

I press my lips together, but I can't hide the smile. "You're so hired."

"I'd like to start immediately." He stands in front of me, reaching out his hands for mine, and I tuck the paper into my bag and stand. Once we're face-to-face, he wraps his arms around me and pulls me close. "I know we're in the airport, but"—he looks around—"there's hardly anyone here, and I really want to kiss you right now."

I hear the question and quickly look around. He's right. It's practically empty in the terminal of this small airport. "I don't really do PDA"—another cursory scan of the space— "but . . ." I grab onto his jacket, tugging him close. "For you, I'll make an exception."

He smiles against my lips, then kisses me, full and deep, hands threading through my hair, and I let myself get lost.

Lost.

That's how I've been for so long.

Crazy that it took a flight halfway across the United States to be found.

Halfway through the kiss, Finn takes my hand and holds it out, placing his other on my waist.

He moves slowly, back and forth, and all at once, we're dancing in the middle of the airport.

And, for the first time in my life . . . I let someone else take the lead.

THE END

Want to read a special bonus deleted scene to see where Finn and Raya first met?

Grab it when you sign up for my email list!

https://BookHip.com/XVQZDAQ

A Love Letter

From the Author

Dear Reader,

When I tell you that this book was a challenge to write, it's the understatement of the year. It was a combination of fear, pressure to "get it right," and life just doing what life does. I wanted to write a book that you would love, but also a book that did this character justice...

Raya is the sister that is the most like me. And her journey is the closest to my own.

In 2012, during the release of my very first book, after moving our family across the country into a rental house, then moving again once we bought a house, I landed in the emergency room. My symptoms were identical to the ones described in Raya's "episode" and the diagnosis was also the same. Severe migraine brought on by stress. When I tell you I thought I was having a stroke, I mean it—it was terrifying. And I, too, was embarrassed to be wheeled out of my house and driven off in an ambulance.

The prescription—rest—felt like a joke. I mean, seriously? Did these doctors know I had a book to get out into the world and another one to send to my editor? Did they know the amount of pressure I was putting on that book to do well? Did they know how scared I was that I would fail?

Work makes me happy. I love my jobs. But over the years, I've learned that deep, soul rest is crucial... and there is a whole lot more to this life than checking things off my to-do list. It hasn't been an easy lesson to learn, which is maybe why taking Raya through this journey was difficult.

I'm even more stubborn than she is. And in a lot of ways, I'm still learning.

In the end, giving her a happy ending was so incredibly satisfying. She deserved it. She's overly protective and a little too cynical, but at the core, she is *good*. And her motivations come out of a great love for her people.

I hope you enjoyed the cherry on top of the Holidays With Hart series, though even as I type that I suspect...I'm not quite done with these sisters yet. After all, there's a wedding on the horizon! ;)

As always, I am SO grateful to you for reading my books. I know how many choices you have when it comes to the books you read, and to think that you picked up one of mine? The best feeling in the world.

For every single reader who reads this book, shares it with a friend, requests it at a local library, reviews it online, talks about it to anyone, anywhere. . .THANK YOU. **You** are why I get to keep doing this.

I'm so, so grateful.

Please don't hesitate to catch up with me via email: court ney@courtneywalshwrites.com or come hang out with me on Instagram (@courtneywalsh), which is where I spend all of

my procrastination time! I love to chat with my readers &
make new friends!

Courtney

Acknowledgments

Adam—For talking me off the ledge more than once and for forcing me to slow down, celebrate every success, and pay attention to the world around me. You are my favorite.

My kids—None of you will ever read this, but I'm so incredibly lucky to know you all. You each inspire me in different, amazing, wonderful ways, and I'm SO glad I get to be your mom.

My parents—Thank you for encouraging me to go after dreams that seemed crazy. And if you ever thought they were crazy, for not saying so out loud. And to my mom for always making Christmas special.

Becky Wade & Katie Ganshert—How'd I get so lucky to have two best friends like you? For the brainstorming, the cheerleading, the listening, the chatting...for reminding me I'm not alone, thank you.

Our Studio Kids & Families—Do you have any idea how special you are? You make my "day job" nothing but pure joy. I'm so thankful for each one of you!

Sarah Smith—Your copyediting skills are invaluable. Thank you for helping me with this one!

Leslie Brown, Tarah Curry, & Heidi Robbins— Thank you for your eagle eyes in the beta reading phase. I'm so thankful for each one of you!

About the Author

Courtney Walsh is an award-winning author of several low spice, small town romance novels. She's committed to creating stories that bring joy and always promises a happy ending. Her debut novel, *A Sweethaven Summer*, was a *New York Times* and *USA Today* e-book best-seller and a Carol Award finalist in the debut author category. In addition, she's written two craft books and several full-length musicals. Courtney lives with her husband and three children in Illinois, where she co-owns a performing arts studio and youth theatre with her business partner and best friend—her husband.

Visit her online at www.courtneywalshwrites.com

www.ingramcontent.com/pod-product-compliance
Lightning Source LLC
Chambersburg PA
CBHW011914130726
47903CB00016B/2838